D1462290

Also by Tina Folsom

AMAURY'S HELLION

(SCANGUARDS VAMPIRES #2)

TINA FOLSOM

Amaury's Hellion is a work of fiction. Names, characters, places, and incidents are the products of the author's imagination and are used fictitiously. Any resemblance to actual events, locales, or persons, living or dead, is entirely coincidental.

2010 Tina Folsom

Published in the United States

Cover design: Elaina Lee, For the Muse Designs
Cover photo: Bigstockphoto/Curaphotography & iStockphoto
Author Photo: © Marti Corn Photography

Printed in the United States of America

1

From his vantage point on the mezzanine, Amaury LeSang gazed over the heads of the crowd in the trendy nightclub. The sea of bodies swayed to the loud and monotonous techno rhythm. His skilled eye surveyed the clubbers writhing against each other, looking for a female in need of company.

Too many emotions slammed into his mind in this busy place—the reason he preferred his own company to that of the crowd.

A bolt of pain assailed him.

. . . should have never gone out with the jerk . . .

. . . ask her to dance, or maybe talk to her friend first . . .

. . . idiot. As if I cared. I'll show him . . .

Blocking out the random feelings of the individuals on the dance floor became increasingly difficult and painful the longer he stayed. Less like words and more like thrusts with a sharp blade, they sliced into him—not one after another, but all at once. The impact would knock a lesser man on his ass.

But Amaury was stronger than others.

He focused on those females who appeared to be unaccompanied. All he needed was a lonely woman welcoming his attention. Somebody who was at the club to get laid. He was more than willing to oblige.

There, the unassuming brunette. Not only did she feel lonely, she was desperate for a man's touch.

He strode down the stairs and waded across the dance floor, letting her feelings guide him straight to her. The woman rocked to the music and looked up at him when he stopped in front of her lithe body.

Amaury unleashed one of his most charming smiles. Combined with his handsome dark looks and blue eyes, most women couldn't resist him, a fact he always used to his fullest advantage.

Dance with me.

He moved his lips and sent his thought into her mind. She would believe he'd spoken, when in reality she couldn't have heard him over the din of the music.

She smiled and nodded. A little shy, yes, but welcoming nevertheless. Snaking one arm around her waist, the other around her shoulder, he drew her close. Her head only reached to his chest, making her at least a foot shorter than him.

Falling into the rhythm of the music, Amaury moved his body against hers. She molded to him, and he enjoyed the feel of her warm flesh through her skimpy clothes—thighs brushing, loins grinding.

Surrounded by the mob of people, the pressure in his head built, and the stabbing pain in his temples intensified. Like a migraine crippling a human, the pain dictated his actions. Nevertheless, he fought not to succumb to its demands for as long as he could, constantly pushing the boundaries of his mental prison.

Amaury didn't particularly like dancing, and this was definitely not his taste in music, but he forced himself to dance with her for one entire song, before he made his move.

"I want to be alone with you," he whispered into her ear, inhaling the natural scent of her glistening skin. He could, of course, fuck her right here on the dance floor, but then he'd have to do more damage control, something he wasn't in the mood for.

He underscored his words by slipping his hand onto her ass and stroking her rounded cheeks. When she looked up at him from under her lashes, he read the desire in her eyes as well as her mind. She wasn't particularly pretty, except for her generous dick-sucking lips, but she was willing. Willing was all he needed. He had no other expectations.

His cock was already fully erect, tenting his cargo pants, which he wore commando. With his hand on her lower back, he led her through the crowd, picking up on random emotions around him.

A stranger's envy sliced through him.

. . . did she catch that hunk? So not fair. What a hottie!

Amaury looked at the woman whose lusty and jealous feelings he'd captured. Clearly, she wanted to take the brunette's place. He could always come back for seconds if necessary.

Only a few more minutes and he'd feel better. His chest rose in anticipation as he inhaled deeply and quickened his stride, steering the brunette through the side exit.

The alley was quiet and dark. Several pallets with boxes stacked at various heights lined one side. Amaury's gaze swept over the area to establish they were alone. A homeless man hung around the entrance to the alley, rummaging through trash containers.

Get lost.

Amaury verified that the man had obeyed his unspoken command and shuffled out of view, before he pulled the woman into the corner behind the boxes.

"What are you doing?" She giggled.

"Kissing you." He lowered his head to hers. "You have the most gorgeous lips I've ever seen."

The compliment worked. His lips met no resistance when he crushed hers, searing them in a demanding kiss. His tongue slid through her parted lips and dueled with its counterpart within seconds.

Without hesitation, he laid his hand onto her breast and kneaded her through the thin fabric, working her responsive nipple into a hard peak. He'd read her right: she craved his touch—so much so, she arched her breast into his palm and demanded more.

"Oh, baby," he murmured against her lips. "So sweet." From experience he knew women were more responsive when physical actions were interlaced with verbal endearments.

Her body welcomed him as his hand tunneled under her short skirt and found its way into her panties. His fingers slid through her curls and met her wet folds.

Amaury captured the moan she released. It wouldn't take long. He realized how starved for sex she was and let his fingers do their magic. Caressing her, rolling her clit between his thumb and forefinger, he could feel her excitement rise. He would make it worthwhile for her.

The aroma of her arousal drifted into his nostrils, and he inhaled sharply. The scent helped him drown out the emotions bombarding him from inside and outside the club. But it wasn't enough. His head continued throbbing with pain.

Without releasing her little nub of pleasure, he slipped a finger into her wet channel. Her muscles were deliciously tight. Nobody had visited her clenching sheath in a long time.

Moving his finger back and forth, aided by her plentiful juices, Amaury worked her into full-blown arousal. It was the least he could do in exchange for what she would do for him in a few minutes.

She gasped as he added a second finger, and he knew she was close. A few more skillful strokes and she came, raining more cream onto his hand while her muscles went through spasm after spasm.

"Mmm," he hummed into her ear. "You all right, baby?" His male pride was satisfied, but the rest of him wasn't, at least not yet.

"Oh, God, yes!" she answered, panting heavily.

"I bet you could make me feel good too. Let me feel your mouth on me, baby."

Without waiting for her answer, he opened his pants and let his cock jut out. Despite its weight it stood erect. Slowly, he took her hand and guided it to wrap around his shaft. Soft hands which didn't close around him completely—too much flesh, too much girth.

"You're so big."

Amaury shook his head. He was perfectly proportioned, but being the size of a linebacker also meant his dick was supersized. "I'm the perfect size for your beautiful mouth."

Without any further objection, she dropped onto one of the boxes and moved her mouth toward him. He felt her tentative tongue touch the tip of his erection a second later.

"Oh, yes, baby. I bet you can give me the best blow job I've ever had." Encouragement never failed.

Her tongue licked all the way down his shaft before she finally wrapped her lips around the bulbous head and slid down on him, taking him in to the hilt.

Nothing felt better than the warmth and wetness of a woman around his cock. His breath rushed out of his lungs at the tantalizing sensation. He steadied himself by placing his hands onto her shoulders and began to move his rod back and forth.

"Oh, fuck, baby, you're good."

Finally, he was able to forget the din of emotions. Peace and quiet filled his mind. He relaxed as the pressure in his head eased and the invading feelings started withdrawing.

Amaury looked up, and for the first time this night he noticed the canopy of stars in the night sky. Beautiful and peaceful, a mirror of what his mind could be like. Clear and unobstructed by any fog or clouds, the stars stood watch over his actions.

As temporary as this feeling of tranquility would be, he needed it to keep his sanity. Only sex could shut out the emotions that assailed him every minute of his life.

The brunette's mouth worked him beautifully. With every stroke and every lap of her tongue he grew harder. She sucked him deeper into her mouth, and he moved faster, forgetting the pain in his head.

Instead, he concentrated on her wet heat engulfing him. The softness of a woman, the promise of a few moments of bliss. A few seconds of contentment was all he needed, knowing happiness was outside his reach, a state he could never attain.

"Baby, yeah. Almost there. Oh, yeah, suck harder."

He could virtually sense his impending release. So close. So deliciously close.

Amaury's jacket pocket vibrated. He ignored it. Gripping his shaft at the base with one hand and cupping the back of her head with the other, he fucked her mouth more frantically, desperate for release. He couldn't stop now, not when he was only seconds from his goal.

Need it. Now.

His cock pulsated with desperate need.

"Squeeze my balls," he demanded. Her hand took his testicles, the gentle touch sending a hot flame through his loins as her fingernails scraped against the tight sac.

His cell phone vibrated again. This time it wouldn't stop. Releasing his rod, Amaury shoved his hand into his jacket pocket and wrenched out the phone.

"Ah, fuck," he hissed when he checked caller ID.

The woman stilled instantly.

"Not you, baby, don't stop," he ordered and flipped the cell open.

"What?" he breathed into the phone, his voice hoarse. With his hand on her head he continued pumping his shaft into her, as she resumed sucking him deep into her mouth.

"Why don't you answer your fucking phone?" Ricky bellowed.

"Asshole." His colleague's timing sucked. "What do you want?"

"Crisis meeting at Samson's in fifteen minutes."

He knew better than to blow off a meeting with his boss and best friend, Samson. And if it was a crisis meeting, some shit was going down.

"Fine."

Amaury flipped the phone shut and shoved it back into his pocket. Fifteen minutes was barely enough time to get to Samson's, but he had to finish this.

He closed his eyes and concentrated on the feel of her tongue sliding along his shaft, the softness of her mouth, and the intensity of her sucking motion. Again, he gripped his erection and fed her more of himself, filling her mouth with so much cock, she almost choked on it.

But she kept going. Her wet mouth pulled on him tightly, while her warm tongue ran along the underside of his swollen flesh, just the way he liked it.

"Oh, yeah, baby. You like my big cock, don't you?"

Her hummed response reverberated on his skin, teasing his senses. The peach scent of her shampoo drifted into his nose. He felt a thin coating of moisture build on his face and neck. Tiny rivulets of sweat formed and ran along the ridges of his muscled upper body, catching in the light dusting of chest hair.

Amaury's heart beat faster. His lungs pumped more oxygen through his system as his blood charged through his veins, thundering in his ears in a violent crescendo akin to Beethoven's Fifth.

And then he felt the rush of his semen shoot through his shaft and into the woman's mouth in quick, pulsating explosions.

His orgasm was short, but powerful. It cleared his head, and for a few minutes he would be at peace. He wouldn't be able to sense the feelings of people he came in contact with and could feel his own heart and the sense of stillness that spread within it.

Only for a few moments. Then he would be invaded again by everybody's pain, hunger, anger, and other emotions people carried with them. And he would perceive their love for someone and be reminded of the things he couldn't feel. But for now, he was at peace.

Reluctantly, he pulled himself out of the woman's mouth and put his still half-erect cock back into his pants.

"You were spectacular," he praised and drew her up into an embrace.

Her lips glistened with his semen, and she looked beautiful to him. Amaury brushed her hair aside and exposed her lovely neck, her pale skin calling to him like a beacon of light guiding a sailor home. His lips touched the tender skin, before his tongue darted out to lick her.

She moaned: a sound so soft and sweet, only a satisfied woman could release it. "Come home with me."

Amaury appreciated her whispered invitation, but had no intention of accepting it. He wanted something else entirely. Her vein beat against his lips, the movement so subtle a human would barely notice it, but his senses were sharper than those of a mortal.

His fangs lengthened, pushing past his lips.

"Baby, let me take from you."

The sharp tips of his fangs sank into her neck and broke through the delicate skin. For a split-second she struggled against him, but his arms imprisoned her. He hauled her body against his, crushing her breasts to his chest.

As her blood coated his dry throat, his cock sprang back to life, but he didn't have time to indulge a second time, as much as he wanted to bury his shaft in her slick heat.

Amaury didn't take much of her blood, only enough to sustain himself. When he felt his hunger subside, he released her neck and licked the puncture wounds. His saliva closed the two little holes instantly. In the morning she would have no visible marks of his feeding, no side effects.

Then he looked into her eyes and sent his thoughts into her mind.

You never met me. You never saw me. Nothing happened. Go home now and sleep. And be careful. Don't ever let a man take advantage of you. You're beautiful. You deserve better.

Her eyes glazed over, and he knew it had worked. He'd wiped her memory of him. If she met him on the street tomorrow, she wouldn't recognize him. Not even the ghost of *déjà vu* would remain.

2

Amaury rushed through the streets of downtown San Francisco before he reached a Cable Car stop and jumped onto the antique streetcar, which took him up the steep hill toward Samson's house.

He liked the city's collection of neighborhoods which masqueraded as a metropolis and where it wasn't difficult to hide being a vampire. With a population as eclectic as the inside of a pawn shop, San Francisco was the perfect playground for modern-day vampires. Being eccentric or weird was nothing unusual in this city, where even the mayor was one of them.

The vampire population of San Francisco grew steadily, attracted by many of the same attributes humans liked about the foggy city: beautiful architecture, stunning views, and tolerant inhabitants.

Many vampire-run businesses had sprung up. There were several hip nightclubs, a newspaper—the *SF Vampire Chronicle* which was discreetly distributed to vampire households—investment companies, and of course Samson's nationwide security company, Scanguards. It provided bodyguards and security guards to individuals and corporations, foreign dignitaries, politicians, and celebrities.

By the time Amaury reached Samson's Victorian home in the exclusive and rather expensive neighborhood of Nob Hill and let himself in with his key, everybody was assembled. Before he even heard their voices, he sensed the tumult of emotions in the house: anger, disbelief, confusion.

His relief hadn't lasted long. The next wave of pain was already building like a tsunami approaching the Pacific coast. He braced himself as he stalked along the wood-paneled corridor toward Samson's private office in the back of the house.

Plastering his usual smile onto his face, he walked into the room, keeping his torment to himself like always. While his friends knew about his so-called gift, they had no idea about the pain it caused him daily and the things he had to do to keep his head from exploding. He didn't want their pity.

They all thought he was a sex maniac out to screw every female he could get his hands on, just for the fun of it. In reality, without sex he would have gone on a crazed rampage long ago, killing everyone and everything in his path. Sex equaled survival—for him and those around him.

"Amaury, finally," Samson greeted him, a pinch of displeasure in his voice. Being well over six feet tall, but with a much slimmer build than Amaury's broad frame, the same black hair, but piercing hazel eyes, his boss looked every inch the powerful man he was.

"Samson, guys," he replied and looked at them. Everybody was there: Ricky, Thomas, Carl, all vampires like himself.

Even Oliver, Samson's human assistant, a fresh-faced twenty-four year old, was present. And of course, Delilah, Samson's human wife, his blood-bonded mate.

Amaury gave her a warm smile, which she returned as she swept her long dark hair over her shoulder, her petite body looking even tinier standing next to her man.

He noticed Samson putting his hand on hers, a gesture so instinctive Amaury doubted his friend had even noticed. The love radiating off the couple almost brought him to his knees. He pulled his shoulders back.

"What's the crisis?" he asked instead.

"Thomas, patch in Gabriel," Samson ordered.

Thomas typed something on the keyboard and stepped back from the screen. As always, Scanguards' resident IT genius was dressed in his favorite biker outfit: leather, leather, and more leather. "Gabriel, you're on."

A second later, Gabriel Giles, head of operations in Scanguards' New York headquarters, appeared on the computer monitor which was turned for all to see.

His commanding presence filled the screen. His long brown hair was tied back in a ponytail, and the scar which stretched from his chin to his right ear seemed to pulsate. Nobody had ever dared ask him how he'd obtained it. And Gabriel wasn't one to volunteer information which was nobody's business. Amaury only knew that it stemmed from when Gabriel was human, since a vampire's skin didn't scar.

"Evening everybody," Gabriel's booming voice came through loud and clear. "We've just been alerted to a problem. There's no easy way to say it, so here it goes. A second bodyguard has killed a client and then himself."

The collective murmurs and gasps of disbelief were quickly subdued, while the emotions continued to simmer beneath the surface.

"As you all remember, over a month ago, one of Scanguards' San Francisco bodyguards killed the millionaire he was protecting and then committed suicide. We thought it was an isolated incident. Unfortunately, with this second murder, which concerns another San Francisco employee, we don't have the luxury of chalking this off as just an individual gone berserk. Somebody's messing with us."

Samson nodded. "Gabriel and I spoke earlier tonight. The late evening news will break the story. We have to be ready to do damage control. Tomorrow the papers will be shredding us to bits. Nobody will shrug this off as a coincidence. And we're pretty sure it isn't."

"Some vampires gone into bloodlust?" Thomas asked.

Amaury listened up. Bloodlust—they all feared it, the uncontrollable urge to take more blood than they needed, which ultimately led to murder and madness.

Gabriel shook his head. "No. Both bodyguards were humans."

"Any connection between the two?" Amaury interjected.

"Negative," Samson answered quickly, "at least nothing we could determine this quickly. Apart from the fact that they were both hired here in San Francisco, they have nothing obvious in common."

"I knew Edmund Martens. I hired him," Ricky said. While he fancied himself a California Beach Boy and had adopted many habits of his new country, he couldn't really be mistaken for anything else but the lad he was: his red hair, freckled face, and decidedly Irish last name, O'Leary, gave him away. "God, Eddie showed such promise. But when he killed that client last month, I thought he'd gone off the deep end and reverted back to his old ways."

"What ways?" Amaury asked.

"Bad childhood, ran away from his foster family, turned to crime— the usual. Never thought he'd go so far and kill someone. He didn't seem the violent kind. But then, sometimes it doesn't take much for somebody to slide deeper. I just thought he'd finally pulled himself out of all this."

"Maybe he did." Samson's concerned look spoke volumes and told them he didn't believe that the two human bodyguards were at fault.

"Who's the second guy?" Ricky wanted to know.

"Kent Larkin."

Ricky's jaw slackened. "He was just a kid. He can't have been working for us for longer than six months."

"A little over five months," Gabriel confirmed.

"What evidence do we have that Edmund and Kent actually killed their clients?" Amaury needed facts. He didn't want to jump to conclusions.

"An eyewitness in Edmund's case and the smoking gun in Kent's."

"Do we have anybody on the inside with the police?" Delilah suddenly asked. Everybody's gaze settled on her. "Well, we'd better make sure we know what they know before it becomes public knowledge."

Ever since Delilah had blood-bonded with Samson, she had started taking an active interest in the company. As a blood-bonded mate, she was entitled to everything Samson owned, and the fact that she'd started sharing in important decisions didn't seem to disturb her man in the slightest. After all, she was his equal.

Amaury was surprised at the change he'd seen in his old friend. After two hundred years of solitude, Samson had had no problems adjusting to marriage to a strong woman. Amaury doubted that he himself would adjust as easily as Samson had, not that this question was anything else but academic. Amaury knew he would never bond, because he could never truly love anybody.

"I'll talk to G," Samson said, referring to the mayor. "I'll make sure he'll keep us in the loop." He looked back at the screen. "What time are you landing?"

"Everybody's on their way to the airport now. We'll touch down about an hour before sunrise."

"Don't you think that's cutting it a little close?" Ricky asked.

"It couldn't be avoided. I had to mobilize the troops first and get ready myself."

"You're coming out here yourself?" Amaury asked in surprise. Gabriel rarely ever left New York for anything. If he was leaving the East Coast for this, he clearly expected these events to turn into a major problem. And if he was risking being out in the open so close to sunrise, Gabriel's assessment of the situation had to border on catastrophic.

"We can't trust anybody in the San Francisco branch. I'm bringing three of my best people with me: Quinn, Zane and Yvette. We'll conduct the investigation our way. Outside of this group, nobody can be trusted. Nobody."

"Gabriel is right," Samson confirmed. "If two of our human guards killed their clients, somebody has their hand in this. And until we know who and why, we have to be tight-lipped about it. The employees will want an explanation. Ricky, you'll call a staff meeting once Gabriel and his people are here. Everybody at Scanguards is under suspicion—humans and vampires alike. Carl, pick them up from the airport."

Carl, Samson's devoted butler, driver, and man about the house, nodded instantly, his slightly heavy body as always neatly squeezed into a dark business suit.

"Amaury, you'll go with Carl," Samson ordered.

Amaury nodded. He hadn't seen his friends from New York in ages, and catching up with them would distract him from his pain. Not that he was overly keen on seeing Yvette again. She was probably still pissed at him.

"Thomas," Samson continued, "I want you to upload complete background checks for all employees and run them in a matrix against each other. Let's see what Edmund and Kent had in common, and then let's run those criteria against the rest of the employees. We need to see who else might be vulnerable to whatever is happening."

"No problem," Thomas accepted. "I'll get right on it. I'll be working downtown."

"Oliver, you're the only one here who can get around during the day. I'll be relying on you heavily. You'll be our liaison."

Before Oliver could respond, Delilah interrupted. "Hold on; I can go out during the day too."

Even though Delilah was a blood-bonded mate and drank blood from Samson, she remained entirely human, except for one thing: she didn't age anymore as long as her man was alive.

"Out of the question," Samson snapped. "You won't get involved in the investigation."

"It's my company too." She braced her hands at her hips.

"I don't deny that. But you won't put yourself in danger, not in your condition."

"Condition?" Amaury heard himself ask and instantly sensed the answer to his question.

Everybody else in the room gave the couple a curious look.

Samson grinned proudly. "I guess the cat is out of the bag." He pulled Delilah into his arms. "Delilah is making me the luckiest guy on this earth. We're going to have a baby."

The man was a lucky bastard. Amaury shook his head. "Congratulations."

As their friends threw in their best wishes and congratulated them on their happy event, Amaury watched Samson hold his wife tightly while whispering into her ear. He didn't need to hear what he'd said, because the emotions emitted by the two hit him like a brick falling from a skyscraper.

The pressure in his temples increased. If he didn't get out of their presence soon, his head would explode.

Love was the most devastating emotion screwing with Amaury's head. He was by no means jealous of Samson, because he had no interest in his lovely mate, but he simply couldn't stomach their company for too long. Whenever other people's love bombarded his mind, the pain he felt was virtually unbearable. Being cursed never to feel love in his own heart again, his mind couldn't handle this emotion and only reacted with pain and rejection.

Unfortunately, the meeting wasn't over yet. He'd already arrived late. Leaving early would be out of the question. After all, he was an officer of the company and had an interest in it. This crisis had to be dealt with.

Amaury gripped the massive antique desk behind him for balance and tried to distract himself from the thunder pounding in his head. Letting his mouth curve into another fake half-smile to disguise his inner turmoil, he addressed Gabriel via the monitor, "Have any of the other branches reported problems?"

"I'm sending reinforcements to Houston, Seattle, Chicago, and Atlanta. We don't know yet whether this is going to be confined to San Francisco or not. But we can't be too careful. The faster we find out who or what's behind this, the better for all involved. This mustn't spread. We'll be ruined if it does."

Samson gave a grim smile, Delilah still tucked into his side. "You're right. The company can't survive this kind of publicity. And if the police or the press dig too deep, we're in trouble. None of us can afford to be exposed for what we are. So, at the slightest breach of security by any human, wipe their memories. It's crucial. No exceptions."

"And we can't have any more people dying," Delilah added.

"Until this is over, we should all minimize our contacts with humans."

Samson didn't have to look his way, but Amaury knew the jab was aimed at him. Easy for his friend to say—he had his human wife by his side day and night.

He got the message, and it was loud and clear. Amaury was to stay away from human women. And what did this leave him with? Having sex with those female vampires who hadn't kicked him out of their beds yet?

It wasn't that he didn't deliver when it came to sex, but many of the vamp ladies had started making emotional demands. Why they had all suddenly turned into needy, clingy creatures, he had no idea. For sure, mainstreaming was to blame. As if emulating humans was the goal.

He sure wasn't going to turn into one of those blithering idiots, going all gooey eyed over some woman, not even *if* he were capable of loving, which, of course, he wasn't.

3

Nina pulled the hood of her dark sweatshirt closer around her head. For the hundredth time this night she tucked an errant dark-blond curl back behind her ear. If she let her hair grow longer, she would be able to pull the unruly locks back into a ponytail. But long hair was impractical, especially in a fight.

In any case, she wasn't girly. At five foot eight, she certainly wasn't petite, a fact she was grateful for, particularly since she was up against some big bad guys.

The fog had dissipated hours earlier, making this a gorgeous, starry, yet moonless night. Almost peaceful in its stillness, it guarded the sleeping city.

Nina continued watching the beautiful Victorian house from her hiding place across the street. Over an hour ago, she'd seen several of *them* enter, and none had come out yet.

Them. She knew what they were. A month earlier, she'd gone through her brother's possessions and pieced together what at first she'd thought was impossible. She'd immediately dismissed her findings as ludicrous. But the more she went back, the more she dug, the clearer everything had become.

She'd found notes in Eddie's datebook, drawings of weapons and weird symbols. And in the margins of a book about the paranormal he'd made more notes. Then under his mattress she'd found a list with names. Next to each name he'd written either *Human* or *Vampire.*

The moment Nina had read the word, she'd thought he'd gone crazy. And for a short while she'd believed that he was guilty of what he'd been accused of. Mental illness would explain it. But there had never been a sign of instability in him. Eddie wasn't crazy—no way would she believe that.

So she'd dug deeper and followed those he'd classified as vampires on his list. Most worked for Scanguards.

Nina sniffed and wiped her nose on the sleeve of her sweatshirt. Her dark clothes made her frame melt into the doorway behind her. Nobody would be able to notice her even if they looked in her direction.

Several weeks of following those she suspected of being vampires had turned into a crash course in stealth. Until now, she'd stayed far enough away from them to be out of danger. Tonight, she would have to get close.

The sound of a door opening pulled Nina out of her thoughts. A quick glance at the person exiting the large Victorian home confirmed it was one of the vampires, the biggest of them, Amaury.

She'd followed him several times, figured out where he lived and tried to find his weak spot. She wasn't particularly keen on him being the first she would have to take down, but maybe this was how it should be. Get rid of the biggest, *baddest* vampire first; the rest would be easy pickings by comparison.

Nina watched him stagger down the front steps, almost as if he were drunk. On the sidewalk he stopped and braced himself against the gate to his right. The light from the streetlamp illuminated his face. Instead of the broad smile he so often sported in the company of others, his face was distorted, deep grooves around his mouth and eyes creating a mask of pain.

Pain? She frowned. From everything she knew about vampires, she was almost certain they didn't feel much pain, if any at all. Yet Amaury looked as if he was in the throes of a migraine, the heels of his hands pressed tightly against his temples.

With bated breath she watched his chest rise and fall as he inhaled and exhaled deeply. There was something so human, so vulnerable about him, it made her own chest tighten in sympathy. She instantly shook the thought from her mind. A few seconds passed before his body finally straightened, his face normal again.

Nina remained at a safe distance behind him as she followed, the damp pavement absorbing the sound of her soft-soled shoes. From the direction he took, she realized he was heading home. Why he lived in the Tenderloin, one of the shabbiest neighborhoods of San Francisco, when he could surely afford a much better place, was a mystery to her. His clothes, while casual, looked expensive. And once she'd seen him in his car, a Porsche.

As she trailed him down the hill, slowly entering the less savory parts of the city where so many of the homeless and drug addicts congregated, she had already decided on a place to take him down. Patiently, she bided her time, each step bringing her closer to the spot which would give her a definite advantage.

Nina stepped around yet another homeless man passed out on the sidewalk. The scent of alcohol and urine assaulted her senses. Suddenly, the drunk twitched and grunted, startling her. Adrenaline pumped through her veins. She glanced down at the man, ready to defend herself if necessary, but he was out cold. When she looked back up, Amaury had just turned a corner. She only caught sight of a flap of his long coattail.

Immediately, she quickened her stride. She couldn't afford to lose him when she was so close to her goal. Two blocks farther was the location she'd scouted out days ago.

The old obsolete stairway she'd discovered led over the roof of an abandoned one-story building. At the diagonal corner of it, it provided a clear viewpoint above a narrow alley—an alley Amaury liked to take. He would pass by it, and she would be able to jump onto him from above, stabbing him at the same time.

Nina slipped her hand into her pocket and touched the stake. The wood felt smooth in her hand as she caressed it like a lover, fitting it to her palm.

Amaury LeSang, you'll be one dead vampire in a minute.

Such a big man, yet such a small object would bring about his death. It was almost poetic. For all their strength and power, vampires were surprisingly vulnerable to something as simple as a piece of wood. There was justice in this world after all. She would call on this justice tonight.

She rounded the corner he'd turned only seconds earlier. The narrow street was dark and—empty. Nina skidded to a halt. Had he noticed her after all and started running once he'd been out of her direct line of sight?

She scanned the sidewalk and doorways. Nothing, except for a couple of homeless men arguing and a teenager lurking in the shadows, probably waiting for his drug dealer, if he wasn't one himself. No sound or sight of anybody else in the vicinity. A cold shiver traveled down her spine, spreading unease in her body.

A block farther was the turn-off to the alley. Maybe he'd already reached it and taken it. A few steps ahead to her right she ducked under the small arch which led to the old stairway. Taking two steps at a time, she climbed it. If she hurried, she could still be in place in time to strike.

Nina picked up speed and ran up the last few stairs before it made an abrupt turn. A short sprint across the roof and she reached the vantage point which exposed the narrow alley beneath. She knew he liked taking this shortcut to his home. She'd seen him do so several times.

Only this time, he wasn't in the alley. She'd missed him. All her work for the night was for nothing. A complete waste.

Damn!

Nina stomped her foot in frustration and pushed the air out of her lungs. A faint sound behind her made her spin on her heels. Only her quick reaction saved her from being grabbed from behind, but the large hand still caught her arm. Her breath hitched, and fear clamped around her throat at the unexpected contact. Without even looking up at his face, she knew whom she was dealing with.

Amaury was built like a tank: hard, unyielding, and unstoppable. She felt his raw power send electrical charges along her skin. Genuine worry hummed through her. Without the element of surprise on her side, she had no chance of winning a fight against him. He could easily steamroll her, and she'd be giving him as much resistance as a blade of grass in the wind.

Escape was her only option at this point. She wasn't proud or stupid enough to stick around.

With a swift move she twisted her arm out and jerked it away, making him lose his grip on her. A firm kick into his shin, and she darted past him, muffled curses chasing her. When she felt his hand grab her sweatshirt, she kicked back with her leg, then spun on the other foot and used both her arms to twist his to force him to release her clothing. But she had underestimated his strength—or the strength of any vampire for that matter.

"Who the hell are you?" Amaury bit out. The deep rumble of his voice sent a tremor through her body and made her skin prickle. "And why were you following me?"

His imposing frame towered more than half a foot over her, crowding her senses. One hand still on her sweatshirt, he wrenched her hood off with the other, ignoring her flailing arms. Her curls tumbled out. Nina tried unsuccessfully to shake his hand off when he used it to tip her chin up, forcing her to look at him.

"You're a woman!"

His eyes widened as he looked at her. She used his moment's hesitation to twist out of his grip and run for it. She didn't even make two steps before his arms snatched her again and held onto her. Tighter this time, hauling her against his hard frame. He turned her around.

Pressing her lips together in a thin line, she glared up at him—and stared into the bluest eyes she'd ever seen.

Nina had always observed Amaury from afar, always from a safe distance. This was the first time she was within inches of his face and his massive body. He was tall and muscled, big-boned, and broad-shouldered. But there wasn't an ounce of fat on him. His hair was as black as a raven, not quite shoulder length, and curling slightly at its ends.

But it wasn't his hair or his strong body that captured her, not even the hands that kept her imprisoned against her will. It was his eyes. As blue and as deep as an ocean they stared at her—hypnotized her.

Maybe she could have shaken off his hands somehow, but not his eyes. Nor the sensual curve of his mouth, the fullness of his lips, or the strong outline of his jaw. Even his nose was in perfect proportion to his size, long and straight, almost Greek.

Never in her life had she come face to face with a man so ruggedly handsome and sensual at the same time. Despite the precarious situation she found herself in—captured by a vampire—she didn't struggle to get out of his arms and away from his body. Rather, she found herself inching forward, moving ever closer to him to savor the heat that radiated from him. Amaury smelled of earth and leather, purely male. Her belly clenched in response. Her body's wanton reaction sent an alarm bell ringing in her head.

What in hell was she doing? She should be kicking his sorry ass from here to Alcatraz, not ogling him like a star-struck groupie. He was the enemy, one of the men responsible for the destruction of her little family. Why was her body not moving when she should have at least tried some of her karate kicks to escape his hold?

His narrowed eyes were sharp and assessing, watching her with suspicion, yet he said nothing. She didn't think he could still be shocked by the fact that a woman had followed him, but something was restraining his tongue.

Nina lowered her lashes to gaze at his mouth and saw his lips part as if in invitation. Firm and sensual lips which beckoned for a brush against them, if merely to confirm she wasn't dreaming the perfection in front of her.

No. Still the enemy. Bad vampire.

She could resist this temptation. She was strong—until he exhaled, and she took in his breath—musky and earthy. His scent was intoxicating, drugging, as if it contained a secret substance designed to make her dizzy. Moistening her dry lips, unable to think clearly now, she stretched upwards and tilted her face toward him. Was he leaning toward her now, or was it an illusion?

Really bad vampire.

Yet, so enticing.

No!

She had to fight this, fight him.

Improvise!

Yes, she had to turn this around, make it her advantage. Find his weakness.

Think! You're a smart woman, damn it, think!

That was it: a woman. She was a woman, and his weakness was women. She'd seen him in the company of many of them—yes, she could use that. It could work.

Or blow up in your face.

Nina didn't listen to her doubting inner voice. Instead she inched forward once more, closer to his perfect face and pressed her lips to his.

He appeared startled, his lips remaining rigid for a moment. But then his hands released their deathlike grip on her arms, and he pulled her to him. One hand circled her waist, the other steadied her head, his strong fingers burying themselves in her curls the way a lover would. Her heart leapt with relief—it was working. She would be able to distract him and escape.

But the moment his lips responded to hers, and his tongue invaded her, her body took over. His kiss flipped the off switch to her brain and shut out every sane thought she'd ever had—wiping her brilliant plan from her mind as if it had never existed.

***

Amaury drew the human female closer to him, crushing her breasts with his chest. Her short blond curls felt soft under his hand, like silk.

As soon as he felt her lips part under light pressure, he responded with a guttural moan. And then he kissed her back. She welcomed his tongue dueling with hers, encouraging him to explore her. He wouldn't disappoint her. Angling his head, he sought a deeper penetration and found her eagerly accepting his demand.

In her shapeless clothes he'd mistaken her for a juvenile delinquent, not the warm and willing woman she turned out to be. But what had really thrown him for a loop was the fact that he couldn't pick up on any of her emotions, which was more than a little unnerving and—fascinating.

For once he could kiss a woman without focusing on his release. It felt like a gift from heaven to be able to enjoy a kiss like the one he now shared with her. A kiss full of fire, passion, and desire. He had no idea why she kissed him, who she was, or what she wanted, but her body pressed against his felt utterly right.

Of its own volition his hand dipped below her waist, splaying over her rounded derrière. With a groan, Amaury hauled her against his growing erection and took charge.

Her lips tasted of vanilla blossoms, of innocence. He inhaled her scent, taking it deep and letting it fill him. Waves of pleasure poured through his body, igniting the lust he kept barely checked within. Her taste was intoxicating, purely female, and indescribably sexy. Unwilling to hold back, he ravished the caverns of her mouth like an invading barbarian, wild and savage.

Instead of withdrawing from his assault, she flung her arms around his neck as if to ensure he wouldn't stop. No chance of that happening, not as long as his cock throbbed with need and her tongue sent tiny shock waves through his body every time she stroked against him. The woman knew how to drive a man insane with her kiss.

Her sweet taste was like ambrosia to him, like a long lost delight he had forgotten about. She reminded him of emotions long buried and stirred his flesh like no other woman had in four centuries.

Under his greedy hands, he captured the warmth and softness of a female overflowing with passion, a woman who could match his own needs. The sounds of pleasure coming from her were like bursts of little fireworks to him, stoking his desire even more. It made him want things he'd never dared acknowledge: closeness, affection, warmth.

Amaury caught her next moan and swallowed it down where it ricocheted in the cavities of his chest, bouncing off his lungs and against his cold heart. And for one instant, a spark ignited where his pounding heart lay almost frozen.

The next second, his heart beat faster than it ever had before. A moment later he heard a sound behind him.

Danger!

Out of reflex, he released her instantly and swiveled. Behind him was only darkness. Nobody else was on the roof but the two of them.

The moment he turned back to her, she'd already moved away from him and sprinted toward the edge of the building. A second later she was gone. He heard the loud *thump* and followed the sound. As he reached the edge, he looked down. Beneath him was the alley he so often took on his way home, and there, at the end of it was the woman, running away from him.

"Wait," he called out to her. "Who are you?"

But she'd already rounded the corner and was out of sight. Amaury swallowed. He could still taste her on his tongue, still feel the ghost of her soft form pressed into his body. What the hell had just happened?

He shook his head. Generally he was the one doing the seducing. But this time, a woman had turned the tables on him. And he liked it. A lot. It was a shame she hadn't gone any further. Why had she suddenly run when everything was going so well?

And why hadn't he been able to sense her emotions, not a single one of them, when only minutes earlier his head had throbbed painfully?

The only reason he'd discovered her following him was because he'd heard her footsteps, but her mind had been completely and utterly silent. As if she had no emotions. Yet, her passionate kiss had said differently.

Maybe something was happening with him. Was it possible that the sessions with his shrink Drake had somehow helped? It could be a start, a sign his curse was waning.

As he turned and walked back toward the stairs, he stumbled over something, but caught himself instantly. He bent down and picked up the item. His breath caught, and his heart beat in his throat. The instant his fingers touched the wooden implement, he knew what it was. Its shape was known to him and any vampire and feared by all of them.

A wooden stake.

4

Despite his relentless efforts for the remainder of the night, Amaury could not find a trace of the mystery woman by the time he was due to meet Carl. In fact, he'd spent so much time on the search he'd neglected his other assignments. The darn woman was screwing with his head, and he was getting increasingly testy about it.

That rotten little bitch had kissed him with full knowledge that he was a vampire. And why? So she could kill him. She had completely distracted him. With a kiss!

He of all people should be utterly immune to such distractions, given he was an expert concerning sex and all things ancillary to it. To play him like he was some randy idiot! The gall the woman had.

She was in for a severe spanking once he found her. And he would find her—eventually. And then the gloves would come off, and he would give her what she deserved. She would be in for a lethal dose of Amaury.

Nobody made a fool of Amaury LeSang—or at least, nobody got away with it. Least of all a human woman.

A honking horn alerted him to Carl who had pulled up with the car. Amaury opened the door to the black limousine and got into the passenger side.

"The car looks dirty," Amaury admonished.

Carl had an annoyed look on his face. Perfect. Two pissed-off vampires together in one car. The night couldn't possibly get any better than that.

"I know. That useless construction crew blocked the entrance to the garage, so I had to keep the car parked outside. I wouldn't be surprised to find scratches on the paint."

"Yeah, sucks." His comment wasn't meant for Carl, but for himself. Where the hell was that woman hiding? Why kiss him like that, with such passion as if she meant it, when all she wanted was to kill him? Even hours after her kiss, he could still taste her, and it drove him insane.

"Did you preview any homes tonight?" Carl asked.

As Samson's personal broker, Amaury took care of all of Scanguards' real estate investments, as well as Samson's properties.

Amaury shook his head. "Something came up."

Yes, his dick.

Which, by the way, was *still* up. Just thinking about the little blond devil kept him in a permanent state of readiness.

"I didn't get a chance. But there are a few houses that just came on the market. Some of them might work for Samson and Delilah. I'll check them out tomorrow night. With the baby coming, they'll definitely need more space."

He reached into his jacket pocket. In anticipation of previewing homes he'd taken his lockbox key with him. It would give him access to vacant homes for sale without making it necessary for the listing agent to be present. A neat system, especially since he could only view homes at night. And luckily, the medieval myth that a vampire needed to be invited into a home was simply untrue, otherwise being a real estate agent wouldn't be the smartest career choice for a vampire.

In silence, they rode to the private airport several miles south of San Francisco. Scanguards had its own planes, specially equipped to transport vampires during daytime hours. Taking commercial planes was too risky.

Carl parked at the edge of the tarmac, killed the engine and looked at his watch. "They should land in a few minutes."

Amaury drummed his fingers on his thighs. He wasn't in the mood to meet his old friends anymore, since it took him away from his search for the human woman who had so thoroughly kissed him. It irked him that so far he'd been unable to find her anywhere. As soon as he could, he would resume his search. He didn't have much to go by—only her scent—but she would not escape him.

The roaring sound overhead announced the descent of the private jet. Minutes later it came to a complete stop at the other end of the landing strip. Carl drove the car up to the plane as the doors opened.

Gabriel was the first to step out. Always with a flair for the dramatic, he emerged clad in black jeans, dress shirt, and leather coat. Coupled with his large scar, he represented authority and confidence. And as New York's number one, he wielded considerable power within the company. Only Samson was more powerful.

Amaury was on equal footing with Gabriel. In the past, their internal power struggles had caused some strife. However, ever since Amaury had moved to California, their fights had subsided, and their friendship had taken priority.

Amaury jumped out of the car to greet his old friend. They clasped each other's right arms. "Good to see you."

"It's been a long time," Gabriel replied.

"Not long enough," a female voice came from the steps.

Amaury looked into her direction. Yvette, as sexy and ravishing as ever, glided down the stairs. Leather pants and a tight pink top accentuated her alluring curves. Her short black hair was styled back, away from her flawless face. Women would kill for a face like hers.

"Still sore?" Amaury forced himself to grin. He wasn't going to allow her to get to him.

"Don't flatter yourself, Amaury."

She stepped down with her long and sexy legs, the same ones he remembered all too well being wrapped around his waist a long time ago. Amaury shook the image off and focused his eyes back on the present.

Yvette stopped next to her boss, maybe a little closer than their work relationship would suggest was necessary. "You're not *that* memorable."

He knew he was, but he'd gain no satisfaction from trying to prove it to her. It was better to let sleeping lions—or lionesses—sleep before their claws came out.

Gabriel turned to the jet's door. "Quinn, Zane, what the hell is keeping you? We've gotta beat sunrise."

"Coming!" came the answer. A second later, Zane appeared in the opening, two bags in hand. "Luggage. Hey, Amaury, can you give me a hand?"

"Allow me," Carl interrupted and reached for the bags Zane handed down.

"Thanks, Carl."

Having rid himself of the luggage, Zane shook Amaury's hand. His head was shorn bald, and despite the lack of hair, he was a handsome devil. Lean and tanned, dressed in faded blue jeans and a white long-sleeved polo shirt, he had a casual air about him. But Amaury knew better.

Zane was a mean fighting machine: fast, ruthless, and lethal. He would never want to get on his bad side, not that Zane had a good side.

"Good to see you," Amaury addressed him. "I feel better knowing you're joining the fight."

Zane's mouth twisted, but it didn't quite amount to a smile. "Anything for a good fight. Gabriel rarely lets me get into the action."

A sideways glance at Gabriel showed Amaury that the New York boss gave them an impatient look, his mouth twisting to one side. "And Zane knows exactly why."

Sounded like a reprimand in Amaury's ears. Zane seemed to shrug it off as if he were made of Teflon. "It'll be like the good old days."

"I don't recall the good old days being all that good," came Quinn's voice from inside the plane. A second later his strawberry-blond head popped out. He had a light complexion, light hazel-colored eyes, and a boyish smile. His age was frozen forever at slightly north of twenty. He took it as liberty to behave his apparent age, even though he was well over two hundred years old.

"Maybe not for you," Zane retorted, "but for Amaury and me, things were pretty entertaining."

Not quite sure which one of their many battles his old friend referred to, Amaury only nodded. Not that he'd call it entertaining. Gruesome was probably a better word. Most fights Zane was involved in turned into a mess of blood and gore.

Quinn finally stepped out of the plane, a garment bag slung over his shoulder. "I'm ready."

"About time." Gabriel looked at his watch and furrowed his brows.

As soon as they were piled into the limousine, Carl turned the car back toward San Francisco. Amaury made sure he wasn't facing Yvette who'd already stared daggers at him earlier. With Quinn sitting between him and her while facing Gabriel and Zane, Amaury was saved from both physical and eye contact.

For a moment there was silence until Gabriel finally spoke. "Samson must be ecstatic."

"Never thought I'd see him like that," Amaury confirmed.

"It doesn't happen to many of us, but when it does, it's life changing." There was a sad look in Gabriel's eyes. He'd not yet found his mate, and Amaury knew instantly that the loneliness was getting to him. It was stronger now than when he'd last seen him face to face a few years earlier.

While they would often talk through video conferencing, Amaury hadn't been aware of how intense Gabriel's emotions had become. Amaury's gift didn't work over the wire. He needed a certain physical proximity to hone in on people's feelings.

Quinn bounced a confused look between them. "Ecstatic about what?"

It appeared the New York boss hadn't yet filled his employees in on the latest developments in the Woodford household.

"Samson's going to be a father," Gabriel replied. "Didn't waste time, did he?"

Only three months earlier, Samson and Delilah had bonded.

"They are good together." Amaury cast a wistful look out the window as he ran his palm along the cool, smooth mahogany inlay on the door.

He would have preferred it if Gabriel had chosen to talk about work rather than make small talk. He needed to get the image of the happy couple out of his mind. Talking about other people's happiness was too much in contrast with his own empty life.

"Wow, that's great," Quinn commented.

Amaury needed to terminate the chit-chat.

"Have you put together a strategy, Gabriel? What's your plan?" Action was a good way to get his mind onto other things.

"I called Ricky from the plane. First, we'll hold a staff meeting. We'll keep in the background and let Ricky run it, but we'll be using our powers to scan their minds. Basically, it's you and me, Amaury. I'll try to unlock their memories and go through them to find anything useful, and you'll get to their emotions and find out what they're thinking," Gabriel explained.

Amaury shifted in his seat. He saw a major headache approaching, literally and figuratively.

"There's a big difference between thinking and feeling," Amaury pushed back. "You know as well as I do that I can't read people's minds. Sure, I can figure out roughly what they might be thinking based on what their emotional state is, but it's in no way reliable or detailed. Your gift is much more precise. Maybe we should just rely on yours."

Amaury was so used to sensing emotions that his brain had started translating them into thoughts for him, but he had no idea if his brain was doing a good job or not.

"No, we need you for this," Gabriel protested.

The tone of Gabriel's voice told Amaury that he wouldn't be let off the hook. And right now, he was too tired for a verbal fight which he wasn't sure he would win at the best of times. "We're talking several hundred people here. We can't do it all in one session." There was no way he could take in that many emotions all at once. The pain would be excruciating.

"We'll break them up into smaller groups. How many can you handle at one time?"

Preferably one at a time.

"Twenty-five, maybe." He would never risk being seen as a wimp. "How about you?"

"Twenty-five will be just fine. I'll instruct Ricky. We can't get all of them together at the same time anyway. We'll have a few busy nights ahead of us."

Amaury realized Gabriel was right—those would be busy nights. There wouldn't be much time to hunt for a fresh meal or get enough sex to keep his pain at bay. He would have to find time to sneak away, otherwise things would get dicey for him. Anywhere close to forty-eight hours without sex and he'd start climbing the walls.

"What will the others do?"

"I'll be at the staff meetings with you and Gabriel," Yvette responded. Amaury raised his eyebrows, but didn't say anything. He caught Gabriel's gaze on him.

"Yvette will be useful. She has a photographic memory like Samson."

Now *there* was a tidbit of information he didn't know about her. How had that ever escaped him? Great, and she'd seen him naked. Did she still carry that particular image in her mind? Amaury cringed. "Perfect." He tried to keep all sarcasm out of his voice, but wasn't so sure he succeeded.

Zane cleared his throat. "I'll be infiltrating the criminal elements of the city to listen to the grapevine. I'm sure I'll dig something up."

"I should help you with that," Amaury offered. Navigating the underbelly of San Francisco was much more up his alley than being cooped up in a room with twenty-five employees and their emotions. At least he would get to kick some ass. Being out with Zane virtually guaranteed it.

"We'll need you at the staff meetings," Gabriel insisted, his tone growing increasingly annoyed. "As I already said, we need your gift."

Gift, my ass! It's a curse!

Before Amaury could respond, a loud noise jolted him. In the next instant, smoke rose from underneath the car's hood and entered through the vents.

"Carl, what was that?"

"Don't know, but it's not good. Hold on everybody," Carl yelled.

They were already on a residential street in the outskirts of San Francisco. Carl jerked the car toward the shoulder, but seemed to have difficulty steering as the engine suddenly petered out.

"Carl, talk to me," Amaury ordered, gripping the handle bar above the window.

"Engine blew, brakes are sticky, and the steering is stiff. What else do you want? A running commentary?"

For the first time since he'd known Carl, he saw him lose his temper. His shoulders drawn up, the skin on his neck muscles pulling into tight horizontal lines, Carl was as close to panic as Amaury had ever seen him.

The car flew over a bump on the road and landed hard, lifting everybody out of their seats before they landed hard on their butts again. Vampires weren't into wearing seatbelts.

Another wild steering maneuver and Carl brought the vehicle over the sidewalk. Both the curb and the thick brush the car grazed helped stop it inches before it hit a low fence.

Amaury looked at his colleagues. Everybody appeared a little disheveled, but nobody was hurt.

Immediately, Carl pulled the lever for the hood and jumped out, Amaury on his heels. He heard displeased grunts behind him as he joined Carl who'd already propped the hood up. With his hands Carl waved the smoke and steam away, before he started inspecting the engine.

"Damn," Carl exclaimed after several seconds.

"What?"

"Here, see this?" Carl pointed to a hose, not that Amaury knew exactly what it was. It appeared to be blown to bits. "This didn't just happen on its own. Somebody made sure it did. This was no accident." Carl's grave look was worrisome. He wasn't one to spurt baseless accusations.

Amaury trusted Carl's assessment, even though he himself couldn't confirm it. Other than driving a fast German car, he wasn't really into the mechanics of it. He left that up to people who found tinkering with an engine interesting.

Carl pointed at some tiny items hanging off the shredded hose. Amaury followed his finger. Two wires.

"Looks like somebody didn't want us to get back. Somebody set a charge."

"Shit." Amaury raised his head to scan the horizon and then looked at his watch. "Fifteen minutes to sunrise."

5

The New York vampires scrambled out of the car and congregated around the open hood. Quinn gave the engine a more than cursory look as he bent over it and sniffed.

"The engine's shot. We can't rig it here. We need parts." Quinn gave Amaury a knowing look. "Explosives."

Amaury nodded.

"What now?" Gabriel asked, his voice tense.

"I'll call Oliver to pick us up in the blackout van." Carl flipped his phone open.

"No time. We'll be toast before he gets here. We need to hide," Amaury said.

"Where?" Yvette asked, looking around the quiet neighborhood. "You don't suggest we break into a house and scare the shit out of the inhabitants, do you?"

"That's exactly what we'll have to do," Zane insisted. "There's no time for your misplaced sensitivities." There was a dangerous undertone in his voice.

"Exposure is to be avoided at all cost," Yvette retorted.

Zane took a step toward her, going nose to nose as he let out a low snarl. "Would you rather be exposed to the sun? That can be arranged."

"Shut up, Zane, and leave her alone," Amaury defended her. He had a better idea. "Let's go. Keep up with me. There's a house for sale about four blocks up."

"As much as I like California, I don't think this is the time to buy a house, Amaury," Quinn interrupted. As always he was the most relaxed among them.

"You don't have to buy it, but I'd like to show you guys the inside. Right now."

Amaury launched into a jog. His friends joined him as he ran along the sidewalk.

"Don't you need an appointment to show a house?" Quinn asked in a casual tone.

Amaury pulled out his electronic lockbox key from his jacket pocket and waved it at Quinn. "Not if you have a key to it."

"We'd better be prepared to use our powers in case somebody's there," Gabriel advised.

"It's vacant. I was going to check it out for Samson and Delilah. We can hide out there until Oliver can come and get us."

Yvette pulled up next to him as they continued running down the street. "I didn't expect you defending me against Zane." Was she going to thank him? Now *that* was a departure from their previous interactions. "In any case, I can take care of myself."

No, didn't sound like a thank you after all.

Amaury gave her a sideways glance. "It means nothing." He didn't want her to get the impression he'd gone soft. Zane had been out of line, and Yvette's concern was valid. That was all that was to it. Other than that he didn't give a rat's ass about what she thought of him.

"Still keeping up the same old face, huh?" Her voice had a mocking tone in it he didn't appreciate.

"It's the only one I got." Before Yvette could come back with another smart remark, which he sensed was coming any second now, Gabriel's voice interrupted them.

"Is this it?" He pointed at the large Georgian-style home with a FOR SALE sign on the front lawn.

Amaury sprinted to the gate. He found the familiar blue lockbox bolted to it. Swiftly, he punched his PIN into his electronic key and pointed it at the lockbox. A faint beeping sound indicated the two devices were communicating.

He glanced over his shoulder. In a few seconds the sun would breach the horizon.

Finally, he heard a click and pressed the container. It released a cradle and with it the key to the house.

"Got it."

When he looked up, he saw his five companions already hovering at the entrance door, their eyes pinned on the horizon. They made way for him to get to the lock. A few seconds later the key turned, and the door opened.

"Quick, pull the blinds and the curtains shut," he instructed as they rushed in, each of them running into another room to close the drapes and blinds, shielding them from the rising sun.

"There are no blinds in the kitchen," came Quinn's voice.

Amaury had already slammed the entrance door shut behind him. "Shut the kitchen door."

A quick survey of the house showed him that the best place to wait was in the den, which not only had dark drapes, but also backed up to a sheltered yard with lush trees. The property was tastefully staged with rented furniture, even though it was unoccupied.

"We made it." Gabriel sighed with relief.

Amaury overheard Carl talking on his cell, instructing Oliver to pick them up.

"Samson obviously has other things on his mind if he can't even ensure the security of his own people," Zane chided, clearly needing an outlet for his anger at the situation.

Amaury shot him a warning look, but Carl was faster when it came to an answer.

"Mr. Woodford doesn't deserve your disrespect, and, not that it's any of your business, circumstances—"

"Nobody should have ever gotten a chance at placing an explosive charge in the car," Zane shot back.

Amaury felt Carl's indignation physically, and quickly turned to hide his face from the group as their collective emotions crashed into him. This pain would never change. Even his shrink had practically given up on him.

During his last session a week earlier, Dr. Drake had suggested taking a break. Amaury could still hear his voice. "It's got nothing to do with psychoanalysis. Your problem is not psychological."

Amaury had shot up from his chair and jerked his coat from the hanger, toppling the flimsy metal coat stand. "Thanks a lot. After spending a fortune on these sessions, *now* you have the insight that it's got nothing to do with my psyche? That's rich!"

"Listen, Amaury. We've explored every possibility. It's time to concede to the inevitable. You were cursed, and none of my medical skills will help you lift this curse. You need a witch to help you, not a psychiatrist."

"You forget that witches don't exactly like us."

In fact, witches and vampires were sworn enemies. Not many of the modern vampires remembered how this animosity had started, but when it came down to it, the two factions were at war. It was all about witches being good and vampires being bad, which was all a bunch of horse crap anyway.

"I can't help you anymore as a professional. And we both know that alleviating the pain with sex is only a temporary measure. You'll need to find something permanent." He'd paused, before he'd suddenly changed his tone. "There's one thing I can do though."

Amaury had looked at the doctor as he'd lowered his voice, as if he was afraid of being overheard. With two steps Drake had crossed the distance between them.

"There's a witch who owes me a favor. I'll talk to her on your behalf and see whether she knows how to release you from your pain. But I can't promise anything."

Amaury had shaken the doctor's hand, grateful there was a glimmer of hope, no matter how faint. Over a week had passed since, and still there was no reply from Drake.

An angry voice pulled him back into the present. "Whoever it was, we'll get the bastard," Zane replied, rage rolling off him.

"You okay?" Gabriel asked suddenly.

Amaury jerked his head. "Yeah, sure." But he wasn't certain for how long he would be all right. Already the ride in the car had taxed his mind. If he had to spend another half hour with them and feel their agitated emotions invade his head, he'd go crazy.

"What did Oliver say?"

"He'll be here in about twenty minutes. He said he had to MapQuest the address first. The GPS in his car is broken," Carl explained.

Amaury rolled his eyes. MapQuest? What would these young kids do if they didn't have a computer? They wouldn't find their way around their own back pockets. When Amaury had grown up, there had barely been any accurate maps of an entire continent, let alone a neighborhood.

Amaury shook his head and glanced at his colleagues. The four vampires from New York sat slumped in the chairs and on the sofa. Carl stood to the side as Amaury continued pacing back and forth. He needed to be alone and rest his mind.

"Are you thinking what I'm thinking?" Carl whispered to him.

He nodded.

"It wasn't a coincidence that you had to park the car outside the garage. It gave somebody the opportunity to mess with it. Somebody planned this."

Amaury leaned against the wall and closed his eyes. It was pretty evident. Somebody was trying to stop them from getting reinforcements in. Which meant somebody was watching them and knew their every move. They would have to be on their toes every minute of the day and night.

"You wouldn't have any bottled blood on you, Carl, would you?" Yvette asked.

Carl pulled out a flask from his jacket pocket and handed it to her. "There isn't much. It's just my emergency stash."

Yvette pushed the bottle back into his hand. "Keep it. I can hold out for a little while longer."

"No, please, I don't need it. I fed earlier," Carl insisted and handed the bottle back to her.

To Amaury's knowledge Carl had never fed from a human. He'd been *raised* on bottled blood and was comparatively young. He'd been a vampire for only eighteen years, sired by Samson who'd found him dying after a vicious attack. Carl was the only vampire ever created by Samson.

"No, thanks, that's okay." When she tried to hand the bottle back to Carl, Zane jerked up from the couch and snatched it.

"Take the damn bottle, Yvette, and shut up! We all know how cranky you get when you haven't fed, so do us all a favor and drink." Zane gave her an exasperated look as he shoved the flask into her hand.

Inwardly Amaury had to grin. She could be an absolute pain when she was hungry. At least *he* didn't have to be the one she would be annoyed with for the next few hours. Zane had just taken over that favorite spot.

Yvette grunted something incomprehensible and put the flask to her mouth. Amaury smelled the blood and felt his own stomach constrict. He normally fed only once a night, but the search for his mystery woman had drained his energy more than usual, and he hadn't had time to feed a second time before he and Carl had left for the airport.

Amaury felt his cell phone vibrate in his pocket and pulled it out. He wandered into the hallway and, after checking the caller ID, answered the phone, keeping his voice low.

"Samson, you heard?"

"Yes, Oliver called me. He's on his way. What's going on?" Samson's voice sounded concerned.

"Somebody tampered with the car. I'll arrange for it to be towed to one of our mechanics to check it out, but from what Carl's saying, it pretty much looks like somebody didn't want us to arrive at our destination. Quinn thinks it was explosives."

"Damn! A mole?"

Samson's guess didn't come out of left field. After they had been betrayed by Thomas's lover Milo only months earlier, nobody was above suspicion. Milo's betrayal had resulted in life-threatening injuries to Samson, and only the quick thinking and selflessness of Delilah had saved his life.

"We can't eliminate the possibility. I'll look into it."

"You don't think that one of our New York crew did this?" Samson asked. "How did Quinn know it was an explosive?"

Amaury didn't want to put a black mark against any of them, but anybody could be a traitor. "I noticed him sniff. Could have smelled the residue, especially if he's familiar with plastique. Is he?"

"He did a stint with a bomb-disposal unit a few years back if I remember correctly," Samson confirmed. "How about the others? Anything suspicious?"

"They were in just as much danger as Carl and I, unless one of them had an alternative plan. Zane sure was eager to break into any house to beat sunrise. Thank God, it wasn't necessary. I had my lockbox key."

Samson chuckled. "I can always count on you to multitask. So, what's the house like?"

"Definitely worth a look. I think you and Delilah should check it out. Only, it's a little suburban. Is Delilah up for that?"

Samson let out another soft laugh. "If it were up to Delilah, we'd be staying in our current house even if we had five kids, which frankly, could happen. But we'll need the space, so this is one decision I'll be making."

Amaury let his grin spread over his entire face. "Sure, if you say so." Like his friend had any chance once Delilah made up her mind about something.

"Not funny, Amaury."

Of course it was funny. Ever since Samson had bonded with Delilah, he had softened when it came to anything to do with her. In business he was still the tough guy he'd always been, but his wife was definitely his soft spot.

"I'll check in with you later."

He disconnected the call and walked back toward the den when he heard the engine of an approaching vehicle. Quickly, he went into the living room and slid back the curtain to peer out the window. A ray of sunshine grazed his hand.

"Ouch!" he hissed and jumped back, letting the curtain fall shut again. The smell of singed body hair filled the air. He glanced at his burnt hand. It shouldn't have happened. He was getting sloppy.

Somebody had to go and open the garage door from the inside, so Oliver could drive the van in. Throwing a look back at the den, Amaury shrugged. If he wanted something done, he'd better do it himself.

He opened the door to the garage and hit the electronic garage door opener just to the left of the door. Expecting the garage door to lift automatically, he instantly stepped back into the hallway and closed the door behind him.

Nothing happened. Amaury waited several seconds, but the expected sound of the garage door lifting didn't come. Impatiently, he went back into the garage and pressed the button again. Nothing.

Then he noticed the sign next to the switch.

Fellow Agents,

Please do not use garage door opener. Garage door is jammed and has been bolted. Repair is scheduled for Thursday.

Amaury pulled out his cell and dialed Oliver's number.

"I'm outside, Amaury. Can you let me in?" Oliver's voice answered immediately.

"That's a problem. The garage door is broken."

"Oh, boy!"

Yes, oh, boy.

He and his fellow vampires wouldn't be able to board the van in the safety of the garage, away from the burning rays of the sun. This day sucked—major.

His colleagues liked the news even less than he did when he explained the situation to them after letting Oliver inside.

"You can't be serious," Yvette grumbled, pulling herself straight in her corner of the couch. "I'm not going outside while it's daylight. Pick me up tonight. I'm staying here." She crossed her arms over her ample chest and pouted.

"I'd like to see you try," Zane provoked her. "Already now you're thirsty. How long do you think you can hold out without blood? Or are you planning on sucking on one of us?"

"Fuck you!" Yvette hissed.

Amaury growled. He was sick of the bickering. No matter what anybody said, he and his colleagues wouldn't be able to remain in the house for long.

"Blood is not the issue: we could always get it delivered, but still, staying here is not an option. There's a broker's Open House starting at nine thirty. The listing agent is going to be here by nine o'clock. We can't stay," Amaury informed them.

"We can wipe his memory when he gets here and do the same with any of the buyers who're coming. They'll never remember we were here," Yvette suggested.

Amaury let out a mirthless laugh. "I guess you don't go to a lot of Open Houses, Yvette, otherwise you'd know that the first thing the broker will do is open the curtains and let the light in. You don't show a house in the dark."

Yvette's mouth turned into a thin line. He knew how she hated to be outsmarted.

"Amaury is right. We can't stay," Gabriel's calm voice responded. "It's just a short dash. Yes, we'll have some burns, but we'll survive. When did you all turn into wimps?"

"Can't we fix the garage door?" Yvette asked.

"I don't know about you, but I'm not an electrician," Quinn remarked without malice.

"We'll stick with Amaury's plan, and that's that." Gabriel put his foot down.

At least one person was on Amaury's side. He knew his plan wasn't great, but the alternative was worse. Even if they prevented the broker from opening the curtains by using mind control on him, somebody else might slip through the cracks. Staying here was too risky.

Amaury turned to Oliver. "Back up the van as close to the front door as you can, then open the back doors."

"There are rose bushes blocking the entryway," he advised.

"I don't care. Drive over them." He could send somebody later to take care of the damage and have everything rectified before the listing agent arrived. "Call my cell when you're ready."

Oliver turned to leave.

"I could slap you for getting us into this situation. I should have known you'd screw up." Yvette jumped up from the couch and trained a sour look on Amaury.

"Oh, go ahead. Take a swing if it makes you feel better. As if I give a shit."

He shrugged as he listened to the front door opening and then closing again. He knew Yvette all too well. She was all talk and no action. Soon she'd run out of steam and deflate again. It wasn't worth wasting his breath on it.

The kick to his stomach had Amaury revise his opinion of her. He doubled over. She'd obviously perfected her karate moves and decided to hand out the beating he'd been due for years.

"Bitch!" He didn't have enough breath for a wittier response while his body dealt with the unexpected assault.

"Yvette, that's enough," Gabriel reprimanded. "We all know what this is about."

Amaury pulled himself straight. His stomach muscles readjusted. Her kick had nothing to do with the present and everything to do with the past.

He made a mental note never to fuck a colleague again, no matter how desperate he got. It was definitely better to stick to nameless, faceless women whose memories he could erase and whom he would never see again.

"Guess we're even then," he said, and nodded to her.

"We'll see," she hedged.

The woman sure could hold a grudge. Same damn memory as an elephant.

"I'll go first," Quinn volunteered cheerfully as if to diffuse the tension. A few seconds later, Amaury's cell phone rang. Oliver was in place.

***

An hour later, Amaury was back in his top-floor apartment in the Tenderloin, tending to his second- and third-degree burns. The dark in his place soothed him. His electronic blinds had closed automatically seconds before sunrise. They were programmed to lift again shortly after sunset.

The neighborhood was sleazy, but it suited him. At least here, the chance of constantly being surrounded by people in love was remote. Anger, despair, and hunger were the predominant emotions circulating in the neighborhood.

His physical wounds would heal while he slept during the day, but he needed blood to help the process. Unlike many of his friends, he'd never taken to bottled blood and therefore had no ready supply in his home.

But there were tenants in the building, tenants he'd selected carefully himself. As their landlord he knew that most of them would be out during the day, but there was one who was almost always at home.

Amaury dragged himself through the dim and windowless stairwell, commanding his aching legs to make it down one flight of stairs. He rang the doorbell and waited. It seemed to take forever until he heard the shuffling of footsteps on the other side. A chain was released a moment later, then the door swung open fully.

The old lady looked as if she'd just woken up. She tightened the belt of her bathrobe around her waist.

"Good morning, Mrs. Reid," Amaury greeted her.

"Oh, Amaury, did you just come back from night shift?" Only now she seemed to take a good look at him and flinched instantly. "Oh, dear, another accident at the factory?"

He'd made up a cover story many years ago, telling her he worked as a night supervisor at a foundry in the East Bay. It would explain why he slept all day and would occasionally come home with injuries.

He nodded. "I'm afraid so."

"You look terrible. Have you seen a doctor?" The old dear was all concerned and sweet.

Amaury hated himself for what he had to do, but he had no choice. He needed blood to heal.

He would make it up to her later. He could lower her rent and even cook her one of his best French dishes. She would like that.

Amaury employed mind control and let himself into her apartment. As soon as he closed the door behind him, he sank his fangs into her neck. Only when her rich blood coated his throat did he realize the extent of his need to feed. Desperate to still his thirst and regain his strength, he took big gulps from her vein.

6

Nina blamed her informant. He'd clearly sold her out. Why else would she be standing in an alley, staring into the ugly faces of two vampire dudes flashing their fangs at her and bent on kicking her ass? She'd unknowingly walked into a trap.

Well, at least one mystery was solved: not all vampires were handsome. In fact, the taller of the two was butt ugly. His nose was tilted too far upwards, showing his nostrils the way a pig's snout would look. She certainly wouldn't have any scruples turning him into dust— that was, if she got a chance. At the moment, that chance looked pretty remote.

Instead of meeting with some low-level criminal who had information on the vampires, her contact, that shitty little weasel, had purposely let her run into a trap. If she got out of this alive, she would beat the shit out of that rotten lowlife, even if it was the last thing she did.

Nina didn't need to glance behind her to know she was at a dead end, literally and figuratively. She stood in one of the many little alleys in the Tenderloin. There was a constant stench of urine, vomit, and alcohol in the neighborhood. The sidewalks were always littered with trash.

Gripping a stake in each hand, she gritted her teeth. Nina was no stranger to fighting. She was extremely agile and was proficient in kickboxing—down-and-dirty style, the way it was fought on the streets, not in the *dojos* or the fancy gyms. She'd kicked more ass than Jean-Claude Van Damme in any of his B-movies. But this fight wouldn't be even. One of the bloodsuckers she could probably defeat, but two at the same time was a challenge she wasn't keen on facing.

Her palms were sweaty, her heartbeat erratic, but she had no choice. She had to fight. A glance toward the only exit of the alley told her that while there were plenty of cars passing by on the main road, nobody was stopping. The cavalry wasn't coming.

She knew she had to be smart about it, use brain instead of brawn.

"Aren't you two pretty ones?" Nina mocked. She wouldn't show them how scared she was.

The shorter vampire let a snarl rip from his throat. "Hmm, looks like delicious dinner."

Dinner?

Not if she could help it. "More like an *amuse-bouche*. There's hardly enough for one of you, let alone two." Maybe she could get them to fight amongst each other. "Look, there really isn't much of me at all."

She stretched her arms out to the sides to show off her slender body, while covertly adjusting her stance to fighting mode.

"It'll be plenty," Butt Ugly assured her and flashed his fangs.

"Now, I hope you brushed your teeth this evening. There's nothing worse than a vampire with bad breath," she chided. Was it smart to provoke him? Anything to gain time so she could work out a strategy was fine with her. Even if it meant making them mad.

"Sassy, I give you that. I'm sure your blood will taste quite spicy. What do you think, Johan?" One side of his mouth tilted upwards and turned into a smug snarl.

His companion grinned. "I think we should do her first." He moved his pelvis in a way which left little to her imagination.

Great! Now they wanted to do her.

Why did men always have to think about sex when they couldn't control a woman any other way?

"Typical man! Can't defeat a woman with his intellect, so he's got to whip out his dick. That's really manly, wow." She flicked her middle finger at them.

Johan took a step closer, but Butt Ugly stopped him. "The boss said to get rid of her and stop her from snooping around any longer, so that's all we're gonna do." He paused and angled his head as if assessing her for the first time. "Well, no use wasting a good snack." He smacked his lips together in an unmistakable gesture.

Nina didn't like the sound of it. No wonder her informant had sold her out. Somebody was after her. And she had an idea of who had sent these goons. Amaury had obviously realized after their encounter last night that she knew he was a vampire and was now taking action.

If she hadn't completely lost it during his kiss, maybe her hand wouldn't have twitched and accidentally dropped the stake. He'd most likely heard it fall to the ground and found it. It didn't take much to put two and two together. She couldn't dwell on it. Her half-baked plan of distracting him with a kiss had backfired, and now she was going to pay for it. Dearly.

If she was going down, at least she would try to take one of them with her. Apart from her life, she had nothing else to lose.

"I failed you, Eddie," she whispered to herself. A second later she lifted her head and locked her jaw. One deep breath to fill her lungs with oxygen, and she was ready for her last fight.

Nina launched into a sprint, gained momentum and jumped, kicking her foot into Johan's chest, Bruce-Lee style. The vampire was taken by surprise and stumbled backwards. Without taking a breath, she landed firmly on both feet and instantly turned back, facing the second vampire.

Butt Ugly sneered. His right hook connected with her shoulder, before she had even seen it coming. Her body whipped back as the pain radiated downwards. For a moment, black dots clouded her vision. Her lungs fought for breath, fighting against the burn charging through her cells.

Damn, the bastard was fast!

A sound behind her warned her that Johan was on his feet again. Guessing what was coming, she took a roll to the side before his claws could grab her. It didn't save her for long. Butt Ugly reared his head and jumped toward her.

Nina lunged onto the dumpster and escaped his reach by jumping off on the other side.

"Go around it," Butt Ugly ordered his companion.

Now they both came toward her, one from the right, one from the left. Remembering her gymnastics training, she did a cartwheel and vaulted over the bins a second time. Her shoe caught on the bin and she slipped, landing hard on her side.

Searing pain ripped through her. Her ribs felt badly bruised; she would be lucky if they weren't broken. But she had no time to check. Her attackers were already upon her. A claw dug into her shoulder and pulled her up, lifting her off the ground.

"Now we've got you," Johan said, triumph coloring his voice.

"You bastards!" she screamed at the top of her lungs and kicked her legs at him, still suspended in the air. With her right arm she tried to grasp for any part of his body where she could do damage, but only now did she realize that she'd lost one of her stakes with her evasive maneuvers. Her left hand still held the second stake, but Johan had immobilized her with his painful grip to her shoulder.

She kicked again, earning herself a swipe of his claws across her chest. A burning sensation hit her. The bastard had sliced through her shirt and skin. She could feel the blood seep from the gash on her breast. It stung like hell.

For an instant, she feared nausea would overwhelm her and knock her out cold. She pushed back the feeling.

"That smells nice," Johan said and moved his head to her open wound.

Nina thrashed harder, but his grip tightened. He would suck her dry, and there was nothing she could do. She had no chance of getting out of his hold. Panic coiled through her body, her heart beating as fast as a high-speed train.

A split second before his fangs dug into her breast, he was pulled away from her. A moment later she landed hard on her butt. She stared up at the melee, expecting to see Butt Ugly fighting with his vampire friend. Instead, she was looking at the broad back of a huge man. Even without seeing his face, she recognized who was fighting her two assailants now.

Nina scrambled back onto her feet. In disbelief, she watched Amaury land kicks and blows against the two vampires, keeping them at bay. Why was he fighting off the two vampires he'd sent to kill her? This didn't make any sense at all.

"You gonna help me or what?" Amaury called out. Was he talking to her? "You, the blonde who kissed me last night."

So, he *was* talking to her. After all, she was the only blonde in the alley, and she doubted either Butt Ugly or Johan had kissed him.

She rushed to his side.

He acknowledged her with a sideways glance. "About time!"

With a quick high kick she fought off Johan to give Amaury a chance to beat the crap out of Butt Ugly. But Johan came back instantly, charging at her more fiercely now. When she tried for another kick, he was faster and grabbed her foot. She twisted, but lost her balance, falling backwards against Amaury.

"Duck," he called out. In the same instant he turned behind her. Instinctively she crouched down, and looking up, she saw Amaury land a heavy right hook into her attacker's face, slamming him into the wall five feet away.

"Thanks," she gasped.

"Don't mention it." He turned back to his own attacker. Nina caught the moment when Butt Ugly's claws beat into Amaury, forcing him to the ground. Helping her had distracted him and cost him the upper hand. The attacker pinned him and raised his arm.

"No!" She heard Amaury's scream and saw the stake in Butt Ugly's hand glint in the faint light coming from one of the windows facing the alley. Without thinking, Nina jumped behind the nasty vampire and landed on his back. Just as the tip of his stake reached Amaury's chest, she slammed her own stake into the vampire's back and hoped she'd found the spot where his damn heart was located.

As the bastard dissolved into dust, she landed right on Amaury, her legs straddling him. He wore his light jacket open, as well as cargo pants and a shirt, which brought her into much closer contact with his body than the night before when he'd worn a long coat. For a moment, the warmth of his body startled her. How could he be so warm? He was a vampire—vampires were supposed to be cold.

"You're w—"

His hand snapped around her wrist which still held the stake. He nudged the offending item away from him while he pinned her with a surprised stare.

"Careful, you could hurt somebody with that," he said, smirking.

Smartass!

Nina didn't get a chance to reply. From the corner of her eye she saw Johan approach, a knife in his hands. He lifted his arm and aimed it straight at her, ready to release it with a quick flick of his wrist.

Before she could move, Amaury twisted underneath her, wrapped his arms around her, and shifted. Instead of the knife hitting her chest, it grazed her shoulder, slicing into the top layer of her skin. The pain was overridden by the adrenaline shooting through her body.

She noticed Amaury's furious look before he unceremoniously dumped her on the ground and jumped onto his feet. Obviously Johan had picked up on the same look and instantly turned tail.

With the immediate danger over, the pain from her wounds suddenly crashed over her, and she let out a frustrated moan. Amaury immediately turned back to her instead of pursuing the other vampire.

"You okay?" Was that worry in his voice?

He crouched down next to her, a concerned look on his face. Was it such a good idea to be so close to a vampire when she was a walking advertisement for his favorite food?

"What's it look like?" She figured it was better not to show him that she was worried about the fact that she leaked blood like a self-serve soda fountain. Would he try to bite her now that he could surely smell her blood? Even her own nose picked up the metallic scent of it.

"You look pretty beat up to me. Let's go and fix you up."

He took her arm to pull her up, but she wrenched free from him as soon as she stood.

"Don't touch me." An instant later her stance faltered, and dizziness overwhelmed her.

"You can't stand on your own," he commented, a smug tone in his voice, and picked her up as if she were as light as a bag of groceries. "You're coming with me."

"No!" Nina protested and tried to wiggle out of Amaury's arms, but her strength was quickly draining. "I'm not going with a vampire."

"Tough luck—I'm the only one here. And I'm not leaving an injured woman in the street where she can get attacked again." His voice sounded firm and unyielding. Great, not only was he a vampire, he was also a Neanderthal on steroids.

You Tarzan, me Jane.

"So, do you have a name?" he asked, carrying her undeterred through the night.

"Hmm," she growled. He wouldn't get a peep out of her.

"Fine, I can just keep on calling you The Blonde Who Kissed Me. By the way, nice kiss. Were you going to repeat that any time soon? 'Cause if I call you The Blonde Who Kissed Me, I might get ideas." The exaggerated waggle of his eyebrows was almost comical, had she been in the mood to laugh.

The man was a pill. But she didn't want to be reminded of that kiss every few minutes. It was going to be hard enough, being pressed against his strong chest. With every step he made, his muscles shifted and rubbed against her, sending the most delicious sensations through her aching body. It was truly irritating.

"Nina. My name is Nina," she finally admitted. "And you're welcome." She lifted her chin and set her jaw.

He cocked an eyebrow.

"Hey, I saved your sorry ass back there," she elaborated. His short-term memory was clearly in need of jogging.

"Only after I saved yours, so in my book we're even."

He was right, but she'd rather bite off her tongue than admit it.

"I can say thank you if you can." His look was a challenge.

"You first." She wouldn't get tricked into thanking him, if he didn't thank her first.

"No, you first," he retorted and kept walking, carrying her as if she weighed nothing.

A young couple passed them on the sidewalk and gave them perplexed looks. Nina restrained herself from telling them to mind their own damn business.

"Forget it."

"Brat!"

"Whom are you calling a brat? Look at yourself, you oversized jerk!"

Big, hunky, sexy oversized jerk.

"Well, this oversized jerk came in handy a few minutes ago, don't you think? And besides, you didn't find me to be such a jerk when you kissed me last night. I remember distinctly how you were all over me."

Embarrassment swept through her, making her cheeks flare with heat. She needed no reminder of her wanton behavior of the night before. It wasn't how she normally reacted to men. They were to be used just the way they'd used her—nothing more, nothing less. And it had always worked for her: no emotional involvement, no abandonment of her good senses, well, not the way it had happened the night before anyway. It was merely a slip, she assured herself. Even the most determined alcoholic fell off the wagon occasionally. Now all she had to do was get back on it and forget what had happened.

As if it was that easy with the way her body tingled under his touch. His scent of leather and spice alone made her stomach spasm—and she wasn't talking menstrual cramps, no, she was talking orgasmic spasms. She'd do well staying away from him.

"Do you need a reminder?" Amaury lowered his head.

Hell, no!

She remembered all too well. "Don't you dare!" Nina yelled, more at herself than at him. If she allowed him to kiss her again, she'd completely melt and turn into a lump of putty. She couldn't afford for that to happen to her. Once had been sufficient, thank you very much.

He grinned down at her with his bad-boy charm that turned her insides to mush.

"Maybe later?" he asked and continued walking along, seemingly unaffected by her outburst.

Nina glanced around, trying to get her bearings. They were still in the Tenderloin and only a block from his place.

"Where are you taking me?" She could guess, but wanted confirmation.

"My place. I doubt you'd want me to bring you to a hospital. Am I right?"

A hospital wouldn't be a good choice. With her injuries, she was sure they'd involve the police. Not only was she not going to be able to explain to them that she'd been in a fight with vampires, but her own background would come up in the process. And she preferred her background to remain where it was—in the dark.

"Care to explain to me what a girl like you was doing fighting two vampires?"

"How about you explain it?"

His stunned look appeared genuine and surprised her. "You're not suggesting I had anything to do with that?"

"Well, did you?"

Amaury slowly moved his head from side to side. "I'm not the kind of man who sends two guys after helpless women like you."

"I'm not helpless."

He raised a mocking eyebrow. "Whatever. I do my own dirty work. I don't hire others to do it for me and then jump in to defend you against them."

"I see."

"I don't see how you could." He paused. "I was looking for you. Seems somebody else found you first. Wanna explain to me what they wanted from you, besides the obvious?"

How much of the pre-fight discussion had he heard? Was he aware that Johan had wanted to have his fun with her? "I wouldn't know. I was as surprised by the two as you were."

"Believe me, vampires don't attack indiscriminately. There's always a reason."

He couldn't be serious. Vampires attacked whenever they felt like it or found an easy target. As if they needed a reason to do harm. Did he think she was gullible enough to believe vampires had some sort of moral code they operated by?

"Since they were the ones attacking me, maybe you should ask *them*."

"Dead vampires don't talk."

"One's still alive. How about you go after him, rather than abduct me?"

"I'm taking care of you first, whether you like it or not."

They entered a six-story apartment building, and effortlessly, Amaury carried her up the stairs to the top floor.

"Can you grab my keys out of my right jacket pocket, please?"

It would be easier if he'd drop her onto her feet, but he seemed to have no intention of doing so. Nina bent toward his side and stretched her arm to reach into his pocket. The action brought her head closer to his. She felt him inhale sharply. Was he sniffing her hair?

She quickly took the keys out of his pocket and reached toward the door. Within seconds they were inside. Nina took in the large apartment. The ceilings were at least twelve feet high, and the style reminded her of the 1920s, which was probably when the building was erected. To her right were floor-to-ceiling windows with a view into downtown and the Bay Bridge.

There was a small office alcove and a sitting area. In another corner she saw a punching bag suspended from the ceiling, something she'd expect to see in a boxing gym, not the home of a vampire. Not that she'd ever been to a vampire's lair.

Amaury placed her on the couch. When his arms released her, she felt strangely cold and shivered instantly. It confirmed what she'd felt when straddling him earlier: his body was warm. And now that she thought of it, when he'd kissed her the night before, his lips and tongue had been downright hot. How could that be? She'd always assumed that a vampire's body was cold—in fact, she knew that from the movies. But no way would she ask him why. For all she knew, over-confident as he was, he'd think she was interested in him, when she was anything but!

"You've lost some blood. Here." He handed her the afghan which had carelessly lain over the backrest of the armchair.

"Thanks." She took the blanket with shaking fingers and covered her lower body with it. Nervousness crept through her body at the knowledge that she was alone with him in his place. This was his home turf—he had all the advantage he could ever want.

"See, you do have some manners." He walked toward one of the doors and disappeared behind what she assumed was either the master bedroom or a bathroom.

"You oaf!" she grumbled under her breath. The man was infuriating. He treated her like a child. And she was anything but that.

Leaving her last foster home with her little brother in tow had ensured she'd grown up fast. Stealing, cheating, and fighting her way through adolescence had done the rest. And now she was a self-sufficient grown woman of twenty-seven. Definitely no child!

"What are you mumbling?"

He'd surprised her with how fast he'd returned, a bowl of water and a towel in hand.

"I'm not mumbling anything."

"Move over," he ordered. "I'm going to clean your cuts."

"I can do it myself. You're not getting anywhere near my blood." Did she have "naïve" tattooed on her forehead? Like she didn't know what he wanted.

"Ah, I see the issue. You're worried I'll bite? If that were my intention I would have done it where I found you. Trust me, take-out is fine by me. I feed on the go."

He compared her to take-out food?

"Those fangs of yours aren't coming anywhere near my skin." She underscored her answer with a warning glance which the big bad vampire completely ignored.

"And here I thought you liked me, considering that kiss . . . "

He had the gall to throw that issue back into her face.

Jerk!

7

Amaury suppressed his urge to smile. Nina was quite a fighter and sparring with him at every turn. He'd been out wandering the streets in search of a meal after his burns from the day before had healed when an intoxicating scent had drifted his way. Instantly, he'd recognized it as the scent of the woman who'd kissed him the night before.

As he'd followed her trail, he'd suddenly heard a scream. Instinctively, he'd known it was she even though he'd never heard her voice before. Once he saw the dilemma she was in, there had been no hesitation on his part. He had to protect her no matter what.

He didn't know either of the two vampires she was fighting and was pretty damn sure they were new in town. Nina had proven to be quite good with the stake, and luckily she hadn't used it on him. However, when she'd suddenly straddled him after she'd dusted that bastard, his heart rate had doubled. Amaury wasn't sure whether the reason was the stake in her hand or the position she had taken above him.

Despite her protests now, he sat down on the couch, nudging her aside with his thigh against her hip. And he had his answer: his heart was pounding again. It was the contact with her body, which made his heart rate spike, just as it had when she'd straddled him, and during that first kiss.

First?

Yes, because there would be a second and a third and a . . .

Amaury cleared his throat. "Nina, let's get that shirt off you." He liked using her name. It suited her right down to the short, honey curls and those plump lips that were made for kissing. He promised himself right there and then that she wouldn't leave his place until he'd tasted those lips again.

"No! I'm not wearing anything underneath."

His heart stopped for an instant as a vision of her naked skin appeared in his mind.

Even better!

"Well, that saves me from having to liberate you from your bra." Could she hear the desire in his voice, feel the heat in his body as anticipation of seeing her naked raised his temperature?

"Jerk!"

She could shout at him all she wanted. He knew she had no other weapons on her—well, at least none which could hurt him. The knife she carried on her hip was of metal—thankfully not silver—and would do no damage to him, which meant at least tonight she wouldn't try to kill him. It was a definite improvement over the previous night.

"How do you expect me to take care of your wounds if you don't want to take off your shirt?"

"I can do it myself."

"Are you always this stubborn?"

No answer.

"Will it kill you to let somebody help you?"

Nina pressed her lips together into a thin line, then gingerly pushed one side of her tattered garment off her shoulder, revealing a large gash. Her skin was pink. The scent of blood wrapped around him, engulfing him in her essence. How could he possibly not be affected by this tempting creature? Resistance was futile, surrender inevitable. The jury was still out on who would surrender to whom.

"Looks bad." He made a corner of the towel wet and gently patted the wound with it, soaking up the blood which kept seeping from it. She winced despite the fact he barely used any pressure on the wound.

"I'm sorry, but I'll have to clean it out, so it won't get infected. Luckily the knife only grazed you."

When he'd seen the vampire readying himself to throw the knife, he'd reacted out of pure instinct. Because she'd straddled him—a position he had enjoyed for far too brief a time—he hadn't been able to move fast enough to prevent her from being hurt.

Amaury lowered his head, pretending to inspect the wound. In truth, he enjoyed her closeness. "It's not too deep."

"Don't you have any rubbing alcohol or something?" she asked.

"I'm afraid not. I don't exactly keep a first-aid kit around, since I don't need it myself."

His own wounds from the day before had healed without the aid of any man-made medication while he'd slept.

"Right; being a vampire, I suppose, has its advantages," she remarked in a clipped tone.

The way she said it didn't sound like she considered this to be a good thing. His ability to heal quickly was one of the things he liked most about being a vampire. Injuries sucked.

"What else do you know about me? Should I introduce myself or is that unnecessary?" he asked. For a second he reconsidered his decision of bringing her into his home, but since she knew what he was anyway, there was no use in hiding. Maybe she already had a whole dossier on him. He wouldn't mind helping her add some details to it, such as what he liked in bed.

"Amaury LeSang," Nina answered simply.

It didn't surprise him that she knew his name. Since she'd followed him the previous night and had come prepared with a stake, she probably knew more than just his name.

"This is the first time I've had my own little stalker. I'm quite flattered." Unless, of course, she tried to kill him again, if that was what her intention had been the previous night.

"I'm not a stalker." Her defiant glare hit him like a punch in the gut. There was so much pain in her eyes, he wanted to merely wrap her into his arms and squeeze her tight. His own reaction surprised him. He wasn't the cuddly kind.

"What do you call it then when you follow me around at night?"

Again her mouth distorted into a thin line. Nina obviously didn't like to be cornered. No answer was forthcoming. Was she pissed now and not talking to him anymore?

"You mean I'm not the only one you stalk? Well, now I'm hurt. And here I thought you were interested in me."

"Oh, you're such a pompous ass!" she spat.

"Pompous ass or not, it got you talking." Amaury smirked. He loved the way her cheeks reddened and could almost feel the heat in them radiate outwards. She was lovely when she was angry. Maybe he should continue provoking her.

He felt her warm skin under his hand where he held her shoulder to keep it immobile. He let his thumb stray, slowly gliding over her skin. The motion heated the natural oils on her skin, and the intoxicating scent drifted into his nose. She was like a heady perfume, making him dizzy. That and the aroma of her blood played havoc with his body and mind.

His fangs twitched, ready to descend and drive into her flesh, hungering for a taste.

"What are you looking at?" Nina suddenly asked, her voice edgy. Had she caught him staring?

"We'll have to close up the wound, otherwise it won't stop bleeding."

Good save, Amaury!

"You wouldn't have a Band Aid lying around?" Her tone was sarcastic. She clearly didn't trust him further than she could throw him, which wouldn't be very far at all. Not with his massive proportions. He perused her pretty frame. She wasn't petite, but compared to him, she looked fragile. Her body was well proportioned: generous curves, strong muscles, yet feminine.

"Do you?" Her voice made him lift his eyes to look at her wound again. Band Aid? No, he didn't have such a thing.

"I've got something better than that." What the hell, he'd just do what he would normally do: close the wound with his saliva. Use the tools he had.

Amaury lowered his head to her shoulder and felt her pull away from him. "What are you doing?" Panic laced her voice, and her eyes opened wide.

"I'll lick your wound. My saliva will mend it." It was simple enough and would be delicious. He'd get a taste of her blood after all.

Nina jerked backwards, scrambling to get away from him, but he pulled her back with both hands.

"Trust me, it won't hurt." He infused his voice with a soothing tone.

"Do you think I'm stupid?"

"Not at all. Actually, I think you're quite smart. Very few humans have figured us out, but obviously you have."

"That's right. And that's exactly why I'm not going to let you near my blood." There was a hard tone in her voice, mirroring her icy look. Melting that ice had just turned into the most important task on his agenda.

"Don't get hysterical. I won't bite you. You can hit me if I do," he offered with a roguish grin. Then he pulled her closer while he continued to watch her eyes. She was still scared. She didn't trust him, but she allowed him to come closer. Without haste, he lowered his lips onto her skin. So soft, like silk, like velvet.

The scent of blood almost drugged him, but he pushed back his hunger. "You'll feel my tongue. It will tingle. Ready?"

There was no reply, but he could feel her holding her breath.

Slowly, his tongue darted through his lips and lapped at the cut. Her blood leapt onto his tongue and ran down his throat as he licked upwards to the end of the wound. Nina tasted of vanilla and spices. He'd never tasted anything as good. If he had a choice, he'd be feasting on her every night and never try anything else again.

He licked over the cut once more, even more slowly this time to savor the moment, but already he felt the skin close and mend. No more blood seeped from it. She would have a small scar, but the wound had already healed. Unable to tear himself away, he placed his lips on the spot he'd healed and kissed it.

"Is that part of it?" he heard her ask.

It wasn't, but for her he would make it part of the healing process. "Yes." Amaury planted another feather-light kiss on the wound.

He looked up and met her gaze. Did she know he was lying?

Nina inspected the spot and for the first time gave him an approving look. "Wow, that's impressive."

"Didn't hurt, did it?"

The question made her blush. She suddenly looked soft and vulnerable, not like the tough fighter he'd met in the alley.

"Let's check your other injuries."

Amaury tried to be as professional about it as he could, but was sure he could barely disguise his eagerness. He hoped he'd find many little cuts he could seal. Any excuse to touch her skin and kiss her. He wanted to do this all night. Lick every square inch of her enticing body, explore each fold and every ridge.

"I'm fine. That was the only injury," Nina assured him and straightened.

Amaury looked down at her shirt and noticed the torn fabric over her breast and the bloodstains on it. "Liar."

He opened the top button of her shirt, while Nina tried to push his hands away.

"Hold still. I'm just trying to help you." There was nothing wrong with him getting a bit of action in the process.

"Right!" she hissed.

"Come on; think of me as a doctor." He'd be more than happy playing doctor with her, especially if he got to examine her naked. And if she was shy, he'd help her over her shyness by getting naked himself. In fact, he'd ask her to undress him.

Undeterred, he opened another button. Nina's hand came up to stop him. Gently he brushed it away and continued. As he eased another button open and glimpsed the curve of her breast, he sucked in a sharp breath.

Air conditioning. He should have switched on the air conditioning. It was getting far too warm in the apartment.

When the last button was undone, he pulled back the right side of her shirt, exposing her breast to his view. Ignoring the cut for a second, he noticed the perfect roundness, the size of a small grapefruit, waiting for his caress. A ripe fruit ready for harvesting. He was one lucky son of a bitch.

Again, Amaury had to clear his dry throat. "It's a bad cut. I'll clean it with warm water first." He had to keep talking, so he wouldn't fall over her and devour her. "I think he got you with one of his claws."

He looked up and noticed that Nina had turned her face away from him as if she couldn't watch. His gaze went back to her breast. The cut was about three inches long and had barely missed her nipple. It continued bleeding.

Slowly, he took the wet towel and started cleaning her wound with one hand, while his other one cradled her breast from underneath to hold it still. She jerked at first when he settled her soft globe into his palm, but said nothing. He liked feeling the weight of it in his hand, realizing it was the perfect size for him. He gave it a barely noticeable squeeze. A perfect combination of firmness and softness greeted him.

"I'll have to close the cut now. You're losing too much blood." He spoke in a low voice, not wanting to alarm her in any way, not wanting to destroy this perfect moment.

Nina finally met his eyes. "Do it." He was surprised by the huskiness in her voice.

The moment Amaury dipped his head to her breast, he knew he would do more than heal her cut. The desire coursing through his loins had him in a tight grip. At the first lap of his tongue over the injury, he grew hard. He let the blood run down the back of his tongue and forced himself to take it slowly, so he could prolong the moment of sheer and utter bliss he felt. Twice already he'd licked over the cut and it had sealed, but he was unable to stop.

"Nina," he whispered as his tongue strayed from the cut and lapped over her hardened nipple. *Hardened?* Was she aroused?

And then he felt her hands in his hair, as if to hold him in place. His lips locked around her nipple, and slowly he suckled. His hand kneaded her gorgeous breast as he sucked her nipple deeper into his mouth. He couldn't get enough of her. She tasted like heaven, like a dream, a fairy tale.

Even the way she played with his hair turned him on. When she suddenly released a moan, he thought he would come right there and spill in his pants. His cock yearned for her soft center, giving him a painful reminder that he hadn't had sex in over twenty-four hours.

Amaury released her nipple, only to lavish his attention on her other breast. He dared not use his teeth to tug harder, lest he scare her. But he wanted her—no, *needed* her—underneath him. He pressed her back into the sofa cushions and shifted his own position, nudging his heavy thigh between her legs.

***

Nina felt his weight on her and his thigh pressing against her sex, as he continued to use his talented tongue on her breasts. With every lap, he sent bolts of fire down to her core, liquidizing everything in its path. She felt her panties soak with the evidence of her desire and was unable to stop her body from responding to him. The same way he responded to her: his erection pressing against her hip was impossible to ignore. Too big to overlook, too hard to wish away, even if she wanted to.

Nina arched her back to force him closer and slipped her hand onto his firm ass. His muscles bunched under her touch when she squeezed him. Would his skin feel soft or rough? Would it be smooth, firm, and warm? Without thinking, she let her hand glide underneath the loose-fitting cargo pants to explore.

She gasped when skin met skin. The man didn't even wear underwear. Just the thought of it turned her body temperature up by five degrees.

He groaned loudly when she grabbed him firmly. Amaury released her breast just long enough for an excited "Oh, yes" to pass his lips.

Then his mouth blazed a trail of molten lava from her breast to her neck, before he looked at her. The moment he pressed his lips onto hers, she noticed his eyes flash red. His lips urged her to surrender, as his tongue teased her. Resistance would be impossible. Her tongue met his for an unequal duel. As he gained ground, she suddenly felt how he pressed her harder into the cushions, until—her tongue touched his fangs! What the hell was she doing? Sleeping with the enemy?

Nina shrieked and pushed back with all her strength. Instantly, a wave of pain raced through her ribs again. "Ahh!" she cried out in agony.

She was stupid, stupid, stupid!

Amaury pulled back and lifted his weight from her. "What's wrong?" He looked concerned, but she wasn't fooled. His eyes were flashing red like alarm beacons, and his pointy teeth peeked out from beneath his lips. If she'd ever had any doubts about what he was, all of those were extinguished with one look at his sharp fangs.

Holding her ribs to counteract the pain, she glared at him. She couldn't form a coherent sentence, still too dazed from his touch and kiss.

"Why didn't you tell me you had another injury?" he accused her and touched her side with his hand.

Nina flinched, not because it hurt, but because she didn't want to feel his touch. It made her dizzy and stupid. Only a stupid woman would be making out with a vampire—and liking it.

"Don't touch me," she barked.

Amaury gave her a startled look. "I'm sorry; I didn't mean to hurt you. You should have said something before."

He reached for her side and placed his hand over her ribs. She wanted to pull back, but he shot her a warning glance. "Keep still."

His gentle movements, testing whether her ribs were broken, were unexpected. How could a vampire with such large hands have such a soft touch? Maybe she'd hit her head during the fight and was hallucinating.

"Nothing seems to be broken. They're only bruised." When he looked at her again, she noticed that the red in his eyes had disappeared and been replaced by a deep blue. Did the man have to look this gorgeous?

Nina nodded. "It hurts like hell."

His hand came up to stroke her cheek so softly that she couldn't reconcile this side of him with the glimpses of vampire she'd seen.

"I'll be more careful in the future." Amaury's lips curled into a roguish grin. "So, where were we?"

His mouth approached her, but she pulled back. The man was obviously so overconfident that he thought he could just continue where he'd left off. As if she were some grateful damsel in distress who'd go all gaga over her rescuer.

Arrogant prick!

"We were right at the end. And it's not going anywhere from here."

Nina had to stop this madness and get out of his place. He was most likely using some vampire trick on her, some sort of glamour or control.

Why else would she have let him touch her and kiss her so intimately? That had to be the reason, for sure. She wasn't the kind of woman who'd just let her hormones rage and melt the moment a hot guy showed her some attention. No, she was always in control. Vampire or not, he was a man, and men were not to be trusted.

"Maybe you should rest a little. Can I get you anything?"

What was Amaury up to? Maybe he was planning to drug her. It wasn't safe here. She should have never allowed him to bring her to his apartment.

His lusting gaze reminded her that her shirt was still gaping open, exposing her breasts. She quickly pulled it together in the front and caught him frown.

"Can you bring me an icepack for my ribs to keep the swelling down?"

Amaury got up from the couch, bringing his crotch to eyelevel. His huge hard-on was impossible to overlook. Was he doing this on purpose to tempt her? Her womb clenched at the thought of what it would feel like to have his cock inside her.

"Sure. Give me a minute."

Nina watched him as he walked to the kitchen. She figured she had less than a minute before he would be back with the icepack, and she used it wisely.

In under ten seconds she was at the entrance door, opening it quietly. Luckily she hadn't taken her shoes off. She didn't bother with buttoning her shirt, but scurried out the door without looking back.

Amaury was dangerous, and not only because he was a vampire. He was a man who could get to her, penetrate her defenses, and devastate her. She could never let that happen. All these years she'd carefully guarded her heart so nobody would ever hurt her again. She wouldn't let her guard down now. Not for him or anybody else.

And he was still the enemy. She couldn't betray Eddie's memory by consorting with the very man who, together with his partners, was responsible for his death. She felt like a traitor for having felt pleasure when Amaury had touched her. She would never allow it again.

8

The door connected with the weasel's face and knocked him backwards into the kitchen of his sorry excuse for a studio apartment. The place stank. Nina tried to ignore the unpleasant odors of stale smoke, mold, and spoiled food, and concentrate on the man in front of her.

With an angry jerk of her foot, she slammed the door shut behind her. Her informant held his bloody nose and gave her a shocked look. She kicked him in the balls for good measure, and he doubled over. Who was the weaker sex now?

"Stop it," he begged.

She hated beating up people who were smaller than she, but this time she had no pity. He'd sold her hide to those vampires, and she needed to know why.

"Now, we'll talk," she announced. Nina knew Benny had a strange sense of what he considered the truth, and the only way to get it out of him would be to beat it out of him. Something she was definitely in the mood for tonight.

Still holding his balls, his face twisting in pain, Benny held up one hand in surrender. Nina wasn't fooled. The moment he recovered, he would fight back. But she wouldn't let him recover—not this time.

She'd already figured out that Amaury couldn't possibly be behind the attack on her. After all, the butt-ugly vampire had nearly killed him, and Amaury hadn't looked the least bit remorseful or pissed off when she had staked the bloodsucker. Unless he'd set all this up to trick her and make her trust him—which would make no sense. She dismissed the idea outright.

Benny straightened. Without hesitation, she balled her hand into a fist and hit him in the gut, his untrained stomach muscles providing no real resistance.

"Ugh!" he grunted as he tumbled backwards and landed against the kitchen counter. Utensils scattered onto the floor.

"There's more where that came from. Now I want an answer."

He gave her one of his fake innocent looks, raising his eyebrows in mock surprise. "What answer? You haven't asked me anything yet."

"Don't play as dumb as you look, or I'm gonna turn you into a eunuch." Somebody like Benny should definitely be taken out of the gene pool. Darwin would thank her for it.

Benny looked around the kitchen. She noticed his gaze zeroing in on a set of kitchen knives just within his reach.

"I wouldn't do that if I were you," she warned in a low tone.

Nina knew he wouldn't listen. He wasn't exactly the sharpest tool in the shed and had obviously still not learned that disobedience would earn him further injuries.

The moment Benny seized the knife from the counter and pointed it at her, Nina had already pulled out her own blade from her pocket. She never left home without it.

"Benny, Benny," she scolded and shook her head in disapproval.

He gave her a smug grin, looking from her knife to his. "I think I have the bigger one."

Typical man! "Size doesn't always matter. It's what you do with it that counts."

"Come and get it, Nina." His free hand motioned her to approach. The idiot had watched entirely too many bad movies and clearly fancied himself as the next Rambo—well, the next really small Rambo without the muscles or the brains anyway.

"Why did you do it?" she asked.

Benny gave her a nonchalant look. "Why not? You don't exactly pay premium when it comes to the information you want. A man's got to live."

Her old dilemma—money. Nina was aware she couldn't always pay enough for the things she needed. Ever since Eddie's death, she'd barely kept above water. Her brother had been the main breadwinner, and she'd gone back to school to improve her chances of getting a good job. But now that she had to avenge him, she clearly didn't have time to get a job or continue with school. She barely had enough time to figure out where she could steal the necessities she needed to survive. The little savings she'd had were gone.

"You little rat." Nina took two steps toward him, her arms stretched out to her sides, ready for combat. "Go ahead, take a swipe at me. Winner takes all."

"Fuck you," he replied.

She gave him a once-over. It was time to show the little jerk that he shouldn't mess with her.

With a shout, Benny suddenly launched himself at her. She dove to the side and avoided him by a hair's breadth. Her side hit the wall and brought back the pain of her already-bruised ribs, but she had no time to dwell on it. She swiveled on her heel and faced him as he lunged at her again. Her arm blocked his knife not a second too soon.

"Ready to give me an answer?" she grunted through clenched teeth.

"You haven't won," Benny countered and pulled back only to wield his knife at her again.

Nina gave as good as she got. Stab after stab she avoided, just as he escaped her attempts to do damage. For a while they were evenly matched.

She felt exhaustion overwhelm her. The pain in her ribs hindered her flexibility. Maybe she should have postponed her showdown with Benny until she'd recovered. She wasn't in top condition tonight. The fight with the two vampires had taken too much out of her already, and resisting Amaury had done the rest.

The next stab of her opponent's knife landed on target. The gash on her arm was only a flesh wound, but the resulting pain wasn't as fleeting as the stab had been.

"Fucking bastard," she yelled and charged toward him, utterly pissed off. The pain gave her another badly needed shot of adrenaline, revving up her engine.

As she aimed her knife at him, her leg landed a well-placed kick at his shin, taking him off balance. He buckled. She took the second's advantage and sliced through his hand, making him drop the knife as a result.

"You bitch!" he bit out.

Nina grabbed his injured hand and twisted it, kicked her knee into his back, and held her knife to his neck. His body quivered. Good—he should fear her.

"Maybe now you're ready to talk. You've got ten seconds."

Her ribs pulsated with pain, and she only had a few more minutes of energy left before she would collapse. She was out of time.

"They'll kill me if I talk."

"Guess what—I'll kill you if you don't. And I'm right here. You've got a choice: die now, or die later," she offered and hoped the idiot was smart enough to choose later.

Benny breathed heavily. "Okay. Just don't hurt me anymore."

"Talk fast. My hand's twitching, and who knows what'll happen if I slip," she warned.

"When I asked around for you, this guy approached me, said he'd pay me triple what you paid if I sent you into that trap."

"Who is he?"

"I don't know. He didn't give a name. Paid cash right there. I didn't ask anything."

"That's not good enough. Why?"

"Why what?"

"Why did he want to get rid of me?"

Benny's shoulders moved as if he was trying to shrug. "Said something about you putting your nose into something that's none of your business."

Nina shook her head. It was her business to find out what had really happened to her brother. She couldn't accept that he was a murderer. "You must know something else."

"No. That's all I know."

"Use your damn brain," she hissed and pressed her knee harder into his back. He groaned.

"I heard him say to his friend that he's going to a staff meeting tomorrow night."

"What staff meeting?"

"Some company with scanners or something."

Nina blinked. "Scanguards?"

"Yes, yes—that's the one. He said he'd be at a staff meeting at Scanguards."

She knew it. Her hunch had been right. It was somebody within Scanguards, just as she'd suspected. Amaury and his friends had to be involved. "What does he look like?"

"Ordinary. Tall, dark."

Amaury was tall and dark, but he sure wasn't ordinary.

"That's not very helpful. I think you'll have to come with me to identify him tomorrow night."

Benny tried to wriggle free from her grip, but she held on. His protest was instant. "No way. I'll be a dead man if I do."

"We'll see about that."

Nina felt her strength seeping from her. She didn't have any more time, otherwise he'd turn the tables on her. "Tomorrow," she promised, before she pushed him to the floor and rushed out the door.

She sprinted down the stairs and out the building, ducking into the next dark doorway to catch her breath. Clutching her ribs, she inhaled and felt the sting of her lungs brushing against the bruised bones. The cut on her arm was still bleeding. Nothing Amaury couldn't fix for her, but she wasn't going back to him.

He might not have sent the vampires after her, but one of his friends or colleagues had. They were all working together. Just because Amaury might not have been involved in every detail didn't mean he wasn't ultimately to blame.

He was the enemy.

The realization hit her harder than expected. Before, she'd only suspected him of being involved; now there was more certainty in her assumptions. Scanguards was definitely involved, which meant, Amaury was involved. Had he fooled her all along and played the passionate and caring rescuer to pursue his agenda? But why? He'd had every opportunity to kill her, yet he'd defended her instead. Why?

With her last ounce of strength she made it home. The one-room apartment was located in Chinatown. It was dark and small. She kept it as clean as she could, but even the cleanliness couldn't distract from the fact that the place was shabby. The furniture was old and worn, a mishmash of styles and eras, but she didn't care.

This was better than the foster homes she'd lived in as a teenager. At least she was alone. Nobody would come to her room at night. Nobody would watch her. Nina banned the memories from her mind. She had survived. It was all that mattered.

She shut the door behind her and set the chain. After pulling off her shoes, she collapsed onto the bed. She was too exhausted to get up to the fridge to pull out the ice tray for an icepack. Instead she turned her face to the picture on the nightstand. A young man grinned back at her, his dimples deep, his sandy hair shaggy.

"Oh, Eddie, I'm all alone. What am I gonna do?"

When tears formed in her eyes, she let them come. In the safety of her own four walls she allowed herself a moment of weakness, hoping the tears would wash away her pain and loneliness, yet knowing they wouldn't.

9

Whenever Amaury needed to think, he cooked. The activity relaxed him. Of course, he could never eat the dishes he prepared, but that was beside the point. He had a lot of thinking to do, so he decided on French cuisine.

He had no idea why Nina had run out on him. For any other man this would be a common occurrence since no man ever really knew what a woman was thinking or feeling anyway. But Amaury always knew what everybody was feeling, so of all people he should have known what she felt. Only, for whatever reason, he was unable to sense her emotions.

This had never happened before.

Just like the night when she'd kissed him, he had at first not even noticed the absence of emotions that normally bombarded him. During the street fight, he had felt the determination of the two vampires to kill her, and his reaction to save her had been automatic. While he'd carried her to his apartment and then taken care of her wounds, he'd been so overwhelmed by the effect she had on his body, he hadn't noticed anything else. Not even the fact that his head was clear of any foreign emotions. And he hadn't even had sex with her.

Unfortunately.

Amaury threw a sprig of thyme into the broth-and-wine-mixture which he'd already poured over the skinned chicken legs and breasts. The familiar smell of *coq au vin* wafted into his nose, and he drank it in. What he'd give for a nice meal, tasting a juicy steak again, or an aromatic casserole.

He closed the lid and set the burner to simmer. As he proceeded to arrange the sliced potatoes neatly into a dish to prepare a gratin, he turned his thoughts back to Nina.

He was still hard just thinking of how sweet her blood had tasted and how soft her skin had felt under his kisses. While he'd touched and kissed many human women in his time, none knew what he was. If they did, they would have never responded to him.

But Nina knew what he was. Hell, she'd killed a vampire right in front of his eyes. And while she had struggled against him at first to let him take care of her, she had surrendered to his touch. He hadn't used mind control on her. It was her decision to respond to him. Okay, so maybe he'd used all his persuasive powers as a man to help that decision along, but he hadn't used any vampire skills.

His centuries of experience with women had taught him what women liked, and he was never shy about using what he'd learned. When it came to sex, he was prepared for just about anything a woman could throw at him. And always game for more.

But something had suddenly changed Nina's mood, even though her body had hummed like a well-tuned piano. He would have liked to compose a symphony on it, had she given him a chance.

A soft *ping* announced that the oven was preheated to the correct temperature, and he placed the gratin dish onto the middle rack. A quick stir of the pot on the stove assured nothing was burning. Nothing, other than his desire for Nina.

He would find her. Now that he'd tasted her blood, he had an infinitely better chance of tracking her down. Like a bloodhound's, his sense of smell was so well developed she wouldn't be able to evade him if he only got within a quarter mile of her.

Amaury's lips curled into a smile. And once he found her, they would finish what they'd started. The only little problem he now faced was his colleagues. If any one of them found out he was seeing a human woman and had not wiped her memory clean, he would be in the doghouse. Their warning still rang in his ears: *exposure has to be avoided at all cost.*

Well, it wasn't his fault. Nina had already known about him being a vampire before they had even met. Who knew how much of her memory he had to erase, how far back he had to go? It was impossible to know. No, the best way was to find her, talk to her, find out what she knew and then decide.

He could definitely justify his approach. And if in the process of it he got a little horizontal action, surely nobody could fault him for that. Any hot-blooded male would do the same. After all, she was a desirable woman with gorgeous breasts and a sassy mouth. Who wouldn't want a piece of her?

He sure wouldn't mind spending a whole night with her, setting the sheets on fire. Now that was something he hadn't done in a long time.

Sure, he had sex every night—just not in bed. That location was reserved for somebody special—and he got the feeling she'd warrant an invitation to his bed. And the next time he'd make sure the door was locked, and she wouldn't get away so quickly.

By the time the food was ready, Amaury had set out his plan of how to find her. Assuming she lived in the city, he would patrol in a grid pattern, starting with all downtown neighborhoods before moving farther out into the suburbs. It would take him a few nights at the most.

Amaury spooned the food into serving dishes and placed them onto a tray before he left his apartment, then made his way down one flight of stairs. Mrs. Reid's apartment looked dark, but he knew she was normally up late, so he rang the doorbell and waited.

A minute passed, and nothing happened. He rang the doorbell again and listened for any sound from inside her apartment. Behind him, he heard another door open.

"She's not in," a male voice said.

"Oh, out that late?" Amaury asked, turning to Philipp, one of the reclusive tenants in the building.

"Didn't you hear? She's in the hospital."

Amaury felt a stab in his chest. He'd fed from her the night before, and now she was in the hospital. What had he done?

"The hospital?" A chill crept up his spine.

"Yeah, she's in bad shape." Philipp craned his neck to look at the tray in Amaury's hands. "That smells good. Is that French food?"

"Yeah, sure. Take it."

Amaury pressed the tray into Philipp's hands and turned away before the man could even thank him. He rushed up the stairs and back into his apartment, slamming the door shut behind him.

The poor woman. The sweet old lady. He'd taken too much from her, and now she was paying the price. What if she didn't recover? What if she died?

His strength left him, and he fell to his knees, guilt blasting through him. He'd lost control. He'd taken too much. It was true, he was a monster. And it was happening again. He was killing again. Just like back then. He hadn't changed at all. After four hundred years he was still the same cruel monster.

A murderer.

***

France, 1609

Amaury's struggles to support his family would soon be over. He'd made a decision. The offer he'd received a week earlier was as good as any he would ever get. And for all he knew, the man who'd introduced himself only by his first name, Hervé, would pay for something Amaury wouldn't even need to deliver. He only half believed the story anyway.

The moonlight helped him find the path to the small bridge where he'd agreed to meet Hervé. If everything went well, Amaury would be paid well to let the man feed off him nightly, well enough to make sure his wife and his son would have enough to eat and clothes on their backs. Already, he'd received a few sous *as a token of the man's honest intent.*

It was the love for his family that drove him to this desperate act. So what if some rich man had a fetish and wanted to drink somebody's blood? If he was willing to pay for it, Amaury was prepared to take the momentary pain and endure it. How bad could it be?

The bridge was drenched in moonlight. Except for the tall shadow of a man, nobody else was around. There had been reports of attacks by wild animals, and not many inhabitants were brave enough to venture out after dark. Nobody would witness what was about to happen.

As Amaury approached the man, he wondered whether he was doing the right thing, but remembering the gaunt looks of his wife and son, he knew he couldn't go back.

The moment Hervé's face came into view, he saw the man's fangs gleam in the moonlight. There was no denying it now: he was a vampire, just as he'd claimed. A cold shiver ran down Amaury's spine, and the little hairs on the back of his neck rose.

"Faites-le vite." The quicker this was over, the better.

Amaury held out his hand and felt the cold coins in his palm a second later. The prick of the fangs on his neck was only painful for a split second, then he fell into a state as if he'd had too much wine, a drunken stupor. Not unpleasant.

But when he wanted to pull away from Hervé, he couldn't. The man wouldn't let him go, and despite his own huge frame, Amaury was no match for the man's inhuman strength. The vampire's fangs dug deeper into him, and more blood drained from his body. His vision became blurred, his legs weak, until he collapsed.

Amaury awoke with a thirst the likes of which he'd never known. A thirst for blood. Hervé had tricked him. He hadn't merely wanted to feed off him—he'd wanted to turn him into a vampire. And he had. To build a community, a family of sorts.

But Amaury had a family, a family of his own, and they needed him. He didn't listen to Hervé who warned him that he was a danger to them now. Instead, he ran home, ignoring his thirst.

The first person he found upon his return was his son Jean-Philippe. With his tiny bare feet the boy ran toward him, his arms outstretched, wanting to be lifted into his father's arms.

"Papa!"

But the moment Amaury clutched his son to his chest, the beast in him took charge, and the thirst overwhelmed him.

Not knowing what he was doing, he sank his fangs into the boy. Moments later the lifeless body of his son lay at his feet, and his wife's hysterical screams filled the night air.

There was no way back from what he'd done. And as a new vampire, he didn't know how to save him, how to perhaps turn his son into a vampire too, so at least he could have survived in some capacity.

Only later did he learn how to create a vampire, how he would have had to feed his son his own blood at the very moment where his heart took its last beats.

"Monstre! T'as tué mon fils!" Yes, he'd killed his own son.

His wife's screams were mixed with tears, her voice hoarse. But the way she looked at him when he came out of his momentary trance, when the beast in him was satisfied by the boy's blood, those eyes condemned him to hell. Living hell.

"Tu vas sentir toute la douleur du monde, des émotions de chacun, et tu seras infirme pour l'éternité. Jamais tu vas sentir l'amour du nouveau. Jamais."

What she condemned him to was what he deserved: to sense everybody's emotions, to feel the pain that would cripple him for eternity with no love ever soothing his heart again.

"Mon dieu, qu-est ce que j'ai fait?" What had he done?

Amaury fell to his knees and wept.

10

It was the last staff meeting for the night. Amaury was tired and drained. He could sense Gabriel wasn't faring much better. Using their powers took a lot out of them.

The chairs in the meeting room were arranged so Yvette could see everybody's faces and register them in her mind. Both Amaury and Gabriel stood next to her, off to the side, while Ricky stood at the podium and answered questions after he'd given his standard speech about the incidents.

"That's just what we need, the police digging around in our pasts," one of the employees droned. A collective murmur went through the room.

Ricky held up his hand to ask for silence. "I understand your concerns. Rest assured, we will not release information to the police if they don't present us with a proper subpoena. As we all know, many of us have less than stellar backgrounds. But we're past that. We've pulled ourselves out of it and have reformed ourselves."

Amaury noticed that Ricky used the collective *we*. He was an extraordinary speaker, always knowing what the crowd wanted, how he could win them over to his side. Many of Scanguards' bodyguards were reformed criminals, and while Ricky wasn't an ex-con, to imply that he was one of them was a smart PR move.

"We're in this together. One bad apple won't spoil the entire batch. I believe in you guys. Without you, there would be no Scanguards. Without you, the world would be less safe," he continued his pep talk. "The company needs you to stay strong and vigilant. If you suspect any wrongdoing, I urge you to come to me."

Amaury scanned the crowd and tried to filter out the various emotions bouncing around the room. His head was near exploding, but as always he didn't let on. The emotions which bombarded him were what he expected: fear, dread, anger, disbelief.

"We can't allow these incidents to rip the company apart. Too many people depend on us. Too many jobs would be lost. We all have families that depend on us. Let's not let them down."

"Are there any leads?" a question came from the audience.

Ricky shook his head. "We're not privy to any information the police deem confidential. We will conduct our own internal investigation though, and for that we rely on your input. Many of you knew both Edmund and Kent. So I have a favor to ask of you: if you think there is anything odd that happened to them before these incidents, anything that might be considered strange, or if you know of any problems they had, please talk to me in confidence. Don't fear any reprisals. If you feel you want to remain anonymous, I'll respect your request."

"Will there be a reward?"

Amaury frowned. Typical. There was always one who wanted to gain from a situation like this. He homed in on the man's emotions.

"At this point nothing has been decided. But you all know how we work. The company won't forget your contribution. We're dependent on each other, and we look out for our own."

He really had to hand it to Ricky; he could put a positive spin on anything. The men in the crowd looked much more relaxed now than at the beginning of the meeting. A lot of their anxiety was gone, and their emotions had settled down to a quiet simmer. Still, there were a few more hotheads to be dealt with.

"I can't afford to be drawn into this. I'm on parole," a big guy shouted out and leapt from his seat. Heads turned to him.

"Well, you're not the only one," another from across the room chimed in. "So, shut up."

"You want a piece of me?" the parolee offered with clenched teeth, fists at the ready.

Ricky brought the crowd under control. "Please, gentlemen. There's no need to get physical. Can you imagine the paperwork I have to deal with just to fill out the worker's comp forms? Please. Settle down. None of us can afford to be mixed up in this, but we are. We didn't choose this, but we have to deal with it. I urge you all to keep a cool head. Our first duty is to our clients. They'll be nervous, and rightly so. If one of you loses his calm, our clients will notice. If you want to be pulled off your assignment, you'd better let me know now."

Ricky gazed into the crowd, but nobody spoke up. "I take it this means we're all still doing what we're supposed to be doing. Protecting our clients, doing our jobs. We'll get on top of this, I promise you. Good night, gentlemen. Be safe."

Ricky cast Amaury and Gabriel a silent look. Amaury nodded. He'd had sufficient time to delve into the employees' emotions, but nothing of importance had surfaced. All emotions seemed reasonable for the situation. However, there were a few staff members he wanted to take a closer look at.

As the room cleared and the chatter subsided, the vampires congregated in a corner.

"Anything?" Ricky asked.

"I tapped into their memories, but there was nothing that connected any of them to Edmund or Kent. Yes, some of them knew one or even both, but I couldn't see any incidences that would lead me to believe in foul play. Unless somebody is blocking my access," Gabriel admitted.

"They can do that?" Amaury asked in surprise. He'd always assumed Gabriel's gift was infallible.

"The humans can't. But any of the vampires might be able to. Not everybody can block me, but some of the vampires might have sufficient powers to at least block me partially or veil their memories so I can't access them sufficiently. Don't you have that issue with your power?"

Amaury shook his head and instantly knew he was lying. He'd only recently met the one person whose emotions he could not read, but he was sure it was a fluke. Plus, she was human. "No, I can sense anybody—human or vampire."

And after the long sessions with the employees, he was completely and utterly drained and exhausted. He desperately needed sex to keep his head from exploding. He glanced at his watch. The nightclubs would still be humming right now. He needed to feed, and he needed to continue his search for Nina.

"Well, good for you." If Gabriel only knew. Good wasn't the attribute Amaury associated with his gift. "Anything from your side?"

"I sensed a few people with guilt issues, possibly somebody with feelings of deception and fear, but I can't pinpoint what about." He looked at Gabriel. "Your gift is a lot more precise than mine."

Amaury's gift was open to interpretation, and this time he couldn't rely on guesswork. This was too important for all of them. That was why Gabriel's gift was necessary to complement his.

"We should interview a few of them one-on-one. Show me the list, Ricky," he demanded.

Ricky pulled out the staff list and handed it to him. Amaury quickly made notes next to various names.

"Let's set something up for tomorrow night."

Ricky looked at the list. "Okay, together with the few from the previous meetings, that's eleven of them. Yvette?"

Yvette had been quiet during the entire time. Now she cleared her throat. "I'd like to sit in on the interviews with Amaury."

Amaury raised his eyebrows, but didn't protest. If she wanted a closer look at the guys he'd picked out, so be it. "Gabriel, it's the three of us then." At least with Gabriel there, he and Yvette wouldn't instantly get into a fight.

"Where's Quinn?" Yvette suddenly asked.

"Probably outside. He was supposed to make sure everybody left the building. Let's go," Gabriel ordered. "It's time to check in with Zane."

***

This was the third night in a row Nina was in trouble with a vampire. Maybe she wasn't cut out for this after all. And this was one mean looking dude. His head shorn bald, his body carrying not an ounce of fat, he had her pinned against a wall outside of Scanguards' downtown offices.

His mouth twisted into a snarl only inches from her face as his arm pressed against her neck, making breathing virtually impossible.

Everything had gone well up to a few minutes ago. She had watched the employees leave the building after the staff meeting. Unfortunately, Benny had bolted before he'd helped her identify his contact. It made Nina think her informant had seen the guy amongst the employees at that moment and decided it was safer to skip. Not that he'd come with her voluntarily in the first place. She'd had to use persuasion of the violent kind to drag him with her.

Obviously the weasel had a better instinct of self preservation than Nina did, otherwise she wouldn't be the one in the clutches of that bald vampire right now. The silver chain she carried in her jacket pocket was of no use to her now—she wouldn't be fast enough to wrap it around his neck even if she managed to get free of his grip. And even though she was armed with a stake, it was in her inside pocket and inaccessible at present. She had to play a different strategy.

"Who are you?"

Yes, his voice sounded just as mean as he looked. No doubt about it.

She opened her mouth, but no sound came out. He was crushing her windpipe.

"Talk!"

Easy for him to say. He wasn't running out of air. She gasped and lifted her arm to gesture to her neck. A second later he loosened his grip on her neck, but only marginally. Instantly Nina coughed.

"Now talk fast."

"I was just minding my own business." If he thought she'd spill the beans this quickly, he'd never met anybody as stubborn as she.

He shook his head. "Not in my territory, you're not. You've been spying on us. Who are you?"

"I was just going for a walk, that's all."

He shoved his thigh against her in a display of physical dominance. She wasn't intimidated this easily—well, at least she wasn't going to admit it.

"*Prowling* is the word you're looking for, I believe."

From the corner of her eye she scanned her surroundings for passersby, but they were alone. This late at night, the Financial District was deserted. The restaurants were already closed, and there were no nightclubs in the vicinity.

"This is a free country."

"For some people maybe."

He was different from the two vampires she'd fought the night before. He could have killed her a dozen times since he'd captured her, yet he was intent on questioning her instead. It gave her hope that he wasn't sent by the same guy who'd dispatched the other two vampires.

"Listen, I have no beef with you. If this is your territory, bro, I'll just be gettin' out of your hair, all right?" She tried her best street-gang lingo on him. If she could convince him she was just some low-level con and not scouting out vampires, maybe he'd let her go.

"What do you want?"

Like she was going to tell him. Hell, the guy was insistent.

"Zane!"

His head whipped back to the voice behind him. Several figures came toward them, all still cast in dark shadows. *Great, more vampires.* Her survival chances had just dwindled exponentially.

"What's going on?" the same voice inquired. The man came into view. The first thing Nina saw was the large scar which reached from his chin all the way to his ear. Gruesome. She could tell that at some time in the past he'd been handsome, but the ugly scar had put an end to that.

"This man just attacked me!" Maybe she could create some confusion and appeal to someone's sense of chivalry toward a woman, not that she got her hopes up. They would only get trampled.

"Nina?"

Now there was a voice she definitely recognized.

Amaury pushed into sight, a stunned look on his gorgeous face. Damn, the man was still as handsome as the night before. She hadn't imagined it.

"You know her?" Scarface with the ponytail asked.

"Zane, let her go. Now!" Amaury ordered the vampire who was still keeping her imprisoned. Zane showed no intention of letting her go. On the contrary, it felt as if he tightened his grip on her.

"Don't tell me she's one of your floozies!" The female voice surprised her. Nina glanced in her direction. If there ever was a woman who could be called a *femme fatale*, it was this one. Black leather pants, a tight colorful top, boobs galore. And an absolutely flawless face framed by short black hair. Some girls had all the luck.

"Shut up, Yvette! Zane, let her go," Amaury repeated his command.

"Who is she?" Zane was clearly not willing to give in.

"None of your fucking business."

"It is when she's spying on Scanguards."

"Nina, you weren't spying on Scanguards, were you?" Amaury's conspiratorial look was subtle.

"Of course not. I was just waiting for you." She hoped nobody could hear the shaking in her voice.

"You're dating a human?" The vampire with the ponytail and scar gave Amaury a scolding look. "May I remind you of what we discussed two nights ago?"

"I know what we discussed, Gabriel. No need to remind me. I'll take care of it."

"Really?" Yvette interjected.

"Yes, really." Amaury sounded pretty pissed off.

"You'd better. No exposure." Gabriel made an indication to Zane to release her. Nina felt his reluctance to do so. The bastard had obviously hoped to do a little harm, and he was still blocking her.

"I think I'd rather do it myself," Zane insisted. "I don't think you can be trusted to wipe her memory. You're too biased."

Wipe her memory? How were they going to do that? By drilling into her skull?

Zane and Amaury shot daggers at each other. If looks could kill, well, luckily they couldn't, or at least she didn't think they could. But what did she know about what else vampires were capable of?

"Nina, step away from him and come over here."

She suppressed the urge to give Zane the finger and was only too happy to comply with Amaury's command. Better the vampire she knew . . .

She noticed the look Yvette gave her when she finally stood next to Amaury. Her next comment came as no surprise.

"Is she *that* good that you're willing to betray your friends?" The woman let her gaze travel over Nina's body, making her feel like she was undergoing an inspection she had no chance of passing.

"Stay out of this, Yvette," he growled.

"That good in bed, huh?" Yvette tossed a cold smile at Nina. "Watch out—he'll take what he wants and doesn't give a damn about the consequences."

Nina was at a loss of how to respond. She was glad she didn't have to. Gabriel cut off the conversation.

"That's enough. Amaury, you know what to do. If you don't take care of this situation, I will. Or worse, Zane will. Do we understand each other?"

There was a slight hesitation from Amaury. She noticed how his hands balled into fists. "Loud and clear."

He turned and grabbed her arm. "Let's go." The gruffness of his voice didn't bode well for her immediate future.

Nina had no idea why he hadn't just fed her to the lions, but rather had taken their wrath upon himself to get her out of the precarious situation. She watched him from the side as she struggled to keep up with him, his hand still clamped around her arm in a none-too-gentle manner.

"Where are we going?" she asked him once they were out of earshot of his vampire friends.

"Somewhere where we can talk."

"Talk about what?"

Amaury stopped and jerked her toward him. The furious look he gave her made Nina hold her tongue. "We both know you and I didn't have a date, so cut the crap. You're lucky I could fool my friends. But now you owe me an explanation."

Again he pulled her along.

"Slow down! I can't keep up with you."

"Unless you want me to sling you over my shoulder, you'll keep up."

Nina ignored the shiver rolling down her back.

Caveman!

11

Nina was driving him mad—stark-raving mad. The moment Amaury had witnessed Zane manhandling her, he'd seen red. No—crimson, scarlet, purple! What the *hell* was she doing there, spying on them outside the offices? And clearly she had been spying. No *way* was this encounter a coincidence.

Amaury grunted to himself as he let them into the apartment and locked the door. His decision to get her out of there had been a simple gut reaction. He hadn't thought about the consequences at all. The only thing he could think of was to get her away from Zane.

He knew Zane all too well, and his interrogation methods were anything but gentle. He didn't want Nina to be subjected to his brutality. Zane followed the directive in a straight line, he was loyal and fiercely protective of his brethren, but his methods were questionable at best.

To imagine Nina suffering at Zane's hands turned Amaury's stomach. And not just for the obvious reasons. Even if Zane weren't as brutal as he was, he wouldn't want the other vampire's hands on her.

"Woman, you're giving me a headache."

"If that's the case, why don't I leave you alone?" She made an attempt to brush past him toward the door, but he held her back and turned her body toward him.

"Nice try, Nina—if that's even your real name."

She tilted her head up in defiance. "Like you're on first-name terms with the truth."

Touché!

"And Nina *is* my name," she added.

"You might as well make yourself comfortable, since you're not going anywhere." He released her shoulders before he could give into the urge to pull her against his body and punish her with a kiss.

"Go, sit."

She didn't move. "I'd rather stand."

"Suit yourself. And start talking."

"Looks like the fog burned off—"

He cut her off. "About why you were lurking around outside Scanguards."

"I wasn't lurking."

Her innocently fluttering eyelids wouldn't work on him. Neither would those plump red lips she'd pushed forward in protest.

"You weren't waiting for *me*, that's for sure. Looks like we have a veritable Buffy on our hands."

"You're calling me a slayer?"

"That's what you are, aren't you?" Amaury let his gaze drift over her slender form. She was tall for a woman, well built with muscles that would put the average human male to shame. But she wasn't strong enough to fight a vampire, and especially not one like Zane.

"I'm not a slayer."

"Then what are you doing seeking out vampires and killing them? In my book, that's slaying. And don't even try to deny it. I was there, remember?" But he wasn't thinking of the fight with the vampires; rather, his mind conjured up images from later that night, images of her naked breasts. With an impatient shake of his head he tried to rid himself of the mental picture.

"That's the thanks I get for saving your ass? If I hadn't killed that guy, you'd be dust right now!"

Nina did have a point. Truth be told, he had no idea why she'd saved him when she could have taken the moment to run for her life. Instead, she'd courageously jumped onto his opponent and staked him.

"And my ass wouldn't have needed saving in the first place if I didn't have to come rescue you."

"I didn't ask for your help."

She braced her hands at her hips, pushing her open jacket clear of her chest. Was he hallucinating, or did this simple action make her breasts appear more voluptuous?

"You didn't need to. It was pretty clear from where I stood that you needed help." The recollection of her fighting alone against those two vampires sent an ice-cold shudder through his bones. He could have lost her so easily.

Lost her?

"Arrogant jerk!"

"Insolent brat. I'm in the right mood to turn you over my knee and paddle your stubborn ass." The moment he said it, he felt a bolt of desire shoot through his loins. The image of her naked derrière made his cock twitch in anticipation. How he would love to feel her skin under his palm.

She narrowed her eyes. "I would like to see you try!"

Amaury heard the fury in her voice. Her cheeks colored a deep red, and her chest rose heavily with every breath she made. Every time her breasts pushed against the fabric, he could spot the hard nipples that topped them. He wasn't the only one getting excited by the situation.

"Don't tempt me, woman!" But he was already tempted. "You have no idea what would have happened if I hadn't stopped Zane. Do you think his parents gave him that name?"

He pinned her with a furious look. "That sick bastard chose that name on purpose. His idea of irony. Nobody's quite sure whether he's all that *sane*. You'd do better to stay away from him."

"Like you're any less insane than he is!"

She compared him to Zane? Now she'd have to pay . . .

Before she could even blink, she was bent over his thighs, her behind pointing up.

"Don't you dare!" she screamed at the top of her lungs and thrashed her legs.

The first slap of his palm onto her backside stopped her next word. Amaury didn't trust himself not to pull her jeans down, lest this situation end somewhere else entirely. But if she continued to struggle, maybe he would have to strip her after all.

"You jerk!"

He gave her another slap, this time a little harder. And a third and fourth one.

"Ouch!" Her protest sounded unconvincing.

He slapped her again, then smoothed his palm over the spot he'd just spanked and stroked gently.

"Stop that!"

Amaury realized that her voice had a little less determination in it than when she'd insulted him. He grinned and noticed suddenly that his headache had waned. In the staff meeting his head had been ready to explode, and even outside during the confrontation with his friends, he'd still had a splitting migraine. But now that he thought about it, somewhere between him walking home with Nina and now, his head had cleared. In fact, he felt great!

Nina twisted under his hold.

"Will you behave now?"

Amaury took her silence as a yes and turned her to him so she sat in his lap, which she immediately tried to vacate. He stopped her—Nina sitting in his lap felt right.

"Now we talk." That was if he was able to listen with her delectable derrière rubbing against him as she continued trying to get out of his lap. She could shift all she wanted. He wouldn't stop her. Did she have any idea her grinding was the reason for his growing erection?

"What am I? A child sitting on Santa's lap?" she bristled and crossed her arms.

"Trust me, *chérie*, Santa Claus is not as big as I am." He pushed his groin against her thigh to emphasize his statement and felt the tightness in his pants. If he made another move, he would burst.

She was clearly annoyed now, sending an acid look his way. Maybe she had finally run out of verbal insults to hand out.

"I've had bigger."

Bigger? He'd show her.

"I doubt that very much. Maybe you should do a proper comparison before you make statements like that." Amaury took her hand and pulled it toward him, placing it firmly onto the bulge of his pants.

Nina tried to pull away, but then her mouth dropped open, and he felt her palm squeeze him lightly through the fabric. "Oh."

The warmth from her hand shot through him, and he pushed against her, encouraging her to squeeze again. He could question her later. There was no rush.

"Touch me." He looked at her face, and she finally met his gaze. Then her hand moved along his steely length, exploring him, measuring him. He sucked in a quick gulp of air and with it her scent. Slowly, he moved his head closer to hers until his lips hovered less than an inch over hers.

"I want to feel your hands on my skin," he whispered against her mouth, his breath mingling with hers.

"You're wearing too many clothes."

Her response made him chuckle. "Why don't you undress me then?" He liked the idea of her taking charge, of her hands easing open the buttons of his shirt, lowering the zipper of his pants.

"Maybe later." Her lips brushed against his. "Are you doing this?"

"Doing what?"

"Making me want to kiss you."

Nina wanted to kiss him? No objections here.

"I'm not using my powers on you." Only those which any man would use to seduce a woman. "I don't need to. We both know we want this."

Amaury pulled her lower lip between his and traced it with his tongue. She tasted intoxicating.

"Why?" Her hands came up to grab his shirt.

"I don't know. And I don't care. Let it happen."

He couldn't explain the attraction between them or why he wasn't following Gabriel's orders and wiping her memory of him and all vampires.

"Am I safe with you?"

He pulled back a few inches to look into her eyes. "Have I hurt you so far?"

"Well, you did paddle my ass, as you so elegantly put it."

He grinned. Spanking her had been more than just a little enjoyable. In fact, it had gotten him rather hot—and hard. He wouldn't mind a repeat of it at a later time.

"Which you thoroughly deserved for . . . " *For giving me such a fright seeing you captured by Zane,* he wanted to say, but bit back the words. " . . . for stalking my friends and me."

By his shirt she pulled him close to her. "Next time you spank me, you should do it right. I barely felt a thing through my pants."

Amaury almost choked. Was Nina suggesting he should slap her naked ass? "Are you saying what I think you're saying?" He'd be happy to do anything she wanted to that cute backside of hers. She just had to ask. Actually, she didn't even need to ask; a mere hint would suffice to put him into action.

"Guess, you'll just have to figure that out, won't you?" But she didn't give him another chance to answer and sank her lips onto his.

Her soft flesh met with his, opening a floodgate of sensations rushing through his body. Her warmth seeped into him, travelled over his skin and penetrated his cells. More blood pumped into his loins, making his already swollen shaft even harder. He allowed his hands to roam over her body as his mouth fitted to hers, learning her every groove.

While his hand on her back pressed her closer to him, he let his other hand slide up her neck, caress the soft skin, then cup her cheek. His thumb stroked her jaw and ran along the underside of her chin, feeling the soft muscle below and the warm blood running through her.

Amaury angled his head and requested entrance with his tongue nudging at her lips. With a sigh she surrendered to his gentle demand and parted her moist lips. A searing bolt of lightning shot through his core as he invaded the delicious caverns of her mouth, finding his responsive counterpart, his long-desired twin, fitting perfectly to him.

He released a guttural moan when he started a duel with her tongue. She sparred with him just the way she'd sparred with him verbally. Her talented mouth drew him deeper, asking him to explore her and learn every minute detail of her. It was exactly what he wanted to do.

Nina suddenly pulled away. "You're wearing too many clothes."

Without waiting for an answer, she ripped his shirt open, sending buttons flying. Instantly she dug her hands into his chest, sending electrical shocks traveling over his skin wherever she touched him. When had a woman last shown him such passion?

"I didn't like that shirt anyway." Amaury pulled her head to him again and continued their passionate kiss, while Nina stripped him of his shirt and threw it on the floor. He felt turned on by the way she handled him, confident and assertive. Having a strong woman like her in his arms aroused him more than any of his daily one-night-stands ever had.

Never had a woman made such passionate demands on him, and never had he been so willing to let a female take charge. This was new to him. New and exciting. Whatever she wanted to do to him, he wouldn't object, as long as she was using her mouth, her tongue and her hands the way she was now.

"Take me to bed," she whispered.

His mumbled "yes" was drowned out by her lips. Not that he needed words to respond to her. He merely lifted them both from the couch without interrupting their kiss and walked them to his bedroom. With his foot, he kicked the door open.

The sheets on his bed were a tangled mess, evidence of his nightmare from the previous day. Slowly, Amaury dropped onto the bed. With a swift move Nina pushed him, and he landed with his back on the mattress, feeling himself straddled by her. Not a bad position to be in.

It had been a while since he'd had a woman in his bed. Most of his sexual encounters happened in dark alleys, nightclubs or back rooms of some sort or other. This was different, more intense, more intimate.

Amaury grabbed her hips and pressed his erection against her center. "I want you." He tugged at her jacket, but she stopped him.

"You first. I want to see you naked." Her eyes were clouded with passion and desire as she looked at him from under her long lashes. It hit him in the gut: that look, those gorgeous eyes looking at him as if it meant something.

"Then undress me." He wanted to surrender to her, give her carte blanche, just to see that look in her face that said she wanted him.

Her hands were steady when she eased the button of his pants open as if she'd done this to him a hundred times. A second later he watched her lower his zipper. He breathed a sigh of relief when his engorged shaft sprang free.

She quickly freed him of his pants and boots before she crawled back up toward his center. He didn't let her out of his sight for even a second, watching her every seductive move. There was something kinky about the fact that he was naked while she remained fully dressed. Something almost forbidden.

Her tongue darted out and licked her lips as she focused on his proud cock nestled in a thatch of thick black hair.

"You're beautiful." Nina looked straight at his face. "I want to taste you." Her gaze dropped back to his hard flesh. He'd never been so aware of his maleness than under her hungry look.

Had he just died and gone to heaven? When was the last time a woman really wanted to give him pleasure without him having to persuade her? Was she for real?

Amaury reached for her, wanting to assure himself that she wasn't a figment of his imagination.

"Keep your hands over your head. Hold onto those bars," she advised him and pointed at the metal headboard of his bed. "No touching. I want to do this my way."

Her seductive smile melted his insides and shot another wave of pleasure through his body, all the way down to his toes. She was still fully dressed, and he lay in front of her, sprawled out stark naked and horny as hell. The aroma of her arousal drifted into his nostrils and drove his desire for her even higher.

"No touching?" How could he possibly keep his hands to himself when the woman of his dreams was in his bed?

Nina shook her head. "Not yet. Later."

He did as she said and grabbed the bars above his head.

He could wait, as hard as it was for him. Soon he would rip her clothes off her body and see her in all her glorious nakedness, touch and kiss every inch of her body and bury himself in her. But she wanted this first, and he wasn't one to deny a woman, especially not if she wanted to pleasure him so selflessly. God, he was one lucky son of a bitch.

"Close your eyes and just feel."

Obeying suddenly sounded like the natural thing to do.

Her lips brushed against his thigh, and her warm tongue blazed a trail of molten lava upwards toward his belly. Instantly his breathing sped up, his heartbeat increased. Amaury fought against the urge to grab her, sling her underneath him and plunge into her. With painstaking slowness, the temptress licked her way up his thigh, then stopped just short of the spot where his desire made a clear statement.

His other thigh received the same tantalizing treatment, making his hips jerk upwards.

"Baby, you're killing me." Very, very slowly—and he loved every second of it.

"Not yet."

His response got stuck in his throat when he felt her tongue lick at the base of his cock. Warmth and wetness engulfed him as her lips grazed his skin, planting small kisses where her tongue had licked before. His moans filled the room.

"I like your taste."

Amaury reached for her, running his hand through her hair. "Oh, *chérie*."

Immediately she pulled away. "No hands. Eyes closed."

He was out of his mind with his need for her, but Nina's determined look made him comply with her wishes, and he put his hands back onto the headboard. A moment later he was rewarded by her tongue lapping against his erection, licking all the way from the base to the very tip, where a drop of moisture had impatiently oozed out. She simply licked it off him and hummed against his skin. She was clearly intent on killing him with pleasure.

Amaury arched his hips upwards, yearning to feel her lips wrap around him. Gripping the metal rail of his headboard tighter, he let out a ragged breath. He would die if she didn't soon soothe the hunger his body was grappling with.

The instant Nina took him into her wet and warm mouth and lowered herself all the way down his steely length, he nearly lost consciousness. His heart pounded like a jackhammer, deafening his ears. His skin was soaked in sweat, and his eyes would have rolled back in his head, had they not already been closed.

The feeling of being inside her mouth was intense, intoxicating, and utter bliss. And then she moved.

His body almost lifted off the bed as she slid up and down his shaft, sucking first gently, then firmer. He had received many blow jobs in his time, but boy, Nina was mastering him without any coaching, as if she knew exactly what he needed.

Amaury could barely wait to repay her with the same kind of attention she currently lavished on him. In fact, before he buried his throbbing cock in her, he would taste her thoroughly and make her come in his mouth. He would drink her juices as if it were nectar of the gods.

Tonight, he wouldn't allow her any sleep, but would satisfy her every desire until she collapsed in his arms. Then, and only then, he would allow her to sleep, safely cradled in his arms, protecting her from the evil outside his four walls.

12

Nina sensed his excitement. It was hard to miss. With every move of her mouth, Amaury's moans became louder and more frequent, and his hips pumped harder. She was pleased with how she could reduce this vampire to the brainless man-in-lust he was right now. The only thing he listened to at the moment was his desire. All his other senses were dulled.

Exactly as she'd planned it. Well, almost. She hadn't planned on enjoying this so much. Never before had a man's body aroused her like his godlike form did. But despite the desire he ignited in her, she had to do what she must. Otherwise everything was for nothing.

After her run-in with Amaury's friends, she'd already written this night off as a complete disaster—until the moment he'd started kissing her. Right then, a plan had formed in her mind. She was bent on using this opportunity to get information from him. She could turn this catastrophic night into a positive one.

In the process she would enjoy his amazing body. The guilt this feeling sent through her heart was hard to deny. But she tried to justify it nevertheless.

She gave his erection one last long lick over its bulbous head. Ah, but he tasted good. Sexy, hot, masculine. His spicy scent made her sex clench violently and her womb protest when she released him.

"Come here, I need to be inside you." Amaury looked at her and reached his hands out to grasp her shoulders.

She shook her head. "Didn't I say to keep your eyes closed and your hands on the headboard?"

"Still?"

"Yes. I'm not done with you." No, not quite yet. She wasn't in position yet. She needed about fifteen seconds more.

"*Chérie*, you're killing me."

If he only knew. Like a good boy he closed his eyes again and put his hands back onto the bars of the headboard, clearly expecting more pleasure to come his way. And under other circumstances she would have jumped at the chance of driving him wild with her mouth. Purely for sexual gratification, of course, without any emotions involved, she told herself.

But now was the time for her to act. While her mouth placed small kisses on his abdomen and licked his navel, her hand reached into her jacket pocket. Her fingers felt the cold chain. She was aware that he would hear the rustling, but she knew how to distract him.

"Your body is amazing. So hard, so sexy." Nina let out a fake moan and felt him respond with a stifled moan of his own. She used the moment to pull the silver chain out of her pocket. For a second, she wondered whether her information was correct that a vampire couldn't break a silver chain, but it was too late to go back now. She had to execute her plan.

Licking her way north, her tongue lapped against his hard nipple, where she lingered for a few seconds. She drew the hard nubbin into her mouth and sucked greedily then sank her teeth into his flesh. She bit gingerly, just enough to heighten his arousal and drive him to the edge.

Inflicting the same torture on his other nipple, she lifted herself over him and straddled him. Instantly his hips undulated, and his hard shaft pressed against her center. Damn, it was good to feel his hardness. She sensed her body melt as the wetness between her thighs increased. Her panties were soaked with her desire. If only she could feel him inside her, just once, maybe it would eradicate the ache she felt right now. Maybe the longing would go away, maybe her womb would stop clenching in response to his movements—

No!

Nina released his nipple and moved farther up, kissing the side of his neck he so obligingly offered her, almost as if Amaury wanted *her* to bite *him*. How odd a notion, to bite a vampire, yet she clearly saw the image before her: her teeth sinking into his flesh. The red liquid painting her lips, lapping over her tongue, running down her throat. She blinked and the vision was gone.

It was now or never. She acted fast. It took her two seconds to wrap his wrists with the chain and hook it securely onto the headboard, before she heard his roar fill the room.

With lightning speed she sat up and was hit by his furious glare.

"*What the FUCK?*" His voice was a loud thunder and reverberated all the way through her body.

Amaury rattled the chain, his flesh sizzling where the silver came in contact with his skin. The scent of singed flesh and body hair stung her nostrils as she watched his face distort in pain.

"The less you move, the less it's going to hurt." Good, the chains were holding. Her heartbeat slowed a fraction, grateful the silver worked. At least something went her way tonight.

"You devious bitch!"

"Hey, manners!" she chided. "Now—let's talk." Finally she had the upper hand. She had to use it to her advantage now and keep a clear head.

"Release me!" He pulled on the chain again, but couldn't break it. Instead, it appeared to dig deeper into his flesh. She noticed his jaw clenching as if warding off the pain.

"I don't think you're in the position to order me around right now."

He flashed his fangs at her, his eyes glaring red.

"Ooh, looks like the big bad vampire is angry." And looking even sexier than before. Was that at all possible? A pleasant shiver traveled up her spine and curled around her neck. Her nipples beaded involuntarily.

Traitors!

"Nina, I warn you. Take this chain off me, or you'll be very sorry . . ."

Amaury could growl with that sexy voice all he wanted. She wouldn't release him.

"Empty threats. Cut it out, Amaury. You lost, I won. You're so easy to distract. You shouldn't let your dick rule you."

She looked down to where their bodies were still touching. His cock was as hard as ever and still pressing against her. With her finger she touched its head and lazily smeared a drop of moisture over it. The velvety smooth head twitched under her touch, tilting toward her, asking for attention.

"Stop it!" His order was issued in a hoarse voice, followed by a barely suppressed moan. It pleased her that even tied up and in agony he still wanted her. She could work with that.

"You don't mean that. I think you want me to continue." And were circumstances different, she would capture him in her mouth again and drive him wild until he lost it. And then she would arouse him again and ride him until he could take no more. But circumstances were what they were. He was the enemy, and she had to deal with him now.

"What do you want from me? Damn it!" His eyes blinked shut for a second as he let out a sharp breath. She glanced at his hands where blisters had formed as if acid were burning through his skin.

"I want answers."

His eyes locked with hers, and she could feel his mind working. She heard a voice in her head, invading.

Release me.

Nina sensed he was trying to control her mind, but she pushed back, refusing to listen, trying to shut him out. That sneaky bastard, he was using his powers on her.

Get out of my head!

Suddenly his eyes turned blue again, and he looked at her with wonder in them.

"You're blocking me. How?"

She ignored his question, not that she had an answer anyway. All she'd done was push against him, deny him entry. How it worked she was unable to explain. "I need answers. We can do this the easy way or the hard way. What's it gonna be?"

Instead of a reply, his legs suddenly lifted and hit against her back, pushing her forward onto his chest, bringing her head to head with him. His mouth rocked forward, and he captured her lips. But he didn't bite. His tongue swept over her lips, demanding entry. Did he really think she'd falter this easily? She pressed her lips together, refusing him.

"Release me now, and I won't hurt you." Amaury paused. "Except for a little spanking."

Nina pushed against his shoulders and brought herself upright, away from his tempting mouth and his drugging scent. The thought of being spanked by him like a naughty child sent a tingle through her body.

"Tempting, but no thanks. I'd rather keep the upper hand."

"I'm warning you, Nina. You'll regret this later." His voice was a low growl now. There was something feral about him, something so animalistic, she should be afraid. Instead she felt like answering his growl with one of her own. She shook her head to stop her errant and clearly stupid thoughts.

"There will be no later."

"What do you want?"

"Revenge, justice. That's what I want."

He answered with a surprised look. "I haven't hurt you. I've done nothing you didn't want me to do."

"You've taken what was dearest to me. You and your friends, you've taken Eddie away from me."

"Eddie? Who's Eddie?" The wrinkles on his forehead were witness to his lack of understanding. He appeared completely clueless.

"See, you don't even know. You guys are so callous about human life that you don't even remember what you did. Just another human life, isn't it? Another one who didn't count. How many others are there besides Eddie that you can't even keep track?"

She slammed her fist into his chest, but he barely flinched.

"Damn it, Nina, you make no sense. Who the hell is Eddie?"

"Was. Who the hell *was* Eddie. Eddie's dead. And it's because of you guys." Because Eddie had worked for them and had somehow gotten embroiled in something. Until they got rid of him, somehow.

"I haven't killed anybody. You've got the wrong vampire."

Nina shook her head. "I've got the right one. He was working for you guys, you and Samson. He was a bodyguard for Scanguards. All he did was work for you, and what did you guys do? Betray him, use him."

Recognition lit in his eyes. "Edmund Martens. You're talking about Edmund."

Finally he was catching on. About time.

"He killed his client and then himself," Amaury elaborated. "It's a fact. Ask the police. They have the evidence. Neither Samson nor I have anything to do with his death."

"You guys made him do it. You forced him, coerced him. One of you set him up." Her Eddie would have never killed anybody, least of all himself.

"That's crazy. I barely knew him. We didn't do anything to him. None of us, not I, not Samson."

Amaury was stalling, and she couldn't accept it.

"Eddie wasn't a killer. He couldn't hurt a fly. Yes, he stole, he cheated—because he *had* to. *We* had to. We had nothing else. But he wasn't a murderer, he wasn't evil. He was gentle and kind." She felt tears well up in her eyes.

"Listen, Nina. Maybe you didn't know your boyfriend that well, but he—"

She cut him off. "*Boyfriend*? Eddie wasn't my boyfriend, he was my brother! My baby brother. I looked out for him. I cared for him." She knew him better than anybody. She'd taken care of him after they'd left their last foster home. And then when he'd finally managed to get a real job with Scanguards, he'd taken care of her, so she could go back to school to get an education. But that was all over now. Because he'd gotten mixed up with vampires.

"Your brother? Oh, *chérie*, I'm so sorry."

Amaury sounded so genuine, she wanted to believe him. But she knew better. With an impatient wave of her hand she stopped him from saying anything else.

"You and your friends, you're responsible. You turned him. You did something to him, controlled him with your minds, just like you tried with me a minute ago. You made him do it. And now you'll pay for it."

She pulled out a stake from her inside pocket. His eyes widened when he homed in on the weapon in her hand.

"You can't be serious."

"I'm dead serious." She felt it was her duty to get justice for her brother. He would have done the same for her.

"Nina, your brother won't come back even if you kill me."

She knew that. "But I'll feel better once it's done."

Amaury shook his head. "No, you won't. If it's true what you say, that your brother wasn't a killer, what makes you think *you're* one? You're cut out of the same cloth."

His blue eyes seemed to want to penetrate her. She didn't want to listen to him any longer, because his words began to ring true.

"You're a vampire, you're already dead. It wouldn't be like killing a human."

"I'm not dead. My heart beats, my blood runs through my veins. I breathe." Amaury pushed his hips against her, making her all too aware of the part of him that was even more alive than the rest of him. "I'm alive, and you know it."

That explained it—with blood running through his veins and his heart beating, of course his body would be warm, not cold. But anyway— "It doesn't matter. You're responsible. You'll have to pay, just like your friends. They'll all pay for it. He was just a kid."

"None of us did this to your brother. But I know something about it stinks. That's why we brought in reinforcements. We're investigating this. Nina, believe me, we're trying to get on top of this. We're just as worried about this as you are. We're trying to figure out who did this to him."

"More like sweeping it under the rug."

"No. We know something is wrong, and we're doing everything we can to find out what it is. We need some time. Please trust me. I'll help you find out who's done this to Eddie. I can find who's responsible."

His eyes were pleading with her, but she couldn't trust him. As soon as she released him, he would turn the tables on her and punish her. No, she couldn't go back now. She'd already gone too far.

She gripped the stake tighter. "Somebody has to pay for his death."

"Somebody *will*, *chérie*, I promise you. But don't do this." His voice was the softest whisper. Too soft for a vampire—too gentle for a murderer. "You'll hate yourself for hurting an innocent person. I can help you. Let's work together. I can protect you. You don't want to be out there on your own. Whoever is responsible is dangerous. Please."

***

Amaury didn't understand what he was offering her, but the sad look on Nina's face tore at his heartstrings. Suddenly she looked smaller and more vulnerable, not like the slayer she was trying to portray. Despite the stake in her hand, he knew she had a good heart.

And despite the agony he was currently in, he wanted to help her. The silver was painfully eating into his skin, the blisters that had first formed now breaking open, making any further contact with the silver even more painful. He tried to move as little as possible to confine the effects of the poisonous metal to a smaller area, but it was hard not to shift as the burning sensation became worse.

All he could do was distract himself. Amaury concentrated on Nina and saw a flicker in her eyes, which he recognized as doubt. She wasn't sure anymore that her action was right. He had to use her doubt to get to her.

"Let me kiss you and make it better." He had sensed how her body had reacted to him, and doubted she had faked it all. She wasn't that good an actress. "Please, you know my body doesn't lie. And neither does yours. Do you really think you would have enjoyed touching and kissing me, if you truly thought I was guilty? Trust your instincts."

His own instincts told him she was good, and only desperation had driven her to these extreme measures. Somehow he would get through to her. He had to try.

"Before Zane captured you tonight, we had a staff meeting. My colleagues from New York and I are trying to figure out who knew anything about your brother and what happened. We have some leads." They weren't really leads, just hunches. He'd sensed some oddities about several of the staff present and had selected those to be interviewed separately.

"What leads?"

There was interest in her eyes now. He was getting somewhere.

"Some indication that some guys aren't telling us the whole truth. There's something hidden, and we'll find it, trust me. Finding the truth is just as important to us as it is to you."

"You're just saying that to pacify me."

Her plump lips parted. What he'd give to kiss her right now. She would believe him then.

Amaury shook his head. "If we can't solve this, it'll ruin the company. We'll lose our clients. Nobody wants to be protected by bodyguards who are unstable. Samson spent years building up the company and making it into what it is today. Do you really think he'd throw that all away by driving his staff to commit murder?"

He noticed the expression in her eyes change. Something was getting through to her. Was he making any sense?

"You know what I am, and have I hurt you? No. Because that's not me. I don't hurt women."

Well, spanking didn't count as hurting anyway, especially not when the other party encouraged it.

"I'm a vampire, and you kissed me. You allowed me to touch you, and you shared your passion with me." He dropped his gaze to her mouth. "You have the softest lips I've ever tasted. No woman has ever ignited this kind of desire in me. Your mouth on me gave me more pleasure than I've ever felt before. Nina, you can't tell me you didn't feel that. You didn't fake it. It was real. Now let me show you the same pleasure. Please, let me make love to you."

Amaury searched her eyes for signs of acceptance and wished he could sense her emotions, but her heart didn't release any emotions for him to read. He'd never learned to read people's faces since he never had to, because his gift always provided him with everything he needed to know. Now he regretted his ineptness.

Nina shook her head as if to shake something off.

"No. I can't. I can't betray Eddie. He was all I had. He was the only one who ever cared about me."

She suddenly jumped up and off the bed. Amaury rattled at his chains, but the silver stung his skin. He bit his lips to stop himself from screaming in pain. Shit! His wrists felt like they'd been dunked into a deep fryer.

"Nina, I care about you. Don't leave."

Without another word, she turned and stormed out of the bedroom.

"Nina, come back!"

She didn't answer. He heard her footsteps as she crossed the living area. Then the entrance door opened.

"Nina, damn it! Come back and finish what you've started!"

And he didn't mean killing him.

His cock stood fully erect, the tiny slit in its tip looking at him accusingly. He was aching now, yearning to be inside her, to find his release with her. And he realized that for the first time his pain was different. He wasn't aching for a climax because his head was exploding. No, this time his body was aching for a connection, a connection with Nina.

She was exactly what he needed. With her blunt human teeth she'd bitten his nipples, and in that instant he'd hoped she would draw blood. He'd ached for her to bite him again when she'd worked her way up his body. Quite deliberately he had presented his neck to her, hoping, wanting, and baiting her to drink his blood. It was foolish. He'd never allowed any of his vampire lovers to bite him, never offered his blood to a human, but her tentative bite had awakened a desire in him he couldn't quite explain, yet wanted to explore.

Wait until I find you.

But until then, he would have to figure out a way of getting out of his current predicament. Breaking the chain was not an option, even though it wasn't very thick. The fact that it was made of silver made it impossible for him to do any damage to it. Every time he yanked on it, it only dug deeper into his flesh.

"Fuck!" Amaury cursed, feeling the pain more intensely now that Nina was gone and he had nobody but himself to focus on.

Amaury looked around his bedroom for anything he could use to rid himself of his chains. He shook his head. How could he have completely lost it and not have noticed her taking the chain and tying him up? No woman had ever gotten him into such a state that he'd completely lost all his senses.

In the last decades, he'd rarely had sex for the sake of sex. The only reason he'd had sex was to get relief from the pain in his head. But when Nina had started seducing him, all he had thought about was feeling her and enjoying her. Not because he had to have sex, but because he wanted to. And that hadn't happened in ages.

With the silver eating away at his wrists, he couldn't just lie here and wait until one of his friends came looking for him. There was no time to waste, or the healing process would take days, not hours. Besides, his hard-on wasn't coming down by itself, especially since her scent still lingered in the bedroom. He needed to get out and start looking for her.

Amaury glanced at the phone which sat on the bedside table. It was several feet outside the reach of his hands. He tried to shift closer, but the chain would only go so far. The more the silver damaged his wrists and dissolved his skin, the more he started cursing her.

Wait until I get my hands on you, chérie.

And why was he still using the French word for sweetheart? He shook his head at his own stupidity and set his mind to the task at hand.

Twisting his body sideways, he stretched both his legs toward the cordless phone. If he pulled a muscle because of it, he would make her massage it with her tongue, he promised himself.

The image only intensified his erection which seemed to grow thicker by the minute.

With renewed determination, he grasped the receiver between his feet and pulled it onto the bed. His toes were too big to dial individual numbers, but if he could press redial, he would reach one of his friends. He wasn't sure which one, but at least somebody would come to help him.

His big toe hit the button, and his sensitive hearing picked up the ringing sound. Even though he couldn't put the call on speaker, it would be sufficient for him to communicate.

"Hey, what's up?"

Great. Thomas? Really?

Somebody was having a joke at Amaury's expense.

13

It was just Amaury's luck that he was tied up in bed with a hard-on that could knock out a charging bull and had to ask his only gay friend to come and untie him. Perfect.

"Amaury?" Thomas's voice came through the receiver again.

He swallowed before he spoke. "Thomas. I need your help."

"Sure, what do you need?"

Amaury frowned. "I'm kind of tied up here. Would you mind coming over and helping me out of this jam?"

"What jam?"

"I'm tied up." He tightened his jaw and closed his eyes in an attempt to breathe through the pain.

"Yeah, you said. But what jam?"

If this ever got out, Amaury would be the laughing stock in the vampire world.

"That's the jam. I'm tied up."

There was silence on the other end, then a stifled laugh. "Oh, I've got to see this. Be there in twenty minutes."

The click in the line confirmed Thomas had hung up. Amaury could imagine the grin on his friend's face right now. He looked at the clock. It was just past four in the morning.

Thomas was true to his word. Twenty minutes later, Amaury heard the key turn in the lock and his friend enter with his heavy biker boots. For safety reasons they all had spare keys to each other's homes.

Without much luck Amaury tried to cover himself with the tangled sheets, but they were twisted underneath him and didn't reach to his midsection. He cursed under his breath. A moment later his friend, clad in his customary leathers, came through the door and stared at him in all his naked glory.

"Now that's a sight I haven't had the pleasure to—"

Amaury shot him an annoyed look. It was embarrassing to be checked out by a gay guy, even if he was one of his friends. "Don't even think about it."

"No wonder the ladies are always after you." Thomas clearly examined his erection.

Amaury rattled at the chain, trying to divert his attention. "Do you mind?" he pressed out through clenched teeth.

Thomas stepped closer and pulled his biker gloves from his leather jacket. "I knew you were into kinky shit, but silver?" He *tsked* as he slipped into the black gloves.

"This wasn't of my own choosing."

"Pray, tell." His friend laughed.

"I don't kiss and tell." Amaury pressed his lips into a thin line. "Are you gonna free me or did you come to stare?"

"I thought I'd just stare until you tell me how you got into this. I have time. It's been a slow night. Besides, I'm bored."

Thomas clearly enjoyed himself at Amaury's expense. He sat on the edge of the bed, and Amaury instantly moved in the opposite direction.

"Cover me up with the sheet, and maybe I'll tell you what happened."

"Maybe isn't gonna get you anything. Hurts, huh?"

"The sheet," Amaury insisted tersely.

"Which portion do you want covered?" Thomas grinned from one ear to the other.

Amaury graced him with a sour look, before Thomas finally complied and reached for the tangled sheet.

"And I don't want your hands coming anywhere near my dick."

"How about my mouth?"

"Thomas!"

"Just joking. You should see your face. Go on then, spill." Thomas placed the bed sheet over Amaury's lower body. "Which of your vamp ladies played this little prank on you? She must have been good, given the boner you're still sporting."

Amaury cringed. "You don't know her."

"I know every single vampire female in this town, not as intimately as you do, of course, but nevertheless I do know each one."

"You don't know her."

Thomas took hold of the sheet at if to pull it off Amaury again.

"Keep that right there," Amaury warned and motioned to the sheet Thomas used for his blackmail.

"New in town?" Another tug at the bed sheet.

Amaury shook his head, then he looked his friend right in the eye. "She's not a vampire."

Thomas let go of the bed linen.

"Not a . . . ? Oh, Amaury, what the hell are you doing? A human? You let yourself be tied up by a *human*? Are you crazy?"

Probably.

"Listen. It happened. I survived it. It's over." The less he made it sound like a big deal in front of his friend the better. "Now get that chain off me."

Thomas held up his hand. "Hold on. Not so fast. Did you wipe her memory before she left?"

"Didn't get a chance." Truth be told, he hadn't even thought of it, that's how drugged with desire he'd been. And besides, he suspected it wouldn't have worked. Somehow Nina had been able to resist his mind control. He'd never met a human who was immune to it. This fact intrigued him even more. Why was Nina so different?

"Do I need to remind you about the—"

"Yeah, yeah. I'm not deaf. First Samson, then Gabriel, now you. I know the rules. This is different."

His friend raised an eyebrow. "How so?"

"She knows who we are. She knew even before I met her."

"What?" Disbelief and panic rolled off Thomas in spades.

"Okay, but this will stay between you and me. I'll take care of this, but the others can't find out. Are you with me?"

Their gazes locked until Thomas finally nodded.

"She's Edmund's sister. The bodyguard who killed a client last month," Amaury explained.

"Ah, shit!" Thomas jumped up.

"Exactly. She's been snooping around. Thinks that Edmund couldn't have done this, that he was coerced or something. Somehow she figured out what we are, and she's blaming us. She wants revenge."

How she'd figured them out, Amaury didn't know yet. He hadn't even tried to question her, so obsessed had he been with getting her into bed.

"Shit, she could have killed you. Why didn't she?"

Amaury could venture a guess. After all, the way she'd sucked his cock told him she wasn't entirely unaffected by their encounter.

"I don't know."

"You don't know?" Thomas sounded skeptical and ventured another look at the spot where Amaury's erection was tenting the sheet.

"Fine. There's something going on between us, but it's purely sexual."

Whom was he kidding? Whatever was between him and Nina went deeper than sex. Had it been merely sex, he would have fucked her in an alley and wiped her memory posthaste. That was the drill with all other women. Which reminded him: he hadn't touched another woman since he'd met Nina.

"Amaury, you're so full of crap." He shook his head. "We'd better find her before she causes even more chaos." Thomas used his gloved hands to loosen the silver chain and untie him.

Amaury stared at his injured wrists. They looked like a dog had chewed on them, the angry red flesh bleeding and only partially covered by skin.

"Fuck!"

"Serves you right." Thomas's reprimand stung even more than the effect of the silver.

"Help me find her, and I'll take care of it. It shouldn't be so hard. Log into the background checks. I'm sure Edmund's file has something on her."

Thomas pointed toward his injuries. "You'll need blood." He pulled out a flask from the inside pocket of his leather jacket and handed it to him.

Amaury hesitated, but took it. After the fiasco with Mrs. Reid he wasn't prepared to put anybody else at risk. The guilt still gnawed at him. And his friend was right: he needed blood to heal.

He took several gulps and handed him back the empty flask. "Thanks. Let me get dressed. My computer is on. Can you start on it?"

"By the way, why didn't you just break the wrought-iron bar to break free?" Thomas tilted his head to the bed.

Amaury followed his look and frowned. The headboard of his bed was an intricately woven iron tapestry. With his vampire strength it would have been possible to break it—not easy, but definitely doable. "It's an antique. I bought it only a month ago. There was no need destroying perfectly good furniture."

Thomas shook his head and headed for the door.

Amaury grabbed his clothes from where Nina had dropped them on the floor. Within seconds he was dressed. In hindsight, he was glad Thomas was the one who'd released him. At least he wasn't as much of a stickler for rules as Ricky or Gabriel. And Samson would have really let him have it. He didn't even want to think of Zane's reaction.

By the time he entered the alcove in the living room which housed his little home office, Thomas had already pulled up Edmund's background check.

"Here, next of kin. Nina Martens. Is that her?" His friend looked up from the computer.

"Yes, that's her name. What's her address?"

"None. Just a phone number. Local."

"Can you find out where it's registered?"

Thomas pulled up another window and started typing. Minutes passed. Amaury paced behind his friend.

"Would you stop that? It's making me nervous."

Amaury halted in midstride. "What's taking so long?"

"Hmm." Another minute passed. "Damn."

"What?"

"It's a cell phone. Registered address is a post box."

"Try the DMV. She must have a driver's license," Amaury suggested. He had to find her, no matter what.

Another screen popped open. Amaury watched as his IT genius of a friend hacked into the system.

"Here we are. Welcome to the Department of Motor Vehicles." Thomas grinned broadly. He was in his element. Unfortunately, minutes later he had to concede defeat.

"She doesn't have a driver's license, at least not in California."

"What? How can that be?"

Thomas shrugged. "Hey, she doesn't live in LA where she'd have to drive to get around. San Francisco has public transportation."

"What now?" Amaury frowned. He couldn't give up.

"I can try to triangulate her cell phone, but I can't do that from here. I need my equipment from home." He looked at his wristwatch. "It's getting late. Tell you what. I'll drive home, try to find out where her cell phone is and give you an approximate area. You think you can work with that?"

Amaury nodded. "If you send me within a couple of blocks of where she is, I'll find her." With her blood still in his veins from the night before he would have no problem picking up on her scent if she was close.

Thomas tossed a glance at Amaury's midsection. "And do something about that boner, will you? It's downright distracting."

Before Amaury could hit him over the head, his friend was gone.

By the time Thomas called him from his home, it was close to sunrise. And his friend had bad news.

"Her cell phone is either out of range or switched off."

Amaury cursed under his breath.

"I'll try again later. You can't go out now anyway. We'll have to wait till tonight. You'd better spend your time sleeping so your wrists can heal."

Like Amaury needed a nurse. But there was no need pissing Thomas off with the comment currently sitting on his lips. "Fine. Call me as soon as you know where she is."

He slammed the receiver down and let out a frustrated shout. Once he found her, she would be punished. Slowly, severely, and without mercy.

14

For the second time Nina looked at the text message.

Mezza9 2nite careful he nos who u r, the message read.

Apparently Benny had decided to give her one goodbye present before he left town to save his bony ass. She couldn't tell whether the information was genuine. Most likely it was another trap. She had to assume as much. However, this time she would be prepared. Expecting a trap and walking into it well prepared, she could make it work to her advantage.

It was worth a try.

After the things Amaury had said the night before, she'd developed serious doubts about his involvement in Eddie's death. The sincerity in his eyes had given her pause. And his insistence that Scanguards was investigating internally had chipped away a little more at her previous certainty.

Now she would put all her chips on the man who'd hired Benny to send her into a trap. Since he'd wanted her out of the way because she was looking into Eddie's death, her conclusion was that he was involved. In what capacity, she wasn't sure yet, but she'd find out, one way or another.

But before she was ready to go and seek him out, she would have to stock up on weapons. This time she'd go in armed to the teeth. She needed another silver chain at the very least. Even though she wasn't sure who the person was, she had a hunch he would turn out to be a vampire. And she wasn't going into the lion's den without protection.

She grabbed her leather jacket from the chair and put it on, stuffed her keys into her pocket and released the door chain. As she opened the door and stepped outside into the dark hallway, something massive blocked her exit.

"Going somewhere, *chérie?*"

Nina's heart stopped. Her immediate reaction was to bolt, but she didn't get a chance. Amaury pushed her back through the open door and slammed it shut behind them. In her small studio he looked even larger than usual.

Oh hell, he looked pissed. She hadn't counted on him finding her. Well, at least not this fast.

"What do you want?" She lifted her chin, trying to look brave, when she felt anything but.

He cupped her shoulders and pressed her against the wall. "I want to warn you."

Nina's breath caught in her chest, as she watched his eyes penetrate her.

"Never, *ever* tie me up and leave me aroused without finishing what you started. Do you get that?"

She nodded automatically.

"I'm going to give you another chance to redeem yourself. One mistake, and I'll deliver you right into Zane's capable hands."

She swallowed hard. "Zane?" Hadn't Amaury been the one warning her about Zane? And now he wanted to throw her at his mercy? So much for all the bullshit about him wanting to offer her protection.

"Now, you'll do exactly as I say. Do we understand each other?"

She understood all too well as she caught his gaze sweeping down her body. "Let go of me!"

She jerked against his hold, but his grip was iron-clad.

"Take your jeans off."

"No!" She hit her foot against his shin, but the effect it had on him was negligible.

"Careful, Nina. You don't want to piss me off even more," he warned, his voice tight. "I'm telling you one last time: strip."

His command made Nina shiver. She hadn't imagined this would happen, at least not this way, not here, not with him being so angry. Least of all had she imagined that it would turn her on like it did. Just the way she felt unprepared for the shame and guilt that flooded her. What kind of woman was she that she felt aroused by a man commanding her to strip? Had she no self-respect left? Or was it proof that her sexual history had tainted the way she saw sex, that anything twisted, anything violent was the norm for her?

With shaking fingers she tried to open the top button of her jeans, but failed. A second later she felt his warm hands on hers, assisting her. The button sprung open.

"Pull the zipper down." His hot breath teased her neck. "Slowly."

She did as he asked, unable to fight him or herself.

"Now, push them over your hips." Was his voice getting hoarse?

"Please, don't do this," she pleaded with him, making one last attempt to stop him.

His lips grazed her neck, then nibbled at her earlobe. "You'll have to learn this lesson. Do it."

A few moments later, she'd stripped out of her jeans. She felt naked in her small panties. Amaury's thighs brushed against hers. Strong, powerful muscles.

"Do you remember what you did to me last night?"

"Yes." Her throat was dry. She remembered all too well.

"No, you don't. You've never felt as frustrated as I did last night. May I demonstrate?" He didn't wait for her permission.

His hand stroked her hip before he slipped it between her legs, touching her through the fabric of her panties. She sighed involuntarily. His touch wasn't rough as she'd expected, but gentle, teasing. Had he not come to punish her after all?

"I was so fucking hard for you last night," he continued whispering into her ear while his finger ran along her folds. "I was in agony with wanting to be inside you."

Her breath hitched at the thought of it. He wanted her—he still wanted her. The thought elated her.

Amaury's hand drew up and briefly slipped over her clit, before he let it slide into her panties. Nina held her breath as he traveled through her curly mound of hair, then stroked lower. The heat shooting through her core made her exhale sharply. When his finger touched her naked sex, she realized she was wet and yearning to be taken by him.

"I wanted my cock in you last night. To fill you, again and again. I wanted to eat your pussy and make you come with my mouth."

The images he was projecting, together with his probing finger at her core, made her break out in an instant hot flash. His mouth nipped at her earlobe, not helping either. Instead of trying to stop him, she tilted her pelvis toward his hand. This was madness. But she didn't care. He was different from other men. He hadn't come back to hurt her, he'd come to give her pleasure.

"I wondered what you would taste like," he said and dipped his finger into her. Her hips bucked toward him, wanting more, but Amaury instantly pulled out and away from her. She looked up at him and saw how his finger came to his lips, and how he sucked it into his mouth, licking it clean.

"Delicious."

Nina gasped and felt her knees buckle. He was seducing her, plain and simple, and she had no defenses. They had all crumbled, and she hadn't even seen it happen.

"Amaury, please . . . " She had no idea what she wanted to ask him or tell him. Her brain was mush. His scent was all around her, enveloping her in a cocoon of desire.

Maybe he had understood what she was unable to tell him, because his hand came back, and again he slipped it into her panties. He penetrated her once more, then withdrew instantly and pulled his finger up and over her clit, circling it slowly.

"And I was wondering what it would feel like if you came for me, if your muscles clenched around my cock, milking me, making me spill inside you." Amaury spoke slowly, his voice husky and calm at the same time. This was not the voice of an angry man. He wasn't hurting her with his touch. Instead he was tempting her to surrender to him.

Her hand had a mind of its own as it suddenly reached for him, finding his swollen shaft hidden behind the fabric of his pants. She felt how hard he was for her. Before she could enjoy the heat under her palm, he gripped her hand and pulled it away.

"No touching. Tonight, I get to touch you, not the other way around."

Nina looked into his eyes and was drawn into the blue of them, their depth, their beauty. She wanted nothing more than to kiss him, touch him, feel him inside her.

"Kiss me."

He shook his head and continued touching her. His thumb stroked over her center of pleasure, first very lightly, almost as if by accident. But she knew nothing he did was an accident. While his lips kissed alongside her neck, a neck she offered him without fear he would bite, his finger slipped into her tight sheath. Slowly and steadily he drove deep, then withdrew. Every time he plunged deeper she tried to hold onto his finger by tightening her muscles, but every time he withdrew, leaving her wanting.

"More." She didn't care that she begged. She was beyond foolish pride.

"So you like that?" His voice hummed against the indentation at the base of her neck. "Tell me what you want."

She moistened her dry lips. Finally he'd give her what she needed. "More."

"More of what?" Amaury withdrew his finger completely.

"Please. More. More fingers. Deeper." She was unable to form a coherent sentence. All she could think of was the pleasure he gave her with his touch.

"Like this?" He drove two fingers into her channel.

Nina bucked against him. "Oh, yes!" Her muscles pulsated around him as she tried to stop him from withdrawing. But she couldn't prevent him from his intent to leave her bereft.

"How about your clit? Do you want me to touch it?" His hand hovered and she tilted her pelvis toward him. But he pulled back. "You have to ask for it."

"Amaury, please, touch me." She would say anything to have his touch back, to have him finish what he'd started.

He didn't make it easy. "Where?"

"Touch my clit." Her breath was ragged, her voice low.

A second later, Nina felt his thumb stroke her where she needed it most. She leaned her head against his shoulder, inhaling his male scent. She needed this man, this vampire. There was no reason to deny it. He awoke everything female in her. When she was near him she felt like a bitch in heat. She was disgusted with herself for her weakness, but she couldn't fight against it any longer.

Amaury knew exactly how to touch her, how to create all those delicious sensations that rendered her nearly delirious with pleasure. Without a doubt she wanted him, couldn't wait to feel his strong body claim her, brand her. And she knew it was how it would be: a fierce claiming, a powerful possession. Because he had the power over her body to make her surrender to him.

And surrender she would, not caring what he would do once she did, as long as his body was there to soothe her need, to fill that gaping void, to quell her thirst for more.

"Make love to me," she heard her own voice beg.

***

Amaury heard the words he'd waited for and released her from his embrace. Reluctant, for sure, but nevertheless determined to execute his plan. She had left him aroused and wanting the night before. Now he would return the favor. It was the only way to pay her back.

His cock protested vehemently as he pulled back, but for once he wouldn't listen to his dick. She was ripe for the taking, begging him, but he wouldn't do it, as much as it pained him.

"Good night, Nina."

He turned and stalked toward the door, anxious to leave quickly so he wouldn't lose his resolve.

"You can't leave now!" There was a twinge of desperation in her voice. Had he also sounded like that the night before?

"Watch me." Amaury stepped through the door and shut it behind him. He heard Nina's voice calling after him as he walked through the dark corridor, but he didn't turn back.

When he walked into the cool night air, he braced himself for a moment. God, he wanted that woman. He'd tasted her arousal and her blood, and both were the sweetest tastes he'd ever had. He could lose himself in her.

At first it had seemed like a good plan to do to her what she'd done to him: arouse her and then leave her unsatisfied. But touching her this intimately, tasting her arousal, and feeling her response to him, had gotten him more randy than a sailor after a twelve-month tour at sea. And half as refined. The way he felt right now, he'd do her in the street in full view of the entire city and not give a rat's ass about exposure. Or common decency.

He had to get out of here before he gave into his urges, went back, threw her onto the floor and took her like the savage he was, not caring if she wanted him or not. Only eager to still his own lust.

Amaury clicked the remote for the car and heard the familiar beeps. His black Porsche was parked only a few yards away. Normally, he didn't use the car for short trips downtown, but Gabriel and the others were expecting him for the first set of one-on-one interviews with the employees they had selected during the staff meetings.

The car door was jerked out of his hand and slammed shut just as he opened it. He recognized the foot that had hit the door.

"You're not leaving!" Nina's furious voice was right behind him. He swiveled to face her and wished he hadn't. Her eyes still showed signs of arousal, but now they were interlaced with anger. The combination was lethal. What man would ever be able to resist a woman who looked at him that way?

"Go back home, Nina." He tamped down his urge to grab her.

"That's all you've got to say?" He saw the hurt in her face.

"You should stay away from me." He was no good for her. Eventually he would hurt her, and it would be worse than what she felt now. If he were smart, he would wipe her memory of him right now and be done with it. But all his smarts had deserted him for the night.

"You're rejecting me, after the way you touched me?"

"That's right." His throat felt tight, and he couldn't breathe.

"Fine. Go, leave. I don't need you. There are plenty of men in this city who'll take what I'm offering. And what do I care who it is? As long as he's got a big dick, there's no difference to me anyway! Somebody will finish what you've started." Nina turned on her heels.

Had he heard right? Another man? She was going to sleep with *another man*?

Amaury snatched her by her jacket and pulled her back to face him. She was going to let another man touch her, kiss her, make love to her? Over his fucking dead body!

"Get in the damn car!"

She shot him a surprised look.

"Now!" Before he lost it and took her against the car door to assert his claim.

The moment they both sat in the car, he stepped on the gas and shot into the street. He was reeling. She'd manipulated him, pushed his buttons. The little vixen had made him jealous! Him, the man who couldn't care less about women unless it was to scratch an itch.

A warm hand slipped onto his thigh, and he let out a low growl. "You don't know what you're getting into."

Nina leaned into him, which wasn't difficult considering how small the inside of his Porsche Carrera was. "Neither do you."

Her hand traveled higher up his thigh, playing havoc with his concentration. He sped up and ran a red light. Angry honking behind him followed, but he ignored it.

"You're playing a dangerous game." His warning seemed to go right over her head as her palm suddenly cupped the bulge in his pants. Had there been any space in the car, he would have leapt out of his seat, but all he could do was let out a frustrated moan. "Are you trying to make me crash the car?"

"I just want to make sure you won't change your mind again."

Amaury shot her a sideways glance. "I can make you a promise right now. You won't get away from me until I've fucked you every which way I can think of, and then some. And then I'll do it all over again, because you'll beg me to."

He didn't care that he sounded arrogant. He didn't care about anything at this point. All he wanted was to be inside her. Only then would he be able to think clearly again. Right, that was what he needed. He was sure afterwards things would go back to normal for him.

Her warm palm squeezed his erection as if in agreement, and he let out a stifled groan.

"Damn it, Nina, can't you wait two minutes?"

"Drive faster if you don't want to get arrested for getting a blow job in the car."

His foot pressed the gas pedal in desperation, while he felt her nudging open the zipper of his pants. A block before his building her hand reached in to pull out his cock. He hit the garage door opener and increased the speed, gritting his teeth.

The Porsche shot into the large private garage with not a second to spare, the garage door already closing behind them. The instant he came to a stop and killed the engine, he pulled her hand off and yanked her toward him.

"You know what happens to naughty girls?"

Nina looked almost innocent when she shook her short blond curls, tickling his face with them. Her intoxicating scent wrapped around him. "No."

"They end up with real bad boys."

A flicker of excitement illuminated her eyes. "Like you?"

"Like me." She had no idea what she was getting into and neither did he.

"Are you still angry with me?"

"Yes." But he would redirect his anger and turn it into passion instead.

"Do you want to spank me again?"

He raised an eyebrow. She sounded just a little too eager. What the hell had he started? What if he couldn't handle her? Or was she just what he needed? "I'll think about it."

Amaury gazed at her red lips which beckoned for a kiss. "Let's go upstairs. This car is not conducive to what I have in mind." Because one kiss would lead to much more, and he sure couldn't move in the damn car.

When he got out of the Porsche, he realized his cock was still peeking out of his pants. A cool breeze blew against his flesh. But he didn't bother adjusting himself. The garage was private and the elevator he had built in led directly into his apartment. None of the tenants had access to it.

As soon as he'd pulled Nina into the elevator and pushed the button to the top floor, he pressed her flat against the wall and sank his hungry lips onto hers.

He meant it when he said he wouldn't let her go until he'd thoroughly fucked her. And he wasn't going to waste another damn minute. The elevator was as good a place to start as any. The housekeeper had come by the day before, so he knew even the floor of the elevator was spotless, just in case he decided to make use of it. Maybe he would.

Amaury crushed her lips with his and dipped into her delicious mouth, searching out her talented tongue. Her response was hard and determined, drawing him into her tantalizing depths. Inviting him, pulling him in, then withdrawing so he would come after her. Playing not hard to get, but hard to keep. A challenge he only too gladly accepted.

He released a sigh and foraged deeper, barely able to breathe, yet unable to stop the kiss. She tasted too sweet, too innocent, when he knew she wasn't innocent, not by a long shot. Not the way she'd taken his cock into her mouth the night before or the way she kissed him now.

Nina's hands eagerly tugged at his jacket, pushing it off his shoulders with ease. She seemed to like undressing him, and he welcomed it since his body was heating up fast. The eight-by-four-foot space would turn into a sauna shortly, given the body heat they were generating. Just as well, since he was planning on stripping her naked in seconds.

Amaury liberated her from the leather jacket she still wore, dropping it unceremoniously onto the clean floor. She wore a T-shirt underneath. When he pulled her against his chest, he felt her soft breasts mold to him without a bra impeding them. He appreciated the simplicity of her clothing, her no-frills style.

His hand found its way underneath her shirt, instantly relishing the softness and warmth of her skin. He let the moment sink in, enjoyed the first contact of skin on skin, before he allowed himself to move upwards, where her twin globes beckoned to be attended to.

His fingertips reached her first, touched the underside of her breast, then slid farther north, searching and then finding the hardened little bud which already stood erect as if greeting his arrival. So he returned the gesture by stroking his thumb over it, applying just enough pressure to elicit a soft moan from its owner. A moan he'd anticipated and now captured with his hungry mouth. A moan which now reverberated through his body, awakening cells long dormant, sensations long forgotten.

"Somebody will see us," Nina whispered against his lips. He curled the ends of his mouth upwards. Her concern was unwarranted, but she couldn't know that, and he wouldn't tell her. She seemed like the kind of woman who would like the added risk of being discovered. And he wanted her just as horny as he was right now.

"So what? I promise you, I won't let anybody join in." Not that he had any objections to threesomes, but when it came to Nina, he didn't want to share her. This was just between the two of them. Private. Intimate.

He pushed her T-shirt up. "Take it off, Nina."

"Make me."

She wanted to play? He growled low and dark, then tugged at it with his teeth. One pull and the shirt ripped, gaping open in the middle.

"You're bad." Her voice was breathless, but not accusing.

"I haven't started yet."

Amaury reached for her beautiful round breasts, taking them into his hands, letting their weight be supported by his palms. As he squeezed lightly, he saw her lashes drop to half mast, partially hiding the desire in her eyes. Her gaze locked with his. Again he kneaded the soft flesh in his hands, and she reacted by pulling her lower lip between her teeth.

His cock tilted toward her, and he did himself a favor and pressed his groin against her sex. She answered by slinging her arms around his neck and pulling his face to her.

"Kiss me like you mean it." It was her demand, not his. Her wish, her choice.

Amaury's hand snaked around her back, while the other one slid to the back of her neck. He took her mouth hard and without mercy, forcing her lips open, driving his tongue into her like the spear of an ancient warrior, and he conquered. There was no resistance. She was his.

With one hand he jerked the button of her jeans open, then pulled the zipper down. Like a mirror image she did the same to him. He needed both his hands to nudge her tight jeans down her hips.

"Help me."

Her hands joined in, and seconds later her pants fell to the ground. His own followed moments later and were instantly followed by his shirt and the torn rags which used to be her T-shirt. He didn't have the patience to let her take off her panties, so he ripped them off her. He'd buy her new ones. Actually, on second thought, he would make sure she'd never again wear any underwear.

Naked, they stood in front of each other. The elevator had long since stopped on the top floor, but the door hadn't opened. It would only do so if he used his key which was buried somewhere in the pile of clothes on the floor.

Amaury's gaze swept over her nude form. She was a real blonde, evidenced by the soft blond curls guarding her sex. Without a word he dropped to his knees and buried his face in her thatch of hair, taking in her scent. His tongue darted out, taking its first taste. One lap was confirmation enough that he'd be lost. Her juices coated his tongue and spread in his mouth. His nostrils flared, his fangs itched. She was more delicious than any dish he remembered from the time when he was human. And tastier than any blood he'd ever tasted, except for hers. He let out a deep sigh and dug his hands into her backside to pull her closer to him.

Nina's breathing appeared more uneven now, and his sensitive hearing picked up her rapid heartbeat. He looked up and found her watching him.

"Come down here." He pulled her to the floor with him and placed her flat down before him, spreading her over the clothes. With deliberate movements he opened her legs and let his eyes devour her where his mouth would follow.

Her pink folds glistened with her desire, teasing his senses. Amaury sank his mouth onto her and explored her most intimate center. He realized instantly that he'd been wrong—his life would never go back to normal again, not after a night of passion in her arms.

15

Nina watched Amaury's head dip between her legs, his dark mane obscuring his face. But she had caught a glimpse of his eyes just before she felt his mouth on her. Unbridled lust was etched into them. She'd never seen a man so determined.

God help her if somebody came into the elevator now, for she was certain nothing would distract him from his task, and she'd never felt so vulnerable in her entire life. And so intent on allowing him anything he wanted as long as it meant he would pleasure her.

She was surprised by the gentleness with which this big man, this powerful vampire, worshipped her body. She hadn't expected the kind of finesse his tongue was exerting on her, not from Amaury, who could have easily crushed her with his weight.

But the way his tongue lapped against her eager petals was almost reverent. His movements were so slow, so mindful, as if he was committing every detail to memory. Like a cartographer who drew a map of a newly discovered continent so he could find his way back.

Amaury murmured something against her skin, which she couldn't understand. But the reverberations echoed within her body, sending shivers through her cells. Nina arched her hips to force him to increase the pressure on her sensitive organ.

His response was a greedy moan. "Patience," was all he said before the tip of his tongue sparred with the sensitive peak of her desire. He circled it like a warrior a wagon, then snatched the engorged nub between his lips and tugged. Like a lightning bolt, more delicious sensation shot through her.

A desperate moan escaped her lips. "Oh, Amaury, oh, God!" Her reaction seemed to spur him on, give him new purpose. Again he lapped over her sensitive clit, tantalizing her even more with but a ghost of a touch. She needed more.

Nina shoved her hands into his hair and pulled his face from her sex. His blue eyes punctuated hers. "Harder!"

He shook his head, a wicked grin forming on his lips. Was he going to leave her frustrated once more? Was he playing with her again? She'd kill him if he was.

"I don't want this to be over so soon. You taste too good."

She breathed a sigh of relief when she read his desire not only in his words but also in his eyes. His mouth dropped back to her moist center, but this time he spread her legs wider and parted her folds with his fingers. His tongue a spear, he drove into her, and she welcomed him.

His hot breath fired her center like the inside of a boiler. And then he added more fuel. Was he intent on this boiler exploding?

She felt his finger invade her, and he withdrew his tongue to allow it to travel back to her neglected little nub. With determined strokes he coaxed it back to attention.

Nina had never been with a man who was this talented and this determined to please her. Her sexual encounters had mostly been means to an end, payment for something, or just plain escapism. And many times utterly unsatisfying, at least for her. The men generally got what they came for. But nobody had really ever cared that much about whether she found her own release. So, she'd always found it easier to fake it. And besides, she'd never felt safe enough with anybody to really let herself go.

Yet Amaury seemed intent on showing her that a man could be selfless enough to make a woman feel good. At least for a little while.

"Why?"

When he suddenly looked up at her, she realized she'd spoken out loud. "Why what?"

"This."

He seemed to understand instantly. "Because you need this. And because I can't think of anything I'd rather do than make you come with my mouth."

Hearing his plain words, something constricted in her belly, sending a wave akin to an electrical shock through her body. Hot and pleasant. Was it the knowledge that he wanted to do this, which created her excitement? Or was it simply the way he'd said it: as if it was the only answer possible?

Before she could say anything else, his tongue was back, lapping at her moist folds, parting them, probing, teasing. A vampire's fangs were right where she was most vulnerable, yet her defenses didn't kick in. No warning came that should have told her not to allow what he was doing.

And at the same time she didn't feel the usual twinge of fear, nor the adrenaline shoot through her veins alerting her to danger.

Because right now he seemed to be just a man in lust, not a vampire, not a fighter. She could let go. He would catch her, Amaury, the man.

"Yes, Amaury." She spoke more to herself than to him, telling her body that he was safe, that being with him was good.

He scooped his hands under her backside and lifted her. His tongue drove deep and his moans echoed her own. Nina buried her hands in his dark, silken hair and felt him shudder. Her muscles tensed at the sensations he sent through her body, driving her ever higher. She pushed against his mouth, feeling his tongue increase its pressure on her clit, but not enough.

"Bite it."

A low growl was his response to her shouted demand. A moment later she felt his teeth graze her sensitive skin, then his lips tug at it, gently, then a little firmer.

"Please."

His teeth closed around her engorged button and pressed into her skin, not breaking it, but it was exactly what she needed. With a breathless moan she greeted the waves that crashed over her and swept her away. Amaury's tongue smoothed over the spot he'd so gingerly bitten, only intensifying her climax.

***

Nina's body shook in his arms, her muscles contracting and releasing in quick succession. Amaury lapped up her arousal, becoming addicted to her taste. By the time her body had stilled and her orgasm had subsided, he was already cradling her in his arms, pressing her against his naked body.

He'd never seen a sweeter sight than Nina's satisfied body. It filled him with an unknown sense of pride. His palm smoothed over her curls before it traveled over her back and settled on the soft cheeks of her derrière. And what a cute little ass it was, just like the rest of her. When she was curled up against him, her cheek leaning on his chest, her arms wrapped around his body, she didn't look like the tough fighter he'd first met. Suddenly she was all soft.

He felt a shiver go through her body.

"You're cold. Let's get you off this floor."

"Before somebody walks in on us."

"No chance of that happening," Amaury announced.

Effortlessly he lifted her from the floor, found his key in his pants and let them into the apartment.

He didn't bother picking up the clothes they had shed. Carrying Nina in his arms was a much more important task.

She looked at the apartment, then back at the elevator, obviously finally realizing that it was private.

"You rat! You had me think we could get surprised in there!"

He shrugged his shoulders, but inwardly he laughed. "It didn't stop you from getting naked."

Her slap against his shoulder didn't even register. It was virtually a caress.

"You can set me down now."

No way. Her body felt too good and his shaft had its own ideas of how to continue the night. And for once his cock and he were in perfect agreement.

"Would you rather make love on the couch or in bed?" Personally he'd prefer taking her to his bed, but if she was more comfortable on the other, he'd have no problems going with her choice.

Instead of an answer her cheeks colored a beautiful shade of pink. Could he make her blush even more?

"In the kitchen or the bathroom maybe? On the roof terrace?"

Yes, her blush could go even a shade deeper. And make her look even sexier. How she could possibly still blush after what she'd allowed him to do in the elevator, and what she'd done to him the night before, was absolutely beyond him.

He lowered his face close to hers, looking into her beautiful brown eyes. "It's okay to admit that you enjoyed what we just did. I won't tell anybody that this fierce slayer has a soft side."

Nina met his eyes and didn't flinch. "Then I guess I won't tell that this vampire isn't all as tough and mean as he makes himself out to be."

Of course he was tough! And mean! He should be feared for what he was and for what he could do. Was she suggesting he was weak? He let out a dark growl.

"Yes, yes. You can growl all you want, you big bad vampire."

Mocking him, was she?

"You want big and bad? I'll give you big and bad."

With a determined gait Amaury carried her into his bedroom and dropped her onto the bed. For a moment he just stood there, looking down at her. Then he touched his erection, stroking it suggestively.

"How big do you want?"

Nina appeared fascinated as she stared at him, her eyes glued to where his cock stood upright. He was eager to fill her with it, plunging his throbbing shaft into her until she couldn't take any more.

Her mouth formed just one word. "Big."

Her arms pulled him down to her, and he fitted his body to hers. She felt right, pinned underneath him. And she wouldn't be able to escape unless he allowed it. Luckily, escape seemed to be the furthest thing from her mind. Why else would she wrap her legs around him and pull him into her center?

Amaury welcomed her open invitation, and so did his cock which already pressed against her thigh. The skin-on-skin contact was enough to shoot a wave of heat through him.

In the background, he heard a faint ringing noise, but he blocked it out. For once, he cursed his enhanced senses. He didn't want to be distracted from the pliable body in his arms, the soft fingers exploring him, the sweet scent engulfing him.

Nina deserved his full attention. And she would have it. For a moment, he closed his eyes and blocked out everything else. With joy, he realized that no emotions bombarded him. His mind was clear. Peace.

When he opened his eyes, his gaze collided with hers.

"What's wrong?"

He sensed a twinge of alarm in her voice and shook his head, smiling. "Nothing! Absolutely nothing." For the first time in centuries. No pain. No foreign emotions. It was just him, all by himself.

"Are you waiting for something?"

Impatient minx.

"Yes, for you to shut up, *chérie.*"

Amaury muffled her protest with his lips. His erection settled against her soft core, and he nudged forward, finding her wetness. Tight—oh her entrance felt tight. Would she be able to take him?

Why hadn't he jerked off earlier? While masturbation did nothing in the way of blocking out the emotions and the pain in his head, at least some of his girth would have eased. Right now, he was close to bursting.

Her pelvis tilted toward him, silently asking for penetration, but he pulled back. Couldn't hurt her. Too big. No. He should prepare her better. Maybe another orgasm would help her tight muscles relax. Or better, finger fuck her first, stretch her narrow channel. He didn't want her to associate their lovemaking with pain. Already he had to work against her aversion to vampires. Now pain because his dick was too big? Couldn't do that. No. She would hate him. And for some reason that wasn't the kind of emotion he wanted her to have for him.

He needed patience to get to his goal.

The loud ring from the phone next to the bed startled him, but a moment later his attention was diverted when Nina's hands clamped over his ass, trying to force him to plunge into her. She was certainly impatient, and she obviously had no idea how savagely his cock could damage her tender muscles if he drove into her without her being properly prepared.

Amaury pulled away and took her arms, pinning them next to her body. Another ring from the phone drowned out whatever she wanted to say and made her stop in mid-speech.

"Nina, we'll have to take it slow."

The answering machine clicked on.

"I'm too big. Let me make you—"

His canned voice filled the room. "*I'm not here. You know what to do.*" Beep.

"*Where the hell are you? You were supposed to be here fifteen fucking minutes ago!*"

Amaury flinched. Gabriel was looking for him. And he wasn't in a good mood.

"*Pick up the fucking phone . . .*"

He lunged for the phone, grabbing it off the hook. Then he instantly put his finger on his lips, gesturing to Nina not to say a word.

"Gabriel—"

The response almost pierced his eardrum. "GET YOUR ASS TO THE OFFICE!"

Damn, he'd forgotten the interrogations which were planned for the night. No surprise Gabriel was pissed. "Yeah, I'm on my way."

"Or I'll have a word with Samson about that human woman from last night. He isn't gonna like it."

He was threatening him? "I said I was on my way." He slammed the phone down and looked back at Nina.

"I've got to go, Nina." Amaury exhaled on a sigh. He could think of better things to do than go to the office right now.

She sat up. "Well, I'll get dressed then."

Amaury stopped her from getting out of bed. "No, stay. We're nowhere near done. I'll be back in three hours."

"I should go."

No. He wanted her here when he came back to continue what they'd started.

"Please, stay and wait for me. Make yourself comfortable. Hey, you can even snoop around if you want to." His apartment wouldn't reveal anything about him that she didn't already know.

"I don't snoop!" The indignity in her voice seemed real.

He kissed her on the cheek. "Okay, then don't. But stay." His mouth trailed to her lips and captured them. If he continued like that, he'd arrive at the interrogations with a hard-on the size of a flagpole and draw further suspicion from his colleagues. They couldn't find out that he still hadn't erased Nina's memory. And that he had no intention of doing so. On the contrary, he wanted to make a lot more new memories with her.

Amaury jumped up from the bed and grabbed clean clothes from his closet.

"All right, I'll stay."

Her eyes were on him as he got dressed, and he enjoyed the way she looked at him. A man could get used to a woman looking at him like that.

"But when you get back . . . "

He gave her an expectant look. "What?"

"No more delays. If you don't have sex with me the moment you get back, I'm out of here."

He grinned. "Yes, *mademoiselle.*"

Nina threw a pillow at him which he caught instantly. His reflexes were as sharp as his dick was hard.

He headed for the door and gave her body one last long glance. She didn't even attempt to cover herself with the bed sheets. He would try to make it back in two hours max. "If you're hungry, there's some *coq au vin* in the fridge."

Before he turned and left, he caught her confused look. Amaury chuckled inwardly. Why he had food in the fridge would give her something to think about while he was gone. He was no run-of-the-mill vampire.

16

Amaury kept food in the fridge? What kind of strange vampire was he? Nina shook her head and jumped out of bed. She snatched one of his shirts from his closet and put it on, then walked into the living area.

She felt invigorated. Her entire body tingled in a pleasant way, as it would after a sensual massage. Only she hadn't had a massage, but an amazing orgasm at the very talented hands—and mouth—of said strange vampire, who thought nothing of leaving her alone in his lair and practically expected her to snoop around, which of course, made it so much less appealing. What a spoil-sport.

Three hours to kill before the sexy vampire would come back and finally make good on his promise to fuck her every which way he could think of. "And then some," the arrogant hottie had said. She had wanted to slap him for that, had she not been so turned on by his words.

Amaury's hesitation at actually penetrating her had come as an utter surprise. When had he turned all soft and decided he didn't want to hurt her? And who said she couldn't handle a man as big as he was? And he was big.

The vision of his hard length of turgid flesh, almost purple in color, with thick veins like vines snaking around it, sent her into another hot flash. It felt as if he was bigger than the previous night when she'd had him in her mouth. But maybe she was just fantasizing. He was just a big man all over, and while his cock was extraordinarily large, it was in perfect proportion to the rest of his body.

But she couldn't continue daydreaming about him. She would have sex with him and then forget about him and get on with her mission. Nothing had changed. In fact, having dealt with him and some of his friends had given her more insight into their powers, and if anything, she was now more prepared to fight them than before.

Amaury didn't want to physically harm her; somehow she sensed that, but it didn't mean he would help her out at the expense of his interest in Scanguards. Maybe he was just trying to soften her up so she would give up and not pursue her path. Well, if that's what he was trying, he wouldn't succeed. As if sex would change anything about what was right or wrong.

Perhaps it was better to forget about having sex with him after all. Nothing good would come of it.

Except another spectacular orgasm.

Ah, shut up!

Since when did she think with her pussy? Had the man turned her into a completely hopeless and helpless woman? This couldn't happen. Men couldn't be trusted, and vampires even less. Sure, he was hot, he wanted her, and he hadn't hurt her, but that didn't mean he could be trusted. Not that this fact would stop her from having sex with him. She didn't need to trust a man to have sex with him. One had nothing to do with the other. Maybe it was better this way. She'd trusted the wrong person once before, and it had screwed up her life. She wouldn't make the same mistake twice.

Nina pushed the rising memories of the events in her last foster home from her mind. This was not the time to dwell on pain that she'd tried to forget for over ten years.

Her eyes darted around the living room, and she spotted her clothes on a chair near the entrance. Both her T-shirt and her panties were ripped and unusable. She shook her head. Amaury sure was one passionate vampire.

She didn't understand why he would leave her alone in his lair, unless . . . Nina spun around to the entrance door and jerked it open. No, she sighed with relief, he hadn't locked her in. Did he trust her to wait for him, or was it just plain arrogance on his part? Or had he seen the longing in her eyes before he'd left?

Nina shuddered at the thought of how much of herself Amaury had already seen, not her body—she didn't care about that—but her mind, her soul, and her heart. All the things she kept hidden, because it was safer to hide her true self: the scared, insecure, hurt girl she still was inside. The girl who so desperately longed to be loved, yet was scared to open her heart to anybody. The girl who wanted *forever*, but settled for *right now*, because it was all she was ever offered. The girl who'd never ask for anything, because she couldn't face *no,* couldn't handle being rejected and tossed aside once more.

No, she had to be the strong woman who had a purpose in life.

A vibrating sound from her stack of clothes brought her back into the present. Her cell phone. She pulled it out of her jacket pocket. A reminder blinked.

Damn! The text message she'd gotten just before Amaury had barged into her apartment—she'd completely forgotten about it. Maybe it wasn't too late yet to make it to the Mezzanine to find that guy. At least she had to try. She wasn't exactly dressed for the club, but her place was practically on the way. She could slip into something more appropriate and be on her way minutes later.

Nina snatched her jeans from the chair and put them on without her underwear.

Three hours was plenty of time to get to the club, try to find the suspect, and get some information out of him. If she was fast, she could even make it back without Amaury ever knowing that she was even gone. She'd leave the window to the fire escape open and get back into the apartment that way.

And if her investigation found something that pointed to Amaury after all, well, then she would do what was necessary. She only hoped he wasn't involved in Eddie's murder, and that her reason for coming back to his place would be to finally have sex with him, and not to kill him instead.

***

Amaury went nose-to-nose with Gabriel. He'd had the foresight to use some mouthwash and quickly wipe Nina's delectable taste off his face before leaving his apartment. Not that it would be enough to eliminate her scent on him completely. But with some luck, Gabriel would be too preoccupied to notice.

"I'm here now, aren't I?"

"I realize that you're his oldest friend, but not even Samson will cut you any slack if you don't do what's expected of you."

If push came to shove, Samson would be on his side, Amaury knew it instinctively. They had been through more together than Gabriel could even imagine. Friendship meant something to them.

"Piss off." He was his own master and didn't need anybody to tell him where his loyalties lay.

"Stop it!" the determined female voice cut through the tension.

And there he'd thought Yvette would love to see a physical fight between the two.

"Dial down the testosterone and let's get to work."

Or maybe she didn't want Gabriel hurt? He cut her a quick glance, but her face was impenetrable. If she had any feelings for Gabriel, Amaury couldn't pick up on them.

"After you." Amaury waved his hand to the door of the private office where the interrogations would take place. His head was hurting again, other people's emotions bombarding him as if the short reprieve from earlier hadn't even happened. And he still hadn't had sex. Seventy-two hours and counting. This was not good.

He should have just taken what Nina had offered him, her legs spread for him, her pussy wet and quivering. But no, when had he suddenly developed scruples? He'd never cared much before if a woman felt discomfort or even pain because he was too big for her or riding her too hard. And for sure, he would have ridden Nina hard, because when it came to her, he had no control over his body.

"Let's do this. I haven't got all night." Gabriel's voice cut through the fog in Amaury's head. Neither did he. After all, he had a woman waiting for him in bed. A most enticing one at that.

For almost two hours they interrogated employee after employee without any real results. Neither he nor Gabriel found anything that would have made any of them a suspect. Gabriel instructed for the last guy of the night to be brought in and let out a deep sigh.

"Ready for the last one?"

Amaury raised his head to meet Gabriel's gaze. "Sure. Bring 'im in." He knew he was all bravado, but he wouldn't admit to Gabriel how drained he was. It wasn't good to show weakness, especially not to a fellow vampire. Not only had he not had sex in far too many hours, he hadn't fed since he drank from Thomas's flask.

He was running on empty and getting decidedly grouchy. Before he went back to Nina, he would have to go on a quick hunt to feed. He didn't like the idea. The fact that Mrs. Reid was in the hospital because of him still gnawed at him. What if he was careless again and killed somebody?

"And who have we here?" Gabriel addressed the employee whom Yvette led into the room. As the man sat opposite of Gabriel and Amaury, Yvette took her observation seat next to the door.

"Paul Holland."

Amaury instantly sensed fear in the man. He gave Gabriel the prearranged sign of lifting the water glass to his lips to alert him.

Amaury and Gabriel alternately went through questions about his job and his relationship with the two dead bodyguards, giving each other time to use their powers while the other asked the question.

"So you only knew them casually?" Gabriel asked.

"Yes, occasionally we'd go out for a beer with a whole gang of our colleagues. The usual."

Amaury sensed Paul's fear growing. But it didn't seem to be directed at him or Gabriel. The man was afraid of somebody else.

"Where would you guys normally go?" It was Amaury's turn to ask a question to give Gabriel occasion to delve into his memory bank.

"Just some sports bar."

Gabriel's sign that he had everything he needed was subtle, but Amaury picked it up.

"Thanks, Paul. I don't think we have any more questions."

Paul rose and left the room.

"He's afraid of somebody, and it's not us. What did you get?"

"Not much. It's almost as if somebody is running interference, like static on a cell phone."

"You think a vampire is controlling him?" Amaury asked.

Gabriel nodded. "I'll have Zane tail him. He's right outside." He dialed a number on his cell phone. "Zane, we've got a suspect. He's leaving the office now. Follow him and keep me posted. If you need support, call Quinn." He flipped the phone shut.

"I'll call it a night." Amaury got up and made for the door, nodding at Yvette, who stood.

"Amaury."

He turned back to face Gabriel.

"I trust you've taken care of the girl?"

Shit. He'd better suppress his memories so Gabriel couldn't figure out that he'd taken care of Nina, but not in the way Gabriel had demanded. "It's all done."

Quickly, he spun back to the door and left, feeling Yvette's disbelief following him. She knew he was lying. He couldn't get out of the building fast enough. The moment he stepped out into the cool night air, his cell phone vibrated. Damn, that had better not be Gabriel demanding he come back!

With relief he recognized Drake's number and answered the call. "Doc, what's up?"

"I have an answer to your question." The shrink's voice was quiet.

Amaury's chest tightened. Finally, an answer as to how he could beat the curse. "Tell me."

"Not over the phone. I don't want to be overheard. Meet me on the steps of Grace Cathedral in fifteen minutes."

"I'll be there." The answer had better be good.

Amaury hailed a cab to take him up the hill. His hands felt clammy as anxiety spread in his body. Had the witch come up with some kind of brew he'd have to take, and was that why Drake wanted to see him in person? Why did fifteen minutes suddenly feel like an eternity?

Would this be the night on which his ordeal ended? Hope rose in his chest. To always feel the kind of peace he only felt in those brief moments after sex—could it truly be within reach?

Amaury paid the driver and sauntered out of the taxi as it came to a stop outside the cathedral. The imposing building threw dark shadows over its neighbors, but he found the darkness comforting rather than intimidating. After more than four hundred years of living in the dark, it had become a trusted companion.

He was not alone. He could sense Drake standing in the shadows.

"I like coming here. It's a peaceful place."

Amaury nodded and turned to him. "Yes, I know what you mean."

Drake's lanky figure separated from the wall behind him and approached. "Sorry I made you meet me here and not at my office. But I can't be overheard talking to you about a witch, otherwise—"

Amaury grunted his understanding. "Let's walk."

Their footsteps echoed off the buildings as they fell in step.

"What have you got for me, Drake?"

There was a hesitation, a tensing in the doctor's body. So the news was bad. He should have guessed. No wonder Drake wanted to talk to him in person.

"Go ahead, doc, give me the bad news already."

"It's not all bad, Amaury. It just doesn't make a hell lot of sense at first."

"Nothing really makes sense anyway."

"Well, then you'll appreciate this tidbit. The witch I spoke to—and believe me when I say that she's entirely trustworthy and as knowledgeable as they come—she looked into your dilemma and did some research. She found a way you can reverse the curse. When she told me I immediately questioned her about it, but she insisted it was the only way. She was quite cryptic about it too."

Amaury stopped and turned to the doctor. "Don't beat about the bush."

"Fine. I just wanted you to be prepared for it. There is a solution hidden in it." The man was stalling, and Amaury felt the tight cords of his patience snap.

"Doc!"

"Okay. She said that if you fall in love the curse will be reversed and if the object of your love—"

"That's ludicrous, and you know it."

This wasn't a solution to his problem. It couldn't be, because he was incapable of love. It was part of his curse never to feel love in his own heart again. So how on earth could he ever fall in love?

"Listen, that's not all of it, there are more pieces to it."

"You can stop right there. I can't even fulfill the first condition."

"Wait, Amaury. I know there's a solution hidden in here somewhere. Please listen. The witch said, 'the object of your affection—her love will be unknown.' "

"Unknown? What the hell is that supposed to mean? What exactly did she say?"

" 'He must fall in love with a forgiving heart,' " Drake recited, " 'his control ineffective, her love unknown.' "

Amaury let the words sink in, but they didn't resonate. There was no solution in them.

"Drake, I think you wasted your favor."

Drake shook his head. "No, there's something there. I just haven't figured it out. Yes, there are two parts to your curse. One, that you sense everybody else's emotions, and two, that you can't feel love."

"Have you ever heard of a circular reference? It's a mathematical problem. That's what this is. I can't solve the problem, when solving one part depends on using the other unknown part."

The doctor gave him a confused look. Mathematics were obviously not his strength. "Huh?"

"Forget it, Drake. The woman has no idea what she's talking about."

The hope he'd experienced minutes earlier had drained from his body. He was still in the same old boat, drifting in an ocean without any paddles. And the paddle he'd just seen appear on the horizon turned out to be just another mirage. It was better not to dwell on it.

"Listen, I'll do some more thinking on this." Drake seemed eager to help him.

"Why? It's a waste of time."

"As a doctor, I have a responsibility to my patients."

That was new. Was everybody suddenly developing a conscience? So far, Drake had taken his money whether he thought his sessions helped him or not. Amaury shrugged. Well, it wasn't his problem if the good doctor suddenly had scruples about all the money he'd made off him without producing any tangible results.

"It's your time, not mine."

"I'll be in touch." Drake turned at the next corner and disappeared amidst the shadows of the night.

Amaury tried to push back the disappointment he felt spreading in his chest. He should have never gotten his hopes up. He would just have to continue as he'd done the last four centuries, using sex to ease his pain.

But he still didn't understand why he couldn't sense Nina's emotions. It made no sense, particularly since he hadn't even technically had sex with her, something he planned to remedy tonight. However, in her presence the pain in his head seemed to ease, even without sex. And that was just the medicine he needed right now.

His cell phone vibrated again. What was going on tonight? He looked at the number, but didn't recognize it. A New York number, but it wasn't Gabriel's, thank God.

"Yes?"

"Amaury, it's Quinn. Listen, I can't talk long."

"What is it?"

"I've been helping Zane shadow this employee, Paul something, and we're at the Mezzanine nightclub. Zane's been mumbling something about your girlfriend being here cozying up to some guy. Thought you should know."

"What?" Amaury felt his heartbeat increase and his blood pressure spike. "Where is she?"

"Gotta go." The line went dead.

Nina? At a nightclub, when she'd promised to wait for him in bed? What the hell! Could nothing go according to plan tonight?

17

Nina took another sip from her beer before she looked back at the guy who'd been making advances at her for the last few minutes. From the bar she had a good view of the goings on in the nightclub. So far, she'd spotted several men who would fit the description Benny had given her, but none seemed to show any recognition when she looked at them.

And if Benny's information was correct, then the man she was looking for knew who she was and would show some sign of recognition. That was what she was counting on. It would be the only way she'd recognize him. That, and if he attacked her. Luckily, the club was busy and an attack would not go unnoticed.

In the meantime she had to fend off the man sitting next to her. It wasn't that he wasn't good looking, but she wasn't in the mood to flirt, nor did she want to waste her time when she was on the lookout for that despicable son of a bitch involved in Eddie's death.

"Looks like whoever you're waiting for stood you up." The man on the barstool next to her gave her a knowing grin.

"What makes you think I'm waiting for someone?" Maybe she should move to a different location in the club to get away from the thick-headed guy who couldn't take a hint.

"You've been looking at every man who's come in here in the last half hour. Looks to me like you're expecting someone. Can't be worth it though if he keeps a pretty girl like you waiting for so long. What if someone else staked his claim instead?"

Now the man had just crossed the threshold from annoying to creepy. She cast him an icy look. "Nobody is gonna stake a claim on me, not that it's any of your business."

Nina turned away from him.

"I'd say somebody already has." A second later she felt his hand on her arm. Nina jerked her head back to him and yanked her arm out from his grip. She caught how he inhaled sharply, as if he was sniffing her.

"You'd better move along before I kick your ass!"

Instead of being offended by her outburst, he answered with a broad grin. That's when she looked at him for the first time and really noticed him.

Oh God, no!

He was one of them. She'd been sitting next to a vampire without noticing because she'd been too preoccupied with finding the guy Benny had described.

"Ah, so you're finally catching on. I was starting to get bored with this little game."

This night was a bust. She had to get out while she could. Good thing was there were too many people around for him to really harm her. She could use the cover of the innocent humans around her to get away. If he was smart, he wouldn't want to risk exposure in such a public place.

"I don't know what you mean." It was best to stick with denial for as long as she could. Maybe he would give up.

"I disagree—for my liking you know far too much. So why don't you and I have a little chat?" He put his hand on her arm again, this time gripping harder. She tried to shake him off, but he pulled her toward him, sniffing again.

A second later she felt herself being ripped away from him by strong hands. She was pressed against a hard chest, one she recognized instantly. While she couldn't see Amaury behind her, Nina saw the reaction on the face of the vampire in front of her. He was pissed to say the least.

"Luther." Amaury's rumble of a voice soothed her nerves more than she'd expected. She let her back relax into him.

"Amaury. Long time no see."

The two of them knew each other? Figured, both being vampires and all. It was probably a small world. She should have guessed.

"Didn't know you were back in town." Amaury's statement sounded like an accusation.

"What, no welcoming committee for an old friend? At least your little girlfriend here was friendly. And I'm sure she would have gotten even friendlier." He gave her a suggestive look.

In his dreams!

Instantly Amaury's arms tightened around her, and his growl rang in her ears. "You touch her again, you won't be walking away alive."

She'd never heard such menace in Amaury's voice.

"Still screwing humans I see. I could smell you on her."

"Nina, we're leaving." He shifted her, pulling her off the barstool, and pushing her behind him where she couldn't see what was going on. The noise in the club prevented her from hearing whether any more niceties were being exchanged.

Seeing Amaury's enraged face when he turned to her got rid of that uncertainty. Maybe it was better she hadn't heard what else was said. She didn't need to add any more choice words to her vocabulary.

Amaury was less than gentle when he pulled her through the sea of people toward the back of the club. If she'd read his face correctly, she was probably in for the spanking he'd promised her. Now that he'd left Luther behind, it seemed he'd transferred his anger onto her. His fingers dug into her wrist as he dragged her behind him, apparently on a mission.

"Where are we going?"

The corridor he hurried her along was dark and led to a flight of stairs. Without answering her question, he motioned her along until they reached a door on the upper level. He pushed it open. She saw the writing on the door, EMPLOYEES ONLY, before he yanked her inside and slammed the door shut behind them.

The room seemed to serve as a locker room for staff. There was an old couch, several chairs, and a table. Shelving on the walls held supplies and various items of clothing.

A lock clicked shut.

"What the fuck were you doing out there?" Amaury's voice could have put any thunder to shame.

"None of your business." She wasn't going to cave in. He had no right to tell her what to do, just because she'd let him touch her intimately. Nina lifted her chin and looked at him. His eyes were glaring red. Oh, yeah, he was definitely mad at her.

His nostrils flared, his chest heaved with every breath he took. If she hadn't seen what gentleness was hidden beneath his rough exterior, she would have truly seen him as a monster. His imposing frame loomed over her, as if he was trying to intimidate her.

"I told you to stay at my place and wait for me."

"You can't order me around. I can do as I please."

"Not if it means you're putting yourself in danger."

"I was in no danger."

He blew out a puff of air, then took a step closer and backed her against the wall. "Oh, no? Then let me tell you something about Luther.

They don't come any more dangerous than him. From now on you will not go out there on your own. Your days of investigating your brother's death are over."

"You have no right—"

He pressed his body against hers, pinning her hands against the wall. "You're listening to me now. I'll be doing the investigating from now on. I'll help you, but you'll no longer put yourself in the path of every damn vampire in this city. Is that clear?"

"Make me." If he thought he could just intimidate her with a few harsh words, he'd have to do better than that. She wasn't afraid of him.

"Watch me."

Amaury ground his cock against her. Damn it—did all vampires constantly have hard-ons, or was Amaury an anomaly?

"What? That's your solution to everything, isn't it? Make the little woman submit."

He was enormous. Getting angry had obviously aroused him. She wasn't far behind. The sheer power he had over her made her insides melt. That, and the intoxicating male scent that was purely Amaury—and if bottled would sell for a fortune.

"That's right." He inhaled sharply. "And it's apparently working."

Did he have to notice that her body was so acutely attuned to him? That all he needed to do was press his taut muscles against her to elicit a purely wanton reaction from her?

He released one of her wrists and dropped his hand to her breast where her nipple had already pebbled at the mere suggestion he was going to touch her.

"I won't stop what I'm doing. Not for you or anybody else." Just because her body was crumbling didn't mean her mind was weak too.

Amaury greeted her defiance with a rakish smile. "I wasn't expecting anything less from you. But I'm not letting you do it alone anymore. You, *chérie*, won't leave my side until this is over."

"What are you trying to do? Imprison me?" Nina lifted her chin in defiance.

"Sounds like an interesting idea. I could chain you to my bed. As we already know, you're no stranger to bondage."

His lewd suggestion sent a twinge of anticipation through her stomach. She felt a trickle of moisture ooze from her core and pool in her panties. He *had* looked yummy when he'd been all tied up. She licked her dry lips.

"You have to do more than chain me to your bed if you want me to give in." At least he'd first have to get her to scream with pleasure, before she'd even consider such a thing as surrender.

"Like what?"

I could think of a few positions off hand.

Instead she said, "Make me a promise."

The spot between his eyebrows twisted into a deep crease.

"I'm not the promise kind of guy, in case you hadn't noticed."

Had he truly misunderstood her, or was he yanking her chain?

"Oh, please, don't even insinuate that I'm interested in you for anything more than a quick fuck," she said.

Or two, or three.

"I want a promise that you will do anything to clear my brother's name."

She looked into his eyes. They were deep blue again, beautiful and sinful.

"Fine. You have my promise. I'll help you. Under one condition."

"What condition?" She held her breath. There was something about the smoldering way he looked at her that made her heart skip a beat or two.

"We'll seal the deal now."

18

Amaury looked into Nina's apprehensive face. She knew what was coming—she was all woman. He wouldn't disappoint her.

"Every promise needs a token. Here's mine." He led her hand to his impatient cock, pressing her open palm against his hard flesh. Even through the fabric of his pants he felt her warmth and softness. Her touch sent his heart racing again.

The woman was driving him insane, and if vampires could have heart attacks, she would surely cause him one. Seeing her in Luther's hold—no, he had to wipe the image from his mind.

"Is that the only thing you can think of?" Her sweet voice was softer now.

He allowed himself to inhale her feminine scent. Was she using vanilla-scented soap or was this her own unique smell her body produced? Just a whiff catapulted his senses into overdrive.

"Apparently when I'm with you, that's what's on my mind." And that wasn't even a lie.

"Can't you wait until we're back at your place?"

"Evidently not." His cock strained against her hand as she tortured him by squeezing. Vixen. Minx. Seductress.

When he'd dragged her into this room, he'd planned on having angry sex with her, but now, he didn't feel that angry anymore. Well, he could always have angry sex with her some other time, since for sure she'd make him mad about something else soon enough. Her compliance never lasted long.

But as long as Nina purred like the sweet kitten she surely wasn't, he would take advantage of the chance to have her without fear of her claws. Not that his pleasure wouldn't be heightened by a few scratches. Or a few bites.

"Do you prefer the table or the couch?" He should at least give her a choice of where he'd finally ravish her. After all, he was old-school and French.

She cast a look at the table, then the couch, then back at him. There was a wicked glint in her eyes, sending a shockwave through his groin. God, she was actually contemplating the table, wasn't she?

"What'll feel better?"

He couldn't suppress a grin. "*Chérie*, no matter how—or where—I take you, it'll be the best you've ever had." He would make absolutely sure of that.

"Amaury, you're so full of shit!"

Now he had to prove something. He wasn't one to back down from a challenge. "Why don't we settle this little argument when you have all the facts?" Oh yes: he'd drive those facts home inch by inch, stroke by stroke.

Amaury lifted her off the floor and carried her to the couch, swiping a clean table cloth off one of the shelves. After spreading the white cloth over the couch, he dropped her onto it. He caught her surprised look. Had she thought he was going to fuck her on the filthy couch, subjecting her to God-knows what germs?

"Nina, you have a lot to learn about me."

"Then let's start with the lesson right now." She pulled him down to her, her arms locking behind his neck. Now she spoke his language.

"What would you like to learn?" He brushed his lips against her cheek then nibbled his way along her jaw. Nina was softer than a vampire woman, her fragrance tantalizing, drawing him in. The aroma of her blood drifted into his awareness and drugged him. He remembered the taste of it from when he'd licked her wounds. How he wanted to experience the same moment again, over and over until he would feel drunk on her blood.

"Everything," she said.

Amaury looked into her eyes, and her rich brown irises sparkled like fire. Nobody had ever looked at him like that, captivating him so easily, stealing his sanity. As he noticed her gaze drop to his mouth, he couldn't help but lick his lips. He was salivating for a taste of her.

Deliberately slowly, he moved his head closer to hers, until his lips all but touched hers. Her breath mingled with his, and he inhaled her scent. Nudging his lips at hers, he made contact and felt her sigh. How could so light a touch create such heat in his body? No woman had ever had this effect on him, as if he was burning up just touching her skin.

What would happen when he finally took her, buried himself in her? Would the heat destroy him? Would his blood boil?

Her lips parted underneath his, asking—no, begging—for his invasion. There was no need to conquer what was freely given. It didn't make the victory any less sweet; on the contrary, when he allowed his tongue to dive into her mouth and tangle with hers, he felt the value of it increase tenfold. A kiss so openly given was a gift to cherish. A gift he rarely ever got.

Amaury ran his tongue along her teeth, traced the inside of her cheeks and dueled with her. With long and deep strokes he teased those endearing sounds of pleasure out of her. How he welcomed them, knowing that each was a direct response to his touch, an encouragement to continue, a confirmation of what she wanted.

He gave her no reprieve, but angled his head for a deeper penetration, unable to get enough of her taste. Rarely had he found kissing alone this satisfying. But the little minx had a way of kissing him back that knocked him out of his boots. Kissing had always been only a precursor to sex, but with her it could easily turn into the main event.

Nina pressed her body against his, her hands clamped together behind his neck, forcing him closer. Was she afraid he'd stop? Didn't she know he would find it impossible to let go of her silken tongue and her smooth lips? Silly little kitten. As though Cyrano would let go of Roxanne. When lips fit so perfectly together, tongues danced in perfect harmony, and breaths mixed to become the most intoxicating French perfume, complementing each other—there was no letting go of that.

Amaury let himself drop flat back onto the couch and took her with him, pulling her on top. His hands went to her back, then slipped lower, resting on the swells of her enticing derrière. Squeezing her firm ass in his hands, he elicited a loud moan from her. How he liked women who responded so freely.

His hands roamed, and he found the zipper of her short skirt and lowered it. Sliding underneath the fabric, he shoved the skirt over her hips and down her legs, baring her ass to his hands. Her tiny panties provided barely a barrier to his touch, but nevertheless, they had to go. It was skin he wanted. Naked, smooth skin. Delicate softness and warmth greeted his needy palms and welcomed his probing fingers.

His attention was diverted from the task at hand when he felt her hands unbuttoning his shirt, her movements hurried, impatient.

Nina sat up, straddling him. "Take it off." Her voice was husky, her eyes appeared glazed, her pupils widened under her half-lowered lids. He rid himself of his shirt in one brisk move.

"You too." Employing vampire speed, he threw her shirt to join his on the floor seconds later. Her twin globes shone like beacons in the dim light of the room. Surely a taste was in order. It had been far too many hours since he'd licked those responsive nipples.

He loved burying his head in between her breasts, being sheltered by the softness of them, taking in the scent of her skin. What man, vampire or not, could resist such perfect roundness?

His lips found her nipples and suckled greedily, first on one, then on the other. Neither would be neglected. He felt like a hungry babe who couldn't quite get enough of the generous meal offered. Such full breasts needed more than a few cursory licks and laps from his tongue.

With his fingers, he tugged at the little buds, making her cry out. She threw her head back and arched her back, offering her breasts for him to continue his sensual assault. He palmed her weight in both hands, then again descended on one of her nipples, his tongue forging ahead, his own deep moan providing the battle cry.

The contact with her hard, erect bud sent more blood surging into his already rock-hard cock. Heat seared through him. Then he closed his lips around her and sucked. His erection added another inch, taking full advantage of his lack of restricting underwear.

Suddenly he sensed her gaze on him and looked up.

"You're still wearing too many clothes."

Amaury made a liar out of her ten seconds later, having rid himself of his pants, lying underneath her, naked now. His impressive shaft stood erect where she straddled him, close enough to feel the tickle of her nest of blond curls. Untamed and natural.

He caught her look as she stared at his erection. Fascinated or frightened? He couldn't tell. Was he too big for her?

A tentative finger brushed over the head of his shaft, where moisture had already collected. Kissing her had done that, as if he were some inexperienced young kid.

"You're big."

"*Chérie*, we'll move at your pace. You'll take me inside when you're ready, one inch at a time." That was why he wanted her on top. If she was underneath him, he would never be able to restrain himself from plunging into her too quickly, without giving her a chance to adjust to his size.

He pulled her head to him and took her lips for a kiss. As she bent over him, his cock rubbed against her stomach, and the little vixen teased him even more by moving up and down along him, rubbing her sex against his length.

The scent of Nina's arousal filled the room and drugged him. Not sure how long he could stand it, he palmed her ass and stroked her bare skin. Slipping one hand along her crack, he found her moist center. She stilled her movements instantly and tilted toward his hand, offering her inviting womanly folds to his touch.

Amaury ran his finger along her warm slit before he slipped it inside. Her tightness was intoxicating. How she would squeeze his cock to fulfillment with her muscles. He could hardly wait. A deep moan dislodged from his chest. She would be his, soon.

When he felt her pull away from him, he didn't want to let her go, but she sat up. She lifted herself onto her knees, and his hands automatically went to her hips to support her. With painstaking slowness, she centered herself over his shaft. Nina eased herself lower until the tip of his cock touched her moist sex. His heartbeat doubled. How he wanted to drive her down onto him! He clenched his jaw to restrain himself.

"So wet for me."

Another half inch, and his bulbous head nudged at her entrance, forcing her nether lips apart to accommodate him. Her breath came in heavy pants, her beautiful breasts moving in unison every time she inhaled and exhaled. Her channel widened slightly, and she inched lower.

Her interior muscles squeezed him, and he ground his teeth together. The sensation was too delicious—almost painful—knowing he had to stay still and not move, when all he wanted was to thrust his hips toward heaven and fill her.

Amaury watched her face for any signs of discomfort when she closed her eyes and suddenly bore down on him, submerging his nine inches of marble-hard cock into her tight body.

Fuck, she was killing him!

He was right at the edge, seconds from spilling, like some green kid. Some juvenile who'd never felt a woman's body before.

His loud grunt was echoed by Nina's guttural moan. When he felt her move, he instantly locked his hands onto her hips and held her in place.

"Not yet." His voice didn't sound like his own. He concentrated on his breathing and tried to settle his thumping heart.

When her lips curled up to form a naughty smile, he gave her a slap on her derrière to warn her not to try anything. What he hadn't counted on was that the reverberation of the light slap reached his cock a split second later, sending a rippling sensation through his body, nearly robbing him of his control.

So much for paddling her ass while he was inside her. He would have to remember that—and use it when he was more used to her body. But for now, it wasn't a good idea. Not if he wanted to last longer than three seconds.

The moment he removed his hands from her hips, Nina started moving. Like Lady Godiva she rode him, her breasts bouncing up and down. She lifted herself as high as she could, only leaving the tip of him inside her, then dropped down again. This time he met her with his own thrust upwards, doubling the impact, almost knocking the wind out of her. She gasped.

Amaury pulled her torso to bend over him.

"Feed me those gorgeous tits." He opened his lips to receive the first nipple she guided to him and sucked it into his greedy mouth, laving it with his tongue.

"Oh, yes." He thanked her for her encouragement by dropping his hand between their bodies to find her most intimate spot as he continued to drive his cock upwards, moving his hips in counteraction to hers.

Coated with cream from her arousal, his finger found her clit and circled it, then flicked it lightly. Her already-hard nipple in his mouth stiffened further. So responsive, so ripe. Like a fruit ready to harvest.

His teeth scraped at her skin, but he didn't bite down. He felt her shudder and instantly stilled. Had he gone too far? Frightened her?

Slowly he released her nipple and looked up at her. She looked like she was in a drug-induced state.

"Do it again."

Amaury stared at her, not sure he'd heard right.

"Your teeth. Do it again."

Capturing her other nipple, he lapped at it with his tongue, then sucked at it thoroughly.

"Please," he heard her say. She was tempting him to bite her.

His teeth glided along her skin, scraping the surface, but only lightly, not breaking the skin, just teasing. When Nina arched her back, thrusting her breast toward him, he sucked more of it into his mouth. In unison with his sucking motion, his pistoning cock surged into her, again and again. And like the experienced rider she proved to be, she held on and moved in rhythm with him.

His fingers played with her clit, stroking, pinching, while his mouth worked her nipples, making them stand up like brave little soldiers. He would have liked to go on forever, but the way her muscles squeezed his shaft, the way he slid in and out of her, deeper every time, he couldn't hold on.

His teeth clamped down on her nipple as he gave her engorged nub another pinch, then felt her channel clench around him, felt the waves of her orgasm hit him, and tumbled with her—over the edge and into oblivion as he came: hot, breathless and with a seemingly endless stream of his seed filling her. He'd died and gone to heaven, and the golden-haired angel looked down at him.

***

Nina dropped her head onto Amaury's chest and exhaled. She hated to admit he was right, but this *was* better than she'd ever had. Without a doubt. Not that she would ever tell him that. A man could get too bigheaded if he knew. And Amaury certainly didn't need to get any more full of himself than he already was.

She felt him press a kiss on her hair. His sudden tenderness surprised her. The man had decidedly too many sides to him that needed exploring. And she was just too exhausted to do any more explorations tonight. As for addressing why she was again sleeping with the enemy rather than fighting him and his vampire brethren, she would go on that guilt trip tomorrow.

"Will you tell me now why you came to the club?"

Nina lifted her head, crossed her arms on his chest and rested her chin on it. "Why do you care?"

"We're working together now. So you'd better tell me what's going on."

She sighed. "Fine. I got a text from my informant, saying that a man involved in Eddie's death is here tonight."

"You think he was talking about Luther?"

She dismissed the thought with a movement of her head. "No. That creep just hit on me. He didn't fit the description I got. Unfortunately, you interrupted me before I could find the guy."

"Luckily, I got here when I did. Zane saw you in the club, and Quinn alerted me. They were following a lead."

"A lead on the bodyguard killings?"

Amaury nodded. "Yes. I think that one of the human employees of Scanguards knows more than he's telling. Zane tailed him to the club. We were trying to figure out if he was meeting somebody here."

"It could be the same guy. If he's an employee of yours it makes sense."

"Why?"

"Because I was also told he was at the staff meeting that night your friend Zane caught me."

Amaury lifted himself to a semi-sitting position without letting her escape his embrace and nudged a pillow behind his back. His hands remained around her back, pressing her to his naked body.

"Are you sure?"

"Yes. The information came from the same informant. Not that Benny bothered staying. He hightailed it out of there before he could get caught. Snake. Especially since he'd already sold my hide to those two vampires you and I were fighting the other—"

"Hold it!" Amaury interrupted. "After he sold you out last time, you took his tip at face value and came to the club tonight? Are you crazy?"

Nina made a dismissive gesture. "This time I was prepared."

Amaury huffed and shook his head in disapproval. "Prepared? Damn it, Nina, you have to stop going around putting yourself in danger."

She completely ignored his reprimand. "Anyway, Benny was the only one who could identify him. His description could have fit any number of guys."

"Where's Benny now?"

"If he values his life, he's left the city."

"What if that guy was here to meet Luther? It would be too much of a coincidence him showing up here, you being given the info to come to the club, and Zane and Quinn tailing our employee here. I don't believe in coincidences."

Nina felt his hand stroke tenderly over her ass, a gesture which appeared entirely subconscious considering Amaury seemed preoccupied with Luther.

"Who's this Luther anyway? He seemed to realize that I knew about vampires."

"That's probably because he could smell me on you."

"What?" She didn't like the sound of that.

"Luther and I go way back. He would have been able to detect my scent on you. Most likely that's why he was toying with you."

Nina frowned. "Old friends, then?"

There was a moment when she thought she detected a grain of pain in his eyes. But it instantly disappeared.

"Not quite. We used to be. Unfortunately he blames Samson and me for his mate's death."

"Mate?"

"Luther was blood-bonded to a wonderful woman and was probably the happiest vampire I knew then."

"Hold on. Don't throw words around I don't understand. What's 'blood-bonded'?" She tried to pull away a fraction, but Amaury didn't release her from his embrace. Instead, he made her snuggle even closer to him. She hadn't pegged him for the cuddly type.

"It's like a marriage, only it's for eternity. A vampire blood-bonds with his life mate, and they're connected forever. They can sense each other. It's an incredibly close connection between two people. It also assures that the blood-bonded human will live as long as her vampire mate and won't age."

"Wow." Stunned about this revelation, Nina wondered what it would be like to live forever. At the same time, she felt awkward hearing him talk about marriage and love while he still held her against his warm body. A body that only minutes ago had joined with hers in a union so perfect she'd not known it was possible.

"He and Vivian were expecting their first child, when—"

"Child? I thought the undead couldn't have children." Amaury threw more incredible things at her than she thought she'd be able to handle. Vampire children? No—way too weird.

"Undead? Where do you get those expressions from? And Luther's mate was human. As a vampire blood-bonded to a human he was able to impregnate her. It's the only time a vampire can father children, if his mate is human."

His hand stroked absentmindedly over her back, up and down, sending delicious shivers along the way.

"And their children, what are they?"

"Hybrids. Half vampires, half humans. They have traits of both species. They can be out in the sun without burning, but they drink blood in addition to human food and have the strength and speed of a vampire. And they are immortal."

"That's just so bizarre."

He smiled. "It's rare. But it happens. Luther was working with us, with Samson and me. He was working for Scanguards. He was a great guy back then. Loyal, dedicated. And he loved Vivian. And she loved him. But there were complications with her pregnancy. One night she started bleeding. Luther was away on an assignment. We called him, but he didn't make it in time. She was losing the baby, and we were losing her. There was nothing we could do. By the time Luther came back, she'd died. He blamed us."

The blue of his eyes couldn't hide the sadness in them.

"But why, when you couldn't do anything?"

"We could have turned her into a vampire to save her."

She hadn't thought of that possibility. "Oh. He wanted you to do that?"

"Yes. He wanted to be with her for eternity. He loved her."

Eternal love—what a frightening, yet strangely exciting concept.

"But if you knew that, why didn't you turn her?"

Amaury's eyes had a sad look in them. "Because she didn't want to."

Realization set in. "She didn't?"

"No. We offered it to her, but she said if she were a vampire, she couldn't have children. She'd just lost the baby. She preferred to die."

Nina pulled back from him slightly. "But then why is he still blaming you when it was her choice? I don't understand. You and Samson did nothing wrong."

"He doesn't know that she refused."

"You never told him?" Why would they keep such an important detail to themselves?

"No. How could we? He loved her. Do you know what it would do to him to find out that his mate, the woman he loved more than anything else in his life, chose death over him?"

Suddenly she understood, and tears welled up in her eyes. "Oh my god, so you and Samson decided it was better he hated you than her?"

Amaury nodded. Nina touched his cheek in a tender caress.

"Does he hate you and Samson enough to want to destroy you and Scanguards?"

"I'm afraid that's possible." He paused. "I think we'd better go and talk to Samson. He needs to know that Luther is in town."

She sat up. "Yes. I think you're right. Besides, we'd better get out of here before somebody finds us and throws us out."

Amaury gave her a roguish grin. "I doubt that'll happen. I own fifty percent of the club."

Nina's mouth dropped open, then she boxed him in the chest. "How many more secrets do you have up your sleeve?"

He raised his hands. "No sleeves, see? I'm naked."

She let her eyes gaze over his body. "I can see that."

"Uh-oh. You've got that look again. We'd better get dressed before you have your way with me again."

"Me? *Me* have *my* way with *you*? Now if that's not the pot calling the kettle black!"

His response was a throaty and way-too-sexy laugh. This vampire was seriously dangerous.

19

Never in her wildest dreams had Nina imagined entering Samson's house on Nob Hill. But there she was at the entrance door, Amaury a step ahead of her, waiting for the door to open. She shifted nervously from one foot to the other. Was this a good idea? Amaury she could handle. He lusted after her and was therefore not interested in hurting her, but what about the others? Nina hadn't forgotten that Amaury had received an order to wipe her memory.

A beam of light illuminated Amaury as the door opened halfway.

"Forget your key?" a male voice asked.

"I didn't want to intrude unannounced. I'm not alone."

The door opened wider, and light flooded onto her as Amaury pulled her next to him. She met their host's gaze and recognized him as Samson. Her pulse fluttered.

She noticed him raise an eyebrow at Amaury as if to chastise him. But a second later he turned into the perfect host.

"Please, do come in. I don't think we've met. I'm Samson Woodford."

Samson stretched his hand toward her, and she shook it, wondering if he noticed how damp her palms were. His introduction was formal as if they were at the Queen's tea party.

"Good evening," Nina said. She hoped that was appropriate; what exactly was the correct greeting when being introduced to a vampire? "I'm Nina."

"Pleased to make your acquaintance." Samson led them into the living room. He remained stiff then turned to Amaury. "May I have a word with you in private?"

Yes, Samson was clearly displeased about her presence. She didn't have to be a mind-reader to figure that out.

"That won't be necessary." Amaury's reply elicited a frown from his friend. "Nina knows who we are."

There was silence so thick she could have cut through it with a knife as Samson eyed her up and down, pressing his lips together tightly. His displeasure with Amaury was evident. Maybe this wasn't a good idea after all. What if he expected Amaury to "take care of her" now that he'd given away their secrets?

Nina noticed how Samson sniffed and felt heat rush to her cheeks. If Luther had been able to smell Amaury on her even before they'd had sex, she could only imagine what Samson could scent now. Under his scrutiny, her face burned with embarrassment right down to the follicles of her hair. She searched for the hole that she wished would open up right in front of her to swallow her up.

"Care to explain why you brought one of your women to my house?" Samson's voice was sharp and unyielding.

One of his women?

She absolutely hated the sound of that. Sure, whatever Amaury and she had wasn't going to be anything permanent, but to be classified as "one of his women" made her sound like a slut. And she wasn't a slut. Well, not really anyway. Her morals weren't any looser that Amaury's, that was for sure. Not that it seemed to be such a high standard to attain.

"She's not *one of my women.*"

She could have hugged him for his defense of her morals. Nobody had ever defended her. Maybe he was truly a good guy.

"She's Edmund Marten's sister out to slay vampires to avenge her brother."

Or maybe not. Amaury had decided to throw her to the wolves— after he'd slept with her. Perfect. He'd gotten what he wanted, and now he went back on his promise. Why had she believed him in the first place? Was she completely delusional?

"Well, that explains things. Yvette mentioned you were with a human," Samson answered, his voice much more relaxed now.

"Figures." Amaury let out a grunt.

Samson held up his hand. "She's only doing her job." He looked at Nina and pointed to the couch. "Shall we sit?"

"Samson, darling, did you see the pregnancy book I brought down earlier? I can't find it." A petite woman swept into the living room then stopped in her tracks.

"Oh, I'm sorry. I didn't realize we had company. Hi, Amaury."

"Evening, Delilah. Sorry to intrude."

Delilah's gaze rested on Nina. Nina returned it. Was she a vampire too? She looked decidedly normal.

"Aren't you going to introduce me to your friend?" She stretched out her hand. "I'm Delilah."

Nina shook her hand.

"This is Nina Martens," Samson said.

"Martens?" Delilah gave her a look of surprise, and Nina nodded.

"Edmund Martens was my brother."

"Oh, dear. I'm so sorry." A second later Nina found herself embraced by the pretty woman. Not knowing how to respond, she looked over Delilah's shoulder and saw Samson's and Amaury's stunned expressions, until Samson's lips finally curled up into a smile.

"Sweetness, you're making our guest feel uncomfortable."

Delilah released her and responded to her husband with a suppressed smile. "I get so emotional these days." Then she looked back at Nina. "It's just the hormones. Sit down. I'll have Carl bring us some refreshments."

Before she could turn back, a stocky man dressed in a dark suit appeared behind her.

"Miss Delilah, may I bring some cold drinks?"

"That'd be great, Carl."

Minutes later they were all seated, drinks in front of them. Nina looked at Delilah as she sat close to Samson, her hand leisurely draped over his thigh, his hand stroking hers.

"Delilah, it appears that Nina knows we are vampires," Samson said.

"Oh!"

"And seems bent on avenging her brother by slaying some of us." Samson looked directly at Nina, giving her the feeling she was the bad schoolgirl being hauled in front of the strict principal of a reformatory school. Yet there seemed to be no menace in his voice. He rather sounded like he was mocking her. Did he not realize she could fight vampires? She'd killed one of them already.

"I think I've been able to convince her that we're not the bad guys," Amaury interjected. "But that's not why I've brought her here tonight. We have a bigger problem on our hands than this little wannabe slayer."

"Hey! I'm not a wannabe slayer!" Was nobody taking her seriously?

Amaury laughed off her protest.

"You promised me you'd let me take charge of this. And I will. So, no more slaying." He took her hand and squeezed it before he looked back at Samson and Delilah. "Luther is in town."

"Luther?" Samson shot up from his seat and started pacing.

"Yes. Nina found him. Or rather, he approached her tonight when she was looking into her brother's death. He was at the Mezzanine."

"Isn't that where Zane and Quinn tracked your suspect to?" Samson asked.

"Yes, and it's also the place Nina's informant told her to find the man who had his hand in Eddie's death."

"You think Luther's got his hand in this?" He let himself fall back onto the couch.

Amaury nodded. "There's no reason for him to come back to San Francisco other than to exact his revenge. I'd thought we'd seen the last of him."

"I guess not. Did Luther see you?"

"We exchanged a few words. But what's worse is he knows Nina is with me."

With him? Didn't that sound just a tad bit possessive? Just because she'd slept with him didn't mean she was *with* him. She'd better explain that to him.

Amaury continued, "He's up to something. I could sense it."

"Did you read his emotions?" Delilah asked.

What an odd question. How would he read somebody's emotions? Nina gave Amaury a sideways glance.

"No. For some reason I couldn't. Maybe he veiled them from me to hide what he's up to."

"I thought nobody could veil their emotions from you." Samson's stunned look swept over him.

Amaury shrugged. "Not sure about that lately."

What the hell were they talking about? Curiosity got the better of Nina. "What do you mean by reading emotions?"

Samson raised his eyebrows. "I guess Amaury hasn't told you about his gift yet."

She caught Amaury giving Samson a look as if to cut him off, but his friend continued, undeterred, "Amaury has a psychic gift and can sense emotions of people around him. It's come in more than useful many times."

A psychic gift? Did this mean he knew what she was feeling all the time? Oh no, that sounded terrible. She felt exposed, naked, and vulnerable all of a sudden. Had she known he could read her emotions, she would have never slept with him. He had an unfair advantage. No wonder he was playing her like a string instrument. What else did he know? Could he tell what she truly felt in her heart?

She felt his hand squeeze hers lightly. "Don't worry. I'll explain later."

She yanked her hand out of his grip. What was there to explain? He could see through her as if through a glass wall. Now he knew everything about her, her fears, her hopes, and worst of all, how she felt about him—the feeling she hadn't even admitted to herself. No, this wasn't good. This wasn't good at all.

"I'll get in contact with Gabriel and warn him to look out for Luther. Did Zane not see him in the club if he followed Paul Holland?" Samson's voice was calmer now than when he'd first heard about Luther.

"Zane's never met Luther before. I'll make sure Gabriel distributes his picture. We should also try to find out if Paul is the guy Nina's informant pinpointed."

"Agreed," Samson said.

"I have an idea," Nina interjected.

"No." Amaury's command came with barely a second's hesitation.

"You don't even know what my idea is."

"The answer is still no. You've put yourself in enough danger for one night. That's all I can handle right now."

That's all *he* could handle?

Nina caught Samson's grin. "Maybe we should listen to Nina's suggestion. After all, it's because of her we were alerted to Luther."

Amaury's annoyed grunt filled her with satisfaction. Finally, somebody stood up to him. She liked Samson. He seemed to be a pretty levelheaded guy—for a vampire, of course. And his wife was sweet and so tiny sitting right next to him. Whereas the asshole next to her. . . well, she'd deal with him later. But he sure wouldn't get away with leaving such important details as his psychic gift out of the conversation.

"I was thinking if we confirmed that he recognizes me, then we know he's the right guy."

"Not a good idea. It would be better to find Benny and have him identify the guy." Amaury's voice sounded gruff.

"Benny's skipped town. There's no telling which hole he's hiding out in now."

"Benny?" Samson raised an eyebrow in inquiry.

"My informant."

"Let's put one of our guys on him, see whether we can locate him." Amaury looked at Samson, obviously trying to get his approval.

"Waste of time." Nina knew it would be useless. "It could take days to track him down. Do you really want to wait that long?" she addressed Samson, ignoring Amaury completely. Right now she was too annoyed to deal with him—which shouldn't be a surprise to him since he was reading her emotions. Damn, she hated that!

"She's right. I'll talk to Gabriel and have him set something up." Samson cast Amaury a determined glance.

"Fine, but under one condition. Nina will not leave my side." As if to assert his statement, he took her hand again.

"Fine," Samson agreed.

Was that a smirk on Samson's face? It seemed so. When she looked at Delilah she saw her, too, suppress a grin. It had to be an inside joke, because Nina could not figure out what the two were finding so funny.

20

"Unacceptable. She'll be too far away for me to rescue her if something goes wrong." Amaury let his frustration out on Gabriel, looking up and down the downtown street. Despite the late hour, there was still the odd car about.

"I can take care of myself," Nina protested.

"Yeah, I've seen that the last two nights." He was in no mood to see her putting herself in danger again.

"You don't have a choice. If I let you go with her, we won't be able to tell if Paul recognizes you or her." Gabriel's voice had a schoolmaster's tone to it. Amaury didn't need a lecture right now. He wanted Nina nowhere near the suspect.

His frustrated grunt only got him a shake of Nina's head. Did she not realize he was only trying to protect her?

"Okay, in positions then. Quinn is hidden in the doorway at the other end. Nina, you know what to do," Gabriel instructed.

She nodded and turned to leave.

"Wait." Amaury couldn't just let her go. "You can change your mind. You don't need to do this."

She spun around, gave him a stern look and flipped him off. A second later she crossed the street.

Amaury felt heat shoot through his veins. Before he could stalk after her to paddle her insolent ass, Gabriel's hand clamped down on his arm.

"You can teach her manners later. We need her to do this now."

Gabriel even had the audacity to chuckle. Amaury shot him a displeased glance, but it didn't deter the New York boss from making yet another disrespectful remark. "Should have wiped her memory when you had the chance, but no, you didn't listen. Now she's got the upper hand. Serves you right."

Served him right?

Where had he heard that before? Yeah, right, Thomas had made the same comment.

Amaury curled his hand into a fist and leveled it at Gabriel. "None of your fucking business."

"What is it with you and human women anyway?"

"None of your business." Gabriel was getting downright annoying now.

"Listen, let me give you some advice."

"I don't want your advice."

"Well, you're gonna get it anyway. A woman like her can get under a man's skin. I've seen it before. Already now she's got you all worked up, and how long have you known her? A week, a month?"

"Three days, not that it's any of your fucking business."

Gabriel's surprise was evident. "Three days? Oh, boy, you've got it bad."

Didn't he know it! He needed no colleague to tell him that. And it irked him to no end. The little insolent minx was pushing all his buttons as if he had "fuck me" written all over his forehead. How she had brought out this possessive side in him—a side he thought he didn't have—was beyond him. Why couldn't he just fuck her and leave her as he did with all other women?

Already now everybody made fun of him. Samson's smirk hadn't escaped his attention. What was it? *Schadenfreude?* Like everybody was happy about what was coming to him. Could they all tell that he was turning into some pussy-whipped idiot?

He couldn't go on like this. Tonight, he'd fuck her once more, and then he'd turn her loose, wipe her memory of him and be done with it. He could not allow her to screw with his head like this. And besides, something in her attitude had changed, and he couldn't figure out what it was.

A sound on the other side of the street had him whip his head around. Somebody was approaching her.

"It's just a homeless guy," Gabriel said next to him.

A moment later an airport shuttle approached and came to a halt in front of them, obstructing their view. The din of emotions suddenly hit Amaury and he pressed his hand against his temple. Almost the entire evening he'd felt barely any pain or discomfort from his gift; in fact, he'd barely sensed anybody's emotions. He attributed it to his extremely satisfying interlude with Nina in the staff room of the club. It seemed that sex with her kept the emotions at bay longer than any of his previous sexual encounters ever had.

He tried to look past the shuttle van to the other side of the street.

"Can you see what's going on?"

Gabriel grunted. "No. Don't worry; she can handle a homeless guy."

The van was stopped for entirely too long, as the driver helped a handicapped person into it. Who the hell left for the airport at four in the morning? Amaury was just about out of patience. Ignoring his colleague's displeased look, he stepped around the van and trained his eyes on the scene on the opposite side.

The homeless man was gone. And Nina was nowhere to be seen.

"Ah, *shit*!"

Without waiting for Gabriel, he rushed across the street, dodging a car and its furious driver. His eyes, well equipped for the dark, darted along the street, checking every doorway, every entrance. At a faint sound, his ears perked up. His reflexes set in, and he swiveled. Two steps and he was at a narrow alley leading to the tradesmen entrance of a building. He could make out two figures struggling.

Despite the dark, Nina's golden hair was hard to miss. Amaury leaped at them and pulled the man off her.

"Bastard! Get your fucking hands off her!"

The mere thought that the homeless guy was touching her turned his stomach. He slammed his fists into the man and threw him to the ground. Behind him, Amaury heard footsteps. Gabriel and Quinn. They could take care of the bastard now.

Amaury brought his attention back to Nina. She was still on the ground, but moaning. Damn, he should kill the bastard for hurting her.

"Nina, *chérie*, don't move. I'm here."

He crouched down next to her and ran his hands over her, testing for injuries.

"What are you doing?" Her voice sounded less than pleased.

"Keep still. I'm just trying to see if you're hurt."

She pulled herself up to sit and wrenched free of his hands. "I'm fine."

Something was wrong. He couldn't find any physical injuries, but there had to be a reason why she was so annoyed with him. In fact, she'd been pissed at him ever since they'd left Samson's house.

Before he could ask her, he heard Gabriel behind him.

"Well, hello, Paul Holland."

Amaury spun his head around. Now that he looked at the homeless guy closely, he realized that Paul Holland, their suspect, had disguised himself. How had he known that Nina was waiting for him here? All Gabriel had done was send Paul on an assignment that would take him past the place where Nina was waiting. So, how had he known to disguise himself?

"I guess this proves that he's our man. Take him back and interrogate him." As much as he'd love to beat it out the bastard himself, he needed to take care of Nina now. "On second thought, have Zane do it. I think I'm all out of nice for today."

Gabriel raised his eyebrow, but didn't object outright. "Don't you want to do it yourself?"

"I'm taking Nina home."

"I can go home by myself." Nina's protest would have no bearing on his actions tonight.

"No, you can't, because you're coming home with me."

Gabriel and Quinn restrained the suspect. "We'll leave you guys to it."

Amaury barely nodded at them and watched as Nina got up, her legs a little shaky. Instinctively, he reached out to steady her. She pushed his hand away.

"What the hell is wrong with you?" Amaury snapped.

"Why don't you just read my emotions?" She gave him a defiant glare.

So that was the problem—she thought he could sense her feelings. What was it she didn't want him to know?

"Nina, I can't sense your emotions."

"Liar. Samson told me that's your gift. You were there, and you didn't contradict him."

He took her by the shoulders and turned her fully to him, even though she continued to struggle under his grip. "I can't sense *your* emotions. Everybody else's, yes. But not yours. And I don't know why."

"You can't?" Her voice was softer now, as if she was trying to figure out if he was lying.

"I have no idea what you feel, and it drives me crazy." Even more so now that he suspected there was something she didn't want to share with him. What the hell was it?

"Oh." It was all she said, before she dropped her gaze from his face.

"Come, let's go home. You must be tired."

Amaury felt drained. Worrying about her had zapped his energy. Or maybe it was because he hadn't fed since the night Thomas had untied him from his bed. How long ago was that? Was that last night or the night before? He couldn't remember. Too much seemed to have happened since then.

There were still a few hours of night left, but all he cared for right now was to crawl into bed with Nina securely locked in his arms. Nothing less would do.

In the cab ride home he put his arm around her shoulder, and finally the stubborn woman leaned against him.

"Are you hurting?"

"Just a little."

"Are you sure?" He tipped up her chin to make her look at him. "You'll have to let me know when something bothers you, because I've never learned how to figure out what a person is feeling just by looking at their face. I've always relied on my gift for that."

"I guess that makes you just like any other man then."

"That's not a consolation."

"You'll get used to it. All men do."

"I'm not all men." To prove it, he took her lips with his mouth and kissed her. When he released her, she was breathless. "Still think I'm like all other men?"

"Not sure. Could you give me another demonstration?"

The wicked glint in her eyes was back. That was something he could work with. Wicked, he knew how to handle. Amaury sunk his hand into her locks and cupped her head to hold her to him. His mouth fitted perfectly to hers. He'd missed her sweet scent and her hungry tongue.

The moment Nina welcomed him into her moist heat to dance with him, he lost all sense of time and place. He scraped his teeth against her lips just enough to elicit a shudder, before he used his tongue to smooth over the tender spot and soothe her.

"You okay now, coming home with me?" He spoke against her lips, not breaking the contact completely.

"Why?"

"Because I can't bear to know you're out there on your own. When you're with me, at least I know you're safe." He inhaled her breath and nipped at her lips.

"Is that really why?"

Amaury sighed. "I want you in my arms. Is that so terrible?"

"Why didn't you say so in the first place?" Her tongue traced the outline of his mouth.

"Because you drive me so mad sometimes, I don't know what I'm doing anymore." He'd never been this honest with any woman. But he couldn't lie to her. Nina was driving him nuts, constantly, making his head spin, and at the same time she calmed his mind, blocked out other people's emotions for him, as if she'd put a shield around him.

She deepened her kiss, and Amaury pulled her into his lap, angling his head so he could get more of her—more closeness, more warmth, more Nina. Just how much would be enough?

21

Nina eyed Amaury when he led her into his apartment and locked the door behind them. She was back in the lion's den and getting more comfortable by the minute. Only four nights earlier she'd tried—unsuccessfully—to kill him. Now this thought was the furthest from her passion-clouded mind.

In the taxi, his kisses had practically knocked her socks off. Amaury had pressed her so close to him, she'd barely been able to breathe, let alone think.

He'd proven over and over that he wanted to protect her, even after she'd intentionally provoked him when she'd given him the finger. She'd been so pissed off thinking he was able to read her emotions that she'd been spoiling for a fight. It wasn't right that he'd known what she felt, when she wasn't at all sure about her feelings herself.

"Are you hungry?" His question was unexpected.

"Actually, I haven't had any dinner. But it doesn't matter." She could hold out until the morning, even though her stomach immediately started grumbling.

"I have some leftovers in the kitchen."

She wrinkled her nose. "I'm not into blood."

"In that case, how about some *coq au vin* with Potato Gratin? You're not vegetarian, are you?"

He took her hand and walked toward the kitchen. Nina had no choice but to follow on his heels.

"Why would you have human food in the house?" She remembered now that he'd told her about the food earlier in the evening, but she'd thought he was pulling her leg.

"I like cooking." As if that was the most normal explanation there was. A vampire who liked to cook.

"But you don't eat."

Amaury motioned her to sit down at the kitchen island and opened the fridge.

"That doesn't mean I don't like the smell of food."

While he took out various containers and spooned their contents onto a plate, she watched him and noticed how comfortable he seemed in the kitchen.

"Who eats the food if you don't?"

Amaury placed the plate in the microwave and switched it on. "My neighbors or some of the homeless in the neighborhood."

She stared at him. He had a charitable streak? "Oh." Now that she was thinking of it, it had been a while since she'd seen him in his vampire form. Maybe her memory was failing her, and he wasn't a vampire after all.

"Are you sure you're a vampire?"

He put the warm plate in front of her and handed her some utensils. A smile spread over his entire face. "Would you like me to flash you my fangs?"

"Maybe later."

"Chicken." His insult was spoken in too soft a voice to carry any weight, and accompanied by his grin it almost turned into a caress. Warmth spread around her heart.

He took the barstool next to her as she ate.

"So, about your gift." She needed to know more about his strange skill. She had wanted to ask him about it in the taxi, but once he'd started kissing her, there'd been no way of stopping him.

"What about it? I already told you, I can't read your emotions. You believe me, don't you?"

She nodded. For some reason she knew he wasn't lying to her. "But can you block out other people, too, like you block me out? I mean, do you hear everybody all the time?"

She caught a sad look in his eyes.

"It's not something I can block out. Whenever I'm physically close to people I sense their emotions. And I'm not blocking you out—God knows the only person's feelings I would really want to sense are yours. But for some reason I can't."

Nina's heart skipped a beat. He wanted to know what she felt? What would he do with it? The thought was both scary and exciting.

"What does it feel like when you sense other people?" She couldn't even begin to imagine how her head would feel if she would constantly receive excessive sensory input from outside. Was it as if somebody was constantly banging at a door to be let in?

Amaury shrugged. "How's the food?"

She'd never tasted anything better. "It's excellent. You're a great cook, and you're changing the subject."

"There's nothing much to talk about."

There would be a hell of a lot to talk about if this were happening to her head every day. His gaze collided with hers.

"Do you hear people's thoughts?"

Amaury shook his head. "No, it's not like that at all. I can't read minds. I feel them: I feel the people and their emotions. They're impressions, not words that come to me. My brain sort of translates them into words for me, but it's not their words. It's their feelings put into my own words. I can't really explain it. It's very intense."

Nina took in a sharp breath, suddenly remembering the night she'd followed him, how he'd held his temples as if he had a migraine.

"It must be so painful. How do you keep your head from exploding?"

Surprise flashed in his eyes. "How do you know?"

"It can't feel good to constantly have your mind invaded with all kinds of powerful feelings. How do you cope with that?"

He brushed his knuckles over her cheek. "Do you know that you're the first person who's ever asked me that?"

"But your friends—they know about it, right?"

He shook his head. "They don't know about the pain. I've never told them what it feels like."

"Why not?"

"I don't want their pity."

"Tell me. I want to know." She took his hand and held it against her cheek. His warm fingers instantly caressed her skin. Too soft for a vampire, too soft even for the hard man he portrayed. No, not the hard man, merely the hard shell. For inside, she suspected, was something different entirely. The softer the inside, the harder the shell had to be to provide protection. Was that true in Amaury's case?

"You don't want to know."

"Please." She turned her head and kissed his palm.

Amaury closed his eyes for a long moment. "It's like somebody is sticking needles in my head. Continuously. Big ones, the kind you'd use to inject an elephant." He opened his eyes. "It's a constant noise in my head. Incessant pounding."

It was worse than she'd imagined. "How do you get any relief from this?"

His eyes, when he met hers, seemed cautious, as if he'd revealed too much already. But she wanted to know all of it. She wanted to understand him.

"There must be some way to get a break from it." How could a person function with this going on in his head all the time?

"There is. It's sex."

"Sex? You're kidding me."

He shook his head, but said nothing.

Then it sunk in. "How often?"

"Daily."

Every day? He had sex *every day*? Nina stared at him, mouth gaping open, unable to say anything. She'd had sex with a man who was sleeping with other women on a daily basis—hundreds, thousands maybe.

"You wanted to know." He gave her an apologetic look. "It's not by choice. And it means nothing."

It meant nothing to him?

Nina felt an uncomfortable twinge in her left side. He'd slept with her to alleviate his pain? That was it? He'd used her. And she'd been so stupid to let herself feel something. He wasn't any better than any other man, if anything, he was worse, because he had lulled her into believing that he was on her side, that he wanted to help. What was she to him? A painkiller?

"You're telling me that *after* you had sex with me? That it meant nothing to you? That's just what a girl wants to hear. Thanks a lot!" With a loud thud she slammed the fork on the counter and pushed away her nearly empty plate. She had to get out of his presence before she broke down in front of him, before she would shed tears of disappointment.

She dropped from the barstool, but before she could stomp out of the kitchen, he'd already grabbed her arm and flung her around to face him.

"It meant nothing with any of those women. It means something with you."

"Save your lies for somebody who's a little more gullible than I am." She wrenched her arm free and walked into the living room when she suddenly heard a loud noise. She turned and saw the steel blinds come down over the large floor-to-ceiling windows.

"Lockdown," he explained behind her. "Sunrise is in thirty seconds. I've programmed them to close before sunrise. They'll lift again after sunset."

"Well, I don't care, 'cause I'm not staying. You can play your little games with somebody else." The best way to shield herself from the pain she felt was to attack. She couldn't let him see how hurt she was.

She made for the door and was surprised that he didn't hold her back. Well, it just proved that their intimacy had meant nothing to him.

She jerked at the door, but it wouldn't open. Her hands went to her hips as she spun back to face him. "Open the damn door."

"I can't."

***

Amaury smirked as he watched Nina try to open the door. It was programmed to lock at the same time the blinds came down. A security measure he'd put in place so nobody could invade the place while he slept. Of course, he could override the system in an emergency. But he had no intention of doing so—this wasn't an emergency, at least not for him. Nina was staying, whether she wanted to or not.

He should have never revealed to her what his gift did to him and how he was able to relieve the pain. Now he had a mutiny on his hands. The little wildcat didn't like the fact that she was one of many women he'd slept with to soothe his pain. He'd have to somehow convince her of the truth—that she was different, that being with her affected him. He craved her company, not because he wanted sex, but because he wanted her. It was high time to admit it to himself.

"It won't open, however long you try, until sundown. Nina, please, we need to talk."

"I have nothing to say to you. Open the damn door!"

"No, I won't. You belong here with me."

"What for? Did you run out of aspirin?" she barked.

Amaury shook his head. "When I'm with you, I'm not in pain, whether we have sex or not. I don't know why. I just know that I want to be with you."

He stretched out his hand, but she crossed her arms over her chest.

"But I don't want to be with you. I'm not interested in being with some sexoholic who can't keep his hands off other women. And I don't need someone who's using me. Been there, done that."

He crossed the distance to her and brushed her cheek with his knuckles. "I'm not using you, *chérie*. I'm with you because I *want* to be with you. If that weren't the case, I would have wiped your memory a long time ago and you wouldn't even know who I was."

Amaury wasn't entirely sure whether he was telling the truth about the memory part—since she'd been unreceptive to his mind control, he suspected that trying to wipe her memory wouldn't have worked. Not that it mattered, because he had no intention of wiping her memory— ever.

"Says the man who's slept with millions of women."

Millions? Not quite. Thousands was more like it. Okay, tens of thousands. Many tens. But if Nina was willing, he'd happily make that just one.

One?

Was he really willing to only have her? No others for variety's sake? The mere thought that he was contemplating this should have sent him running for cover, as if the sun were about to rise. But he wasn't inclined to do anything of the like.

"You're exaggerating a little."

"Am I? How old are you?"

He realized what she was getting at. She was trying to estimate how many women he'd had. "Old enough to know not to answer that question."

"Ha, I knew it. You're constantly hiding things. You can't be trusted."

Amaury had to suppress the urge to sweep her into his arms and kiss her to convince her otherwise. It wouldn't be the right way to do this. He needed her to believe him, not because he was kissing her senseless, but because he could reason with her.

Again he stroked her cheek with his thumb. "I know it's not easy to trust somebody you've just met, but you and I, we've been through a lot together. We've fought together. My life was in your hands, and yours in mine. Don't you think you could at least try to give me a chance? Yes, my past isn't exactly as squeaky clean as that of a choir boy, but I haven't touched or even thought of another woman since I met you. That's never happened to me."

Nina's eyes met his. "Never?"

"No. All I can think of is being with you."

Finally he saw her soften. She dropped her arms to her sides. He inched closer.

"I'd like to kiss you," he said, "but I don't want to do anything you don't want me to do." Amaury searched her eyes for consent.

"Amaury, I'm so confused. I don't know whether I can trust anybody. I don't understand what's happening to me when I'm with you." Her eyes grew moist. "You make me mad one minute and—" She swallowed hard. "—and weak another."

"Weak?" He shook his head. "You're not weak. You're the strongest woman I've ever met. And yet . . . "

Nina raised her lashes and looked at him expectantly.

He sighed. "I can't help myself, but I want to protect you even when I know you can take care of yourself. Crazy, huh?"

A faint smile stole around her lips. "Maybe we're both a little crazy—or just a little tired."

Amaury took her cue. "Come, you need to sleep. We both do. And I want to hold you in my arms. I promise you, you'll be safe with me."

Ten minutes later he had his wish: Nina was in his bed where he held her closely. He sighed contently. There was no wild sex, no passionate kissing, no frantic touching this time. Having her in his arms was enough tonight. Enough for him, the least likely vampire to cuddle? He shook his head in disbelief. Clearly, something strange was happening to him if he felt satisfied with merely having her in his arms. The only time he'd ever held a woman in his arms was when he was fucking her. This—this was different. And he couldn't get enough of this newfound intimacy with her.

"*Chérie*, why do you make me feel this way?" he whispered, but Nina didn't hear him. She was already asleep.

22

Lights were ablaze in the bare underground interrogation room at Scanguards. Gabriel stood back, Quinn by his side, as Zane took over the questioning of the suspect. He rarely allowed Zane to unleash his brutality on anybody, but this time even he felt it necessary. Paul Holland, the man who'd attacked Nina and who was somehow involved in the bodyguard murders, wasn't talking.

Samson had ordered that nobody was to interfere when it came to Amaury's relationship with the human woman. When he'd issued his directive, Gabriel had heard the grin in Samson's voice, as if he was extraordinarily pleased with himself. He hadn't questioned his boss, but he sure wanted to know what had brought on this turnaround, especially after everybody had been advised days earlier to minimize their contact with humans.

He shook his head in silence and turned his attention back to Zane and the suspect. The bald vampire was as much known for his utter lack of compassion as for his convincing torture techniques which bordered on medieval. Scanguards' interrogation room wasn't equipped for torture. Rather, it was a training room for bodyguards. But Zane didn't need many tools.

While Zane would have probably enjoyed stretching the man on a rack, there were certainly more subtle ways to dig up information.

Rumor had it that Zane had extensively studied the interrogation techniques used by the Nazis during World War II and adopted some of their methods. Therefore, when he pulled out a simple pair of pliers from his long coat, Gabriel showed no surprise and only winced inwardly. He abhorred violence, but knew in this case it was necessary.

Paul's eyes flickered briefly when he caught sight of the instrument, but a second later he had himself back under control. For a human he appeared extraordinarily fearless. Gabriel had yet to figure out what gave him this mental strength.

"Did I mention that I really don't care if you survive this or not?" Zane's voice was calm and expressionless.

A snort was the answer. Was the man mocking his tormentor?

Gabriel forced himself to watch his second in command as Zane gripped the suspect's wrist and applied the pliers to his thumb.

The instrument tightened over the tip of the man's digit. "Who's behind this?"

No answer, but a huffed breath. Paul's disobedience was greeted with an evil grin by Zane and an instant tightening over the suspect's thumb. The sounds of bones cracking and muscle being pulped into a bloody mess were drowned out by Paul's scream.

"Who's turning our guards into killers?" Zane's voice was as calm as if he were asking the time.

The suspect's mouth pressed together into a thin line, indicating his unwillingness to divulge any information. Gabriel sensed a short flicker of a memory appear in the man's mind. But it was too brief for him to hone in on it. He nodded to Zane to continue. Even if Paul was unprepared to talk, he could be weakened enough to release information via his memories.

Gabriel was unclear how, as a human, Paul was able to shield his memories from him. Whoever his master was—and he knew there had to be a master—had to be either a vampire, a witch, or a demon. No other creatures had powers sufficient to block his gift of unlocking memories.

Zane applied the pliers to Paul's index finger, this time pulling on the fingernail and ripping it clean off. Blood splattered as the suspect let out another scream. Paul's eyes watered, the pain evident on his face.

"I can do this all day." Zane was right. They had time. It was already daytime, and there wasn't much else they could do anyway. Whether it took them five minutes or five hours to get him to talk didn't matter much.

Defiantly, Paul looked up at Zane and spat. "I won't tell you anything." His voice was labored. The man was in undeniable agony, yet he showed tremendous strength.

Under other circumstances Gabriel would have admired him. After all, Paul was a Scanguards bodyguard, and they were known for their stamina, determination, and grit. They'd been trained to cope with torture. And this one had been trained well. Too well.

"You will. They all do when I'm through with them." Zane was clearly enjoying himself too much at the man's expense.

Thirty seconds later another bloody fingernail landed on the concrete floor. The room positively reeked of blood now. Zane's fangs had lengthened, and Gabriel noticed the bulge under his associate's jeans. He'd always assumed Zane got turned on by violence, but now he knew for certain. Gabriel shot him a warning look, which Zane ignored.

Another scream echoed in the small room as Zane crushed Paul's ring finger with the pliers.

"Whom are you working for?"

Paul slumped forward, breathing heavily. He mumbled something incoherent.

"What?" Zane pushed Paul's shoulders back and jerked his face up to look at him.

"Luther."

Gabriel's heart sank. It was true then. Up until now he'd still hoped their suspicions were unfounded.

Zane continued his questioning. "Who's Luther?" He set the pliers again, but Gabriel pried them from his hands before he could clamp down.

"That's enough."

Zane's furious glare hit him. "We're not done."

"I know Luther." Unfortunately, yes, he knew him, their former friend and partner. The man who'd turned against them after his blood-bonded wife had died.

Gabriel turned to Paul. "He was seen in town last night. What does he want?"

Paul shrugged, seemingly unwilling to give away anything else. The back of Gabriel's hand hit him straight across the cheek. Blood instantly seeped from Paul's mouth.

"He wants to destroy Scanguards."

Gabriel nodded. He had guessed as much. "What's he paying you?"

Paul's surprised gaze struck him. "Paying? This isn't about money."

"Is he forcing you against your will?"

He shook his head. "He offered me immortality."

Immortality? Gabriel's heart skipped a beat. Luther was planning to create a new vampire?

"You don't know Luther. What makes you think he'll keep his promise to you once you've done for him what he wants?" Gabriel shook his head.

"He'll keep his word. I know he will." Gabriel was surprised at Paul's firm belief. There was no reason, unless . . .

"Why are you so sure?"

"He did it for the others."

Gabriel's breath hitched. This couldn't be happening. Ever since Luther had turned against them they'd wondered what he would do, but creating new vampires to build his own army? Was that his plan? Had he gone completely crazy?

"The whole story. Talk fast or—" He turned to point to Zane. "—I'll let him continue."

23

Nina jerked and was awake instantly. It was dark. Only a small nightlight from the open bathroom door illuminated the bedroom. The mattress moved, the person next to her thrashing violently—Amaury. His screams had woken her.

Nina reached for the nightstand to find a switch for the lamp, knocking a book off of it in the process. The small lamp spread a soft glow over the room.

Her gaze turned back to Amaury, who continued thrashing, having already tossed the blanket off his body. Sweat beaded on his naked body. He mumbled in French, a language she didn't speak, his head whipping from side to side.

It was evident he was in the middle of a violent nightmare. She hadn't even known vampires could dream, let alone have nightmares. Nina placed her hand on his shoulder, trying to wake him.

A loud snarl ripped from his throat, making her jolt back instantly. She saw his fangs protrude from his mouth.

"Amaury, wake up!"

He didn't seem to hear her, but continued to thrash about. It appeared to get worse by the minute. She had to wake him up no matter what. She was fully aware of her own naked body, and for a moment it made her feel vulnerable.

Nina swung herself over him, straddling him, and in the same moment held down his arms. But even in his sleep he was strong.

"Amaury, you need to wake up. Please."

She pressed her full weight down on him, when a growl filled the room. His eyes flew open, glaring red at her. Her breath caught in her throat as she tried to pull back from him. But in a split second he'd flipped her and pinned her underneath him, flashing his sharp fangs at her, snarling like a beast. She'd never seen anybody more frightening in her life.

"*AMAURY*," she screamed, his face only inches from her. "It's *me*, Nina. Please, stop!"

As quickly as he'd attacked her, he let go and pulled back, dropping back onto his knees. She pulled her legs up and scrambled backwards to brace herself against the headboard.

Amaury looked stunned and confused, breathing hard. "What happened?"

When she stared at his face again, his eyes had gone back to their brilliant blue, and his fangs had receded. "You had a nightmare."

He averted his eyes. "Oh, God, I'm sorry. I should have never made you stay." He looked back at her. "Did I hurt you?"

His eyes ran over her body, seemingly looking for any signs of injury.

"No. It's fine." Only her heart was still beating violently.

He shook his head. "No, it's not. I put you in danger. I could have maimed you or worse. I'll go and sleep on the couch. Lock the door behind me."

Amaury rose, but she took hold of his arm, making him stop in mid-movement. His gaze first fell to her hand then rose to her face.

"Stay," she said.

There was a sad look in his eyes. "Nina, I don't want to endanger you. If I'd known this would happen, I would have asked you to lock yourself in here in the first place."

Nina pulled herself closer to him. "It wasn't your fault. Please, come back to bed. I feel cold without you."

She ran her other hand up his chest. She felt a strange sense of protectiveness toward him. Protectiveness toward a vampire? "Hold me and tell me about your nightmare. I know a lot about nightmares. You shouldn't be alone right now." Her own nightmares had always frightened her, and being alone after she'd woken up in the middle of the night had frightened her even more. Why would it be any different for a vampire?

Amaury's reluctance to come back to bed was evident, but nevertheless he let himself be pulled back. She molded her body against his warm skin.

"How come you didn't know?"

"I knew of the nightmares, of course, but not of how violent I'd turn. I always sleep alone."

Realization hit her. "None of those women ever stayed here with you?"

Amaury shook his head. "I never felt the need to actually sleep with a woman. And when I say 'sleep,' I don't mean sex. I haven't slept with a woman in my arms since I was human."

"Oh." All her anger about the many women he'd had sex with dissipated. Suddenly she felt too shy to ask him why he never spent the night with a woman in his bed. Or maybe it wasn't shyness. Maybe she merely didn't want to read too much into it. She didn't want to get her hopes up that something special was growing between them.

She raised her hand to stroke his cheek. "Tell me about the nightmare."

"I'm not sure this is something you'd want to know about me."

"Why not?"

"Because it's something I did in my past, something evil."

Given that he was a vampire, she didn't think there was anything that could really shock her. "We all have demons in our past. Maybe it's time you talked about yours."

"You sound like my shrink."

His revelation surprised her. "You have a shrink?"

"I did, but he couldn't really help me."

"Then what have you got to lose by telling me?"

He looked at her for a long moment. "Nothing, I guess. One day, you'd have to find out about it anyway. Why not now?" Amaury pressed a kiss on her forehead. "Promise me something."

Nina gave him a puzzled look.

"Promise me that whatever you might think of me after this, you won't run away. I'm still here to protect you—even from myself if need be."

"I won't run."

He nodded and swallowed hard before he looked straight at her.

"I committed a terrible crime. I killed my young son."

For a moment there was utter silence in the room. Amaury didn't breathe.

"Oh, my god." Her throat was too dry to say anything else. The revelation sank deep into her.

Nina felt him pull away, but she tightened her grip on his arm. She knew instinctively that rejection was the last thing he could handle right now. "How did it happen?"

"It was my first night as a vampire. I had no idea what the change would do to me. The craving for blood, the terrible thirst—I didn't know how to fight it. Jean-Philippe was only three years old. He trusted me." Amaury's voice broke.

Nina hugged him tightly, stroking her hand over his broad back. He was a father—he'd had a wife, a child. She would have never guessed. Suddenly she saw him with different eyes. He'd cared for somebody before. He'd loved somebody once. "You didn't want to do it. The vampire who turned you is to blame."

Amaury pulled away from her. "No. I'm to blame. Maybe I didn't ask to be changed, but I provoked it."

"Provoked it, how?"

"I thought I would be helping my family. I couldn't provide for them, but then a man made me an offer. I took it, thinking I could make things better for them and for me. He made it sound so easy. He would pay me for allowing him to feed off me, but he didn't keep to the arrangement and turned me instead. I didn't know about the thirst, how it would control me. When I got home that first night after my change, Jean-Philippe was right there at the door, greeting me. I was ravenous, famished."

Amaury ran his hands through his hair, a haunted look in his eyes. "I fell into bloodlust. Nina, I sucked him dry. *My own son.* I'm a monster."

Nina wanted to give him comfort, but he held her back as if he didn't feel he deserved compassion.

"When my wife saw what had happened, she cursed me. And then she flung herself off the church tower. She killed herself because she couldn't bear the loss of our son. She had every right to hate me. I hated myself." He paused. "She was the one who gave me this so-called gift."

"Gift?"

"The fact that I can sense others' emotions. She cursed me. Even though she wasn't a witch. There was a belief back then that if you wished evil upon someone with all your heart and soul, and then killed yourself, your wish would turn into a curse. That's what happened. She cursed me, just as she cursed me never to love again. Now you know."

"Never to love again?"

Amaury nodded and swallowed hard. "Do you know why I live in the shabbiest part of town? Because I don't deserve any better. At least among the less fortunate people in this city I feel at home. I sense their pain, their anger. There isn't much love in the Tenderloin. I don't get reminded often of what I can't feel. It makes it easier."

Nina took his large hand into hers and squeezed it. "Amaury, why are you so hard on yourself?"

"Why? Because every night I remember what I've done, and every night I wish I could turn back time and bring him back. Bring them both back. But I can't. I've killed them both."

She rested her head against his shoulder. "Haven't you repented long enough? When did all this happen?"

"Over four hundred years ago."

Nina gasped. "Even human murderers often get out after thirty or forty years. You've been in this prison for over four hundred years."

"And it doesn't get any easier. Nothing has changed. My son is still dead, and I'm still his killer."

"You were not in control of yourself. In a human court they would have called it mitigating circumstances."

"That's not an excuse."

"No, but it's the reason why it happened. You didn't do it on purpose."

"How would you know?"

"Because when you're in control of yourself you don't hurt people. You didn't hurt me."

Regret crept into the blue of his eyes. "I almost did."

"The point is you *didn't*. You are *not* a monster."

"Since when are you the one defending vampires?"

"Since I got to know one." She never thought she'd say such a thing and find herself in the position of defending him. A hell of a lot had changed in her world in the last three days. The pain she saw in his eyes hurt deep in her chest. Why was it that she was so affected by what he felt? Why did it hurt her so much to see him in pain?

"Nina. I'm damaged goods."

"We all are. You've suffered long enough. Don't you think it's time you forgave yourself?"

"Forgive myself?" Amaury's voice sounded shocked. "I can never forgive myself for what I've done."

She lifted her head and looked into his eyes. "If you can't do it for yourself, then somebody else has to. You can't go on like this. I forgive you, Amaury."

24

Amaury stared at Nina, stunned, not understanding for a moment what she had said. She forgave him for what he'd done four centuries ago? No, he couldn't accept forgiveness. He didn't deserve it.

He tried to speak, to protest, but no words came past his dry lips. Her hands wrapped around his frame and her naked body pressed into his. She should be appalled by him, disgusted, recoiling from him. Yet she wasn't. Instead, her hands soothed him, stroked tenderly over his body and planted small kisses on his neck and shoulders.

Of their own volition, his hands pulled her closer, hugging her tightly as he eased them both back into the sheets.

"I don't understand." Why was his little fighter suddenly going all soft on him? He was the strong and scary vampire, the same who'd attacked her in his sleep, yet she soothed him with her touch and her tender kisses.

"You're too hard on yourself. It was an accident, a terrible accident. It's time to let go of the guilt."

Amaury didn't know whether it was her words that made him feel better, or the way she said them. Or maybe it was just the way she snuggled into him, trusting him not to hurt her. But he felt calmer now, and the sadness that had overtaken him earlier had all but vanished.

He kissed her forehead, then looked into her eyes. "Who are you?" Not only did she block out the emotions bombarding his head, she seemed to understand him on a deeper level. She knew what he needed when he needed it. Was it even possible?

Nina shook her head. "I'm nobody. But I recognize pain when I see it."

And he understood. Having been raised in a foster home couldn't have been easy. "Tell me about you and Eddie. I read in his file that you guys grew up in a foster home. Must have been hard."

Nina closed her eyes for a moment before she spoke. "One foster home? Make that three."

Amaury tucked her closer to his body and pulled the blanket over them. "Tell me what happened. I want to know what turned you into such a tough cookie."

"You think I'm tough?"

He smiled. "Yes, and I mean that in a good way. I like strong women."

"My parents were on their way back from their anniversary dinner." There was a faraway look in her eyes, a look which spoke of sadness and longing. "The babysitter let me watch TV while she put Eddie to bed. That's when the police showed up at the front door."

She paused and took a few breaths before she continued. "A drunk driver, they said. He ran a red light. I remember my parents like it was yesterday. But Eddie was too small. He would cry sometimes at night because he couldn't remember what our mother looked like. The first foster family we were placed with was nice to us, but then our foster dad lost his job, and they couldn't afford to keep us. Eddie was heartbroken, but Social Services just took us away."

She sighed. "They wanted to split us up at first, because they thought it was easier to place just one of us, but I wouldn't let go of Eddie. I screamed at everybody who came close to us."

Amaury brushed his knuckles over her cheek, wanting to comfort her.

"I was twelve when we were sent to another family. I was big for my age and I already had boobs. And that was a problem."

Amaury's stomach twisted. He didn't like where the story was going.

"One day I caught my foster father watching me when I got dressed. He played it down, but I knew that look he had. At first I didn't say anything because my foster mother was so nice. Eddie really liked it there, and he had friends at school. I didn't want him to have to move again. But it happened again and again. Until I couldn't stand it anymore."

Nina looked at him with big eyes. "I found photos. Not just of me, but also of other girls. The perv was taking photos of us—naked, in the shower or the bath, or when we were getting dressed. He had spy holes all over the house."

"Oh, my god. What did you do?" Amaury's hands balled into fists. He knew exactly where he wanted those fists to land.

"I started barricading my door, but my foster mother got suspicious. By the time I was fourteen I wore clothes that would disguise my figure, so he wouldn't look at me anymore, but he didn't stop. Then one day I'd forgotten to lock my door and he came in. He touched me, but I kicked him. He was so mad. I knew he would come back that night and hurt me. I picked Eddie up from school and told him we were going camping."

Amaury planted a soft kiss on her hair. Why couldn't he have been there to help her when she needed him? *"Chérie."* It was all he could whisper to her.

"Social Services found us three days later, but in the meantime I'd already sent some of the photos to my foster mother, anonymously of course. When we got back, I saw she'd been crying. A week later Social Services came and picked us up again. She chose her husband over us. She stayed with him, with that perv. And she threw me and Eddie out. How could she choose him over us? We were good kids. He was a bad man."

Nina choked back the tears. "They blamed me. Eddie did too. He didn't understand. He was only eleven. They kept us at the orphanage for a while, and I wish we'd stayed there. But Eddie was a cute kid and popular, so they found us another family. After the last one, I didn't think it could get any worse."

Amaury felt anger build up inside him.

"Nina, you don't have to tell me anymore. I know this is painful for you. I understand."

She shook her head. "No, I have to tell you. I've done something very bad. And you should know."

Amaury kissed her lips softly. "Whatever you've done, I'm sure it was warranted."

"I stabbed a man, and if I'd had the courage I would have cut his dick off."

He winced, his body instinctively jerking at the image she projected. His jaw dropped open, and all he could do was stare at her.

"Yes, I took a knife and almost castrated my third foster father. He came to my room one night and raped me. I knew nobody would believe me if I reported it—he was an upstanding citizen, well respected in town. I knew he'd do it again. But I was prepared the next time."

Amaury listened with bated breath.

"When he touched me again with his filthy hands, I reached for the knife underneath my pillow and stabbed him. There was so much blood.

Only my cowardice saved me from actually cutting his dick off. Instead, I just twisted the knife in his stomach. He screamed, and my foster mother came running just as I'd thrown him off me. I threatened her too. And then I played back the recording I'd made on my little hand-held tape recorder. I always used it in school to tape my teachers, but I kept it close-by because I knew I would need it as evidence one day. On the recording my foster mother could hear what he'd been trying to do to me.

"I made sure she realized that I'd destroy them and their precious reputation if either one of them ever touched me or Eddie again. And I had the proof to make it happen."

"What happened to the bastard?" If he wasn't dead yet, Amaury would be happy to do the deed himself. He felt a swell of fury rise in his stomach.

"He survived. She called an ambulance and told them what I told her to say: that her husband surprised a burglar and was stabbed by him. I made sure all the evidence pointed to it by the time the police arrived: I broke a window from the outside and hid my bloody sheets**. Of course they didn't find the guy, and of course they tried to sniff out what was going on, but all they had to go on was our testimony. There was nothing they could really do.** By the time he got out of the hospital, I'd brought a copy of the recording to a safe place with instructions to make it public if anything ever happened to me or Eddie."

"A safe place?"

"A mail box at one of those mailbox places in another town with instructions to open the box and send its contents to the county sheriff if anything happened to me."

"And then?"

"I had almost two more years left to my eighteenth birthday. Those months living with them were hell, but he didn't touch me, too afraid I'd make good on my threat. When I applied to become Eddie's guardian on my eighteenth birthday, they supported my application. I had two jobs by that time; working constantly, I could support us. They wanted me gone, so they did everything to help me leave."

Amaury swallowed hard. How could an eighteen-year-old girl take on such responsibility while dealing with her own pain? How much had she suffered? "How could you even stay with them after what he did to you? Why didn't you go to the police?"

"I had no choice. I couldn't risk a long drawn-out trial. I stabbed a man. It would have taken months to prove that I acted in self-defense. I couldn't risk being separated from Eddie. They would have sent him somewhere else while all this was going on. No, it was too risky. I needed to stay with Eddie. It was the only way."

"Don't you think it was riskier to assume they'd give you guardianship of your brother? You were only eighteen, for God's sake." What were the chances of her application not just being tossed out immediately?

"As I said, my foster father was a respectable citizen, and he knew people. He pulled some strings with the judge, that's how badly he wanted all this to go away. I was a thorn in his side. As soon as I became Eddie's guardian, we left. We moved around a lot until we landed here in San Francisco."

Amaury grunted. He wished the asshole had bled to death rather than survived. He didn't deserve living, raping a sixteen-year-old. Putting her—his sweet Nina—through horror like that. He felt his body tense and harden at the thought of wanting to kill a man.

"So, you see. I did a terrible thing, stabbing him, wanting to kill him. I did it on purpose. I knew what I was doing, and still I did it."

Nina turned her head away from him and buried it in the pillow. He didn't know what to do. Pull her into his arms? Give her space? Why couldn't he read her emotions so he would know what to do now?

"I'm sorry, Nina." Amaury couldn't find any words, not when rage coursed through his veins. Somebody had hurt her, and he wanted to retaliate, hurt that man even more. He put his hand on her shoulder and flinched, pulling it back instantly—his fingers had turned into sharp claws. He felt his jaw itch and his fangs push through, unable to prevent his vampire side from appearing. No, he couldn't let himself go like that in front of her. The last thing she'd want to see right now was another violent man, especially after he'd nearly attacked her in his sleep. He had to tamp down his anger first before he could pull her back into his arms.

"Sleep a little longer. I'll let you rest."

Amaury turned his head away and avoided looking at her. He knew his eyes flashed red. He glanced down at his hands—lethal weapons. No, he couldn't touch her right now, as much as he longed to comfort her. He wasn't in control of himself. "I'm sorry."

He got out of bed and, naked as he was, walked into the living room, pulling the door shut behind him.

In one corner, his punching bag hung suspended from the ceiling. He headed straight for it. That was what he needed: if he couldn't punch her rapist or any of the other men who'd hurt her, to punch *something*. Amaury slammed his fists viciously into the bag. He would kill any man who hurt her. Nina was his to protect now. Nobody would ever hurt her again. He'd make sure of that.

***

Amaury hadn't come back to bed after Nina had told him about her past. She could easily guess why: he was horrified by what she'd done. And what was probably worse, she'd been raped, and what man wanted to deal with that? Nobody wanted that. Least of all a man like Amaury, who could have any woman he wanted. He could have a woman who didn't carry the kind of emotional baggage she did.

He probably already regretted having slept with her. His "I'm sorry" had dripped with pity. She guessed he'd spent the remaining hours of the day thinking about how he could extricate himself gracefully from this relationship. Nina would make it easy on him. She wouldn't stay where she wasn't wanted.

As Nina let the warm water of the shower run over her body, she knew she should have never opened up to him. She'd been lulled into feeling safe by his gentle words and by his admissions of his own past. At first it had been a shock to hear what he'd done, but she had found it in her heart to forgive him, because he'd not been himself. The pain in his eyes when he spoke of his son had cut deep into her own heart.

But when it had come to her own guilt, Amaury hadn't been able to do the same. She'd instantly felt his hesitation at even touching her, until he'd finally pulled away completely—as if he was disgusted with her. In the moment where she'd needed his touch most, he'd denied her, he'd withdrawn.

He'd rejected her, just as everybody else had done so before him— as her foster mother had rejected her after she'd exposed her husband as a pervert. Even knowing that her husband was abusing young girls, she'd still chosen him over Nina. Her self-worth at that point couldn't have been any lower—until now. Being rejected by Amaury after opening her heart to him was even more painful.

Nina dreaded facing him now. She didn't want to see the pity in his eyes or the regret. Maybe he'd keep her around for a little while longer so it wouldn't be too obvious that he didn't want her anymore, but she would know.

She wouldn't let this happen. She would leave—on her own terms. And there was only one way to do it: defend her aching heart by attacking him. She couldn't let him know how much she hurt. It would only make it worse.

Nina stepped out of the shower and dried off before she dressed in the clothes from the night before.

She found Amaury in the living room where one corner doubled as a small gym. He was dressed in gym shorts. His upper body was bare, his muscles flexing with every move he made, his skin glistening with sweat.

He greeted her with a cautious look. "You're up."

"Yes, I took a shower. I hope you don't mind."

"No. No, of course not."

Was this nervousness he displayed? He wiped his face with a towel then took a few steps toward her. Midway he seemed to change his mind and stopped.

"Can I leave you alone for an hour? I need to go feed."

The words didn't immediately sink in. "Feed?"

He nodded, his eyes remaining cautious. "I didn't feed last night, and the night before I barely had any blood."

So she had understood right after all. Amaury was planning to go out and drink somebody's blood. Good—it provided her with just the right ammunition to make her exit.

"You're going out to bite somebody?"

The look he gave her could only be described as stubborn. "I need blood to survive."

Nina knew what a vampire needed. "What's wrong with mine?" Would he take the bait? Would he go in for the fight she tried to pick so she could leave with her head high?

His eyes wide, he stomped toward her and grabbed her shoulders. "Are you crazy? You don't know what you're saying. You can't possibly want me to bite you."

The moment he said it, a realization hit her like a thunderbolt.

She wanted him to bite her.

She wanted him to drink her blood.

Her life wouldn't be complete without Amaury taking her. And in that instant of realization, she felt more fear clamp down on her than ever before in her life.

With the strength she thought she didn't have, Nina shook off his hands. "Get away from me!" If she stayed, she would become his toy, something he could push around any which way he wanted, because she would have no strength to resist him. She couldn't allow this. She could never again be at the mercy of a man, no matter how much she desired him. No matter how much her heart ached for him.

Amaury's face took on a puzzled look. "Nina, what is this about?"

"I don't . . . I can't—" Her voice broke. She spun around and fled, yanking the door open.

"Nina!"

She heard him yell after her, but she was already in the stairway and kept running. She had to get away from the only man who had cracked the door to her heart open—leaving it exposed to be hurt.

25

Amaury stopped at the top of the stairs and looked down. Nina's rapid footsteps echoed in the hallway. What had just happened?

He ran his hands through his hair.

Had she really tried to offer him her blood?

It was what he'd fantasized about for the last few days, ever since he'd licked her blood off her wounds. It had haunted him, the knowledge that he was lusting not just after her body, but also after her blood. He wanted Nina, all of her.

As he ran down one flight of stairs, he stumbled over a package in front of Mrs. Reid's door. He instantly stopped in his tracks. The old lady was still gone—all, because of him.

As crazed as he felt right now—thirsty from the lack of blood—his brain kicked in, and fear spread in his chest. What if he hurt Nina like he'd hurt Mrs. Reid? What if he couldn't control himself? The way he wanted Nina right now, he wasn't sure he'd ever be able to stop drinking from her.

He remembered the sweet taste of her blood on his tongue, the intoxicating scent, the smooth texture when it had coated his throat. His cock went rigid at the mere thought of tasting her again, drinking from her, more this time, much more. His hands balled into fists as he fought back the urge to run after her and dig his fangs into her.

His desire collided with the guilt pulsing through him. He had to set something right first, had to assure himself that Mrs. Reid was going to live. The burden of another death at his hands would be too much to carry, and he couldn't go back to Nina, knowing his conscience wasn't clear. She'd forgiven him for one murder—he didn't believe even she would have it in her heart to forgive him for another.

If he could save Mrs. Reid, only then did he deserve another chance. If not, he wasn't good enough for her, not good enough to take what Nina offered him.

***

An hour later he'd found out where the old lady had been taken and had snuck into her hospital room.

Mrs. Reid looked fragile, lying there surrounded by tubes and machines. Amaury took a seat next to her bed and just looked at her. Her skin was pale, and there were lots of bruises. Had she fallen because he'd weakened her too much?

His gut twisted in disgust at himself. He was a despicable creature, feeding from the weak and vulnerable, a monster. Amaury let his head fall into his hands, not knowing how to go on.

A sound at the door made him jerk.

"You can't be in here. Visiting hours are long over," the young nurse said. She stood at the door, hands at her waist and a scolding look on her face.

"I'm sorry. I just only got into town."

"And you are?" He sensed the suspicion she treated him with.

"Her grandson," he lied, knowing that if he didn't claim he was family, she'd get security to throw him out instantly. "I'm sorry. I was so worried about her and didn't want to wait till tomorrow."

Her look softened, and she gave him a pitiful smile. "Have you talked to the police yet?"

Amaury stiffened. "The police?"

She nodded and stepped farther into the room. If she was going to drag him to the police, he'd have to use mind control and wipe her memory. "Yes, I think they have a lead on the guy who did this."

He swallowed hard. They were onto him? How? He'd wiped Mrs. Reid's memory. There'd been nobody in the stairways when he'd entered her apartment to feed from her. Amaury stood, ready to do whatever he needed to do. His body hardened as he prepared to use his powers.

"You mean they haven't told you yet? It's really awful what he did to her. Nice lady like her, and that thug just robs her and beats her up when she's on her way to cash her social security check. I don't know what the world is coming to."

"She got robbed?" He cast another glance back at Mrs. Reid. Her arms sported black and blue bruises.

"You mean nobody told you?" The nurse tossed him an incredulous look. "She was attacked right outside her building."

Amaury shook his head. "Nobody told me. I just came out here as soon as I heard she was in the hospital." He hadn't caused this? This wasn't his fault? He felt a boulder the size of Mount Rushmore lift from his shoulders.

"Will she be all right?"

"She'll pull through. She just needs some rest. You should go home now. Come back tomorrow during visiting hours."

He nodded. "Just a few more minutes?"

"I didn't see you."

He smiled at her as she left the room and closed the door behind her.

Amaury approached the sleeping Mrs. Reid and stroked his hand over her cheek. He hadn't hurt her after all. It was terrible what had happened to her, but at least he was free of guilt. He could feel her pain, and he knew he could help her.

Swiftly, he pricked his finger so a small drop of blood appeared. He guided it to her mouth. With his mind he sent his thoughts into her.

Open your mouth and take the medicine.

In her sleep her lips parted, and he let several drops of blood drip into her mouth.

Swallow.

A few drops would be enough to help her heal faster. By tomorrow, the black and blue bruises would be gone, and her aching bones and muscles would feel less sore. There would be no adverse effects. Vampire blood was a cure for many human ailments, and if scientists only knew, they would be hunting him and his brethren. Luckily, they didn't even know vampires existed.

Sleep now.

Amaury kissed her forehead. With a last look at her face which already took on a more natural color than before, he left her room. His step was lighter than when he'd first entered the hospital.

26

Gabriel rushed through the entrance door Carl had opened for him.
"He's in his office."

He didn't even break his stride as he headed for Samson's office in the back of the house.

Samson looked up from his desk and motioned him to come in as he finished a call.

"Thanks, Thomas, and when you're done with it, we're meeting here at—" He looked at his watch. "—eleven o'clock. Call Ricky and Amaury for me, will you? Gabriel just got here."

He disconnected the call and stood up.

Gabriel hadn't taken a seat yet. He preferred standing.

"Give me the lowdown."

Samson always came right to the point. Gabriel appreciated that in his boss. No beating about the bush, no politics.

"We're sure it's Luther. Paul Holland confessed after a little persuasion by Zane."

Samson raised an eyebrow, but didn't say anything.

"After he broke, I was able to get through to him. Luther wants revenge, that's pretty clear, and not at all surprising, given what happened."

Samson nodded. "Understandable. After he lost Vivian and his unborn child, he nearly went crazy. There wasn't anything we could do to help him. He needed to blame somebody."

"Don't you think it would have been better if you had told him the truth?"

Samson shook his head. "Amaury and I decided it was better to keep the truth to ourselves. It would have killed him. When he disappeared, we first thought he'd followed her into death. Well, he didn't. Somehow I always knew he'd come back when he'd collected his strength. We knew we'd have to face him one day."

"Now what?"

"We prepare as best we can. I don't want him harmed, but we have to defend ourselves. Has Paul given you any indication as to what he's planning?"

"I doubt he knows. I couldn't find anything in his memories that would suggest he does, and Luther certainly is smart enough not to divulge too much information to his men. But you know him. He has a plan. He always did. We can be sure of that."

"Then we'd better have a plan, too. Have you alerted your people to him?"

"Yes, they all know now who he is. Everybody is working on finding where he's hiding out. We have a pretty good idea where he is. I found some hints pointing to a warehouse in Paul's memories. We're confirming it right now."

"Once my guys get here, we'll mobilize our side. Whom can we trust?"

Gabriel gave him a cautious look. "That's just it, we can't be sure."

"Why's that?"

"He's creating new vampires."

He could see his boss's jaw drop. "He *what*?"

Creating new vampires willy-nilly was a grievous offense in their society. One didn't just run around and turn people. It was irresponsible. "What's gotten into him? It's one thing to want to take his anger out on Amaury and me; it's another altogether to go around creating vampires."

"He's using it to gain loyal supporters. If they prove themselves loyal to him, he turns them, as a reward so to speak. At the same time he makes sure he's got some dirt on them, so they have no way of turning against him."

Samson looked straight at him.

"What kind of dirt?"

"He has them commit a crime for him, makes sure everybody knows who the culprit is, then saves and turns them. And thus he's created a loyal follower, somebody who owes him big. I think he's collecting an army. And he'll need it if he wants to destroy Scanguards."

"Is that what Paul thinks?"

"Yes. It looks like he wants to take the company down to hurt you and Amaury."

"Damn! How many does he have?"

"We have no way of knowing, but I suspect that our two bodyguards who killed their clients are some of them. I believe it was all a set-up."

"But they committed suicide."

Gabriel shook his head. "That's what eyewitnesses said, but the dead bodies couldn't be identified. The first one was burned to a crisp; the other bodyguard jumped into the Bay according to witnesses, and the body has not been found. The eyewitnesses could have been tampered with. For all we know, Luther used mind control to plant false memories into their minds so they would testify that they saw the two die."

"And they would even pass a lie-detector test," Samson continued, "because they wouldn't know they were lying. Clever."

"Yes, Luther was always smart."

"So for all we know, Edmund and Kent could be vampires. And supporting Luther. Who knows how many others he's turned before those two. Any idea?"

"Paul had no information on it."

Samson balled his hands into fists. "We have to stop him. He's gone crazy. Who is with us?"

Gabriel glanced at his boss. "I'd say only the inner circle. I suspect that Luther's been planning this for a long time."

"You're right. I'll assign my guys to the search. We'll coordinate with Zane and the others. Amaury can run the show."

Gabriel sighed. "About Amaury . . . "

"What about him?"

"I think his loyalties are divided right now."

Samson frowned. "Amaury's loyalty to me is without question."

"The woman," Gabriel said.

Samson paused and closed his eyes for a moment. "I hadn't thought of her. Damn, you're right. I'd hoped that finally something would change for Amaury. I don't know how much longer I can pretend I don't know what he's going through."

"What he's going through?"

"Yes, his gift." Samson sneered. "As if he can fool anybody."

"You know of his pain?"

"He's my oldest friend. I wouldn't be much of a friend if I didn't know the pain he's going through every day."

Gabriel gave Samson a surprised look. "And I thought I was the only one who knew, because I sensed his memories, as much as he was trying to shield them from me."

"When I saw him with Nina last night, I could feel that he was much calmer than usual, as if he was at peace. Whatever she's doing, it's good for Amaury. He needs a break. But I'm afraid we can't let him continue this, as much as I feel for him."

"Do you think she knows her brother could be with Luther?"

Samson clearly contemplated Gabriel's question. "If she does, then the reason she's with Amaury isn't his good looks."

"Shit." Gabriel didn't like that idea at all. If she was in her brother's camp, she would be a danger to Amaury and all of them. "He needs to know."

Samson nodded slowly. "I think you're right. We can't trust her. If she was as close to her brother as she claims, he would never have kept her in the belief that he's dead. We have to assume she knows."

"Then she's been using Amaury and us to help Luther."

"That's a distinct possibility." Samson looked straight at his second-in-command. "We have to contact Amaury and warn him."

27

"I know you're in there. Open the damn door, or I'll kick it in."

Impatiently, Amaury hovered outside of Nina's front door. The place was a dump. Sure, he didn't live in the best area of town either, but there was no way he'd let her continue living in this vermin-infested place. At least *he* had a good reason to live where he did.

"Go away." Nina's voice came from inside the apartment, the first sound he'd heard in the five minutes he'd been banging on the door. It was a start.

He lowered his voice, relying on his persuasive powers, knowing mind control didn't work on her. "Please, Nina. We need to talk. Let me in, *chérie*."

A moment later he heard a chain being released and the door being unlocked. Finally.

"Nina, please let me come in."

Nina opened the door and stepped back. He glanced at her face and recognized that she'd been crying. Had he done that? He felt like a complete and utter jerk for making her cry.

Quickly, before she could change her mind, he went inside, closed the door behind him and locked it.

"What do you want?" There was a good dose of defiance in her voice, and she served it up straight without any disguise. He deserved as much.

Amaury shifted his weight uncomfortably onto the other foot. It was critical that he didn't make a mistake with her. Despite the fact that he couldn't sense her emotions, he knew she was hurt. He was the reason for her big brown eyes reflecting sorrow and resignation. He realized he'd messed up. With his tendency of acting like a bull in a china shop, the odds of mending what he'd already screwed up weren't in his favor. No self-respecting bookie would take that bet.

"I want to apologize." Now there was a phrase he hadn't used much before. It felt strange coming from his lips, but it was the first thing that came to him.

Nina didn't answer. Instead, she looked at him with her big brown eyes, the hurt sitting deep within. It hit him in the gut, as if she'd punched him.

"I only wanted to protect you," Amaury tried again. "I was scared I would hurt you."

"You didn't want me."

How could four little words cause such pain? Didn't want her? That's what she thought?

"What did I do?"

"Nothing, you did nothing."

He didn't understand. Damn, why couldn't he sense her? Why couldn't he figure out what was wrong? "Please, Nina, talk to me, tell me what I did wrong."

She sniffed. "After I told you what I did, you didn't . . . " Her voice broke off.

"I didn't what?" he probed.

"It doesn't matter anymore. Please go."

"The hell I will. I won't leave. Nina, I'm not moving one inch until you've told me what's going on."

His statement seemed to get her dander up—good. He preferred it when she was fighting him rather than running away from him.

"What do you want, Amaury? Haven't you slummed it long enough?"

"Slummed it?" He grabbed her upper arm and pulled her close. "If you're referring to yourself when you talk about slum, I suggest you stop it right now."

"Give it up. You don't have to pretend you care. If you'd cared at all, you wouldn't have left me alone when I needed you. There, now you know. Now, go."

Amaury sighed with relief. That little misunderstanding had gotten her all riled up? If only everything were as easy to fix as this.

"You silly little kitten. Don't you know that I wouldn't have wanted anything more than to hold you in my arms?"

"Then why didn't you?" she barked, clearly not believing him yet.

Despite her resistance he pulled her into his arms. "Because my hands had turned into claws and my fangs itched for a bite. I was angry, *chérie*, and I wanted to hurt the man who did this to you. But I didn't want to hurt you. I couldn't hold you—please believe me. I wasn't in control of myself."

"I thought you didn't want me anymore because you know my past. You know I'm trash."

Amaury pulled back and looked at her face. "You, Nina, are the only good and innocent person in this room. You're not trash."

He kissed her softly on the cheek. "I will kill anybody who hurts you."

"I don't want you to kill for me. They're not worth it."

He shook his head. "You are the most confusing woman I've ever met. I need to know something." Amaury paused, knowing her answer was more important than anything. "Did you mean it when you offered me your blood tonight? Did you want me to bite you?"

He felt his heart lurch into his throat as he waited for her to respond.

"You didn't want it." It wasn't a straight answer, but he could work with that.

"How would you know?"

"Because you said so."

"I said I didn't want to hurt you."

"You won't hurt me."

"You have that much faith in me?"

She nodded. "You've protected me. Why would you hurt me now?"

"A woman's logic. How can I argue with that?" Amaury paused. "Nina, why do you want me to take your blood?"

She pressed her lips together.

"Why? Please tell me."

"Promise me first that you'll take my blood."

"Believe me, I'm so far gone, I won't be able to resist. I just want to know why."

"I don't want you to touch anybody else."

She was jealous? His heart skipped a beat. She was jealous! And possessive!

"You . . . I . . . oh, God." He had no words to express what he felt. Instead, he tightened his arms around her and brushed his lips against hers. They molded to him instantly.

"You're mine."

Mine.

So utterly right it felt to realize she was his, that no matter what, he wouldn't let go of her. Amaury took her lips in a fierce kiss, branding her, searing the memory of it into his brain. His lips felt raw when he released her, and Nina breathed as heavily as he did.

"You'd better tell me that you want me too." He searched her eyes for an answer.

"I do, but—" she started.

His heart leapt. She wanted him. "No buts. If you want me, you'll have me. All of me. And I take all of you. No reservations."

He felt her arms wrap around his torso as if she would never let go of him again.

"I'm—" He started to say "blessed," but he wouldn't let such profanity pass his lips. "Please tell me you want to be mine." He needed to hear it, needed to know he wasn't dreaming, he wasn't misinterpreting her.

Nina pulled away an inch and looked at him. "Amaury, I want you, but I'm scared you'll toss me aside when you've had enough of me."

"Silly woman. I might be an idiot, but I'm not stupid enough to let go of the best thing that's ever happened to me."

"Are you hungry now?" There was a wicked glint in her eyes.

He was ravenous. "Yes, hungry for your body and your blood."

"Does it hurt?"

Amaury smiled. "No. It will be like an orgasm rippling through your body." He shuddered at the thought of it. Soon, his fangs would dig into her vein and he would drink from her, while he impaled her on his shaft. There would be nothing better than to drink from the woman he desired while he made love to her.

Amaury took in a deep breath and inhaled her scent. She would be his woman. He'd never been so sure of anything else. Nina gave his mind peace and his body pleasure. As for his heart? If he didn't know any better, he'd say she was defrosting his heart too.

***

Nina felt self-conscious, the way he was devouring her with his eyes. No man had ever looked at her that way. Amaury looked imposing as he stood in her small studio, yet this powerful vampire had just confessed that he wanted her. Her, a nobody.

His hard body pressed against hers, and she could sense every muscle, one in particular. He desired her, and the evidence of it nudged against her stomach, hard and huge, begging for attention.

She knew she'd gone completely crazy, yearning to be with a vampire. Not just any, mind you, but Amaury. As if she had the same fascination with vampires as she'd recognized in Eddie's incoherent scribbles. And what had it gotten him? An early grave. Would her fate be the same if she played with fire—that fire being Amaury?

What if he was right and he couldn't control himself when he bit her? Would he bleed her dry? Yes, she was scared, but she was even more frightened of *not* being with him. Under his touch she'd been alive, and finally felt a connection to somebody. A connection she wasn't willing to give up no matter what it meant in the long run.

Nina wasn't thinking of a future. It was dangerous to dream of a future. It created expectations, and she didn't want that. She didn't want to expect something and then be disappointed. It only led to more pain.

If Amaury wanted her now, she would take that and hold on as long as she could, but brace herself for when he would realize that this wasn't meant to last.

She recognized the lust in his eyes and the hunger for her blood, but she didn't delude herself. He was a vampire, he was gorgeous, and he would remain young forever. She had nothing to offer him but her body and her blood. Maybe for a few weeks, or even a few months, he would be hers. And then he'd move on to another conquest.

But she wouldn't think of it, not tonight. Tonight she'd make a few memories she could keep for herself for when she was alone again.

"Are you gonna kiss me?" Nina asked him.

"Only if you tell me what's going on behind that furrowed forehead of yours. Are you having second thoughts? We don't have to do this if you don't want to. I'll be with you even if you don't want to give me your blood."

Nina shook her head. "No. I don't want you to do this with anybody else." Her objection came out harsher than she'd anticipated.

A huge grin spread over his entire face. "There's no need to be jealous."

"Jealous? Who's jealous?" She didn't want to be seen as some needy, nagging girlfriend. Men ran from that first chance they got.

"You, *chérie*. You're jealous." Amaury kissed along the edge of her jaw. "It's lovely." His lips trailed down her neck, planting feather-light kisses along the way.

She tilted her head to give him better access and held her breath. She would feel his fangs any moment now. Heart racing, her pulse beat a violent *tat-TAT-tat-TAT-tat-TAT* under her ribcage, and blood pounded in her ears.

Suddenly, he chuckled and lifted his head to meet her gaze. "You didn't think I was going to bite you just now?"

Nina tried to pull herself out of his arms. He was toying with her. "You—"

"Shh, Nina." He put his finger on her lips. "When I take your blood, I want to be making love to you. I want to feel your naked body joined with mine. I want you to remember this moment for the rest of your life and think back on it as the most amazing pleasure two people can ever experience together. This will be special for both of us. There's no way I'd rush this. Trust me, I want this more than you can even imagine."

Her heart leapt at his admission. She eased back into his embrace and moved her lips over his. "You can't possibly want this more than I do."

His soft laugh tickled her mouth. "If you want this only half as much as I do, I'll die a happy man."

"But aren't you immortal?"

"Pretty much. I guess I'll just have to be the happiest man alive then."

"You mean this will make you happy?"

"Not this, but *you*, *chérie*. Only you."

Amaury's kiss was soft and tender, almost reverent, as if he worshipped her. His mouth fitted to hers, nibbling gently on her lips, teasing and tasting. Nina inhaled his scent, a mixture of earth and leather, and she catalogued it. She would recognize him anywhere just by his lips and his scent.

Her senses were attuned to him, taking in every detail: how his skin felt, how he sounded, even the heartbeat she felt under her hand which she'd rested on his chest. The heartbeat of a vampire. A heart which beat rapidly and unevenly against her hand as if he wanted to tell her of his feelings in Morse Code. Just as farther down, his need pulsed against her in a different rhythm. His long, hard cock ground against her with every breath he took, assuredly and evenly.

She felt secure in his arms as he held her, one hand cradling the back of her neck, the other snaked around her waist. Only now she noticed that her feet didn't touch the ground. He'd lifted her up and kept her suspended in midair as if she weighed nothing.

"Am I dreaming?" she mumbled against his lips.

"If you are, then we're having the same dream. And I'd rather not ever wake up from it." His lips claimed hers, and this time he kissed her with more urgency, nudging her lips apart with his probing tongue, until she surrendered to his demand.

Nina felt him move, and moments later he lowered them onto the bed. As Amaury rolled to the side, his hand went underneath her T-shirt. The moment his fingers touched the naked skin on her back, she felt as if she would spontaneously combust. She couldn't stop a moan from escaping her lips, all the while turning into a puddle of unbridled desire.

His skillful tongue tunneled deeper and coaxed her body to feel more pleasure, while his thumb stroked upwards along her spine. Her trembling hands worked on the buttons of his shirt, but his mouth was too distracting for her to concentrate on anything else. She was unable to make her hands work in a coordinated fashion.

Nina released a frustrated sigh.

He instantly pulled away to look at her. "What's wrong?"

"I can't get those damn buttons open."

Amaury's chuckle sounded like music in her ears. It felt like a drizzle of warmth descending on her, calming her. "Why don't you just rip them open? I know you're good at that."

She didn't need another invitation. His damaged shirt landed on the floor a few seconds later. Before she could cuddle back into his chest, though, he pulled her T-shirt over her head.

"Much better," he commented, his eyes landing on her naked breasts. Under his hot gaze she felt her nipples turn hard. Nina noticed his wicked smile as he looked back at her face.

"Oh, yeah, much, much better. I hope you have no other plans for tonight, *chérie*, because I have no intention of ever letting you escape from my arms again."

"Promises, promises." She ran her fingernail over his chest, drawing a leisurely circle around his nipple. While his muscles were hard, his skin was surprisingly soft.

"You can take that promise to the bank; it's as good as gold."

"If I had a nickel for every promise—" She didn't get any further, but instead found herself pinned down by his body, his warm mouth kissing her lips.

"Be still, *chérie*, and let me love you." She'd never before heard him speak with such tenderness.

***

Amaury felt Nina's warm body underneath him, her delectable breasts crushed into his chest. The heat from her body seeped into him and ignited his cells. The draw she had on him was irresistible. Her scent created a cocoon around him, as if to shield him from everything else. She was the only woman he wanted to be with.

His hunger for her was palpable now. With difficulty he pushed it back, not wanting to cheapen this experience by haste. This would be a memory they would both cherish, an event they would look back at with joy.

Had any other woman ever given him such joy, sent such pleasure through his body? Her soft moans and sighs alone stoked the fire burning in him.

Amaury settled between her trusting thighs and let the hard ridge of his cock stroke against her center. Even through the clothes he could feel her wetness and her heat, as she responded to him by undulating her hips. Oh, yes, the little firecracker wanted him just as much as he wanted her. Even without sensing her emotions, he knew this little fact with certainty. And she would have him.

He drew back slightly to give his hands a chance at palming her gorgeous tits. The hard nipples screamed to be touched. Erect little buds, pink and hard, greeted his fingertips.

"Promise me, you'll never hide those from me under a bra." He wanted those ripe fruits always accessible to his hungry hands, never impeded by any restricting garments. All they should ever feel were his hands caressing them, his lips kissing them, and his mouth suckling greedily. Maybe even his fangs taking blood from right there, feeding from her. His cock jerked violently at the erotic image.

"Don't you like undressing me?" Nina was a tease, but he didn't mind.

"Oh, I like undressing you, but I don't want anything or anybody to cup those beautiful tits but me. I don't want a bra having more contact with them than I will. I could get jealous." He would be envious of the bra which would hold her twin globes all day as they bounced up and down. No, he should be the only one allowed to do that, to support her weight, to hold her, squeeze her, massage her.

"Is that an order?"

Amaury rubbed his fingertip over her nipple. "Let's just call it a . . . suggestion." He knew how little she would respond to an order.

Nina arched into his hand. "Any other . . . suggestions?" The sultry look she gave from under her lashes made his heart stop momentarily. Was she actually baiting him to make more demands? He had a few other requests tucked away which he wouldn't mind her complying with.

"A few. If you're up for them." Slowly he kneaded the pliable flesh in his palm. Then his lips descended onto her silken skin, and he let them slide over her nipple. His tongue lapped against her flesh, and his breath followed, ghosting over her damp skin.

Nina expelled a strangled moan while her nipple turned into a rock hard-peak. "Are you trying to kill me?"

"On the contrary, I'll make you feel more alive that you've ever been." Briefly he looked up from his delicious task to meet her gaze. "And *that's* a promise."

And he'd keep that promise.

Minutes later he had them both stripped naked. Nothing could get in the way of his eager mouth and hands now.

He was teetering on the edge of his control when he had her body beneath his once more. Her arousal was like a beacon leading him to a long-sought buried treasure. Amaury took a deep breath, inhaling her fragrance, letting it tease his nostrils, coat his tongue, and permeate his lungs. What sweet scent, what powerful drug she was to him.

For a moment, he kept himself still above her, his weight braced on his knees and arms, as he took in the sight. Nina's face was glistening, her honey curls rumpled, her eyes wide open, expectant, but not afraid.

"Please," was all she said, but her actions said more. Her legs wrapped around his waist, and slowly she pulled him down to her until his erection settled at the entrance to her core.

Warm moisture greeted him, inviting him. His body coiled with tension, anticipating her tightness, her heat, as he held himself back for another second just to savor the moment. Amaury felt the rightness of his decision, the determination in himself of what he needed to do.

"You're mine." His claim was like a battle cry, as he forged ahead and impaled her on his shaft, letting her tight muscles clamp down on him, imprison him in a cage he'd never be able to escape, would never want to.

"Oh, baby," she whispered breathlessly. Nobody had ever called him *baby*.

"Too big?"

Nina shook her head. "Perfect."

It was all he needed. Amaury withdrew from her tight sheath, let his cock slip out but for the bulbous head, before he plunged back into her wet heat. With every stroke his balls slapped against her flesh, only adding to the enticing sensation of her muscles gripping him.

Nina threw her head back and arched toward him, meeting his thrusts one for one. Her sensitive neck was exposed to his view, the vein under the pale skin throbbing, beckoning him, inviting him.

"Nina, I need you." He sank his lips onto her neck. A startled movement was her response. Had she changed her mind? Before he could pull back, he felt her hand on his neck, pressing him closer to her.

"Yes, Amaury."

Her words were like a symphony in his ears, like angels singing. He could smell her blood, almost taste it. His fangs lengthened, and then, without any haste, the sharp tips pricked her skin and drove in.

The scent of her blood assaulted him instantly, almost robbed him of his senses, so intense it was. The thick liquid coated his tongue and dripped down the back of his throat. Warm, sweet and plentiful it spread in his mouth. His first swallow was like a feast following a long famine. Rich, nourishing, and intoxicating.

His cock throbbed violently as the blood replenished his body, and the rhythm of his hips increased. Amaury heard her moan, uncontrolled and wild. Nina's nails dug into his back as she bucked against him.

The moment he felt her mouth on his shoulder and her teeth digging into him, he knew what he needed. Her blunt human teeth would never pierce his skin, but he could do it for her. He couldn't stop his next action. It was as if his heart had immobilized his brain and dictated his body's movements. His mind wasn't master anymore. For the first time in his life as a vampire, his heart ruled supreme.

As if in a trance, Amaury removed his fangs from her neck and pulled back. Nina instantly let go of his shoulder. "Don't stop, please, don't stop," she begged.

"I won't." With his nail, he cut into the skin of his shoulder. Seconds later blood seeped from the cut. He looked into her passion clouded eyes. "Drink from me, *chérie*, please, let me be yours."

He watched her expression change, first to surprise, then to interest. But there was caution in it too, and doubt.

"It won't turn you into a vampire, you'll stay human. But I'll be yours." And she would be his, forever his mate. Blood-bonded for eternity. Bound to him. For him to protect forever. His heart had made the decision for him. There was no way back from it. He would explain all details to her later, but right now he couldn't stop this magical moment.

Nina's mouth descended onto the cut. Her tongue darted out and lapped at the blood, before she locked her lips around it and started suckling.

Her action sent a thunderbolt through his body. Amaury's chest released a triumphant growl. A moment later he sank his fangs back into her neck.

"Always."

And then he could feel her, finally sense her emotions. Now it was a different hunger he needed to still, not the need for blood to nourish him, but for her blood to complete him, to establish their unbreakable bond.

Nina's blood filled him and mixed with his own in a process that would change both their DNA, mysteriously, irrevocably. If she wanted to, he could father children with her. But most of all he would always be aware of her, sense her, know what she was feeling, just as she would with him. Their souls would be connected.

The sense of peace spreading within him warmed his heart. Nina was his.

Amaury released her neck and withdrew his fangs. His tongue smoothed over the incisions and sealed them instantly.

Nina's mouth still sucked on his shoulder, and he was caught up in the sensation it caused in him. She was taking his essence into him, accepting him for what he was.

"Yes, take me inside you," he whispered into her ear.

With every drop of blood she took from him, he felt her excitement grow. She was so slick, his cock slipped back and forth in rapid succession, pumping into her, hitting her sweet spot with every stroke.

He used every last ounce of his control to hold back his release until he finally felt her breathing become erratic and her body tense up. A second later her climax crashed over her, and her muscles clenched around him. With a last thrust, he stabbed into her, touching her womb and flooding her with his seed. His cock pulsated, releasing stream after stream into her warm sheath.

Nina's mouth went slack on his shoulder. She'd stopped drinking from him.

Her eyes were closed when he looked at her.

"Nina, are you okay?"

She blew out a breath, a drop of his blood on her swollen lips. "Hmm."

Amaury kissed her softly.

Mine.

28

Nina felt different. Never had sex affected her like this. If she didn't know any better, she'd say Amaury was a magician, not a vampire. Strange feelings swarmed her head, making her feel almost dizzy. Sensations of possessiveness, affection, and satisfaction invaded her thinking. Were those her thoughts? Why was she suddenly thinking in such terms?

After all, this was just sex. She knew men well enough to realize that even if they found a partner who could fulfill their sexual needs, it didn't mean they would not stray and try to find variety with somebody else. She wasn't naïve.

Nina tried to shake off the strange emotions. Maybe her blood-sugar level was low and she needed to eat. That would explain why she felt so woozy. Of course, a mind-blowing orgasm such as the one she'd had thanks to the tremendous skills of one super-sexy vampire could also cause said wooziness.

She lifted her head from Amaury's chest to look at him. He'd pulled her on top of him, sprawled her over his body moments after his climax had shaken him violently. She'd never seen a man lose control like that. As if he'd let go of all walls, all protection, all pretense.

"You've slayed me," he said without opening his eyes, his mouth curling into a smile.

"That was pretty good." Nina downplayed their lovemaking. She wouldn't fall into the trap of becoming a clingy girlfriend now. For sure it would make him run faster than if she were chasing him with a stake. Sure, he'd said amazing things to her—that he wanted to be hers—but that was during the heat of passion. She never put much weight on what a man said in bed.

Amaury's eyes flew open, and he pinned her with an intense stare. "Pretty good?" His chest muscles bunched underneath her. "That's all you've got to say?"

Oh, now she was in trouble. The man wanted to hear more than just a "pretty good" for his efforts. She never knew he'd turn into such a hawk for compliments.

"Well, it was very good."

He propped his head up. "Very good?"

Evidently "very good" wasn't sufficient either.

"How about 'spectacular,' 'out of this world,' 'mind blowing'?" he coaxed.

Nina's heart leapt. He'd felt that too?

"God, woman, are you trying to give me an inferiority complex?"

His exasperated huff made her chuckle. Making him mad turned out to be great fun. "Inferiority complex? You? I don't think I could succeed even if I tried. You're just way too full of yourself."

A second later she found herself underneath him, pinned between him and the mattress, a position she increasingly enjoyed. "Full of myself, huh?" Amaury nudged his already swelling cock against her. "Shall I show you again what it feels like to be *full* of me?"

There wasn't the slightest doubt in her mind as to what he meant.

"Are you sure I need another demonstration?"

His breath ghosted over her cheek. "*Chérie*, I'm going to give you as many demonstrations as you need, until you're ready to admit that I fulfill your every need." His hips moved, settling his heavy cock at her sex. Nina moved against him, making his erection slide over her still sensitive clit. A hitched breath escaped her.

"Tell me, when my cock strokes you like this, do you want me to go slow, or would you rather I fuck you hard and fast?"

Sweat beaded on her brow. It became difficult to breathe with the vivid imagery he projected. "Do I have to make a decision right now?"

His hips circled, drawing his erection over her center of pleasure once more. "No. You can just let me take care of you as I see fit."

"Are you always this possessive?"

"Possessive—*moi*?" He grinned unashamedly. "It's definitely a first for me."

Amaury drew his hips back and slowly slid into her moist channel. Involuntarily, Nina bucked against him, welcoming his hard shaft as he filled her.

"Do you always have to be on top?"

"Not always, but right now I want to see your face when I make you come. There's nothing more enticing than watching how your eyes go all dreamy." He punctuated his word with a thrust of his cock. "And your lips part." Another thrust. "Your cheeks flush." He plunged deeper.

"I think I get your point," she rasped. He did have a way of supporting his explanations with examples.

"Of course, there's also much to be said for other positions," he hedged and withdrew his erection.

"Such as?"

He pulled back from her and masterfully flipped her onto her stomach. "Such as the view of your sexy derrière when I fuck you from behind."

He palmed her round cheeks, sending a shiver through her body. "I believe I still owe you a spanking," Amaury announced.

"What for?" She sounded far too eager in her own ears. Would he notice that?

"You flipped me off last night. Such lack of respect can't be tolerated."

"I understand." Nina lifted her backside slightly toward him in anticipation. "I was bad."

"Really bad," Amaury confirmed. "But I'm not cruel."

A wave of disappointment swept over her. He wasn't going to punish her? Now that she'd gotten all excited about it. "No?"

"No. So, for every slap you endure without protest, you'll be rewarded."

"How?" Her voice echoed in the small room. The thumping of her heart reached her ears, almost deafening her.

"That's for me to decide." His hands stroked suggestively over her ass, before one slipped along her crack and swept over her female folds. One long finger dipped into her heat, wringing a strangled moan from her throat. Nina clenched her muscles to hold onto him, but as quickly as he'd invaded her, he escaped.

***

Amaury gazed at Nina's nude body, the enticing swells of her sexy derrière arched toward him. He'd truly struck gold. His blood-bonded mate wasn't only gorgeous and strong, she enjoyed the same diversions in bed that he loved to indulge in.

His chest swelled with pride when he looked at her and contemplated his fate. She'd accepted him, taken his blood and bonded with him. The knowledge that she was his forever couldn't be compared to anything else he'd ever experienced.

And he'd start off their relationship right, by asserting his claim on her and showing her what she could expect from him in the coming centuries: mind-blowing sex, utter devotion and his protection to the death. He'd start it off with a bang, or rather, a slap.

Amaury pulled her onto her hands and knees. A moment later his flat palm connected with her flesh, making her ass jiggle. Only a suppressed moan came over her lips.

"Good girl," he praised and centered himself behind her, nudging his cock at the entrance to her hot channel. Her pink folds glistened like flower petals after a spring rain, and her juices coated the head of his shaft as he slid an inch deep then stopped. Nina tried to shift toward him to take him deeper, but he held her in place.

"No, Nina. You'll only get as much as you deserve." He clenched his jaw, trying to fight the tightness with which she squeezed the tip of his cock. He only hoped he'd last long enough to make her come. The way he felt right now, he had serious doubts. He felt like an untried youth who spilled the moment he felt a woman's touch.

"More," Nina demanded, her voice husky. God, how she turned him on with just a sound. Like a siren's call.

Amaury answered her with a quick slap on the other cheek. A little harder this time, leaving a faint palm print. He felt the movement extend to his cock as her muscles clenched around him. It sent a delicious tingle into his balls which instantly drew up and tightened. In the same movement she pushed back and took him deeper.

Amaury paddled her backside immediately to make her aware of his disapproval. "Stop it, Nina." And for good measure he slapped her once again, left, right. She moaned into the mattress.

His hand went into her hair and he drew her head up. "Let me hear you. There's no shame it admitting you like it rough. " In fact, he welcomed it, the knowledge that Nina wanted what he had to offer.

His cock was halfway inside her, and he didn't have the willpower to pull out. The vibrations each slap sent down his cock and into his balls were too much to resist. With every wave her sheath gripped him tighter and drew him deeper.

"Damn it, Amaury, do it again!" His vixen was going all wild on him, just how he liked it. Now she was ready for him.

"That's my girl." With the next stinging slap to her delectable derrière, he drove his cock into her to the hilt, his balls slapping against her pussy. He realized he would come too soon. Snaking his arm around her front, he dropped his hand to the juncture of her thighs and found her sensitive little nub of pleasure.

Amaury moistened his fingers with her juices and drew the engorged button up, tugging on it gently. Her muscles clenched around his shaft in response. Damn, but she was tight.

"Fuck, Nina, you're killing me."

She let out a gurgle of a laugh and met his next thrust with even more ferocity. He repaid her by pinching her clit in the same instance, tearing an uncontrolled scream from her throat. The little temptress was trying to steal his control, but she didn't know him well enough yet to realize that he wouldn't allow himself to come before he'd sent her over the edge.

"Come for me baby—you want this," Nina teased.

"You first!"

Amaury lowered his head to her neck and sank his lips onto her skin, kissing her as he continued to torture her engorged nub with his fingers. His teeth scraped against her neck, eliciting a shiver from her.

"Not fair," she complained and moaned.

"All's fair in love and war."

Love?

He had no time to contemplate it. A moment later a visible shudder went through her, and then he felt it, the ripples traveling through her and hitting his body. With a triumphant groan he drove into her again and tumbled over the edge, finding his release in her shaking body, robbing him of all his senses.

29

Amaury found himself cradling Nina in his arms, her back tucked into his chest, her derrière fitting perfectly into his groin. Had he fallen asleep after their lovemaking? Well, he was awake now, and so was his cock which for some reason was slowly sliding back and forth along her pussy. The moisture oozing from her soft petals coated his shaft. Was that what had woken him?

Damn, but he was randy. Could he not even keep away from her in his sleep? He brushed a lock of hair out of her face and trailed his fingers over her neck. His bite marks weren't visible anymore, but her blood was coursing through his veins and his through hers.

He would never take blood from anybody else again. Nina would be his only source for life now. Vampires blood-bonded to humans—rather than to other vampires—rejected all other blood. Only the blood of their mates could sustain them as long as they were bonded. It ensured absolute fidelity, trust, and devotion for the blood-bonded couple. Not that Amaury thought he would ever want to touch another woman but Nina, not even without the blood-bond.

His sleeping beauty had no idea what power it gave her over him. He would explain it to her once they'd settled into their new life together.

He smoothed his palm over her shoulder and kissed her pale skin.

Nina stirred. With long, slow strokes he moved his hips back and forth, sliding languidly along her warm entrance.

"Are you trying to take advantage of me while I'm asleep?" her sleepy voice asked.

"Would you like me to?"

Instead of an answer, Nina lifted her leg slightly and with her hand guided his erection into her. Her sheath was drenched with her juices and his seed. He'd never known a more welcoming feel.

"I took you hard earlier. Aren't you sore?" He slowly moved in and out, letting her body's rhythm guide his movements.

"And your point is?"

A loud bang at the door prevented him from answering. Then the sound of a familiar voice. "Amaury!"

Amaury cursed under his breath. Nina turned her head, an anxious look on her face. "Who is that?" she whispered.

"I know you're in there."

"Hold your horses, Thomas." He gave Nina a reassuring look. "It's nothing to worry about. He's a good friend." Amaury kissed her. "We should get dressed." His friend had better have a good reason for showing up at Nina's place. For sure, his timing sucked.

Minutes later, Amaury let an impatient-looking Thomas into the apartment. Thomas nodded curtly at Nina then addressed Amaury.

"You didn't answer your cell."

Amaury remembered having set the ringer to silent because he didn't want to be disturbed. "How did you find me?"

"Let's just say I had a hunch where you'd be when I didn't find you at home." His gaze went to Nina. "Excuse me, I haven't introduced myself. I'm Thomas."

He stretched his hand out to shake Nina's. Amaury's stomach twisted when he saw his friend touch her, despite the touch being innocent. Was this how he would feel from now on when another male came close to her? Damn, was he in for a rollercoaster ride.

"Nice to meet you, Thomas. I'm Nina."

He recognized how Thomas inhaled sharply then pinned him with a surprised look. Before his friend could comment on what he'd observed, Amaury continued the conversation.

"Why were you looking for me?"

Thomas' gaze drifted around the room, clearly examining the messy bed. "It's not I who's looking for you. I'm here on Samson's orders. We have a lead on Luther."

"What's the plan?"

"We're going in." Thomas looked at his watch. "Let's move. It's already taken me over an hour to find you. Everybody is assembling at Samson's."

Amaury looked at his mate. "Nina, get your jacket. You're coming with me."

Thomas raised an eyebrow. "I don't think that's wise."

"I'm not leaving her unprotected."

"Amaury, I can stay here if your friend doesn't—"

He cut her off. "No, you're coming with me." He gave Thomas a warning look. There'd be no way in hell he'd leave her alone while Luther was out there. If Thomas could smell that he'd bonded with her, so could Luther. He'd just put her in more danger than she was ever in before. By making her his, Amaury had given his enemy another front on which to attack.

Nina turned to the closet next to the bathroom.

Thomas took a step toward Amaury. "You blood-bonded with her?" He kept his voice low so Nina couldn't overhear their discussion.

"Yes. And it's none of your business."

"Have you gone completely crazy?"

"I said it's none of your business."

"What's none of his business?" Nina's voice came from behind him.

Amaury spun around. He wouldn't communicate Thomas's disapproval of their union to her and taint their happiness tonight. "Nothing, *chérie*. You ready?"

He took her hand and made for the door. "You coming, Thomas?"

A low grumble came from Thomas as he followed them out the door. Amaury imagined what his friend was thinking, but couldn't sense his emotions. No wonder: after the amazing sex he'd had with Nina, he wouldn't be able to sense anybody's emotions for maybe as long as an hour. His head felt great, and not even Thomas's annoyance could change that.

"I'm here with my Ducati," Thomas announced when they stepped outside.

"I have the car here. We'll follow you." At least he would get a few more minutes alone with Nina.

As soon as they sat in his Porsche and drove off, Amaury turned to Nina. "I'll have to leave you at Samson's house so you'll be protected."

"Don't be ridiculous. I don't need protection."

He sensed her resistance.

"You won't win this battle, so you might as well throw in the towel now. You're my woman, and Luther will not hesitate to use that fact against me."

"Your woman? My, where do you get those expressions from? This is the twenty-first century, if you haven't noticed yet. I'm my own woman."

Amaury put his hand on hers and squeezed it. Nina couldn't accept that he was there to protect her? He had to have chosen the most fiercely independent woman as his mate, hadn't he? *"Chérie*, you are mine as much as I'm yours. Get used to it."

Amaury pulled her hand to his mouth and kissed it. He felt himself get hard in response and shifted in his seat to accommodate his swelling cock.

"Do you always have to get your way?"

He gave her a serious look. "Not necessarily. But you have to understand one thing: you're mine to protect, and nobody will prevent me from doing so—not even you."

He brought the car to a stop outside of Samson's Victorian home. Thomas was already parking his motorcycle.

Before Nina could open the door, he pulled her into his arms. "Promise me, you'll stay at Samson's until I'm back."

Her eyes looked at him, searching, questioning, as if she wanted to protest, but then she simply said, "Fine."

He took her lips and kissed her fiercely. Despite her initial resistance, Nina yielded to him and parted her lips. Amaury moaned and dove into her, possessing her mouth, sparring with her tongue, tasting her sweetness. Did he deserve such luck as to have a woman like her?

A knock at the window pulled him out of his bliss. Thomas was getting impatient.

And it turned out he wasn't the only one who was impatient. The moment they entered Samson's house, he and Thomas were commanded to the office.

Samson expected them together with the rest of the gang: the four New York vampires and Ricky. Without giving Amaury as much as a glance, Samson pointed at a blueprint.

"This is the warehouse where we believe Luther is operating from. We think he has at least four or five men with him. Zane and Yvette will take the back entrance, Gabriel and Quinn will come in from the roof, I'll be with Thomas going in the front. Amaury and Ricky, you take the side."

"Weapons?" Gabriel asked.

"Stakes and semiautomatic guns with silver bullets. Ricky, get them out from the arsenal below when we're done here," Samson ordered and threw him a set of keys.

"I want to take him alive, but if your lives are in danger, you know what to do. His men are all new vampires; they are most likely inexperienced. We can use this against them."

Finally he looked at Amaury. "Where's Nina?"

Amaury didn't like the way the question sounded. "In the living room with Delilah."

"You brought her here?" Samson seemed outraged.

Amaury squared his chest. "She needs to be protected."

"We can't trust her. We have reason to believe her brother Edmund isn't dead, but was turned into a vampire by Luther. We think he's working for him."

Amaury felt his throat constrict. "Are you sure?"

"Ninety-nine percent," Gabriel answered in Samson's stead.

"She's most likely a mole and has been handing information to Luther all along," Samson went on.

Amaury shook his head. No. This wasn't possible. Nina wouldn't do that. She was his mate. He would sense if she were betraying him.

Thomas cleared his throat. "Are you gonna tell them, or should I?"

He looked at his gay friend and swallowed hard, before he met his boss's and best friend's inquisitive stare. "I'm blood-bonded to Nina. And as such I will defend her with my life, no matter whose side she's on."

Amaury barely heard the collective gasps and mumbled comments of his colleagues as he looked at Samson's reaction. His friend closed his eyes briefly, then looked back at him.

"Amaury, how? What happened?"

Amaury shrugged, not being able to explain it himself. All he knew was that Nina was his, and she would remain his. If she was indeed helping Luther's side, he would do everything to turn her away from him. And if his own friends wanted to harm her, he'd take her away from here and live in exile with her. As long as he was with her nothing else mattered.

"She's mine, Samson. You of all people should know what it feels like. It was the only thing I could do."

Samson nodded slowly. "You know what this means, don't you?"

"I'm prepared to face the consequences. If she's guilty, all I ask is that you give us a day's head start. I'll sign my interest in the company over to you."

Samson's mouth dropped open. "You would leave us for her?"

Amaury had never been so sure of anything else in his life. He would exchange two-hundred years of friendship for eternity with Nina in a heartbeat.

"She's mine to protect. There's nothing I wouldn't do for her." Amaury widened his stance, ready to prove he wasn't bluffing.

"She's played you," Gabriel accused him. "You of all people. Didn't I warn you this could only end badly? But you didn't want to listen, did you? How did she get you to do it? Is she really that good in bed that you'd give her such power over you? Are you that far gone?"

Livid with rage, Amaury lifted his arm and swung—but didn't connect with Gabriel's face. Instead, he found himself being restrained by Samson. Amaury twisted out of his grip and faced him.

"When I'm done with Gabriel, I'll deal with you!" Yes, he'd given Nina power over him, but he trusted her with his life—she wouldn't betray him. "Nobody gets away with insulting my mate."

A nod of Samson's head and Zane and Quinn took hold of Amaury, their grip viselike. No matter how furiously he tried to shake them off, he couldn't shake loose.

Then Samson shoved a pointed finger at his chest. "You, my friend, listen to me now. We're going to take out Luther, and you can either be with us or against us. Nina will remain here—Carl will watch her. If she does anything suspicious, Carl will restrain her. And there's not a thing you can do about it. Delilah will talk to Nina."

Samson's wife was a former auditor and as such had an uncanny way of finding out information. "We'll see what she can find out. If it turns out she's innocent, you'll get my sincerest apologies, but in the meantime, my word is law. So, what's it gonna be?"

Amaury pulled against Quinn and Zane, but the two didn't give an inch. With defiance he glared at Samson. "I'm with you, but if anybody harms her, God help him, because I'll hunt him down and tear his heart out."

Samson nodded. A moment later the two New York vampires released him.

Samson's basement was a veritable arsenal of weapons. The need to survive two centuries of wars had made it necessary to be prepared for everything.

Amaury took his weapons—several stakes and a semi-automatic with silver bullets—and familiarized himself with the blueprint of the building. Everybody did the same. Nervous energy rippled through the room. Again, Samson made sure each member of the team knew their position.

After they synchronized their watches, they stalked upstairs.

Amaury watched how Samson pulled Delilah into the kitchen for a private talk. Nina stood in the hallway. He saw her look at the vampires as they congregated there. Nobody said a word, yet they eyed her suspiciously. Amaury took her aside and stepped into the living room with her.

"We're going to smoke out Luther." Did she know this already? He searched her eyes, but found nothing suspicious, only concern. For him?

"Take me with you."

"No. It's too dangerous. You're safer here." If she *was* truly on Luther's side, she would interfere and give their positions away. And in the melee? She could get hurt.

Amaury sensed her apprehension and wrapped her into his embrace. Not wanting to be overheard by his colleagues, he whispered into her ear, "*Chérie*, please stay here. If anything happened to you, it would kill me."

Nina lifted her lashes and looked up at him. "You come back in one piece, okay?"

"I promise."

She attempted a smile, but it was miserable at best, as if she knew of the danger ahead. "Can I take that to the bank?"

He chuckled, trying to put her at ease. "Like a cashier's check—it's guaranteed." He took her lips and kissed her passionately. Her arms tightened around him, and her lips responded with the same passion as earlier in the night. No, his Nina was no traitor. She couldn't be. This kiss felt true, not like a lie.

With his mind, Amaury reached out to her, but before he connected with Nina's mind, Gabriel's voice came from the hallway. "Ready everybody?"

Amaury pulled himself out of Nina's arms. It was time to fight.

30

"I'm hungry. How about you?"

Nina turned to Delilah who stood at the door to the kitchen. "How can you eat now?"

The house was eerily quiet now that all vampires but the butler were gone.

"I can always eat. And right now I eat for two. How about I cook us something? Come, join me." She waved her into the kitchen, and Nina followed.

"You don't look fat. I can't believe you're eating for two." She didn't mean to insult her, but Samson's wife truly looked perfectly proportioned.

Delilah laughed. "I'm pregnant. Juice? Water?" She pointed at the bottles in the fridge.

"Water is fine." Nina took a seat at the counter. "I was wondering whether you were human or not, but I guess that clears it up. I'm assuming vampires can't get pregnant."

"Amaury didn't tell you? Men, they often forget the most obvious things."

She and Amaury hadn't exactly had an awful lot of time to talk. They'd barely discussed their own relationship, if it could even be called a relationship.

"Here." Delilah handed her a glass.

Nina took a sip.

"I'm sure he'll explain all important things to you soon. When I first blood-bonded with Samson, there was so much I didn't know—"

"Excuse me, explain *what* to me?" She couldn't follow Delilah's ramblings, as nice as the woman was.

"The blood-bond and everything that goes with it." Her hostess made it sound like that was the most obvious answer.

"That's okay. I don't really need to know anything about that. Once this is all over I'll just go back to my regular life. The less I know the better." It wasn't like she wanted to write a book about the mating habits of vampires.

Delilah's face looked distraught. "But you can't leave him now."

"Amaury?" No, she didn't want to leave him, but there was no future in whatever they had. She wasn't naïve. Amaury had everything. There was no reason for him to saddle himself with somebody like her. Sure, she could try to keep him interested in her for as long as possible, but at some point he would stray and look for something new. "That's really just a fling." She had to downplay what they had. The less importance she gave whatever was between them, the better.

"A fling? Nina, you don't blood-bond with a fling." Delilah's tone was scolding.

"Who says anything about blood-bonding?" How old-fashioned was Delilah? Just because she'd slept with Amaury didn't mean she'd get to marry him. And besides, hadn't Amaury said he wasn't the promise kind of guy?

"But you and Amaury are blood-bonded."

Now the poor woman had obviously gone off the deep end. Was that what pregnancy did to women? "No offense, but what gives you that crazy idea?" Nina reached for her glass and brought it to her lips.

"Amaury told Samson that you blood-bonded."

The water spewed from Nina's mouth as she almost choked. "What?" Something was seriously wrong here.

Delilah gave her a startled look. "You mean you don't know?" Her forehead wrinkled even more.

"I didn't do anything."

Frantically, Nina searched her memory for everything Amaury had ever told her about blood-bonding. She remembered Luther's story clearly, but at no point had Amaury explained how it actually worked. Why would he say such an outrageous thing to Samson?

Delilah came around the counter and sat on the stool next to her. "Tell me what happened earlier tonight when you were with Amaury."

Nina felt heat rise into her cheeks. She couldn't possibly discuss her sex life with a woman she'd met only twice. "Sorry, but I can't."

She felt Delilah's warm hand on her arm. "It's important. Tell me what happened."

With a reluctant movement, Nina opened her mouth. "We had sex."

"That goes without saying. What happened during sex?"

Nina cleared her throat. She wanted details? "Can you be a little bit more specific?" She felt her cheeks flush.

"Did Amaury take your blood?"

The rush of blood to her head suddenly made her feel dizzy.

"Yes, but he feeds from others, and that doesn't mean he blood-bonds with them." There had to be some kind of misunderstanding. She knew for a fact that vampires fed off humans without any aftereffects. In fact, when she'd first started investigating Eddie's death and followed some of them, she'd seen them feeding. That had been proof positive that they were vampires.

She felt Delilah's hands on her shoulders, shaking her out of her thoughts.

"Did you take his blood?"

Nina's cheeks burned with embarrassment. In the heat of passion she had sucked his blood and, by God, she'd found it erotic. But no way would she admit this to a stranger. It was hard enough to admit it to herself. And besides, he'd promised her it wouldn't turn her into a vampire. Had he lied to her?

"Did you?"

Nina looked straight at her hostess. "No, that'd be gross!" The lie rolled off her lips like water.

"It's one of the most erotic things to do with your partner. Whenever I drink from Samson—"

"You drink his blood?"

Delilah nodded. "It's part of the bond. At first, it establishes the connection. Then later it sustains it. Nina, please tell me the truth. Did you drink from him while you had sex, and while he drank from you?"

Nina closed her eyes and nodded.

"You blood-bonded with him. He was telling Samson the truth. You are his mate."

His mate. She—she was Amaury's mate. For eternity. Always. This couldn't be true. "Why would he do that?" Amaury didn't love her—he'd admitted that he couldn't love. She knew their relationship was only temporary.

"He didn't explain that to you? Then I guess, he didn't ask for your permission either?"

Nina remembered the one thing he had asked her. "Unless you consider his question 'do you want me?' as asking permission."

"Hardly," Delilah said. "Did he just bite you without asking you? You could bring charges against him. Samson can bring it up with the council. How despicable of him!" She seemed truly annoyed with Amaury.

"Not exactly. I did ask him to bite me, but I didn't know what it meant." Suddenly she felt true anger well up in her. The arrogant macho jerk had done it again: he'd imposed his will on her. As if his wish was her command! "That son of a bitch! He tricked me! He knew what he was doing, and he did it anyway. He's gonna pay for that. I'll feed him his balls for breakfast, and then I'm out of here!"

Fury coursed through her. He had blood-bonded with her without asking her, without explaining anything, like she was some woman who had no rights. What century was he living in? She'd show that bastard what he could do with his blood-bond.

"Nina, you can't leave."

There was a firm determination in Delilah's voice that made Nina level a gaze of refusal at her.

"I can and I will. This is over! If he thinks he can treat me like some piece of property, he can go right back into the Dark Ages where he's from."

"Seventeenth century, actually," Delilah interjected.

"Whatever. Amaury and me—that's history!"

"Nina. Maybe I should explain something about the blood-bond to you, since obviously nobody else has."

"I know more than I ever wanted to know about it. I don't need to know anything else. It's over!"

Delilah cleared her throat. "Maybe I should pour you a brandy. I think you'll need it."

Suspicion crept up Nina's spine and settled uncomfortably at her nape. "I don't need a brandy. Say what you've got to say."

"A blood-bond is forever. Only death can sever it."

"Ah, fuck! Please tell me you're kidding."

Slowly Delilah shook her head. That's when the realization broadsided her. Amaury had told her that a blood-bonded human lived as long as her mate. It meant that she was bonded to Amaury for eternity. And she hadn't been given a choice about it. He, caveman that he was, had decided for her. This changed *everything*.

"Oh, wait until I get my hands on him!" And that was a promise *he* could take to the bank.

31

The minivan came to a stop half a block from the warehouse. Oliver killed the engine. He would be the lookout while the vampires went in.

"This is the place," Samson said.

"Are we sure?" Amaury asked, glancing out the window.

Gabriel nodded. "It looks exactly like in Paul Holland's memories. This is Luther's base. Paul couldn't lie about it even if he wanted to. Luther should have been more careful about what he allowed him to see. Now we'll get him." The scar on his face throbbed.

"You all know what to do. Let's get into positions. Gabriel calls the shots," Samson ordered.

"Communication equipment on." Gabriel touched the little device sticking out from his ear. The others did the same. "Checking."

Amaury heard the sound of Gabriel's voice in his earpiece. Everything worked fine.

They scrambled out of the van. Amaury stretched his legs and looked around. The neighborhood was industrial and on the other side of the train tracks, if not to say the wrong side of the tracks. A few blocks down was San Francisco Bay, a couple of blocks up the Potrero Hill neighborhood. The streets were deserted. It was better that way. Nobody would call the cops once the fight started.

Amaury tensed. It would be over soon, but so much for him depended on the outcome. Was Nina truly on the other side, or was she just as much a pawn as Paul Holland had been? Maybe drawn in by some promises Luther had made and would never keep? In a short time, he'd know the truth, and it scared him.

His entire future depended on the truth. He would never leave her. She was his mate and he was responsible for her life now, as she was for his.

"Ready?" Ricky's voice came from behind.

Absentmindedly he nodded. "As ready as I'll ever be."

The group split up, every pair making their way to their prearranged place, covering the various entry points to the building. Ricky and Amaury walked side by side, gliding silently toward the side entrance.

The closer they came to the entry door, the more worried Amaury was. He was supposed to help the group by sensing anybody's emotions from the inside, yet right now he couldn't even sense what Ricky was feeling. And the guy walked right next to him.

It had been over two hours since he'd had sex with Nina, and his gift—or whatever one wanted to call it—still hadn't returned. Sex had never blocked out his ability for this long before. At most he would be free of emotions for half an hour, but never this long. If it didn't come back in the next couple of minutes, he and his friends would be at a severe disadvantage.

"Everybody in place?" Gabriel's voice resonated loud and clear in Amaury's ear.

"Zane and I are at the back," was Yvette's reply.

"Thomas and I, ready," Samson said.

"Amaury and I are at the side. Ready whenever you are." Ricky looked at him.

"Any activity from the inside, Amaury?" Gabriel asked over the earpiece.

Should he lie or tell him the truth? "Nothing from the inside."

"What do you mean? Specifics please."

"I mean I can't sense anything." Amaury recognized that he was getting irritable.

"Nobody inside?" Samson asked for clarification.

Amaury huffed. "I don't fucking know, okay?"

Ricky cut him a surprised glare. Several voices came through the earpiece at the same time, before Samson's voice burst through.

"Explain yourself, Amaury."

The earpiece fell silent. "I haven't been able to sense anybody's emotions since I bonded with Nina. Even before that things were getting sketchy—almost like blackouts. I think I've lost my gift." He was certain the moment he spoke. It had started slowly with the first time he'd met Nina. And while at the beginning his inability to sense any emotions had been confined to her alone, it had spread—slowly, but with ever increasing range.

Each additional moment he'd spent with Nina had wiped out more of his so-called gift. The temporary release that he'd only ever felt right after sex, had extended further and further the more contact he'd had with Nina.

He realized now that by bonding with her he'd hammered the last nail into the coffin with which to bury his hated gift.

It was over. His curse wasn't coming back. His psychic ability was lost.

And all he could think of was how free and happy he suddenly felt.

"Fucking perfect timing," Ricky hissed.

"Stop it!" Samson ordered. "We'll have to do without it then. We'll manage. Gabriel, at your command."

"Test your access points," Gabriel instructed.

The side door was locked. Ricky worked on the lock.

"Back?"

"Open," Zane confirmed.

"Front?"

"Thirty seconds," Thomas paused. Then, "Okay, front is open."

"Side?"

"Almost there," Amaury answered, watching Ricky. A nod from Ricky, and Amaury corrected, "Done."

"Ready on the roof. Give us fifteen seconds. Fourteen . . ." Gabriel's voice trailed off.

Amaury counted silently. Ricky's lips moved: *ten, nine, . . .* as Amaury gripped his semi-automatic with both hands. Tense seconds passed.

Now, his friend mouthed and swung the door open silently. Amaury eased inside and pressed himself against the wall next to the door, his eyes scanning the darkness inside. Ricky slid next to him a second later.

There was a musty smell in the warehouse which was stacked with crates. Amaury couldn't hear his friends' footsteps. Good. If he couldn't hear them, neither could Luther or his men. He motioned Ricky to stay on one side, while he crossed the path between the crates and moved along on the other side.

Despite the darkness, he saw clearly where he was walking. At the end of the aisle of goods he stopped and peered around it. Nothing. He gave Ricky a hand signal, then eased around the corner.

Aisle after aisle he worked his way toward the center of the building, with Ricky doing the same on the other side until the rows of boxes and crates ended, and he reached an empty space in the middle. A movement to his left made him swivel on his heels, his index finger on the trigger of his semiautomatic.

"They're gone." Samson stepped in front of him. "The place is empty."

His other colleagues came into view, frustration and disappointment reflecting on their faces.

"Nothing," Gabriel confirmed.

"Maybe Paul's memories weren't that good," Zane insinuated.

Gabriel pinned him with a furious glare. "This is the place. They were here."

"And now they're gone." Quinn's voice was even as he cut in. "They must have known we were coming."

Suddenly several sets of eyes landed on Amaury. If they were thinking what he suspected, they were in for a fight. Nina didn't do this. He took a step toward Quinn. "What are you suggesting?"

His colleague held his ground. "You know what I'm suggesting."

"You leave her out of this," Amaury hissed and glared into the round. "That goes for all of you. She didn't do this. She did not betray me." God help him if she had.

Both Quinn and Zane stepped toward him, meeting his stare. They weren't backing down. Amaury widened his stance, readying himself for a fight. He would defend Nina even though he didn't know what she had or hadn't done.

"There's always the other reason, you know." At Yvette's casual words, everybody turned toward her. She stood there, her leather-clad foot propped on a crate, pretending to check her fingernails for any damage. Several seconds passed.

"And are you going to share this reason with us any time soon?" Amaury finally asked.

She stopped admiring her nails and looked up. "Ah, I see, I have everybody's attention."

"Yvette." Gabriel's voice sounded like a warning.

"Have you guys ever wondered why it was so easy to capture Paul Holland?"

"Go on," Samson encouraged, clearly intrigued.

"I believe Luther wanted us to catch him so he could lead us into a trap. He used Paul to feed us information he wanted us to have and made sure Paul only saw what he wanted him to see. I think it was all a setup."

Gabriel scoffed. "I don't see anybody who's trying to kill us here, do you?"

"Maybe we're not the ones he wants. Paul claimed Luther's plan was to destroy Scanguards, but what if that's not his real goal? What if it was merely a diversion? Maybe he just wanted us out of the way."

"To do what?" Samson asked.

"If he hates you two as much as you say, getting revenge by destroying your company frankly doesn't sound like it's personal enough. I could think of something much more personal than the company, something much more valuable, or shall I say. . .some*body*?"

Amaury suddenly felt a stab in his temple, the kind of stab he would feel when emotions invaded him—only now it was different. There was only one thought, coming from only one person. Nina. He could sense her. But before he could put the thought in his head into words, he heard Samson shout.

"No! Delilah!" Samson pressed his hand against his temple. He shot a panicked look at the group. "Luther's got Delilah."

32

Nina bent over the sink and splashed water on her face.

The first wave of anger over Amaury and his high-handed approach to their relationship had passed. She was much calmer now than during her earlier conversation with Delilah. Maybe she had overreacted a little.

Well, it didn't happen every day that a girl found out she was blood-bonded to a vampire for eternity.

To a very hot and sexy vampire.

But it didn't change anything about the fact that Amaury had obviously spent too many years in the dark ages, where slinging a woman over his shoulder and dragging her into his cave was a perfectly acceptable form of courtship. Even though what had happened in the cave had pleased her very much.

Still, he'd tricked her. No matter how secretly excited she was that this powerful vampire had bound himself to her, she couldn't let his action pass without making him aware that he couldn't treat her like this. If she'd let him get away with it now, then what else would he think he could do? She wanted a partner in her life, not a tyrant.

Hell, they hadn't been out on a single date. He'd never even bought her dinner. All she'd had were leftovers of food he'd cooked for somebody else.

Surely Samson hadn't treated Delilah with such disrespect. She seemed to be all gooey-eyed over her man. And what had Amaury done? He'd treated her like property, nothing more. She was no man's property, no matter how hot he was or how amazing he made her feel every time he touched her. Why couldn't he have asked her like any normal man? Of course, Amaury was anything but normal. Hell, she didn't want a normal man! She wanted him, a vampire. But before she would admit that, she'd teach him first that he had to treat her like an independent woman, not chattel.

And now she'd talk to Delilah about it. The woman seemed to have her head well screwed on, and maybe Delilah would help her figure out how she could teach Amaury the lesson he needed to learn before they started their lives together.

With a determined move she took the towel and wiped her face dry, then looked in the mirror. A loud thump startled her. She listened, but a second later everything was quiet again. She let her hand run through her locks before she turned back to the door and unlocked it.

The moment she opened the bathroom door and stepped out, she heard a commotion in the front of the house. A shriek from Delilah and some muffled grunts mixed with the sound of heavy items hitting the floor made her rush down the corridor.

Nina reached the living room a few seconds later. The picture that greeted her made her heart stop in shock. Delilah struggled to get out of the grip of a man whom Nina instantly recognized as Johan, the vampire who had attacked her a few nights earlier. Carl, obviously in an attempt to help her, was fighting against two others whose backs were turned to Nina.

She gasped. One of the men snapped his head around and spotted her. He released Carl, leaving his companion to deal with him. In shock, she stared at the man who approached her now and whom she'd first met at the nightclub: Luther.

There was a curious expression on his face, almost as if he was surprised to see her here.

"Now look at that. Amaury's little tart."

At first it appeared he had little interest in her. But then she took a step back, and he was suddenly on her. Nina didn't dare move. When Luther took in a deep breath, she instinctively knew it wasn't a good sign. A flicker in his eyes confirmed that her luck had just changed. She cursed Amaury. Had he not brought her to Samson's house for her safety, she wouldn't be in danger now.

"Who would have thought?" He took in another breath. "Yes, two birds with one stone. Lady Luck is on my side tonight. At first you were just an annoyance to get rid of, snooping around in my business, but now. . .your value has just gone up."

Luther took a curl of her hair and twisted it around his finger. Nina turned her head so it slipped out of his grip.

"You're gonna pay for this," she warned him, feeling she had to be brave.

He let out a bitter laugh. "I've already paid a long time ago. Now finally, I'll get something in exchange. I think Amaury will regret having made you his mate, and so will you. He's turned you into a target."

Nina's chest tightened.

By making her his mate, Amaury had handed Luther another bargaining chip. If he wanted revenge on Amaury, what better way than to take it out on his newly bonded mate? She glanced past him where Delilah had given up her struggle against Johan, who held her arms behind her back. She realized instantly what Luther was planning to do to her and Delilah. Her fear tightened her throat, making her unable to speak.

Luther looked back over his shoulder. "Tie her up. This one too. We're taking both."

Johan grunted and tied Delilah's wrists with duct tape. Nina kicked Luther in his shin when his attention was diverted by Carl who still struggled with the other intruder.

"Don't, Nina; it's not worth it," Delilah warned.

"*Bastard*!" Nina screamed the moment Luther pinned her against the door frame, glaring at her.

"Try that again." The challenge in his voice carried a menacing warning, a clear indication that he wanted to inflict pain.

Behind him another figure moved.

"Nina?"

Her ears were playing tricks on her. The voice Nina heard belonged to a dead man. She shook her head trying to clear her mind, but then the man came into view behind Luther. No, it couldn't be true. He was dead. She'd buried him a month ago, buried his charred body.

"Eddie?"

Luther released his grip as Eddie pushed in. "Nina! What are you doing here?"

"Eddie!"

She was dreaming. Eddie was alive. How?

"But, you died." She touched his arm, looked at his face. It was Eddie, but he was different. He looked stronger than before, and there was a strange glint in his eyes. His skin was clearer than before. No pimples, no sign of blemishes, when just before his death he'd been fighting a bout of acne.

Was her mind playing tricks on her?

All of a sudden, a movement she caught from the corner of her eye distracted her from examining the man in front of her. Nina whipped her head to the right. Carl had scrambled to his feet and held a stake in his hand, as he jumped toward Eddie, intent on killing him.

Without thinking, she pushed Eddie out of the way and took the impact of Carl's attack. The wooden stake, while blunt, drove into her arm. It didn't penetrate deeply, but nevertheless managed to break through a layer of muscle. Blood dripped from her. She clamped her good hand over her injured arm, trying to ward off the stabbing pain. To no avail. A dull ache coiled through her body.

When she looked up, she saw her brother's face before her, his eyes red and sharp fangs protruding from his lips. Reality hit her harder than the stake had seconds earlier: her baby brother was a vampire. And not only that, he was working for the bad guy. For Luther, who now restrained Carl.

"Oh, no, Eddie."

His fangs came closer and closer. Nina felt her knees buckle as nausea overwhelmed her.

"Please, no."

Would her own brother kill her? It was too much for her mind to handle. Black blotches appeared in front of her eyes. She wouldn't faint, no, she couldn't. She wasn't some weak girl who'd fall . . .

33

The light from the open door spilled onto the sidewalk. Samson stormed up the front steps to his home just ahead of Amaury.

The hallway and living room were scenes of destruction: overthrown furniture, broken glass, and blood. Amaury's stomach twisted painfully. He inhaled sharply, and the scent of Nina's blood hit him.

No!

He stumbled into the room, almost tripping over Samson. On the floor lay Carl, a heap of torn muscle and blood, but he was breathing, his eyes open.

"Where's Delilah?" Samson asked.

Carl's response was a gurgle. "Gone."

"And Nina?" Amaury's throat was so dry he could barely speak. There was no response from Carl.

Behind them the rest of their colleagues charged into the house, Gabriel barking commands.

"Zane, Quinn—check upstairs. Yvette, Ricky—take the back of the house. Oliver, we need you here."

Samson knelt next to Carl, who'd lost consciousness, blood pouring from his stomach wounds. Why they hadn't outright killed him, Amaury couldn't figure out.

"He needs fresh blood. Gabriel, we need a donor."

Before Gabriel could answer, Oliver pushed through the door. "You've got one."

Without hesitation he crouched down and pulled back his sleeve.

"Carl has never bitten anyone," Samson explained.

"Well, he's just gonna have to bite the bullet now, won't he?" Oliver placed his wrist at Carl's lips.

"He won't be able to. One of us will have to open your vein for him."

Oliver nodded at Samson and stretched his wrist out to him.

"Thank you. But Gabriel will have to do it for you," Samson said and motioned Gabriel to approach.

Amaury instantly realized why. As a blood-bonded vampire he didn't take blood from anybody else but Delilah. Even just piercing Oliver's skin to open the vein would make him taste some of his employee's blood. Samson's body would reject the foreign essence, making him sick in the process.

Gabriel took Oliver's wrist and set his fangs, piercing the skin. A moment later, Oliver placed his wrist at Carl's mouth again and let the blood drip between his lips. The red liquid ran into his mouth, and seconds later Carl's lips locked on the wound. He started suckling.

"Nothing in the back of the house," Ricky announced as he and Yvette came back into the living room. "No sign of them."

Amaury exchanged a terse look with Samson. Their mates had been taken, and any blood-bonded vampire would give his own life to have his mate returned unharmed. Never in the last four hundred years had he ever thought he'd feel what he felt right now: devastation. Not even the pain he'd experienced in his head all these years could compare to it. Nothing felt as painful as knowing Nina was in the hands of a madman.

"We need to find out what happened and where he's taken them." Samson glanced in Gabriel's direction.

"I'm sorry, Samson: I can't lock onto Carl's memories while he's unconscious. We need to wait until he comes to."

Amaury shook his head. "We don't have time. Nina is injured. I smelled her blood."

He paced nervously. What if the injury was life threatening? He could heal her with his blood, but he had to get to her. He needed to do something.

"She must have been fighting him when he took them. Always the fighter," he mumbled to himself. He cast a look at Samson who stood motionless next to Gabriel.

"How can you be so calm?"

Samson's lips pressed into a thin line. "It doesn't help either Delilah or Nina if we lose our heads. That's not how we can save them."

Amaury huffed, but kept his next comment to himself.

Samson put a hand on his shoulder. "I know exactly what you feel right now. I'm going through the same thing." For a moment the pain was evident in his hazel eyes. Yes, he suffered as much as Amaury did, if not more. Not only did Samson stand to lose his mate, but also his unborn child. Even without his gift, Amaury recognized the pain in his friend.

He clasped his hand over Samson's. "I know."

"Upstairs is clear." Zane and Quinn entered the room. "It must have all happened downstairs. Nothing was disturbed upstairs. No sign of forced entry."

"You mean they let him in?" Samson asked.

"That's what it looks like." Zane nodded at the door. "It doesn't look like the front door is damaged."

There was a loud groan from the floor. Everybody's eyes snapped to Carl who'd released Oliver's wrist and coughed.

Samson dropped down to his level. "Carl, we nearly lost you."

"I couldn't stop them." Carl's eyes lowered in shame.

"How many were there?"

"Three. Luther, I recognized him, and two others." His voice was still weak.

"What happened?"

Carl swallowed and accepted Samson's help to sit up. "Miss Delilah was in the living room when I heard the front door open. By the time I ran into the hallway, they'd already stormed in and grabbed her."

"Where was Nina? Was she fighting them? Is that how she got injured?" Amaury interrupted.

There was a pissed-off look on Carl's face when he answered. "Oh, she was fighting all right, but not against them."

"What?" Samson looked from Carl to Amaury.

"No, you're lying!" The implication buried in Carl's words conjured up images that twisted a knife in Amaury's gut.

Carl scrambled to his feet. "I never lie. I was fighting one of them, and she was talking to Luther. And then the one I fought saw her. They knew each other. When he was distracted I tried to stake him, but she threw herself in between and saved him."

Amaury gasped. "No. You must be wrong." Nina wouldn't betray them. He would have felt her treachery, sensed her deceit if there had been any in her heart.

"I'm not wrong," Carl barked. "She took my stake in her arm to save him. She was all worried about him, screamed '*Oh, no, Eddie*'—"

"Eddie?" Amaury's heart knotted.

"Her brother?" Samson asked.

Amaury nodded, squeezing his eyes shut. His mate had betrayed them and taken her brother's side. "She wouldn't do that to me. She wouldn't." But she had. There could be no doubt now. Why had he not seen it?

"Was that why they didn't kill you, so you could tell me what she'd done?" Was that her last cruel deed toward him?

Carl shook his head. "Luther left me alive to give you and Samson a message."

Samson faced Carl. "What's the message?"

"His words were: Vivian needs company."

Amaury felt as if his guts had just been ripped out. For the first time he could see a physical manifestation of Samson's pain. His friend's knees buckled, and he had to grip Gabriel's arm to stay upright.

Zane's and Quinn's inquisitive stares landed on Amaury. They knew Samson wasn't in any condition to answer. "Vivian is dead." Luther was planning to kill their mates. But then, if he wanted to kill Nina, wouldn't that mean she wasn't on Luther's side after all? Or had his plan changed after he'd realized that Nina was now Amaury's mate? Had she in fact been on Luther's side in the beginning, but by bonding with him signed her own death warrant?

"I know where they are," Samson suddenly said. "Let's go." He stepped toward the door, only to be blocked by Gabriel and his New York crew.

"No."

Amaury instantly took Samson's flank, getting into battle position. Why would their colleagues stop them from rescuing their women?

"Get out of my way, Gabriel." Samson's voice was a snarl.

"Can't do that. It's too close to sunrise. Whatever you're planning, we won't have enough time tonight. And besides, we're not going in without a plan."

"He's right, sir," Carl's voice came from behind. Samson and Amaury turned to him.

"If he wanted to kill Delilah right away, he would have done it here. There's a reason he left me alive to tell you." Carl paused. "He's going to wait until you get there, so you'll have to watch when he kills her."

Samson nodded slowly.

And Nina—was nobody thinking of Amaury's mate? Were they all convinced that she was a traitor? Amaury wasn't. He couldn't allow that thought to take residence in his mind. If Luther wanted to kill her, it could only mean one thing: she wasn't on his side after all. Or was it all a big deception? Had Carl misunderstood? Was Luther planning to kill only Delilah and not Nina?

Nina, where are you? Talk to me.

He reached out to her with his mind, but there was no reply. She should hear him. There were only two reasons why she wouldn't reply: she either refused because she was with Luther, or she was dead. Amaury couldn't accept either reason.

34

A familiar voice broke through the fog.

Nina, where are you? Talk to me.

Then another voice, this one closer. "Nina, can you hear me?"

Nina opened her eyes. The light around her was dim. She found herself lying on a cold stone floor.

"Thank God, you're okay," Delilah said. Nina took her helping arm to sit up. Her side hurt. She looked down at her arm. There were no traces of blood on the spot where Carl had caught her with the stake. The wound had closed and healed.

"Where are we?"

Nina glanced around the dark room. It was made of stone and concrete without any windows and only a few wall sconces for light. There was one heavy-looking door, no furniture or decoration. If she had to guess, she'd say it was underground.

"I don't know. They blindfolded me on the way here. But we were in the car for over half an hour, maybe longer."

Nina gave Delilah a cautious look. She didn't appear to be upset with her, when she had every right to be so. After all, she'd prevented Carl from killing one of the vampires, her brother.

"How's your arm?"

"I think it's fine. It seems to have healed already. How long was I out for?" Judging by the state of her injury she guessed at least two days.

"Only a couple of hours. Your brother healed the injury."

So she hadn't imagined it all. Eddie was alive, and he was a vampire—a vampire working for the other side. "I'm so sorry. I didn't know."

Delilah squeezed her hand. "I understand."

Nina shook her head. "I couldn't let Carl kill him. He's still my brother."

"Nina. Please, I would have done the same in your situation. I had a brother once, too. I would have done anything to save him." There was a faraway look in her eyes before she snapped back to the present. "Now we just have to convince Samson and Amaury of your innocence. They think you were working for Luther all along."

Nina swallowed the shock of Delilah's statement. Amaury thought she was a traitor? Yet he'd bonded with her? It didn't make any sense.

"When did you talk to him?"

"On the way here."

"They left you a cell phone?"

Delilah chuckled softly. "Of course not. I communicated with Samson via our bond."

Her expression must have been utterly confused, because Delilah clarified, "Telepathically. All blood-bonded couples do it."

"Oh." She'd never heard of such a thing. "You mean I can do that with Amaury?"

Delilah nodded. "I'm sure he's already tried to reach you, but you were out cold."

"I'm normally not the person who faints." Nina, the self-confessed vampire fighter, had to faint when push came to shove. How embarrassing.

"You were injured; you had a lot to deal with. The shock of seeing your brother. It was just too much for you. Sometimes our bodies just tell us when we've had enough."

Delilah seemed calm considering the situation they were in.

"I didn't know Eddie was alive . . . "

Delilah squeezed Nina's hand. "I know that now. But when our guys got back to the house they found Carl—"

A bolt of guilt shot through Nina. "Carl—oh God, Luther killed him. I'm so sorry." She pushed back the tears.

Delilah shook her head. "Carl's alive. But he told them that you fought on Luther's side when you defended Eddie. That's why they believe you've betrayed us."

"But I couldn't let Eddie be killed, I couldn't. They have to understand that. He's my brother. He's all the family I have." If she lost him, she'd have nobody.

"They'll understand—in time. Amaury will understand."

Amaury. Would he really understand? The man who jumped to conclusions in two seconds flat? He would condemn her.

"Unfortunately, they also think you let Luther in the house. I didn't have a chance to tell Samson before our communication ended. He's going to be so upset."

Nina stared at her. "About what?"

"Luther used mind control on me and made me open the door," she explained.

"Can't you contact him now?" Nina asked.

Delilah shook her head. "I can't get through. Either he's too occupied with preparing a plan to get us out, or we're just too far apart."

"Oh no. What now?"

"I know Samson and the guys are coming for us."

Nina had to admire her confidence. She herself didn't feel this sure of anything right now. There was just too much to come to grips with. Her brother was alive and working for the enemy. She was in some sort of underground bunker with no means of escape, and the men who were supposedly on their way to rescue them believed she was a traitor. Where would she even start to fix things?

"How are they going to find us?"

"Trust me, they will. A blood-bonded vampire will never give up on his mate. If he does, it will be his own death."

This sounded far too dramatic to be true. "What do you mean?"

"Samson can only feed off me. The longer he's away from me the longer he won't feed. A blood-bonded vampire can't metabolize foreign blood. He can only live off his mate's blood. As long as I'm alive he'll need my blood. Only when I die, will his body accept blood from somebody else."

Delilah's words were spoken with calmness despite the fundamental implications they carried.

"But that can't be."

"That's how it is. Without our blood, our men will die."

Nina swallowed hard, but the lump in her throat didn't disappear. "You mean Amaury would starve without me?"

Delilah nodded. "I'm sorry."

"Why then? Why make me his mate if that makes him dependent on me?"

"There's only one reason why a vampire chooses a mate: he loves her and can't live without her."

Nina choked back a tear. How she longed to hear those words from him, even though they couldn't be true. "But Amaury can't love anybody. He told me so himself. He's cursed never to love again."

Delilah shrugged. "Something must have happened. I can only tell you what I know from my own experience. No vampire takes a blood-bonding lightly. It is forever. And it is for love."

Nina put her head in her hands. "Delilah, there's something I have to tell you about Amaury and me."

Delilah's soft palm stroked over her hair. "You love him, don't you?"

"Promise me you won't tell Samson—I need to be the one to tell Amaury." She paused. "If I ever get the chance."

***

Nina jerked out of her sleep when she heard a sound at the door. She looked at Delilah who lay next to her on the stone floor, asleep. Nina remained still, pretending to be sleeping while she watched the door open. There was a sliver of light penetrating the dim dungeon, silhouetting a tall figure at the door.

She would recognize the man anywhere.

"Eddie," she whispered and jumped up.

He looked behind him, then slipped into the room and closed the door. "Nina."

A second later she wrapped her arms around her brother. "Why didn't you tell me?" She swallowed back a tear. "How could you let me think you were dead? I buried you, I cried for you."

Eddie's familiar hand brushed over her curls, as he'd done ever since he'd grown taller than her. "I couldn't, sweetie. I wasn't myself. The first few weeks were agony."

She pulled away to look up at his face. "Did he force you?"

"Force me? Who?"

"Luther. He forced you."

He held her a foot away from him. "Of course not. He would never force anybody."

It didn't make sense to Nina. Eddie would have never made her suffer like this without even trying to let her know he was alive. "I don't believe you. You could have told me you were alive."

Eddie shook his head. "I couldn't. The days after the transformation were painful. I had to come to grips with the thirst. I had to learn how to control my urges and my strength without harming anyone. For the first few weeks I could barely think straight. I didn't dare come near you. I was too afraid of hurting you."

Nina recognized the sincerity in his voice.

"Why did you do it? I thought things started to work out for us. Why would you throw this away?"

"Throw what away? Just barely scraping by? Never quite making it? Always looking over your shoulder?" She could sense his anger and frustration.

"It wasn't like that."

But she knew her own protest was weak at best. They had struggled.

"It was always like that. Don't lie to me, Nina. No matter how you tried to shield me from things, it was always like that. You can't tell me you were happy the way we had to live."

"But we had each other." Her protest drowned in his angry huff.

"Yeah, we had each other. Because you always sacrificed yourself for me. Do you think I wanted that?"

"What do you mean?"

"I know what you had to do. I woke up that night. I heard what he did to you. You should have killed him. But you didn't. Instead you stuck it out for me. You lived with this asshole day in and day out. Did you think I was blind? That I didn't see how hard that was for you? And I couldn't protect you. But now I'm a vampire, and as a vampire I'm finally strong enough to protect you from assholes like him."

She shook her head in disbelief. He knew she'd stabbed their foster father? He was aware of the ghosts of her past?

"Yet you let me believe you were dead."

"I was, for a while. But I would have come for you. I'm here now."

She looked behind her at the sleeping Delilah. "I don't call that coming for me. Luther kidnapped us."

"He had his reasons. He wasn't after you. Believe me, he was as surprised as the rest of us to find you there. All he wanted was that bastard Samson's wife." He tossed a look into Delilah's direction.

"He can't just go around kidnapping people. I can't believe you're on his side. This is wrong."

Eddie looked at her as if she was crazy. "You have no idea what that man did to Luther. Samson destroyed his life. He let Luther's wife and child die. No matter how you look at it, this has to be punished."

"Is that what he's told you? That Samson let Luther's wife die?" Nina couldn't believe her ears. That's how Luther had convinced Eddie to help him, by telling him lies? By making him think that Samson was the bad guy?

"Because that's the truth."

"Luther is lying. It's not how it was."

"How would you know? You weren't there."

Eddie's stubbornness reared its head again and reminded her of the time when he'd insisted as a thirteen year old that he was better at driving than she just because he was a boy.

"Neither were you," she retorted. "Your Luther is not the hero you make him out to be."

"You don't know anything about Luther."

"And neither do you." Nina braced her hands on her hips and challenged him with a stern glare.

"I know enough to know he's not as corrupted and evil as Samson and his men are."

"Well, then maybe you should ask him why he sent those goons after me."

"What goons? He sent nobody after you. We were out to get Samson's wife. You just got in the way."

Nina waved her hand impatiently. "Not tonight. He tried to have me killed several nights ago. By Johan and some other vampire. Why don't you go and ask him?"

"That's not true."

"Who're you gonna believe? Your sister or your new friend? I have no reason to make this up."

"I don't believe it. Luther told me you've hooked up with this bad-ass Amaury. Has he brainwashed you?" Eddie grabbed her shoulders and shook her. "Has he?"

"It's not like that. He hasn't done anything." Well, Amaury had done quite a bit, but nothing she was willing to discuss with her brother. Their issues were private and she'd sort Amaury out later. If she ever made it out of this place.

"Don't lie to me. Luther said you're his woman. Is it true? Are you his? Is that why you're on their side?"

"No! I'm on their side because they're the good guys."

"Don't kid yourself. There are no good guys."

"You're wrong," she insisted. "There are no bad guys, just people living with misunderstandings."

"Nina. Wake up. I can help you. I can guarantee that nobody harms you, but you'll have to trust me. I know what I'm doing. Don't you see what Luther has granted me? A new lease on life, a new chance for something bigger and better. We'll never be poor again. You'll always be safe with me."

Funnily enough, it was the same thing Amaury had promised her, to keep her safe.

"But you can't interfere anymore."

He pointed at Delilah who still appeared to be asleep, even though Nina suspected she was only pretending by now. Their argument was getting heated, and no normal human would be able to sleep through it.

"I can't let injustice happen. How can you expect that from me? Don't you know me at all? Do you think that after what happened to me when we were young, I would allow another innocent to be harmed and just stand aside? No, if that's what you want me to do, then I don't have a brother. Because my brother would not force me to act like this. My Eddie would never do that."

She glared at him furiously. Yes, he was a big bad vampire now, but he was still her little brother, and if somehow she could get through to him, maybe she had a chance of turning this situation around.

"You don't know what you're saying."

Eddie turned on his heels, and before she could come back with anything else, he stormed out. She heard the door lock behind him.

Damn vampire speed!

With her next breath a sob dislodged from her chest.

"I'm sorry, Nina," Delilah's voice came from the floor. "Give him some time. He'll figure it out. You planted some doubts in his mind. He'll come back."

She turned to her and watched her sit up. "Eddie has always been a stubborn kid. I think he's turned into one hell of a stubborn vampire."

35

Amaury carefully slid the silver dagger into its sheath and strapped it to his hip, before he looked back at Samson. They were gearing up in Samson's basement arsenal. The others were busy loading up the vans with everything they'd need.

"I don't think it's any of your business if I'm communicating with my mate." He would not be censured by Samson, no matter what. That Nina had so far thwarted all his efforts to get in touch with her was beside the point. If anything, it made it even more important that he should get through to her, to make sure she was all right. Maybe she didn't know yet how the telepathic communication between blood-bonded mates worked and was confused.

In the sleepless hours he'd spent waiting for sunset, he'd been going through scenario after scenario of why she didn't reply to him. For his own peace of mind he'd settled on the least frightening one: she was unaware or confused about the skill and didn't know how to apply it.

"It's my business when she could jeopardize the rescue mission. If you give away what we're planning, you're putting Delilah in danger. Is that what you want?" The warning tone in his friend's voice gave him pause.

"You know full well that I would never do anything to put Delilah in danger. Nina won't do anything to hurt anybody. I trust her. I love her."

The realization sank in deep. Love? Was it possible after all these years, even with the curse? Had he beaten it? How? There was no rhyme or reason to it other than the knowledge that it was the truth. He loved Nina. Loved her beyond the bond, the lust, the sex. His heart felt too big for his chest, as if it had expanded, enlarged to make space for her. The warmth spreading within it extended throughout his body, seeped into every cell, and tingled on his skin. Amaury was in love.

"If you loved her, you wouldn't have bonded her without giving her a choice," Samson snapped.

Fury reared up in Amaury. "What are you saying?" A tiny twinge of something he couldn't identify flicked sparked in his stomach, but was gone just as quickly. He took a step closer, almost butting heads with Samson.

"You know exactly what I'm talking about."

"Why don't you tell me?" Amaury surprised himself with the menace in his tone. His loyalty to his old friend was overpowered by his love for Nina.

"You didn't tell her what the blood-bond entailed. Nina had no idea what she was getting into."

"That's not true." Samson's accusation stung. At the same time, a little ball of guilt settled in his gut.

"If it's not true then why was Nina so shocked when Delilah made a comment about your blood-bond to her? And why do you think Nina is so pissed at you?"

Pissed? She was upset with him? Was that why she hadn't replied to his telepathic calls?

"You can't be serious," Amaury tried to deny his friend's accusation.

Samson nodded and gave him a hard look. "Delilah told me Nina didn't know you were blood-bonding her. You did it without her permission."

Amaury took a step back and braced himself against the wall. "But I asked her. I told her." He had—well, he'd sort of asked. It hadn't been that explicit, but he was sure she'd understood.

"What exactly did you say?" Samson's voice was calmer now, more controlled.

"I asked her if she wanted to be mine, and I told her I would be hers."

Samson *tsked* with disapproval. "And from that you thought she'd get that you wanted a blood-bond?"

Amaury's heart contracted painfully. He'd been so sure about her that night. The way she'd looked at him, how her eyes had gazed at him with longing, with want. She'd begged him to take her blood, and there'd barely been a hesitation when he'd asked her to drink his. Nina had wanted him, he was certain. They belonged together, they were right together. This was no misunderstanding. It couldn't be.

"But she wanted me. She . . . " His voice trailed off. Maybe she'd wanted him last night, but for how long? This couldn't be happening.

Amaury felt his friend's hand on his shoulder and looked into his concerned face. "You are aware that she can bring this up to the council."

He was aware of the council, the powerful body of vampires from across the country who acted as a tribunal of sorts and dealt with serious infractions within their race. Blood-bonding a human without consent was a severe crime.

"Or she can just leave you."

Amaury nodded. Neither option would free him from the bond. Either case meant death. But he wouldn't think of this now. He couldn't let this distract him from the task at hand.

"Whatever she wants, she can do it. But I have to save her. I can't let her die at Luther's hands."

A world without Nina was unthinkable, and whatever it took to save her, he would do it. By bonding with her he'd pledged his life to her. And he wouldn't hesitate to fulfill the pledge if it was asked of him.

36

Luther gave her the creeps. The coldness in his regard made Nina cringe inwardly. The gray of his eyes looked like ice as they stared at her and Delilah without any expression in them. Did he still have emotions, or was his heart a frozen wasteland?

A chill went through the dungeon with his presence. Nina shivered and felt Delilah grasp her hand in reassurance. But even the knowledge that she had a friend at her side did not diminish the eeriness of his visit.

"Finally the time has come. I would have never guessed it to be so easy in the end. And for Amaury to hand you to me on a platter—priceless."

"You know they'll come for us," Delilah claimed, her voice ringing with unerring certainty, steady and without a tremble.

Luther twisted his mouth into a thin smile. "I'm waiting for them. I promised myself that they shall not miss your deaths. I want them to witness the moment you die—to feel the pain, the agony, the despair. To know the exact moment their grief will grip them."

Behind him, Johan grunted in obvious agreement. Nina cast him a hidden glance. Was there any way of getting around the two and escaping? After having seen how speedily her own brother had made his exit, she dismissed the idea as impossible.

"Where is Eddie?" Nina had a sick feeling in her stomach. She hadn't seen him since their confrontation earlier that day. She wished she knew what was going on in his head. Had Eddie taken some of her words to heart and changed his opinion of Luther?

"Making the last preparations."

At Luther's response, a painful twinge spread in her stomach. How could her brother be complicit in cold-blooded murder?

"He won't let you kill me. I'm his sister." Her protest earned her a bitter laugh from Luther.

"Do you really think he knows what he's doing? I've chosen him because he's so impressionable. He blindly followed the first person who showed him a way out of his misery. I've made sure he can never go back to what he was. I own him."

"Nobody owns Eddie."

Eddie was too stubborn to let himself be controlled by somebody. Having turned into a vampire hadn't changed that stubbornness. Nina had been at the receiving end of it only hours earlier.

"He's changed. The power he now feels, the power that comes with being a vampire runs through his veins. He doesn't know yet how to control it. He looks to me for guidance. I am his father now, and he will do whatever I wish."

"No!" Nina screamed. "I won't allow it."

Luther took a step toward her. "Seeing that you'll be all tied up in a few minutes, I don't see how you can stop me. I will achieve my goal. Your men will lose their mates, just as I lost mine. They will pay for what they've done to me. And your brother will help me, because I control him."

The hardness in his tone slammed through her bones. Nina knew there was only one way to stop him: tell him the truth. "You don't know what really happened to your wife."

Delilah gave her hand a painful squeeze, trying to stop her. Why was everybody so intent on keeping the truth from him, when the truth was what could save them?

He snarled, his fangs protruding from his clenched jaw. "I know every agonizing minute of her end."

"You don't know the truth."

Another tug from Delilah's hand.

"The truth is what I say it is."

Luther spun around and stalked toward the door, Johan on his heels. Before she could say anything else, Delilah shouted after him, "Samson and Amaury will kill you if you harm us."

Luther threw an icy look over his shoulder. "Oh, I'm counting on it. Vivian is waiting for me."

With a loud thud, the door fell shut behind them.

"Oh God, he's crazier than I thought. He's prepared to die." For the first time Delilah's voice was laced with fear.

37

The mausoleum Luther had built to immortalize his beloved Vivian was a gothic contraption of limestone and wrought iron the size of a mansion. Surrounded by mature oak trees, it was sheltered from curious eyes. While there were no gates to surround it, Amaury was certain Luther had already been warned about their approach.

After not being able to communicate with Delilah for hours, Samson had finally received a short message from her before communication broke off again. She had been quite explicit: Luther expected them to try to spring the women from their prison: in fact, he was counting on it. He wanted them to witness their mates' deaths.

Amaury felt his chest contract painfully at the recollection of Samson's words. All day he and his vampire brethren had worked on a plan for getting their women out unharmed. And according to Delilah, Nina was in as much danger as she was. Delilah seemed convinced of Nina's innocence. She had made that clear to Samson when she had communicated to him via their bond.

While Samson and the rest of the group were still skeptical about Delilah's assessment, Amaury felt his heart fill with hope. As a former auditor, Samson's wife had a bright head on her shoulders, and Amaury pinned all his hopes on her belief.

Even though Delilah had been unable to give them the location where she and Nina had been taken to, Samson had suspected immediately where Luther would be.

After Vivian's death Luther had disappeared, but not before he'd erected a monument to her, a shrine of sorts.

Amaury glanced back into the woods where his friends were hidden. They needed no light beyond that provided by distant city lights, stars, and the crescent moon. Their superior eyesight would be sufficient to find their way through the dark. Slowly, they tightened the perimeter they'd formed around the property. With quiet commands over their earphones they communicated their positions to each other.

With all of them essentially trained as bodyguards, they knew they were superior warriors, but unfortunately so were Luther and his men.

Amaury and Samson were still unclear as to how many other vampires were working for Luther. There had been no time to do any detailed reconnaissance.

Amaury listened to this headset and moved a few yards closer to the building. At a copse of trees he stopped and trained his eyes onto the mausoleum. He picked up movements. He concentrated and could make out two figures near the steps leading up to the entrance.

"I see two people," he whispered into his mic.

"I have them in sight," Gabriel confirmed. "Two of them. Going closer now to confirm identity."

Amaury held his breath. Without making a sound, he glided forward, seeking out the next bush, which would provide him with cover.

"Confirmed, Delilah and Nina are on a platform," Gabriel's voice came over the headset.

Amaury looked to his right. Samson was taking cover behind the bush next to him. He nodded to him, before he looked back at the mausoleum. Amaury could make out the platform clearly now.

In front of the steps leading into the mausoleum, Luther had built a large wooden stage. And on the middle of it, Nina and Delilah stood motionless, their arms behind their backs. He was still too far away to make out more details.

"Wires," Thomas said through the earphones, "what's he want with all the wires?"

"I'm approaching from the back," Ricky announced. "Following the wires."

"Any sight of Luther?" Amaury asked. One-by-one his colleagues came back with a "negative."

On the platform, Nina and Delilah didn't move. He trained his eye onto them once more and could now see that their mouths were gagged. Luther obviously wanted to avoid them calling out to their rescuers. Not that it mattered. Both women could still communicate with their mates if they wished to. No gag could prevent them from doing so.

This could only mean Luther was concerned about the women alerting the remaining vampires to something. But to what?

Amaury motioned to Samson that he was ready to approach. His friend nodded and pointed to an opening between two bushes.

Three long strides and Amaury reached the point. He stepped through it. An instant later he heard a click and snapped his head to the source of the sound. He noticed the small round device instantly.

"Fuck!" he hissed under his breath.

"What?" came Samson's quick reply.

"Motion detectors."

There were only two reasons for Luther to have motion detectors: to indicate their approach and to initiate a sequence. A look at Samson who had moved next to him, told him his friend had come to the same conclusion. Something was about to happen.

"Shit!"

***

Nina noticed the ticking sound instantly. It hadn't been there before, she was sure, but suddenly it had started. She twisted her head to look to her side. She couldn't ask Delilah whether she heard it too.

But something was wrong. Well, quite a few things were wrong, starting with the fact that she and Delilah were tied to a couple of poles. But up until a few seconds earlier, nothing had been happening. Now, it appeared something had started with the ticking sound. And a ticking sound was never a good thing. Any movie buff could tell her that.

Nina craned her neck again, and out of the corner of her eye she could see a flicker of light. Twisting her body a little more, she managed to move another inch and finally saw it: a clock, counting down.

Well, that solved the mystery of the ticking sound.

Who the fuck switched on the damn bomb?

She'd seen nobody in the vicinity, which meant somebody was doing it remotely. The wires suggested as much. After Johan and another vampire had tied her and Delilah up, they'd left them alone. That had been over an hour ago if she had to guess.

Nina? Can you hear me?

The voice in her head sounded familiar.

Amaury?

Was this what Delilah had spoken about? The telepathic communication via the bond?

Yes, it's me. Tell me what's happening. We're close.

Nina adjusted to the voice in her head. It gave her a strange sense of calm.

You'd better come closer fast—there's a bomb ticking.

There was silence. No answer came from him. Where the hell had he gone?

Amaury, damn it! What are you gonna do about it?

Another few seconds passed before she finally felt the warmth again that came with the thoughts reaching her mind.

Listen carefully. I think we triggered it by approaching.

Idiots!

Is there a clock?

Of course there's a clock, she answered him.

Can you see the time?

Nina craned her neck once more. *Less than ten minutes.*

Shit!

Before she could concentrate on replying to him, she noticed a movement nearby. She stretched. From the corner of her eye she saw Eddie. But he wasn't walking toward her. He crawled along the bushes that grew alongside the stairs, hiding behind them. What was he trying to do?

Her attention was diverted again when a booming voice behind her spoke.

"I see everybody has finally arrived."

Why was it that every villain had to have his obligatory speech before he blew everything to smithereens?

"Lights," Luther called out, and a moment later the stage was flooded with light, as was the grassy area in front of it. No matter who'd approach them, they would have no way of hiding now.

Luther remained behind her and Delilah, clearly using them as a shield so no vampires trying to rescue them would be able to get a clear shot at him.

***

Amaury looked at the platform. The light gave him a perfect view of the spot where Luther had decided to kill their women. He instantly realized there was no way to get to the platform without being seen. This would not be a stealth rescue operation. This would be all about speed.

Amaury set his stop watch to nine minutes, the time remaining until the bomb would blow.

"We don't have much time," he spoke softly into the mic. "The motion detectors triggered the countdown to a bomb."

"Welcome to my little show," Luther's voice called from across the clearing. "I trust we're all here?" There was a little pause, before he continued. "Good. I wouldn't want to start without you."

Amaury aimed his semiautomatic in Luther's direction and looked through the viewfinder. His target stood right between Nina and Delilah.

His finger tightened on the trigger. Luther moved. Pearls of sweat built on Amaury's forehead as his trigger finger trembled. A look at Nina told him he couldn't risk shooting. What if he missed? No. It was too risky. Slowly, he lowered his arm.

Samson stirred next to him. "I know." Then he spoke into the mic. "We can't do anything from the front. Can you guys get to them from the sides?"

"Working on it," Gabriel's voice came through the ear piece.

"Ricky, anything on the wires?"

There was no response. "Ricky?"

Samson shot Amaury an alarmed look. "Yvette, Zane—check in the back for Ricky."

"Will do." Yvette's voice sounded through the ear phone, then clicked off.

"No matter what you're planning to do, you won't be able to save your mates, just as I wasn't able to save mine." Luther's voice echoed through the night. "I've waited for this moment for a long time. I never thought I'd catch two birds with one stone. Frankly, Amaury, my old friend, I didn't think you had it in you."

Amaury didn't give a rat's ass about what Luther thought. Nina was his, and he would not allow her to be hurt.

Luther turned toward Delilah and brushed a strand of her hair away from her face. A defiant shake of her head was the answer.

"What a lovely mate you have, Samson. When I heard of your bonding a few months ago, I wanted to congratulate you in person. Excuse the delay, but I had things to prepare, you understand. I needed loyal supporters and what better way than to create them myself, don't you think? After all, you turned all my friends against me. In my moment of grief, I had nobody."

Amaury remembered the time well. Only, Luther had been the one who'd turned against his friends, pushing everybody away, accusing everybody of wrongdoing.

"You could have saved Vivian. And you let her die. You had the power, yet you didn't act. But enough of the past. It dies today—with me and your blood-bonded mates."

It was no surprise to Amaury that Luther was prepared to go down with them. He had to know that both he and Samson would hunt him down to the end of the world. Luther was as good as dead the moment he laid hands on Nina and Delilah.

A quick glance at Samson confirmed his friend was thinking the same thing. Amaury looked at his watch: only six minutes left. He gestured to it and made a sign to Samson, indicating the remaining time with his fingers.

"Gabriel, update." Samson's voice through the earphone sounded calmer and more collected than he looked.

"This is Quinn. Found the trigger mechanism. It's on auto. I can't deactivate it from here. I need to find the console."

"Do it."

"On my way. A word of warning though—I think there's a manual override somewhere. In case we disable the auto, he has another way of setting it off."

"I'm looking for it," Thomas replied.

"Less than five minutes," Amaury whispered.

"Good night, my friends. And welcome to true darkness," Luther said. A moment later, he glided back into the mausoleum behind the women, his frame melting into the entryway.

38

Nina shivered. Luther's last words had given her the chills.

She looked to her side to where Eddie had hidden earlier, but couldn't see him anywhere. She caught a look at the clock. Less than five minutes remained.

Out in the distance across the grassy area she could make out some shadows. Were they moving toward her, or was this merely wishful thinking?

Seconds later she saw a familiar shape come into view. Despite the darkness, she recognized him: Amaury. Next to him, a slimmer, but equally tall man appeared: Samson.

Nina looked over the edge of the platform as Amaury and Samson continued their approach, unimpeded by anybody. This wasn't right. It was too easy. Why would Luther leave her and Delilah alone, so their men could come to free them? It didn't make sense. Yes, the bomb was ticking, but five minutes would be plenty of time to free them and be far enough away from the platform by the time it blew up. No, something was seriously wrong with this picture.

It's a trap!

She concentrated on Amaury and opened her mind to him. Frantically, she looked around herself, following the wires.

From the corner of her eye she suddenly saw a movement. Eddie rushed past the platform and toward Samson and Amaury, launching himself onto them. She wanted to scream and stop him, but the gag in her mouth prevented her from it.

Instead she watched as he threw himself against Amaury. They fought while Samson continued to approach. A frantic look by Eddie toward Samson told her that something was wrong. Eddie wasn't fighting to kill them, only fighting to stop them.

Amaury, stop! Don't hurt Eddie! No further! Stop Samson—stop him now!

A second later Amaury's command echoed through the night. "Samson, stay back!"

His friend instantly stilled, and so did Eddie. He stopped punching.

"Thank God," she heard her brother's voice rasp. Exhaustion clearly showing on his face, he pointed to a spot only a foot ahead of Samson. "Laser trigger."

Nina's heart pounded.

Amaury still had her brother in a tight grip, but he didn't appear to intend him any more harm. "Talk. Fast." Amaury's voice reached Nina's ears and felt strangely comforting.

"Once you pass that point, the laser beam is interrupted. It triggers a second mechanism, and you've got sixty seconds for the platform to blow," Eddie explained.

Nina's heart stopped. So that's why Luther had been so confident and left them alone. If the men tried to rush them, they would inadvertently reduce the time on the clock and blow up with them.

She blinked and swallowed hard. This was it. They were so screwed.

"Is there a way around it?"

Eddie shook his head. "There are more lasers on either side of the podium. The only way to get onto the podium without tripping one of the lasers is from inside the mausoleum."

Her brother looked up in her direction. "I'm sorry, sweetie. I didn't realize how crazy he is. When I understood what he was planning, it was already too late."

Amaury looked at Nina, agony and torture obscuring his beautiful features. Without breaking eye contact with her, he addressed Eddie. "Get us into the mausoleum. Now."

She watched as Amaury spoke quietly into his mic, then listened to his earphone. She caught his frustrated look, before he huddled with Samson and Eddie. They were speaking too low for her to hear, but their gestures told her they were in disagreement over something.

"No! Are you crazy?" her brother shouted at Amaury.

"It's the only way." Amaury's reply was just as emotion-laden.

He looked at her, a sad look in his eyes.

Trust me.

Nina heard his voice in her head. Trust him with what? What the hell was he up to?

Several seconds later all hell broke loose. From out of nowhere, Amaury's vampire friends appeared, swarming the area. And then she saw the others, Luther's men.

Johan stalked onto the scene from behind the mausoleum, together with three others she didn't recognize. One of them had helped tie her and Delilah up. The others she'd never seen before.

While she still tried to survey the area to understand what was happening right in front of her, she noticed Amaury and Samson move. Like sprinters they ran toward the stage, only faster than any human could run.

Her heart pounded in her ears. Nina didn't need to look at the clock to know that her last sixty seconds were ticking away. This was how her life would end? Blown to bits? Would it be painless at least?

With a loud thud, both vampires jumped onto the platform and straight toward her and Delilah. One second more and Amaury was behind her.

***

Amaury had pulled the knife out of its sheath in mid-jump and was ready to cut her restraints when he saw them: silver handcuffs.

"*Nooooo*!" His own cry mingled with that of Samson's, who was behind Delilah and had met with the same obstacle.

"Oh God, Nina," was all he could say.

He felt her kick against the pole. In frustration he hit against it—it was made of iron, a metal a vampire could bend and break if he used enough force.

"Samson, the pole—*break it*!"

Save yourself, Amaury, please.

"I won't leave you!"

His anger mixed with determination.

"Bend forward, away from the pole as much as you can," he ordered her. Nina did as he asked.

Amaury kicked against the pole with his leg, then followed it with the blade of his hand. Again the leg, then his hand. In a steady, but rapid rhythm a human's eye would barely be able to follow, he kicked and hit. Another one. And one more. The pole started to crack on one side.

One more, just one more.

He collected all his strength and slammed his foot into the pole. Searing pain shot up his leg, but he ignored it. The metal split. With vampire speed, he reached for her wrists, not even noticing the damage the silver did to his own hands. Wedging the pole up, he twisted it away, letting it fall onto the stage. Tugging her bound wrists upward, he wrenched her free.

Amaury grabbed Nina as he jumped off the platform. The shadow next to him had to be Samson, but he didn't have time to look. With several more steps, his mate clutched to his chest, he was able to put distance between them and the platform, before he felt the explosion rock him. The shockwave threw him forward and onto the ground as searing heat shot over him.

With his last ounce of strength he covered Nina beneath him, cradling her in the safety of his broad body, hoping the fall hadn't hurt her. Her body felt soft underneath his, her breasts crushed against his chest. But she felt cold. How long had she been made to stand up there in the chilly night air? Her breathing was as ragged as his own. Seconds passed before he knew it was safe to lift his head.

To his left he found Samson lying in a similar position, covering Delilah with his body.

Looking behind him he saw his colleagues fight the opposition. They outnumbered Luther's men. It was safe to sit up. Amaury rolled off Nina. Her arms still bound behind her back, she couldn't move much on her own. He helped her sit up before he tugged at the duct tape over her mouth.

"Sorry, *chérie*: it'll hurt."

Her eyes were wide. She was clearly still in shock. Amaury pulled the tape off in one swift move, then instantly pressed his palm onto her lips trying to soothe the pain.

Her muffled groan bounced against his hand.

He couldn't leave her in pain, and, what the hell, he needed to feel her. "I'll heal it."

His tongue traced over her lips which the tape had left tender, soothing first the lower one, then the upper one. A moment later he found himself kissing her and pressing his body against hers. For a brief moment he enjoyed her closeness. He wanted this to last an eternity, but as quickly as he'd kissed her, he released her.

Amaury hadn't forgotten about what he'd done to her. Having saved Nina's life didn't change that. She wasn't his to keep, because he'd never asked her to be his, not in a way she would have understood anyway.

"I'm sorry." Amaury averted his eyes and looked back toward the mausoleum. It still stood. Why hadn't it blown up too?

"Quinn, the mausoleum didn't blow."

Over his mic he could hear Quinn's labored voice. "Sorry, buddy; I cut the wire for the mausoleum, thinking it was for the platform."

"You okay?"

"Could use some help back here: he's got another friend."

"On my way," Amaury confirmed. He stood and cast a glance at Nina. "Stay here."

***

Nina watched as Amaury rushed toward the building. She looked to her side and saw how Samson kissed Delilah softly. His tender voice carried to her.

"I almost lost you."

"Everything's all right."

"And the baby?"

"She's fine."

"She?" Samson's voice was filled with surprise.

"I'll explain later. Can you get these cuffs off me?"

Nina felt her own wrists being chaffed by the handcuffs. "Me too. Amaury chose to run off before he untied me."

Delilah sent her a pitying look. Yes, it hurt, the fact that while Samson took care of his wife, Amaury had chosen to continue to fight rather than take care of her.

"Oliver will bring metal cutters from the van," Samson said.

Nina turned back to the battlefield. Behind the wrecked stage, a dark figure emerged from the mausoleum. Luther. Nobody had spotted him yet.

Her eyes searched for Amaury.

The remnants of the platform were still burning. With difficulty, she was able to make out the different figures fighting in the vicinity. She recognized Johan who fought with Gabriel. Others were obscured by the fire that raged as a result of the explosion.

Nina saw Amaury head toward the back of the building. Unfortunately Luther spotted him at the same time. She saw how his gaze followed him, and he started moving in Amaury's direction. Amaury couldn't see him since he was looking in the other direction.

If she didn't warn him, Luther would strike him from behind without warning.

Nina spun back to Samson. "Samson! Luther—he's after Amaury."

She couldn't point in the direction she'd seen him, because her hands were still restrained behind her back.

"Where?" Samson's eyes traveled swiftly over the scene.

"To the right, there, next to the building. Please help him."

Samson touched his ear then recoiled in shock. "My mic's gone! Fuck!"

Nina's stomach twisted.

"Amaury!" Samson yelled out, but his friend didn't turn. There was too much noise on the battlefield. "He can't hear me."

Panic ripped through her. "Oh, God, no."

She watched as Luther stalked Amaury.

"You have to warn him, Nina—do it!"

Panic made her brain freeze. If he couldn't hear Samson, whose voice was louder than hers, how would he hear her warning? She felt her heartbeat pound into her throat, the lump in it tightening. Desperation immobilized her.

"Amaury!" she croaked.

"The bond," Samson instructed. "Use the bond."

Nina blinked once, then concentrated.

Amaury, behind you, Luther is behind you.

An instant later, she saw him spin around and face his opponent. Luther dealt the first blow, but because Amaury had had a split second to react, it failed to connect directly, and he instantly countered. They were evenly matched, dealing each other blow after blow.

Nina's stomach twisted painfully as she tried to watch their fight. With every blow Amaury absorbed, she flinched. Who was stronger? Would Amaury win?

She was startled when she suddenly felt somebody's hands on hers.

"I'm Oliver. I'll cut your cuffs. Keep still."

A moment later she felt cold metal against her skin. A snapping sound followed, and the cuffs fell onto the grass. Without turning to thank the man, she ran toward the scene in front of her. She had to help Amaury, no matter what.

She stumbled forward when in the corner of her eye she saw Eddie. He was fighting with Zane. And Zane had the upper hand. Looking to Amaury then back to Eddie, she made a split-second decision and ran toward her brother.

"Stop! He's on our side."

But Zane ignored her. He continued pounding into her brother.

"Zane, stop! Don't hurt him," she screamed again and lunged forward, throwing herself between the two. Zane grabbed her and tossed her aside, then reached for Eddie. "He's with Luther."

Her response was drowned out by Samson's booming voice behind her. "Zane, he's with us. Release him."

A disbelieving look came over Zane's face, but he obeyed and dropped Eddie from his grip.

Nina ran toward Eddie and hugged him. Her brother's strong arms went around her and squeezed tightly.

"You're alive," he said.

Because of Amaury she was alive, but now he was in danger. Nina peeled herself out of Eddie's embrace and let her eyes search for her mate.

39

Amaury dodged another of Luther's blows and swung his fist against his arm, momentarily blocking his opponent, and allowing him to pull out his silver dagger with the other hand.

He used his leg to kick Luther's legs from underneath him and felt him stumble. Without hesitation, Amaury pinned him against the wall behind him and lifted the dagger to strike.

For having nearly killed his mate, Luther would have to die. Only then would the beast inside Amaury be appeased.

No! Stop, Amaury!

Nina's voice invaded his mind, and he hesitated.

Please, if you love me, don't kill him.

From the corner of his eye he saw a movement and turned. Nina came running toward him.

"Don't move, or you're dead," he warned Luther and kept the dagger pressed to his throat. The silver bit into his opponent's skin.

"Amaury! Don't kill him, please, don't," he heard Nina call out.

His gut twisted. Why would she want to save Luther when he'd been planning to kill her? He couldn't make heads or tails of it. Amaury gave her a long look, trying to search her eyes for an answer. Whose side was she on?

Behind her, Samson and Delilah came into sight, and a second later some of the others. The fight seemed to be over, but the fire continued to rage.

Amaury felt Luther slacken under his grip, clearly realizing he'd lost. Amaury's hand twitched, eager to finish what he'd started.

"Don't," Nina warned him, "or you're not any better than he is."

"Why should I spare him?" he asked, avoiding her gaze and instead training his eye on Luther's throat, where the silver dagger burned his flesh. He would only have to press a little deeper to end his life, to make him pay for the pain he'd caused.

Recalling the sight of Nina on the platform and the panic that had gripped him when he'd realized her handcuffs were made of silver made his heart beat in a violent rage. He could have lost her forever.

"You're not his judge." Nina's calm voice drifted into his ears.

"No, but I *am* his executioner."

"Then I will be his defense counsel."

Amaury stared at her, his jaw dropping. "What do you mean? He's guilty. We all know that."

"Let's get it over with," Luther suddenly interjected.

"No," Nina said, taking a step forward. "There are mitigating circumstances."

Even Luther's face twisted into a confused frown.

"Mitigating circumstances?" Amaury repeated. He noticed Delilah, who had approached with Samson, reaching for Nina's arm. The two women exchanged a look.

"He needs to know," Nina said quietly.

A sense of dread came over Amaury when Nina locked eyes with him. "If you and Samson had told him the truth back then, this would have never happened."

"Stay out of it," Amaury warned. This was between the men. He and his colleagues would deal with Luther the only way possible. Kidnapping and attempting to murder a vampire's mate called for the only possible punishment: death.

"Quinn, get the women out of here," he ordered. When Quinn looked at Samson for confirmation, his boss nodded.

"No, I'm not leaving!" Nina underscored her protest by bracing her hands on her hips and widening her stance. His little fighter was ready to do battle with him. But Amaury wouldn't allow it, not this time.

"I said—"

Nina interrupted him, her voice furious now. "I heard what you said. And as Rhett enlightened Scarlet: 'frankly my dear, I don't give a damn.' I'll say what I've got to say, and nobody will stop me." Nina leveled a defiant glare at him.

Damn, his woman had balls. And she used them to defy him. If he weren't so busy with keeping his knife at Luther's throat, he'd grab her right now and bend her over his knee for a well-deserved ass-paddling.

Nobody other than Samson had ever truly stood up to him. And he was a six-foot-something tough vampire, not the delicate human woman whose fists where trembling at her waist. No, he hadn't missed that. Nina was nervous, but at the same time she was willing to go through with this. He had to admire her, even if he didn't agree with her this time.

Amaury caught how Samson opened his mouth to speak, but was held back by Delilah. A soft shake of her head and a touch of her hand on his arm stopped him.

"Luther," Nina addressed the vampire at the end of Amaury's knife, "I despise you for what you tried to do to Delilah and me, but I can understand the pain in you. But you should know neither Amaury nor Samson is the source of that pain. It was Vivian who didn't want to be turned even though she was given the choice."

An instant roar tore from Luther's chest as he tried to grab Nina. "*You're lying!*" He struggled against Amaury. "You'll pay for that lie!"

Luther's kick landed in Amaury's groin before he could avert it. The pain shot through Amaury's entire body and made his hand release the silver dagger, before he doubled over. Luther escaped from his grip and lunged for Nina. A startled scream burst from her lips.

Despite the pain and nausea his body was fighting, Amaury jumped after Luther. With horror he saw his enemy clutch Nina by the shoulder.

"No!" A scream ripped through the night, and Amaury realized it was his own. He had to save Nina.

His friends were faster. Within seconds, Zane and Samson had pried Luther off her and had him restrained.

Like a wild man Luther looked from one to the other then back at Nina.

"You're lying! Admit it—*you're lying!*" he demanded.

Nina shook her honey curls, her face sad. "I wish it were a lie."

Amaury noticed a solitary tear dislodge from Nina's eye and run down her cheek. Luther had seen it too.

"No!" A violent scream came from Luther's chest and echoed in the night. "No! No!"

A moment later, Amaury saw him break. Luther's entire body collapsed as he sank onto his knees. "Oh God, no."

Samson turned to his men. "Quinn, you and Yvette, take Delilah and Nina back home. We have to take care of things here."

Quinn nodded.

Amaury noticed Nina send a questioning look first into Eddie's then Luther's direction. He took a step toward her. With his voice lowered, he addressed her. "Eddie is safe with us. I promise."

"And Luther?" she asked.

"We won't kill him. But he will be punished."

For a long moment she looked at him then nodded. He motioned to Quinn and Yvette, and the two led the women away. Amaury followed Nina with his eyes. Would he have a future with her?

When he turned back, he saw Samson crouching next to Luther, a hand on his shoulder.

"We couldn't tell you; I'm sorry." Samson's words were spoken softly.

"I loved her." Luther's voice was laden with unshed tears.

Amaury understood his pain only too well. He turned away. Samson would have to deal with Luther. He didn't have any strength left. It would cost him enough to make it through the next few hours and make things right with Nina.

"What'll happen now?" Ricky asked next to him.

Amaury looked up. "Luther will have to go before the council. He'll have to stand trial for the murders of those humans the bodyguards killed."

"Do you think we can keep Eddie and Kent out of the proceedings?" Ricky asked.

"They'll have to testify, but they'll be held blameless. They were under Luther's influence when they committed those murders, which means the crimes were Luther's."

"What'll happen to him?"

"I don't know, but I know the council is fair. They'll look at motivation."

Amaury looked back at Samson, who'd helped Luther up.

"Are you ready?" Samson asked.

Luther looked first at Amaury then back at Samson. There was something Amaury couldn't put his finger on, but he could see Luther's mind clicking.

"I want to say goodbye to Vivian."

With a nod from Samson, Zane released Luther's arm and allowed him to turn toward the mausoleum. Amaury caught hate glinting in Luther's eyes and realized instantly that this would be no loving goodbye to his dead wife.

Not knowing why, but acting entirely out of instinct, Amaury jumped toward Luther. But he was too late. By the time he reached him and slammed him to the ground, Luther's hand had already pulled out a small electronic device from his pocket.

"THE TRIGGER!" Samson screamed from behind him.

Amaury wrestled with Luther, trying to pry the device out of his opponent's hand. Luther was quicker. His thumb pressed down on the button.

A split second later, the mausoleum was shaken by an explosion, causing the walls to implode in on each other, and sending a cloud of dust up from the rubble.

Vivian's resting place was no more.

40

Amaury's legs felt heavy as he stepped into his private elevator and pressed the button to his apartment. He'd spent the entire night searching for Nina. She hadn't waited at Samson's house for him. She'd simply left without a word.

If he was honest with himself, he wasn't even surprised. He'd been an ass, and convincing his mate to forgive him and come back to him wouldn't be easy. But first, he'd have to track her down. After finding her studio in Chinatown empty, he'd scoured every alley and every club for her. Nothing. She'd vanished. The only reason he was returning home now was the rising sun. Once the sun set again, he'd continue his search for Nina.

The moment he walked into his place, Amaury realized he wasn't alone. At the sight of Nina standing in the door to his bedroom, dressed in his white bathrobe, he froze.

The elevator door clicked shut behind him.

Hallucinations wouldn't set in until his body was in starvation mode, but it was too early for that. Twenty-four hours without blood wouldn't do that to him. He'd gone longer without it before.

"Amaury, you're home."

Even the voice of the mirage sounded like her. And the scent drifting into his nostrils was all Nina. She was real, and she stood in his apartment, looking like she'd just taken a shower. She didn't look like a woman on the run. And if she was trying to avoid him, this had to be the worst hiding place he could possible think of.

"You look like you've seen a ghost."

"You're here." His parched throat hurt as he spoke, but his heart leapt with joy.

"And you're stating the obvious." Nina took a few steps toward him as he watched with caution. She didn't look like she was angry at him. Could it be that she already knew what he wanted to tell her? And how had she gotten into his apartment in the first place?

"I broke in. Fire escape," she answered his unspoken question and tilted her head to the window.

He raised an eyebrow. "Time to upgrade security around here. Anyway, I would have given you a key."

Nina shrugged. "Where's the fun in that?"

"Or you could have just waited at Samson's for me instead of making me chase all over town for you."

"Even *less* fun in that," she countered.

"You knew I was looking for you?"

She gave a nonchalant shrug. "You wouldn't be the Amaury I know if you weren't."

Nina wanted to spar with him? He took a few steps toward her. "And I wouldn't be the Amaury you know if I didn't paddle your sweet ass for that."

She planted her fists at her hips, but mischief glinted in her eyes. "You'd have to catch me first." In a flash she took off toward the window. He cut her off before she even got halfway. Thank God for vampire speed.

With one swift move, Amaury hauled her body against his and locked his arms around her. She gave him a coquettish look. Damn, did it feel good to have her soft form pressed into his.

"So now that you've caught me, were you going to come out with that apology anytime soon, or were you planning on kissing me into submission?"

Damn again! Nina knew him better after a week than his friends did after two hundred years. And within seconds, she'd turned him from a man prepared to grovel into a predator ready to claim his prize without considering the consequences—again.

Amaury let out a deep breath. "You tell me, *chérie*, given that you're holding all the cards."

Nina gave him a long look until her expression changed to serious. "Why didn't you save yourself when I asked you to?"

He gave a slow shake of his head. "Save myself for what, to live a life without you?"

"Next time you'll—"

He framed her face with his hand and put a finger on her lips. "Next time, I would do exactly the same. And you can fight me all you want on that."

"Stubborn vampires are a pain," she claimed.

"That's right, *chérie*, but you know what's even worse?" He paused briefly. "A vampire in love. Because when he gets something into his head, there's no stopping him."

"In love?"

"Yes, *chérie*," he whispered, "I love you."

Amaury took in the hitched breath she released and brushed his lips against hers. "Now, are you ready for that apology I owe you?"

"Kiss first, talk later."

"If I start kissing you, we'll never get to talking. And besides, shouldn't you still be mad at me?" He gave her a curious look. Would he ever figure out what was truly going on inside her pretty little head?

"It's kind of hard to be mad at the man who just saved your life without any regard for his own. And it's even harder to stay pissed off with you, knowing the kind of power you gave me over you."

She could only have found out from one person. "Delilah told you that?"

"Yes, she and I had time to talk. So tell me, why would you do such a stupid thing?"

"What stupid thing?"

"Bonding me without my permission, without knowing whether I would stay with you."

Amaury swallowed away the lump in his throat. Yes, he'd given her power over him, made himself vulnerable, yet he didn't feel weak. "That night, I realized I needed you. For the first time since I became a vampire, I felt something. I wasn't prepared to give up this feeling of finally being complete. And tonight, when you stood up on that platform a minute away from dying, I knew a life without you wouldn't be worth living. Nina, I love you." He closed his eyes for a second, knowing he had to offer her a way out. "But if you don't feel the same for me, I will let you go."

***

Amaury loved her. Her crazy, stubborn, big vampire loved her. Yet was prepared to give her her freedom. Loved her? But, he couldn't, could he?

"But you said you weren't capable of love."

He smiled. "That's just it, I wasn't. And then you came along. I was told by a witch that there was one way to reverse the curse. At first I didn't believe her, but then she proved me wrong. *You* proved all of us wrong."

"What did she say?"

"She told me that the object of my affections had to be a forgiving heart. That could only be you—you forgave not only me for what I'd done in my past, but also Luther."

Nina smiled. "Without forgiveness, life stops in its tracks. It was time for you to move on."

Amaury gave her a soft kiss on her lips. "I know that now. You've helped me see that. But it wasn't the only thing that the witch said. My control over you had to be ineffective. Remember? Mind control didn't work on you."

"You mean when you tried to get me to untie you?"

"That's right. And let's not try this again, at least not with silver. Other materials, I'm open to . . . " The hungry look he raked over her made her shiver with pleasure. "And I still don't know how you were able to do that."

"You mean push you out of my mind?" She shrugged. "I don't know. Maybe I'm stronger than you."

He grinned. "I can live with that."

"So can I."

"But the last thing the witch said was that your love had to be unknown. I didn't understand what that meant, but I think I do now. I could never read your emotions, which meant I didn't know whether you loved me."

She shook her head. "I don't think that's what she meant. A love unknown? It was I: I didn't know I loved you until I almost lost you. My love was unknown to myself." Not anymore.

"And now?"

Nina brushed a strand of hair out of his face. "I love you. Is the entire curse reversed now?"

"Ever since we bonded, my head has been clear. I haven't sensed a single emotion from anybody, except—"

"Except?"

"I'm starting to sense you. I could sense you right after the bonding, but then it vanished. I should have been able to feel you continuously, but I didn't."

"It might have something to do with the fact I was resisting it. When Delilah told me about the bonding, I was a tad angry with you for not asking me and tried to block out everything about you."

"A *tad* angry? I don't think I want to be around when you get really pissed." Amaury stroked her cheek with his knuckles. "I'm sorry, Nina. Believe me. I wanted you so much, my heart just took over. I thought I saw in you that you wanted me too, but I know it was wrong. I should have given you a choice."

Nina put a finger on his lips. "Shh. I wanted you too, I just didn't realize how much until tonight. Come."

Amaury let himself be pulled to the couch and sat down. With a quick move she settled over him, straddling him. Nina gazed into his blue eyes. What a big softy he was, her dangerous vampire. Hidden behind all that brawn was a heart he didn't like to show. A bigger heart than she thought anybody could have.

When he'd saved Eddie during the fight, she'd seen no hesitation in him, as if he'd done it just because she'd asked him. The one time he hadn't listened to her pleas was when she'd asked him to save himself. Of course he hadn't. Amaury never listened to her when it came to his own safety. She'd have to have a word with him about that—later.

And now he'd offered her freedom, to release her from their bond. But there was no release from the bond until one of them died. She sensed that he was prepared to take that step just so she'd be free.

Amaury's final act of selflessness had confirmed what she'd felt spreading inside her: the knowledge that she was his, not because he'd bonded her, but because she wanted to be his.

"Why don't you ask me now?" she teased.

There was a moment when he hesitated, but then the words spilled from his mouth. "Will you bond with me, Nina? Will you be mine forever, and let me be yours?" The blue in his eyes became more brilliant as he waited for her reply.

She should let him wait, but the thrill she felt, knowing she'd brought this man to his knees—well, almost—was exhilarating, empowering.

"Under one condition."

Shock registered in his face. "What condition?"

She pulled the lapels of her bathrobe open to expose her breasts to him. Nina noticed his gaze drop lower as she cupped one of her breasts and presented it to him. "Feed from me, Amaury."

Underneath her she felt his erection grow, evidence of his desire in what she offered. Somehow she knew it was what he'd wanted since the night he'd taken her blood. And she'd give him anything in her power.

"Oh, Nina, *chérie*, you have no idea how happy you make me."

His hand went to her breast, and he stroked it lightly. "I don't deserve you. But I'm glad I got you anyway. You're not going to resist me again, are you?"

"Resist you? You know I always will, because that's what you need."

"I might have to spank you if you do." His wicked smile made her heart skip a beat.

"For that you'll need your strength. And without food, I'm not sure how you can keep up your strength." She dropped her gaze to her breasts and noticed him do the same.

"I like the way you argue your point," Amaury agreed in a husky tone.

His hand brushed over her erect nipple. Without haste, his mouth descended onto her flesh, his lips connecting with her skin, setting her on fire. A lick with his tongue followed, making her entire body tingle. Oh, God, how she loved this man, this vampire.

"Amaury, take me, please."

"I'm yours," he whispered before Nina felt his fangs pierce her skin. His mouth closing over her breast, he sucked and took the life-giving sustenance she would provide him with for the rest of her life.

Their hearts beat as one, their souls connected by invisible tendrils so strong, no forces in this world could separate them. They were one—one body, one mind, one soul.

My mate. My hellion.
Mine.

~ ~ ~

ABOUT THE AUTHOR

Tina Folsom was born in Germany and has been living in English speaking countries for over 25 years, the last 14 of them in San Francisco, where she's married to an American.

Tina has always been a bit of a globe trotter: after living in Lausanne, Switzerland, she briefly worked on a cruise ship in the Mediterranean, then lived a year in Munich, before moving to London. There, she became an accountant. But after 8 years she decided to move overseas.

In New York she studied drama at the American Academy of Dramatic Arts, then moved to Los Angeles a year later to pursue studies in screenwriting. This is also where she met her husband, who she followed to San Francisco three months after first meeting him.

In San Francisco, Tina worked as a tax accountant and even opened her own firm, then went into real estate, however, she missed writing. In 2008 she wrote her first romance and never looked back.

She's always loved vampires and decided that vampire and paranormal romance was her calling. She now has 32 novels in English and several dozens in other languages (Spanish, German, and French) and continues to write, as well as have her existing novels translated.

For more about Tina Folsom:
http://www.tinawritesromance.com
http://www.twitter.com/Tina_Folsom
http://www.facebook.com/TinaFolsomFans
You can also email her at tina@tinawritesromance.com